MIRROR OF TRUTH

By M. A. SENFT

Published by DREAMSPACE PUBLISHING LLC,

Cover Illustrated by: Patrice Becker

www.masenft.com

Published in the United States of America.
First Edition, 2nd Revision February 2023

ISBN – 978-1-7376534-3-1   Paperback
ISBN – 978-1-7376534-4-8   Hardback
ISBN – 978-1-7376534-5-5   E-Pub

DREAMSPACE
PUBLISHING LLC

MIRROR OF TRUTH

By M. A. SENFT

BOOK TWO OF THE
CLINT REEVES, BEYOND THE GRAVE SERIES™

There is a fifth dimension, beyond that which is known to man. It is a dimension as vast as space and as timeless as infinity. It is the middle ground between light and shadow, between science and superstition.

—Rod Serling

For what it's worth… it's never too late to be whoever you want to be. There's no time limit. Start whenever you want. You can change or stay the same. There are no rules. I hope you see things that startle you. I hope you feel things you've never felt before.

—Unknown

The meaning of life is to find your gift. The purpose of life is to give it away.

—Pablo Picasso

DEDICATION

This book is dedicated to my 100-year-old father, Walter. Ellsworth Johnes, who is a writer, and still lives on his own. As I've said many times, he taught me the power of words—their impact, and magic. His longevity has demonstrated as the pages of life turn, chapter by chapter, we face many obstacles, both good and bad. It's how we deal with them that matters.

I also want to thank my husband, Herb, for being the light of my life. He is truly the wind beneath my wings. He encourages me to reach for the stars where the sky has no boundaries. Because of him I have done just that, expressing my untethered mind and spirit through stories based on the paranormal.

And, finally, I want to acknowledge my incredibly gifted cover illustrator, Patrice Becker. She is simply amazing. Thank you for always capturing what I visualize and bringing it into existence. You are simply the best!

Chapter 1
Matters of the Heart

Sunday, November 13, 2005

One thousand and one, one thousand and two, Farley counted, waiting for the clap of thunder to chase the bolt of lightning he'd seen above the trees a second earlier. In the dark, from the living room window, forked lightning snaked across the ebony sky. Flashes burst, illuminating the hickory floor and walls. Even as a child he was captivated by the rumbles thunder produced. Back then he found it fascinating—not so much nowadays.

A crimson dawn had foretold worsening weather was on its way, by late afternoon the storm had materialized, rolling heavy clouds in from the southwest. They grew upward and outward into thunderheads as evening drew nigh.

One thousand and three, one thousand and four...

Eight counts later, thunder rattled the floor-to-ceiling windows of Farley's cabin, and the newly laid metal roof pinged from pelting sleet and hail. Had he made a mistake not to have chosen a more traditional material such as asphalt, clay, or slate? It wasn't like he hadn't been warned. The salesman at Tiptop Roofing—on more than one occasion—mentioned the distinctive sound weather had on metal and how bothersome it could be in extreme conditions. Nevertheless, Farley had followed his heart and moved forward with his red metal roof, delighting in it each time he turned into the drive.

By feel, he navigated the shadows of the house, his slippers shuffling over the designer tile as he made his way into the kitchen and to the back door where he flipped on the porch light for a better view. Icy pellets covered the deck and yard. Leaves, yet to be raked, glistened in the raging storm.

A whispering drone stirred at his feet. The furnace kicked on, pushing warm air through the register. Two hours earlier the outside gauge revealed the barometric pressure had dropped dramatically.

Temperatures had plummeted fifteen degrees since then. November was a fickle month, often changing from pleasant, tepid conditions to brisk, frigid ones in a matter of hours.

Farley navigated his way back into the living room where in advance of the impending storm he had stacked armfuls of logs next to the fireplace. Ready to light, he wedged crumbled newspaper under and around the logs, tucking fatwood kindling between them before striking a match. He preferred the cabin on the cool side, using the fireplace for heat rather than the geothermal he had installed when the cabin was constructed.

Nestled among a grove of jack pines, forty-seven miles West of Louisville, Kentucky, Farley's cozy cabin was situated two miles—as the crow flies—from Highway 150 in Indiana. His home was located a mere ten-minute drive from Salzburg, a quaint Indiana town north of the Ohio River, and West of the Indiana and Kentucky bridge. Building his home at the edge of a forest was the ideal location to recuperate from a grueling year of physical recovery.

This wilderness retreat offered restorative qualities only Mother Earth could provide, ones never imagined prior to living in the country among nature's best. Wildlife had healing properties not found in a prescription bottle. Big city life was all Farley had ever known, born and raised in Louisville. His current rustic log cabin in Indiana was like living on another planet compared to his modest dwelling in Kentucky.

In 2003, two years previous, Farley was taken by ambulance to the emergency room in serious condition. The accident occurred on a blistery November night, ironically days before Thanksgiving. That's when life as he knew it was put on permanent hold.

Consequently, at age thirty-six Farley was forced into early retirement. Resting in the hospital bed that night, with the lights dimmed, he determined a decade and a half of working long, difficult assignments—on the second and third shifts—had taken their collective toll, leading to the damages that ended his career.

Installing, upgrading, maintaining, and repairing utility poles, lines, and towers for a living was a tedious occupation by anyone's standards. The job of a linesman was a solitary, albeit necessary job that Farley enjoyed for the most part, except on the bitterest of nights like the one that had caused his mishap.

Persistent, pent-up anxiety, before and after the fall, was behind Farley's difficulties, fraying his nerves to the edge of brokenness. It had taken a vast amount of discipline to right his sinking ship, but with time, his mental well-being was on the mend, along with his body, thanks to constructing a home close to the national forest.

The only worrisome factor remaining was the unknown, intrusive voice he occasionally heard in his head.

Trekking the trails of Hoosier National Forest had become part of his rehabilitation routine since that dreadful night, a practice Farley conformed to religiously since his cardiologist endorsed it, promoting its importance at every exam.

Farley didn't mind. He rather enjoyed hiking in the forest and found it invigorating, especially on sunny days when shafts of light pierced the forest canopy to create a specialness never experienced in his previous life. Feeling amazingly alive, Farley crisscrossed the forest with keen awareness of his own mortality, thanking God for his survival.

Often, he'd sit on the ground enjoying the scenery, or on a stump to catch his breath when he had pushed himself too far. Mastering the underbrush of fallen, decaying trees, debris, and obstacles became a pleasant challenge. Always watchful of wildlife, unique insects, and birds only the forest housed, his hikes heightened his sense of belonging. When in season, Farley gathered flowers for table arrangements, and berries for his breakfast along the way—a refreshing treat when he returned home.

Farley identified a tranquility felt nowhere other than in the forest. It seemed to caress him when he walked through the woods, a knowledge that somehow, someway, wholeness would, in time, find him. In truth, Farley had come to suspect a guardian angel watched over him. At times he'd swear the sounds of nature exceeded the ordinary. A strong fragrance, sometimes a vibration, not easily described, intensified his surroundings, and his awareness of it.

Gazing at the curling flames in the firebox, Farley revisited the night of the tragedy, returning to November 20, 2003. Thick ice had built up around the power lines. The accumulation was unyielding, and he guessed it was the reason he lost his footing. A transformer had tripped, and Farley was sent out to repair it. Hundreds of homes were without power. While he had no clear recollection of the incident, he was told later what had happened. Knocked unconscious, lying on the ground, a passing motorist who had witnessed the event dialed 911.

No one assumed Farley would fully recover, and they were right. He had not. Far from it. He was, however, acutely aware of his mortality, more than at any other point in his life.

"Your gear saved your life," Dr. Gregory Langley informed Farley when he came to the recovery room.

Langley had been waiting for the anesthesia to wear off. "You have a broken collar bone, two cracked ribs, and a splintered left tibia. All fixable. Plus, your shoulder was dislocated but we slipped it back in place."

Then he dropped the bomb...

"I wish this wasn't so," Dr. Langley spoke in a downtrodden tone, "but, the EKG we ordered while you were unconscious–in preparation for surgery–revealed an abnormality."

Farley, foggy brained, frowned, tilting his head as though he didn't quite understand the point being made. "And… what exactly does that mean?"

"Well," Langley faltered, not wanting to deliver the bad news, "your heart, I'm afraid is damaged beyond repair. Severely compromised, to be accurate. A preexisting condition not related to the fall. One we've overlooked somehow in your annual exams. Who knows how long the problem has existed, but you need to see a specialist soon."

He was too stunned to form words. "How can that be? I'm fit as a fiddle," he fired back using an old-fashioned phrase to describe himself. His face turned grim as he registered the seriousness in Langley's eyes. "You said so yourself. Or so you thought."

A long moment passed. Tears welled as he continued to protest. "I take handfuls of supplements, Doc. Every day! I limit how much red meat I eat. I hate vegetables but tolerate them for my health."

Farley glanced out the hospital window, wearing a pained expression. "None of that suggests an unfit lifestyle. Does it? Certainly, shouldn't lead to heart disease." He gulped, choking down the fear of what any long-term implications might be. "Are you absolutely, positively certain? Maybe you're mistaken, or X-rays got switched?" He furrowed his brow. "You should double check. Something's wrong."

"Farley, the test is accurate. I'm terribly sorry." Langley looked at him with regret, but optimistically noted, "The important thing is we caught it in time."

"So, you didn't just deliver a death sentence?" Farley petitioned, his voice clutching to a sign of hope. "I have time?"

When Langley didn't answer quickly, Farley became alarmed. Any optimism he was clinging to dissolved into resignation of the inevitable–a short life.

"You have a condition called cardiomyopathy, meaning the heart muscle is damaged, enlarged to the point where it can't pump blood properly. It's the leading cause of heart failure. Typically, this condition affects younger people, like you."

Farley drew a sharp breath. Thrusting his hands outward, he spoke in a raised voice, "C'mon on! I run! I jog almost every day, a minimum of eight to ten miles at Shelby Park, in Germantown." Farley's manner grew grave, his tone lowered an octave. "I feed the deer." He looked away so the doctor wouldn't see the tears that streamed down his face. "They come right up to me, eat bread out of my hand." His voice trailed away with nothing more to add.

"Look," coached Dr. Langley, seeing Farley was clearly distraught, "we need to keep a close eye on things. I've written two prescriptions. You can pick them up at the pharmacy after you're discharged. Both will help keep the fluid buildup in your lungs under control. That will reduce any shortness of breath. Hopefully, your condition won't worsen."

Farley appeared frightened but said nothing.

"You'll need to decide if you want to be placed on a heart transplant waiting list. I strongly advise it. You are an excellent candidate. Your heart might not be in the best condition, but your body is, and that's the best we could ask for. When a donor becomes available, you'll be notified which means report to the hospital immediately, without delay."

Farley's expression was one of panic. Bile climbed up his throat. Several minutes passed before the feeling he might get sick, subsided.

"How ridiculous is this?" he proclaimed angerly. "I don't even drink. At best, a handful of beers a year. Maybe a Jack and Coke on a special occasion." Farley was bitter. "I may up my game after this fine piece of news, rather than curtail simple pleasures." Their eyes locked, Farley's resentment apparent. "It's like you're talking about some other guy, Doc, not me."

"I understand," commiserated Langley. "It's a bitter pill to swallow. I even pulled my office records to compare them with Dr. Bayne's. A year ago, nothing would have indicated heart failure, not like this. Your heart was normal size, no abnormality. Unfortunately, these things aren't always predictable. We should be counting our lucky stars, Farley. Had the accident not happened, we wouldn't have caught it. Your fall was a blessing in disguise."

Farley nodded, reluctantly agreeing. "If a donor match doesn't happen, how long do I have?" he inquired.

"Let's not go there right now," Langley stated, cutting off a conversation that had nowhere to go but down. "We'll pick that discussion up later, maybe in my office a week from today. You should be feeling better by then. For now, let's just concentrate on regaining your strength and getting better."

"I apologize. Shouldn't have put you on the spot like that," Farley offered. "You're not a fortune teller. No one would know the answer, except the Man upstairs." He glanced up. "It's just a lot to take in. You know? I guess, whatever happens, happens." Farley looked away, tears streaming down his cheeks. "A hard pill to swallow, indeed." He regrouped so they could conclude their discussion. "I simply need time to adjust. I'll be alright."

"If you want it, I ordered something to help you sleep. Please get some rest. I will check in on you tomorrow." Langley moved toward the door.

Later that night when Farley sat in the dark considering the bleak future that had been laid out, he admitted, in hindsight, that he'd been suspecting something wasn't quite right for some time. Shortness of breath and fatigue were warning signs, Langley had stated. Farley had both and elected to ignore them. Sure, heart disease ran in his family, especially with the men, but he dismissed that knowledge as well. He had taken extra precautions, but apparently, they weren't enough to escape the family curse.

Released three days later, Farley left the hospital a sick man with serious decisions on his mind. In short order he had a will drafted, and then consulted a family services counselor at the nearby cemetery where his mother and aunt were buried. He wrote a check and borrowed against his life insurance to cover the remaining installments for the plot he had previously secured a few years back.

While Farley enjoyed the hustle and bustle of city life–mainly in his youth where on occasion he would stay out late partying, and then report to work the next day exhausted–no longer did he have the energy, nor the inclination, to mingle with the masses. He would spend what time he had left in solitude.

Within days of his follow up conversation with his doctor, Farley was added to a heart transplant waitlist, 1A/1B classification, at three local hospitals, with instructions to keep an eye peeled for *the call.* Day or night, no one knew when the exact donor match would come available.

At his office visits the following year, Langley and Farley set a protocol for what he should expect, emphasizing the importance of a timely hospital arrival. Farley trusted in God, and believed he'd be one of the lucky ones to survive the complex operation he prayed he'd face. In the event he did not survive the operation, he had arrangements ready. Langley advised Farley if he made it to the one-year post-op mark, he'd have an eighty-five to ninety percent chance of cheating death. Seventy-five percent after three years, which to him translated to a promising prognosis.

Thirteen months, and a day after the accident, on December 21, 2004, Farley got the call. At record speed he arrived at the hospital, and within two hours they'd hastily wheeled him into surgery. The unfortunate soul who had died from a gunshot wound supplied Farley with the new heart he yearned for, but it came with a *price. It retained a memory!*

CHAPTER 1

Life changed dramatically since the evening of November 20, 2003. After Farley's misfortune where Dr. Langley pointed out the truth of his situation, his world upended. Two years later life had made an about-face, and now he lived north of the Ohio River near a small town most people wouldn't give the time of day to when traveling US 150 unless they had heard of the Reno Gang treasure discovery and would stop in as a destination point.

Leaving his Louisville residence of fourteen years was difficult, hard to put into context. But, in the larger picture, laying down roots a stone's throw from Indiana's Hoosier National Forest was a godsend, exactly what the doctor ordered.

Fortunately, he'd purchased the land years before his accident. With no intentions of building on the property until his late sixties, Farley never expected to be forced into disability retirement at age thirty-six. The property presented Farley a pleasurable environment to spend his remaining days, and he was truly grateful.

He was young enough to enjoy life's little pleasures, and although fate had dealt Farley a few belly punches, he had heroically endured them all. When the accident occurred, he'd had a sizeable savings squirreled away for rainy days. Now, rain was falling.

When the calendar year turned, he'd accomplished priorities, like selling his house and liquidating finances. Soon after Farley meet with a builder to start construction on his Indiana residence. Adding biweekly deposits from his paycheck into savings over the years turned out to be a brilliant move, providing Farley with a nice-size nest egg.

Not a wealthy man, Farley squeezed funds out to pay cash for his cabin. The excess he tapped into came from an unexpected windfall inheritance his great-aunt, who he thought didn't have two nickels to rub together, left him. Farley's mother and her aunt both died within two months of each other. His mother was penniless. Her Aunt Becky was not.

Who would have known? Farley thought when he was told the amount he was to inherit. Aunt Becky lived in Floyds Knobs in a meager apartment with scant surroundings. Comically, Farley often thought she looked like a bag lady. When she passed, her money went to Farley's mother, who in turn, died eight weeks later, recycling the inheritance to him.

Farley was set for life with legacy money added to his savings. His total funds had accumulated handsomely at Miller's Credit Union, bringing his net worth, combined with the proceeds of the selling his house, to just shy of five hundred thousand dollars.

Great Aunt Becky was, of course, responsible for the bulk of his fortune leaving almost four hundred thousand, but coupled with his savings, Farley had ample funds to build on the property he had purchased as an investment in his youth. Plus, his awarded monthly severance from United Alliance Electric and disability benefits had eliminated any worries he may have had prior to the accident.

Dr. Langley emphasized the importance of a steady exercise routine. Farley soon realized the little slice of heaven he purchased complemented the healing process and road to recovery beautifully. Hiking trails and toting lunches into the forest several times a week brought a kind of inspiration other people, he imagined, sought in a Synagogue or church.

Woodland wildflowers, like trilliums and bluebells in the spring, and fall foliage covering the forest floor in autumn had invigorated him to walk even during the colder months. The land turned out to be the best decision he'd ever made–a fortuitous blessing. And… now his survival was tied to it.

Each night Farley gave thanks to the angels who watched over him the evening he received the donor's heart. That fateful night when a poor soul lost his life. Farley owed his life to the unfortunate man who had passed away.

It had been a long, exhausting year of follow-up appointments and schedules. Doctors and technicians who had probed and prodded, at first, every two weeks, moving to four, until finally his milestone anniversary of six months was triumphantly behind him. Farley journeyed his final leg to recovery.

That's when the voices started. Seeded in his head, Farley was no longer worried about his heart. Mental health had taken center-stage.

He didn't tell his doctors about the anomaly that had been developing over recent weeks, for fear of additional testing, but this time… on his brain. No longer would they merely focus on his heart.

CHAPTER 1

Fervently, Farley prayed for the intrusive mental images to go away and for the bad dreams and voice that entered his thoughts to recede. They had not. To the contrary, his dreams became more disturbing, bleeding into his daytime hours, and the voice was louder and came more often.

Physically, Farley felt sound. Mentally, was a different story.

You're off your rocker, man, he'd scold himself, time and again when the chatter was so invasive he couldn't hear himself think.

To make matters worse, his nightly dreams had become even more lucid, although splicing the vague goings-on together was next to impossible. The images weren't sufficiently coherent to make sense of. In the morning, only a sinking feeling lingered. He kept a pad of paper by the bedstand so he could write down any noteworthy features during the night, but none made sense in the morning's light. Ultimately, he concluded something must be bothering him on a subconscious level, elusive to his conscious mind.

Patient, heal thyself, Farley recited daily believing he could solve the problem. He started brain probiotics designed to improve brain health, but those hadn't worked, nor did any other cognitive supplements. The circumstances in his dreams felt real enough; yet were foreign to his own memory. Strange images flickered of people and places he didn't recognize. It was as though Farley had split into two people. The unfamiliar dream situations got stronger, invading his daytime hours.

Until recently he believed his mental illness was under control, but no longer would it remain fettered at the edge of his thoughts. The voice refused to be silenced. To the contrary, it was getting more insistent with each passing day to the point where Farley became convinced a heart transplant glitch had occurred causing neurological damage. Wires somehow must have been crossed, causing severe brain issues.

Sitting in his easy chair with the lights turned off–an activity Farley thoroughly enjoyed–the sounds of the crackling fire filled the room. With the woodstove door open, he cupped a warm mug of malted Ovaltine.

Temperatures had dropped once the storm rolled through, now snowfall accumulated outside the living room window. He guessed

12

one to two inches. The forest, with its deep rich evergreens and pines stood starkly against the steely gray sky and showcased a typical Indiana November day. It was not unusual for autumn's colorful foliage to begin the month but by mid-November anything was possible, an unseasonal thunderstorm, or for snow to fly.

He leaned back onto the headrest, wishing the answer to his dilemma was written on the ceiling, indicating a clear direction to take.

A half hour later he arose and walked to the mud room, sat down on the bench, and pulled on his boots. The change of temperature would feel invigorating, he figured, after sitting in front of a warm fire.

Closing the door behind him, Farley stepped out into the falling snow. All ambient noise was absorbed, its sound trapped between the snowflakes. The scene underscored the quiet blissfulness of nature. He moved closer to the forest, enjoying the serenity of the moment and appreciating the view of his property.

Abruptly, he came to a halt, perplexed by what he thought he saw. A figure was standing at the edge of the woods. Cautiously he inched forward, focusing his attention on the object.

Based on its stature, I'd say an animal, he presumed. Taking a step backward, the creature gave the impression it *wanted* to be seen.

"No way," he stammered. "That can't be right." He wagged his head, speaking softer. "I don't think so. Black cougars don't live in these parts.

The feline's spectacular green eyes receded slowly into the darkness, back into the forest, its large paws engulfed by shadows.

Farley decided his eyes had played tricks on him. "I must be wrong," he said with unwavering certainty. Deliberating if what he had seen was indeed what he thought he saw.

Just then, a voice, specific, and well-defined, rang out.

Farley stopped, stone cold, his eyes scanning every inch of the space around him.

He saw no one.

But swore he heard, "K, or kid."

Chapter 2
Down the Rabbit Hole

Startled, Farley's heart responded, skipping beats, he dropped to his knees, grabbing his chest. A stabbing pain radiated around his heart.

"Leave me alone!" he shouted, rolling to his side.

"Ann..." the voice said.

"I don't know anyone by that name," exclaimed Farley angrily, his heart aching.

"Ease my pain." The voice spoke, fading into the folds of Farley's brain.

As Farley lay on the ground, watching the snow diminish, spaced between the clouds he saw intermittent stars. In that instant, his clarity of mind returned. Without knowing how, he knew his heart was speaking. The dead man's heart, in his chest, was trying to communicate.

"I have no idea who you are," Farley moaned, trying to calm himself from the severe pain that had radiated from his chest to his extremities. His arms and legs were still numb. "How can I help when I know nothing."

Heavy silence embraced him.

Farley warily got up from the snow-covered ground, brushing himself off and glancing over at the forest, darker and more ominous than before. A frigid gust of night air stung his face as he bent down to pick up the Kentucky Wildcats ball cap that had fallen off.

There was a hush so quiet Farley would have sworn the only sound was the one inside his head, asking–*What just happened?*

He went inside. In the kitchen, he placed a cold glass of milk onto the carousel in the microwave. Watching the seconds tick away, his mind whirled with unanswerable questions. The bell dinged. Farley took the warm glass over to the table. He added chocolate syrup before climbing the stairs to the bedroom.

A restless night awaited.

Monday, November 14

Monday morning, while the coffee brewed, Farley decided he had no choice but to accept what he couldn't change or hide from what afflicted him. Instead, he'd seek information and research the subject of heart transplants.

Surely, I'm not the only heart recipient to experience abnormal lingering side-effects, he assured himself. *Others must have had experiences such as mine.*

I've not visited Salzburg's library. Today is as good a day as any, he reckoned. Almost a recluse, Farley had been hiding at his home and property for far too long, afraid of interacting other than at the grocery and hardware for the most part and at Josie's Diner only twice.

I'll have breakfast at Josie's Diner and then hoof it over to the library afterward, he grinned. *Walking off the extra calories from a hearty breakfast will be good for me. Today is not the time to cut back on comfort food.*

Most of the snow from the night before had melted away by the time Farley got into his Land Cruiser. Living in the country required a dependable vehicle. In his younger days when he fought to put food on the table, and was only able to meet his basic needs, a fancy vehicle wasn't in the cards. Aunt Becky had afforded him a different set of circumstances, of which he was eternally thankful.

Driving into town, Farley made notes on how best to approach his unique circumstance. In the recovery room, the night of the transplant, he was informed his heart donor's name was not public record. Taking that route would lead nowhere. The idea was to research a fifty-mile radius around Grayson Hospital where the transplant took place. Hopefully, he would find useful information at the library or guidance on how to access accidents and fatalities in Louisville on the night of the operation.

He had an urgency to read, in depth, about heart transplants, as well as a determination to locate forums or support groups he could attend. Not having a computer made it difficult to do research for specific information. Mainly, did other heart transplant recipients encounter bizarre experiences afterward, like he had?

As he turned the corner by Josie's, three elderly women were getting ready to go into the diner, followed by four more people. One of the males hurried ahead to hold the door for the older women.

Farley smiled, thinking what a kind gesture. He motored on to parallel park on a side street a block away. Since putting down roots near Salzburg, he'd come to realize Josie's was a gathering place. The quality of ingredients at the diner were topnotch, so no wonder people went there to socialize. Odd for a small-town to have a chef who served such excellent food, but it did explain the ongoing carousel of business. Plus, the cheerful atmosphere was aboveboard.

Farley grabbed a newspaper on the way in from the stand beside the building. A hostess greeted him the moment he walked through the door grabbing a menu and leading him to a booth by the window. He laid the newspaper down next to an empty cup and slid across the bench.

"Would you like something to drink?" the waitress pleasantly inquired.

"Yes, that would be nice. Coffee, please," he answered moving the empty cup to the edge of the table.

"Your waitress will be here in a jiffy to grab your order," she said as she scurried off to the drink island.

Farley removed the scratch pad from inside his jacket pocket and placed it on the table. Once he scanned the headlines, and worked the crossword puzzle, he outlined his concerns regarding last night's episode. Such as, when was the first time the man's voice he'd been hearing became evident?

"Are you ready to order, sir? I can come back if you need more time," the waitress, dressed in 50's diner garb, asked as she topped off his coffee mug. "If you're interested, today's special includes two eggs, a side of ham, sausage, or bacon, a choice of hotcakes, waffles, or buttermilk biscuits served with a choice of potatoes, home fries or hash browns. Coffee and tea are included... all for $8.99."

Farley snickered. "That's a lot of food, lady."

"Depends on how hungry you are, I suppose," she giggled, knowing how much food would be set on the table if he ordered

Today's Special. "If you care to know, a nearby farm, Shoemaker Creamery and Poultry, supplies our chicken, eggs, butter, cream, and milk. Drury's Family Farm delivers our other meats. Everything is local." With a crooked smile, she added, "Pasture, and free range is healthier, I might add."

"That's good to hear," Farley replied, thinking about his heart and overall health. "What I put in my mouth matters a great deal," he stated, smiling back at her.

"Oh, and we have one of the best breaded tenderloins you ever sank your teeth into. Indiana is known for our breaded tenderloins, and Josie's makes the best," Jules said, grinning even bigger, a twinkle in her eye. "I'm done with my sales pitch, if you'd like to order."

"Foods taste better with fresh ingredients. I watch my diet closely and use organic when its available." Farley declared, "I'm sold! I'll have the special."

She picked up the menu, chuckling as she did. "Perfect, you won't be sorry. It's a winning combination. You might not eat again until tomorrow afternoon, but you'll be a happy camper until then."

"May I ask your name?" Farley politely inquired, chortling at her remark. "You are a delightful human being!"

"Certainly, I'm Julie Eileen Reeves." Her smiling eyes brightened the room. She wore a red, white, and blue diner uniform that spoke of patriotism. "My friends call me Jules. And yours?"

"Farley McDougal," he answered promptly, briefly hesitating. "May I call you Jules?"

"Absolutely!" she enthusiastically responded. "Didn't I see you in here a couple months ago? At this same booth?"

"You did," Farley responded amiably, thinking it was nice to be remembered. "I'm not new to Salzburg, but new enough. Been in the area almost a year now. Moved in from Louisville." Farley pointed to his cup. "Great coffee by the way. I must say, Josie's is a nice way to start the day. Coffee, a newspaper, and a hearty breakfast."

"You sound like my husband, Clint. He eats like a horse and never gains a pound. Grates on me something awful." When the door opened, Jules glanced over. More customers were filing in the already jammed diner, their children jabbering in high-pitched tones, making them impossible to ignore.

17

Farley was thoroughly enjoying his and Jules's conversation and hated for it to end, but he knew it was done. He hadn't laughed this much in a long time. "You'll be seeing more of me, I suspect. Good food–good service. That too is a winning combination."

"I hope so," Jules replied sincerely. "Patrick, the owner, enjoys mixing things up. Ivan, our chef, explores exotic cultural recipes from every continent. We note the best sellers. You'll have to come back during the dinner hour. Every week it's something new. We specialized in local, down-home favorites, but also serve European cuisine and puff pastries made with fresh cream. Guaranteed, you'd love those. On Thursday's Patrick bakes Black Forest Gateau, a chocolate sponge cake with cherry filling. That's a must-try!"

"Goodness sakes, you'd never expect such diversity from a diner."

"Yeah, I know," Jules nodded. "Customers come from all over to eat here. Even from your Louisville!" she teased, her green eyes glistening. "New Albany, Floyds Knob, Salem, Paoli. A lot of tourists from French Lick and West Baden venture this way when the places over there are bustling, especially in summer and autumn, when the leaves turn."

She noticed a couple seated at the other end of the diner looking rather impatient. "Sorry, better go," she said.

"Oh, sure. Thanks for the chat," Farley replied quickly as Jules hurried away.

He glanced at the bustling commotion taking place behind the counter. Orders sat in the window for pick-up and, voices called out, mixed with customer chatter. It occurred to Farley he'd made a mistake by not coming into town more often, and to Josie's Diner, in particular. Soon he'd be a *regular,* like Jules's other customers, he imagined.

When Jules returned with his breakfast, she suggested a not so busy hour. "The best time to come for breakfast is between eight and ten o'clock."

"I'll keep that in mind," he said, thanking her for the tip.

"Enjoy your meal. I'll be back to refill your cup."

Farley guiltily grinned. "I drink more coffee than I should, I'm afraid. I'll keep you hopping."

"Never you mind," Jules tittered as she walked over to the coffee machine to grab the pot. "Hope to see you around soon, Farley. Have a nice day."

"Oh, I will, thank you. I'm going to the library. Got some research to do."

"Tell Bonnie–she's the librarian–that Jules said hello. She's a good friend of mine."

"I'll do it," Farley countered with a smile.

After finishing his meal, he dropped the newspaper off on the bench by the door and walked out into the gloomy overcast November day. Little trace of the snowfall of the evening before remained. Few trees held their leaves this time of year, and winter was just around the corner. He wasn't able to pinpoint the reason, but he felt more optimistic than in past years, despite his current concerns.

Salzburg was a charismatic small town with more than its fair share of friendly people. Farley had made a good decision to purchase the property where his cabin was situated. He lived in a dream home, situated on an ideal piece of land bordering a national forest. From that perspective, he lived a picture-perfect life.

Life is going to improve, he vowed. *First things first. I'll take the reins to search for a solution to my mental issue.* He grimaced, *On the verge of madness is not a state of mind I prefer.* He hummed a silly tune he'd heard recently. Every now and then, in the quiet before dawn, Farley heard children singing in beautiful harmony. Sometimes indiscernible chatter, but the song was clear, and he knew it well from his own childhood. A nursery rhyme from a century ago, he struggled to dismiss.

This old man he played one, he played knick-knack on my thumb; with a knick-knack paddywhack, give your dog a bone, this old man came rolling home. This old man he played two, he played knick-knack on my shoe...

Thinking himself crazy, Farley would turn his white noise machine up to drown out their voices until it passed. Glad he didn't hear it more often, usually he'd fall back to sleep without much trouble, but not always. Though not an unpleasant song, Farley was on occasion, forced out of bed, starting his day earlier than anticipated to quiet his mind.

Just ahead sat Salzburg's library, the grandest building in town. The structure featured large smear stones and was of baroque construction, resembling German architecture. Inside, he admired the rich shades and dramatic shadows of light that trickled through the curved windows and spilled light into its spacious interior. Heavy tables and small heavy wooden desks were stationed at each corner and sidewall. At the back stood an elongated table used for spreading materials out.

He walked to the center aisle, past a man and woman speaking lowly. The place smelled of old books and lemon, presumably a polish. At the visitor's desk he waited for an attendant. Shortly, a woman carrying an armful of books and papers slipped by him. Behind the desk, she set her burden down. "Good morning, how may I help you?"

"Hi, my name is Farley McDougal. I'm looking for information on a rather unusual subject." Shrugging his shoulders, he said, "Heart transplants. I know that's a weird request." He grinned boyishly. "I can't find data, so I came here. "Don't have a computer. which I probably need to address."

"Yeah, they are a necessity these days, I'm sorry to say. Fewer people visit libraries when all they have to do is hit a few keys and the information they are looking for, accurate or not, pops up online." She contemplated her words, and then asked, "What specific type of heart transplant information are you seeking?"

"I'm not sure. Maybe side effects?" Farley had no idea where to aim his appeal. He could see the confusion in the attendant's eyes. "I guess I should explain." Farley did a quick scan of the library. Of the few people scattered about, none were paying attention to the front desk. When he felt assured of not being overheard, he said reluctantly, "I had a transplant last year and wanted to understand it better. What to expect going forward.

"I see," replied Bonnie, nodding her head to acknowledge his unease. "You look great by the way." Observing Farley's fair complexion, which complemented his dark gray eyes and chestnut hair, she thought him a handsome man. "So how have you been since your operation, overall?"

"Better, as the months pass, thank you. My land butts up to the forest, so the environment has been a huge help. I've been recuperating there for the last year. Walking the woods and exercising religiously. My doctor insists but I'd do it anyway. I believe I'm pretty much back to normal."

Instinct told Bonnie that Farley was holding a vital piece of information in reserve, not stating everything on his mind. She had learned to read people after years of working at the library. People didn't always realize it, but their voice inflection and body language spoke volumes. *Tells* were easily recognized if a person knew what to look for.

"Well, if I may ask… do you want general articles or more specific accounts, like peer reviews? Technical data or broader, more encompassing papers on the subject?"

Farley put his hands to his side. "That's an interesting question. I suppose peer reviews and articles with more depth, not journals. Expert knowledge would be best." Farley hoped to achieve a greater understanding of the side effects that accompany his condition. A behind the scenes discussion not available to the public. "Is that what you mean?"

"Yes." Bonnie smiled graciously. "Okay, I'll search credible sources with solid investigative studies backing them. It'll take three or four days to gather the material."

"Absolutely," Farley responded, relieved to have assistance. "Call me whenever they are available, anything is more than I have now."

Bonnie turned a pad of paper around toward Farley and held out a pen. "If you'll write your phone number down, I should be back with you in a couple of days. At the latest, by week's end."

"That's truly kind, I appreciate this." With his parting words, Farley gave a nod of thanks and walked to the exit but then, abruptly turned, seeing the attendant he'd been speaking with watch him closely. "I forgot to ask your name."

"I apologize. I should have introduced myself. I'm Bonnie Woodlock."

"Well, Bonnie," Farley's expression brightening, "Jules said to say hello!"

Bonnie tittered, reacting to Farley's jovial spirit, "She did… did she? If you will, when you see her next, tell Jules, Bonnie said, *hello*, back." They laughed.

Standing on the sidewalk, with the sun poking through the clouds, he felt a lightness of foot. His new surroundings in Indiana were feeling more comfortable with each passing day. As he trekked back to his Land Cruiser, an air of anticipation surged.

Chapter 3
Friend or Foe

Farley decided to accept what he could not change. He knew in his heart a deep, profound message was making its way to the surface. He'd silenced the *voice* at every turn, but no more. Now he would embrace it.

So far, the only coherent words to make any sense was what he had heard the night before. Everything else was like turning a dial on an old-fashioned radio. Nothing but static. Still, he distinctly heard the name, *Charlie.*

"Charlie," Farley repeated aloud, wearily laying his head in his hands. "Who's Charlie?"

He took a quick gander of his living room. Was anyone out there listening to him talk to himself? By the fire, he eagerly concentrated on excerpts of vague dialogue he remembered from various dreams. Ones that stood out enough to reasonably recall. He wondered if Charlie was the name of the victim who had died. Even if it was, what difference did it make? Unless...

Why was Farley singled out? In his *heart*, he knew the only way to get answers he desired was to decipher the images from his dreams and messages into something that made sense. He'd have to stop being afraid of his dreams if he expected to get to the bottom of the ordeal.

He'd jot down dreams of significance so he could refer to them later. Recent dreams had become amazingly lucid. So much so, Farley would swear he was experiencing them in real life. Though the people popping up in his dreams were complete strangers, he felt like he knew every single one of them. It was as though he was watching a movie and he was a main character.

Dreams and interpretations might be another avenue to explore, he decided, aware some people specialized in that specific field.

The silence in the living room grew intense. He went to the kitchen, taking his empty cup and saucer with him. Tomorrow was a new day, along with a new attitude to greet it with a solemn pledge of acceptance. Besides… he'd collect his chihuahuas, Winston and Cocoa from the animal hospital the next afternoon where they were being brought up to date on current vaccines and groomed. They always looked so cute when he picked them up. Them excited to see him, him excited to see them.

Farley hated leaving them overnight, but it was unavoidable. The surgery Winston required, on his back leg, meant he needed to be kept under observation. If Winston stayed overnight, so did Cocoa. They were inseparable brothers.

Slowly he climbed the stairs to the upper level of the home, thinking about his ex-wife, Gloria, and how much he ached for her. The dogs missed her too. A sadness washed over him, and tears pooled, formed by the intensity of her memory.

Farley could still see her face, every inch of it, and hear her sultry voice. Amarige perfume—an oriental floral cashmere wood, vanilla, and gardenia scent—was all that remained of their days spent together. He'd purchased the fragrance each Christmas, and the tantalizing scent lingered when she walked out the door for another man.

He remembered the episode well that brought about the end. A trusted friend's daughter who had been watching their children at the time, had gotten distracted while her mother ran to the grocery. When the drowning occurred, she had gone to the front part of the house to chat with a friend and lost track of the time. It didn't take long for the children to succumb to the elements.

The toddlers had wandered outdoors, and with hands clasped, they had slipped into the backyard pool. Scene investigators related the twenty-something daughter hadn't comprehended the twins were missing. The unlocked sliding door was open allowing the children to patter out onto the patio to the full-size, unprotected swimming pool.

After the tragedy, the circumstances Farley and Gloria traversed became insurmountable, a hill they couldn't climb. The unbearable pain of burying two children wrecked an ideal marriage. Losing a child was never easy, but having twins die from drowning proved an impossible feat to overcome. Twice the pain, twice the devastation.

Farley refused to lay blame when Gloria cut her losses. It was his fault for not seeing the powerlessness she coped with. He'd missed warning signs, like neglecting the tiny puppies she wanted so badly. Back then Cocoa and Winston could fit in the palm of his hand.

In the end, the loss was too great to rise above. Gloria told Farley she felt cursed. He supposed they both were. When she found companionship with another man, she not only walked out on him, but she also abandoned her six-week-old chihuahuas. Now, the three of them held each other up in his cabin in Salzburg, Indiana–for better or for worse.

A full moon shone onto the bedspread while at the window he admired the beautiful scenery. The backyard, illuminated–in a strange glow, felt almost magical.

But then, in his peripheral vision, Farley caught a glimpse of movement near the edge of the forest. The shape grabbed his attention immediately he leaned in.

"How strange," he mumbled, not able to make out what he saw.

A silky black cougar strolled into full view, removing any doubt of what Farley had seen. Already certain it was not a bobcat, as he might have expected for southern Indiana, his curiosity piqued.

The second time in two days? What are the odds of a cougar hanging around my property?

He'd been looking for signs, anything out of the ordinary after the episode he had experienced in the backyard the night before. It seemed incredulous to witness the animal again, yet here it was standing in Farley's yard again. He had dialed his internal antenna to the animal's authenticity, wanting to validate his own sanity.

With a close eye on the animal, Farley watched the feline. The cat remained poised for a long while, never shifting its weight, until at last, it stretched forward on its front paws, looking up at the window, almost as though it knew it was being observed.

A gut feeling nudged Farley that this feral cat was somehow connected to what was going on inside his head, the voices, and his dreams. Why… he could not say.

"I'll start a journal this evening," Farley said convicted. "Document everything, no matter how insignificant it might seem."

By 10 p.m., Farley was past fatigued and crawled into bed. He closed his eyes, focusing on the white noise coming from his bedside sound machine. Clearing his mind, he listened to the sound of ambient noise. His reward–uninterrupted sleep.

Wednesday, November 16

Two days had passed since his visit to the library.

He'd picked Winston and Cocoa up from the animal hospital and carted them back home to familiar surroundings, Winston was under observation, whereas Cocoa was loose as a goose charging up and down the steps with endless energy, happy to be home.

At last, the call Farley had been waiting on came. Bonnie had gathered a considerable number of reports and had them for him behind the desk.

When he entered the library, she greeted him right away. "Good to see you, Farley," she smiled happily, "hope you brought your reading glasses. If not, you're going to need a pair before you're done with what I've compiled. I literally had to stop myself from researching more. I was shocked to find so many articles on the subject."

She gave him a brisk pat on the arm. "Have a seat, I'll be right back." Quickly she disappeared behind the counter to where the articles and papers she had accumulated, lay. Upon her return, she said, "Take what you like, some or all of them."

"Thanks, I'll take them all," Farley said, carrying the stack of materials to the back corner table where he sat down, determined to get a handle on the weirdness afflicting him.

For hours he combed through the material, only getting up once to use the restroom. That's when it registered how dark it had gotten. By late afternoon, he knew more about heart transplants than he thought possible. Walking to the front, he waited for Bonnie to appear from the backroom.

"Hey," he said when he saw her, "I wanted to thank you for putting all this together. That was a tall order." He placed his hand on the pile. "I haven't gone through everything but what I have is incredibly useful."

"My pleasure. You're welcome to check all of it out, library policy is one week, but that can be extended," she said with a wink.

"Really?" Farley's eyes widened, pleased to hear he didn't have to consume everything at the library but instead could skim over it from the comfort of his easy chair at home in front of the woodstove. "That would be super."

"I'll make a list of what you're signing out. When you're finished, just return everything. Never know when someone else might be interested in this same subject. I'll already have it available, thanks to you. You'd be surprised what we get requests for around here."

"Will do," Farley agreed, digesting Bonnie's comment.

Farley exited the library clutching an armful of folders. Homework for tonight. Before leaving home, he'd put vegetables in the crock pot to make soup, figuring he might need a ready-made meal. He'd guessed right.

Once home, he settled in with a bowl of the soup and the first folder.

What he read was thought-provoking. *The human heart is more influential, and powerful, than the brain when communicating with the body and nervous system. Hormones are used to transmit information. The electromagnetic field of the heart is more dominant and intelligent than that of the brain. The heart's field envelopes every cell in the body and extends fifteen feet or more outside the body.*

Farley laid the first folder down, amazed at what he had absorbed. He'd make a cup of hot tea before proceeding, letting the information sink in. Tackling the next folder, he read science had begun to examine the heart from an altogether different lens than in the past, due to multiple case studies that had surfaced.

He mumbled into Winston's cocked ears, "Premonitions, feelings, and retained perceptions have been documented, *and validated. Can you believe that?*" He had no problem believing the heart had an influence over the direction a person might take, internally or externally, especially since his was currently influencing him to read the material Bonnie had provided.

He took an apple pie from the refrigerator, fresh baked three days ago with apples from a local orchard. The pie had been difficult not to polish off in one setting. Farley loved pie and found it made the perfect pacifying food anytime, day or night, especially at breakfast. He cut a slice and returned to the living room, ready to devour more.

He opened folder two. "Since 1967, when the first heart transplant was performed, some recipients reported phenomena that defied explanation," Farley read, "such as personality changes, food preference shifts, and unique, yet unrecognized memories."

Farley's attention zeroed in on the last few lines. He reread the entire last paragraph, this time more thoroughly so he fully understood it's meaning.

"The heart has more than forty thousand neurons," he read. The scientific and medical community refer to them as the heart's little brain. "It has its own inherent, complex nervous system where cellular memory is stored. Acting independently of the brain, heart sensory neurites automatically send and receive meaningful messages. Therefore, it has long been suspected memory transfer from donor to recipient is possible. In essence, the heart has an emotional fingerprint that is unique to the host."

Years ago, he had read an interesting article regarding the positive effects that earth's magnetic field had on plants and was stunned to learn geomagnetism impacted all living things, including humans.

His spring garden came to mind causing him to chuckle, visualizing what it would look like to others if he was seen with the plants, talking to them, trying to encourage their growth with baby talk.

If everything carries an emotional imprint, it makes sense organ cells would too, he determined. Given this information, it makes sense my new heart has the capacity to retain a memory, or multiple memories.

From the onset, Farley was assured his donor's identity would never be divulged. However, the peer paper he'd been skimming through stated in select cases, when mysterious behavioral indicators warranted investigation–usually for psychological reasons–profiles were selectively breached.

Farley jumped to his feet, staring at the medical journal he'd just read lying on the seat as though it were the holy grail. *So, it is possible to find out whose heart I have.* He paced fretfully about the room, digesting this new detail. From the kitchen door he stared out into the forest, then he walked back to the sink, then back to the door, repeating the circle.

The article states, in year 2000, 2,199 transplants occurred and in some of these cases, organ donor recipients reported experiencing recurring dreams they believed belonged to the person who had died and donated their heart. Patients claimed, memories belonging to the deceased, on occasion surfaced in them.

The part that put Farley on his heels was when he read: "Furthermore, researchers suspect, theoretically, it is possible for a memory link between the person who died and the recipient to be subconsciously influenced by the transferred heart."

Farley plopped down, weak in the knees from the adrenaline surge that was pumping through his body. And, in that moment, it was as though the words on the paper leapt off the page, bold as life.

"Premature organ harvesting, within hours after physical death is diagnosed, conceivably can intensify the memory transfer from the donor to the receiver, after death occurs. An increasing number of experts believe cellular memories are indeed transplanted from donor to recipient. Likewise, consensus points to the mind extending beyond our brains."

His *donated* heart pounded wildly as though in synchronicity with what Farley had just read. *I'm one of those rare cases they are referring to,* he declared in his mind. *I have dreams, see things, and recall memories that aren't mine. I hear a voice that isn't mine. My transplant is tied to my mystifying artistic talent, which really isn't mine either. It's my donor's.*

Not long after Farley's transplant, he had become aware of an insatiable desire to create artistically. He not only enjoyed pen and ink drawings but also sketching, watercolors, and oils. Several works of art were collecting in the loft, gathering dust, all created since his operation. At times he was so compelled to paint, sleep eluded him, forcing him out of bed in the middle of the night to work on a scene in his mind.

Although he never displayed them, Farley proudly delighted in them, thinking he had developed a dormant talent and never suspecting otherwise. They were *his* creations, and *his* skill had produced these remarkable, professional pieces of artwork.

Still, one was quite unforgettable, a portrait of a woman with silky dark hair and eyes that sparkled, as though she were alive. Farley didn't know his subject, but he had a strong attraction to her, her radiance enhanced with each stroke he put on the canvas. To this day, her eyes haunted him. When he walked into the loft, where her portrait was stored, resting against others, her eyes seemed to follow him. It was as though something in her aquamarine eyes called out to him.

The strangest watercolor he'd painted, however, was of a corner coffee shop. He titled it *Beans to Brew*. He could see every detail in his mind's eye prior to sketching the rough draft. He would have sworn he had visited this establishment sometime in his past... it seemed so familiar.

I suppose I can ditch seeing a psychiatrist, based on what I just read, Farley settled. *I'm not as insane as I thought I was.* He grinned at his interpretation of sanity. *Now, the issue is how do I get this guy out of my head. Force him to stop invading my thoughts!*

So far, Farley hadn't read anything about people hearing their actual donor's voice, although he assumed considering everything else he had ascertained, it too, was plausible. The problem he faced was who to talk to about the issue. The only warm, breathing bodies he conversed with were his two canines Cocoa, and Winston, and they only cared about eating, playing, and cuddling. For the first time in a long time, Farley laughed aloud at the notion he was talking to his dogs like they could carry on an intelligent conversation.

Tomorrow morning, he would ask Bonnie if she could copy what he felt was pertinent information. While at Josie's, he'd order a cinnamon roll as a thank you to give to his first friend in Salzburg.

He turned out the lights and sat by the fire sipping a cup of hot chai, Cocoa snuggled up against him and Winston curled in his lap, both as worn out as he was. Soon they'd all head upstairs for bed, hopefully for a quiet night without dreams.

Chapter 4
Rod's Apothecary & Sundries

Thursday, November 17

Clint Reeves and his wife, Jules, sat at their kitchen table admiring the view of Hoosier National Forest that edged their property through a generous bay window Clint had installed the previous year after they were married.

Dawn manifested streaks of new day sun through the trees and onto the newly painted soft buttercup-yellow kitchen walls, emphasizing the early hour. With the thermostat switched off, their spacious deep fireplace heated the modest home with little effort.

They sipped the first cup of the day, the scent of dark Columbian roast was strong as they talked and nibbled on buttermilk biscuits and peach jam. Clint was saving his appetite for a larger breakfast, along with the morning newspaper at Josie's Diner—in an hour or so.

"Only a half-day today," Jules announced excitedly. "Should be home no later than 2 p.m." She snickered. "I like being my own boss. Never thought I'd be in those shoes."

"Good." Clint smiled, delighted his wife was happy. "Could you join me later today? I need your decorating expertise. Two heads are better than one, especially since I'm red-green colorblind," he joked, thinking about something he'd learned regarding the condition. "Did you know all babies are born colorblind? They grow out of it as their eyes develop? Not me."

"I did not." She laughed. "Thank you for sharing." She buttered her second biscuit and wolfed it down. "Are you referring to your new office at the orphanage? Or the one at Rod's Apothecary? If you mean the orphanage, I've already been thinking about decorating ideas there. The last I heard you weren't sure you were going to use the attic space, other than for storage."

"I'm talking about the children's home. I've asked your brother if his crew could detail out the attic," Clint stated. "I've been thinking

I'd like to take a few things from the barn over to the home. Besides the barn needs sweeping. Randy said no problem, so I let him know what I had in mind. He's wrapping up a job in Jeffersonville now, and could squeeze mine in after that, no more than two weeks out."

Jules eyes turned thoughtful, questioning what he planned to take to the orphanage. "The barn does need reorganizing," she agreed, thinking anything they tossed out would be a step in the right direction. It's a fire hazard! What will you take?"

Clint winced. Since their wedding it had become a serious catch-all with her belongings and his piled sky-high with hardly an inch to spare. They had been discussing renting a dumpster to throw much of it out before spring arrived.

Jules's house had sold in less than a month. Last April, after their nuptials in March, she offered most of her furniture and appliances to relatives and friends or donated it to Goodwill. She had kept Great-Grandma Hamilton's antiques and select items from her Beech Grove home. Dishware, such as her mother's Blue Willow plates and depression glass would remain with her–always. She also put aside the red cellophane Christmas wreaths from her childhood and a six-foot aluminum tree for safekeeping. She still had plans to purchase more wreaths from eBay later in the year to decorate every window in this house.

"The antique mirror," he answered, "my favorite possession." A boyish grin swept over his face. "Other than you, of course." He winked teasingly. "If you will allow me the indulgence of a bolstered male ego, and a politically incorrect euphemism." He chuckled. "Burn me at the stake for blasphemy!"

Jules howled. "*Oh no,* I married a male-chauvinist! *Oink, oink*! You hid this from me until after we were married? That's grounds for divorce," Jules teased.

"I take it back. The mirror *is* my favorite! Not you! Grounds for divorce, eh?" Clint stood, grabbing Jules's hand. "Dance with me." He twirled her, squeezing her tight. "You are my everything. My girl. Gave my life new meaning."

"We saved each other," Jules replied, taking Clint's face in her hands and kissing him. "We were two lonely souls God took pity on. Gave us a second chance at happiness."

"In more ways than one." The treasure he'd discovered two years prior afforded the couple financial freedom. Thanks to Rod Radcliff, Sr., Clint's benefactor, he had become a wealthy man and although Jules and Clint were insanely rich, they opted to utilize their good fortune to benefit others.

Clint took a deep breath, recollecting Rod, Sr.'s parting words. Words branded into his mind for all time… *At last, peace has found me.*

October 23, 2003, was the last time Clint physically laid eyes on Rod, Sr. The two men stood on Grandview, a location where Rod's General Store had once been erected, fifty years earlier. Today, a new establishment occupied that plot of ground–Rod's Apothecary & Sundries. The new building, completed in January 2004, paid homage to Clint's benefactor, Rod Radcliff, Sr.

Replicated to reflect Rod, Sr's great-grandson's storefront, Rod's New and Used Books, and Clint's musings of how Rod's General Store might have appeared, the new building showcased both styles. This was the third time to have Rod's name on a building at this location.

Although Rod's New and Used Books was never authenticated–a mirage by all accounts–it was as real as anything Clint had ever stepped foot in. A figment of his imagination? The problem was how did he explain multiple visits there. He had even bought gifts inside its walls for his grandchildren's treasure hunt, making it easy to recall the floorplan.

"I'd like to have the mirror in my office. It represents an amazing story of exploration and good fortune. I think I'll set up a ruse corner office." Clint grinned, shifting his position. "That'll work for important meetings, but what will be even better is to have an office above the fifth floor. It's been calling me. We could decorate a mock office on the second floor, and then the real one up in the attic."

His voice was laced in humor. A half-grin translated Clint's real desire. Jules clearly interpreted the look. She knew him well. "Feelings should not be ignored. Has Randy started any of this?"

"Nah," Clint replied, "and, that's just it. I don't want much done. He could start basics, like framing both areas out reasonably soon. I want the one on the second floor formal, but the attic is to remain as authentic as possible. Rough and unfinished." Clint fanned his hands. "Truth is, I was thinking about doing it myself, with Randy's help, of course. We could design a turn-of-the century motif not seen anywhere else in the building."

"That's an intriguing idea," Jules considered, appreciative that her brother and husband enjoyed each other's company. They had worked long hours together during the construction stage of the orphanage, and this would be another joint effort. The building had turned into a construction masterpiece. Five stories high, the orphanage screamed of superior craftsmanship, a creation unequalled in children's homes. That could be seen from the highway.

"How terrific. You could hide there when you don't want to be disturbed," Jules teased him. "Maybe you could use the same theme applied at Rod's Apothecary & Sundries, you know, a mid-1900s style."

"Exactly!" Clint responded enthusiastically, realizing Jules saw what he envisioned. "A compelling design. It'll be my secret chamber when I need solitude. Go up there to read, relax, walk out to the cupola landing to stargaze. No one will have the code to enter, other than you and security in a case of an emergency. Reach for the Stars—code: 7387. That will be it."

Jules stood, ready to depart. "See you later at the diner, sweetie. I'll text you when I'm headed this way." She hugged her husband tightly, not wanting to let go but work called. Jules's shifts at Josie's Diner had been cut considerably since she married Clint. Now, she worked at her own discretion. No longer did she clock in five to six days a week.

Jules had worked there since 1999 and was infatuated with the fifties theme and uniform the diner required. Her relationship with the *regulars* felt more like family. The staff had not changed these past six years. She had the best of all worlds. When her late husband, James, was killed in a traffic accident in 1998, on I-465 in Indianapolis—the same night she lost their unborn child—she withdrew into a shell of a person. Her life had shifted dramatically since that night.

Clint watched as Jules pulled out of the drive, waving as she turned the corner. The weather app on his phone indicated temperatures were unseasonably cold for this time of year. It predicted a high of only thirty-three degrees by 4 p.m. He shuffled to the bedroom to pick out an appropriate sweater, which he found and put down beside his favorite pair of jeans, before heading to the bathroom to shower and shave.

Fifteen minutes later, he was on his way to Salzburg where he'd continue his laid-back morning close to his wife. He'd eat a big breakfast, read the newspaper, drink coffee at his designated table, and be served by his favorite waitress. After that, the plan was to stop in at Rod's Apothecary & Sundries where he'd start the process of clearing out his makeshift office over there. Things from there would be moved to storage at the orphanage until construction on the two new offices were underway.

Back when Rod's Children Home's construction-phase began, Randy's crew installed—per Clint's request—a circular staircase to create a hidden passageway behind the top floor wall, leading to the attic. They laughed at the idea of putting one in, and until now, the space remained unfinished. It was rather childish to construct a secret passage, Clint realized, but he liked the idea of having a secret passage to a secret room. The fact it existed at all brought a smile.

He still had snippets of memories of the rooms and hallways at Vincennes Orphanage where Clint grew up. Often, as children, he and Gary, his best friend, would venture into restricted areas, after dark. They speculated on what was behind the locked doors on the top floors. His fertile imagination suggested labyrinths of passages that ran behind the inner walls. Those hallways would lead to hidden treasure or dead bodies, like in his most cherished book, Treasure Island.

He shook the delightful memories of childhood days with Gary aside as he entered Josie's. "Give me an hour," he mouthed, tapping his wristwatch. "I need to make a couple of stops before breakfast."

Jules signaled she had deciphered his code.

Stepping back outdoors, he strolled across the street to Ace Hardware to find a half-moon wrench. After that, he walked down to Rod's Apothecary & Sundries on Grandview, enjoying the walk.

On the sidewalk, facing the storefront, Clint backpedaled to admire the creation in the store's bay window. He had a hard-fast rule not to sell Christmas items or hang decorations before Thanksgiving. One week from tomorrow all turkeys, pilgrims, the cornucopia of vegetables representing the holiday, flint corn, and pumpkins, would be tidily packed into their respective bins until next November, thereby making room for Christmas merchandise.

The **ROD'S APOTHECARY & SUNDRIES'** wooden plaque at the entrance–just as it had been when **Rod's New and Used Books** was here–swung loosely. The new name was boldly stenciled across the display window as well. Each time Clint saw Rod's name on the building it sent ripples of gratitude through him.

The bell jingled overhead when he opened the door, just as it had when the bookstore was here. Everything Clint did at the apothecary was designed to remind him of his adventure in 2003. Inside he checked merchandise. As he moved about listening to the laughter coming from the rear of the establishment, he knew someone would soon come to greet him, unlike when Rod, Radcliff, Jr. managed Rod's New and Used Books. Clint grinned when he recalled how unorthodox his visits had been with that Rod. A surreal sensation rushed over him, knowing this entire building was recreated from the memory of his visits with Rod, Jr.'s bookstore.

Clint moved through the building, acknowledging each employee with a smile before retreating to the antique room–his current office located inside an alcove to the right of the display case.

On his way he wandered the aisles eyeing the store's goods. Gifts, available to donate to the children's home, were placed strategically alongside other historical items relating to the history of the Reno Gang's rampage through southern Indiana. Miniature molded replicas of the shack Clint had used to access Goss Cave sat on souvenir tables. Wooden toy treasure chests, quartz crystals, snow globes, fake gold and silver bars, pouches of coins, and other assorted knickknacks were positioned at eyesight for children to view and handle. All, Clint imagined, he would have played with when he was a youngster. They encouraged orphanage donations, so a cash box sat by the door. The entire focus of Clint's general store centered around the orphans who lived at Rod's Children Home–raising awareness and encouraging adoptions.

Rod's Apothecary & Sundries was a hodgepodge of children's toys and memorabilia in relation to Little Goss Cave and the stolen treasure hidden there in 1868. Everything in the store intertwined somehow with the Reno Gang treasure and Clint's discovery of it, which in time, prompted the existence of Radcliff's Children's Home. Pamphlets described various activities that took place on the three-hundred-acre grounds, art lessons, taught by local and state artists, cooking classes, stage plays, and woodworking courses, all designed to expand the orphans' horizons.

Clint pulled back the curtain that separated the antique room from the main shop. His eyes took a moment to adjust to the amber lights of the corner Tiffany lamp, but when they did, he settled into his rocker. Although it was not an exact facsimile of the room he had wandered into at Rod's New and Used Books, it was close.

Not long after the hoopla died down in 2003, and the media frenzy waned, following the news of the discovery, Clint got to work designing a building to place on his newly acquired land. Instead of erecting the orphanage close to the road, he built it further back on his acreage. A long winding road, trimmed in blue LED lights defined the lane and the home's manicured exterior and an ornate gate secured the grounds. The home's magnificent architecture was a striking view from US 150 and did not go unnoticed.

On Grandview, Clint earmarked five acres for the general merchandise storefront and its parking lot. His heartstrings urged him to erect it with its main purpose to educate those interested in the history behind the orphanage. The bottom-line, main objective, however, was to connect individuals and parentless children. For Clint it was a win-win. A way to support Salzburg and help the children.

Twenty minutes slipped by while Clint relaxed in his bentwood rocker, drinking Dad's Root Beer taken from the cooler by the door on his way in. Every minute in this room was heaven. Finally, he got up and walked over to the filing cabinet. Beside the desk he pulled out a set of blueprints. Time had come to get back to Josie's.

Chapter 5
An Unsettling Paradox

Farley left his house enlightened, albeit disturbed by the predicament he found himself in. His physical health was on the mend, but his head was an altogether different matter. It had turned into a battle zone, congested with a stranger's chatter. The other person, the one on the party-line, was getting more insistent with each passing day, not going anywhere, not to be ignored.

No longer could Farley pretend the dual voices clamoring for attention in his mind were benign, or fixable. No psychiatrist could rid him of the affliction *he* suffered. With nowhere to turn and no one to share his burden, he was resigned to plotting a solution of his own.

Before returning the literature Bonnie had gathered, Farley planned to treat himself to Josie's breakfast special. Craving comfort food, he pulled the Land Cruiser behind the diner, wedging it between two larger trucks. When he walked through the diner door, Jules's bright smile greeted him.

"Farley," she said warmly. "I'm so happy to see you this beautiful Thursday morning." She lifted a menu that was sitting by the door and led Farley to a corner booth. "I hope this'll do. One week before turkey day… everyone is out shopping, getting ready for Christmas and Thanksgiving dinner. It's been mighty crazy lately with the holidays closing in. Can I get you a cup of coffee, tea, or a soft drink?"

Farley wasn't used to such an energetic welcomed from anyone, other than his dogs. "Thank you, Jules. I'm glad to be here. Am I officially one of your regulars, now?" he teased thinking the sound of that fit well.

"I think so." She giggled with delight.

"English morning breakfast tea, please," he answered, scooting over on the bench, "that'd be much appreciated, m'lady."

"Your wish is my command," she countered jokingly. "Be right back."

For the first time in years, Farley felt the heavens smiling down. He had gained two new friends, Bonnie and Jules, both upbeat personalities, which raised his spirits.

For an imaginary, fleeting moment, he saw Jules sitting in the booth across from him. Not there physically, of course, but in his mind's eye she was and he was spilling the beans about his predicament, asking her opinion on what to do, or who to see. What would *she* do if she heard a stranger's voice in *her* head? He closed his eyes, shaking his head, *Bad idea, Farley.*

Just then a dark-haired, striking man walked in, a newspaper tucked under his arm, smiling lovingly at Jules. The man waved at the owner standing in the galley kitchen. The greeting was mirrored. Patrick and Clint were good friends, sharing a long history.

Farley watched Jules go up to the stranger, lean in and kiss him lightly on the cheek. *Must be her husband*, he deduced. *Those two make the perfect couple–her dainty physique and his brawn. What a pair.* He wondered what it felt like to be this guy. Shamefully, a touch of envy entered his thoughts, causing his soul to cry. It had been so long since he felt the adoration of female companionship. To his shock, Jules turned toward him, leading the man to his table.

"Farley McDougal, I'd like to introduce you to my husband, Clint Reeves," said Jules, wrapping her arm around Clint's waist.

Clint extended a hand, "Nice to meet you, Farley."

"Same here," Farley countered. "You have a delightful wife. Like she said when she seated me, *Josie's feels like home*. I'd have to agree. I'm partially here because of her. She has a way about her that makes you want to come back."

Clint turned to his wife. "Yeah, everyone loves my girl. She's a gem." His last comment was used purposely. It tied to their adventures in Goss Cave, his pet name for Jules.

Jules joshed with them, "Stop it! You're embarrassing me."

"Sorry," Farley immediately replied, not certain if she was kidding.

"Don't be," she joked. "Flattery will get you everywhere."

Clint snickered. "She's a pistol, Farley."

The newcomer glanced at the two of them. He could tell they were clearly in love. "It was good to meet you, Clint. I'm sure our paths will cross again."

"I'm certain they will too. I'm one of her regulars." He kidded. "Plus, Patrick's menu choices can't be beat. He and Ivan are exceptional chefs, you'll get hooked on the place, guaranteed."

Jules walked with Clint to the opposite side of the diner where a table was set awaiting his arrival.

Clint sat down. "Nice guy," he declared, studying the man across the diner. "What an unusual name–Farley McDougal. I like it. Sounds stately."

"He is nice. Says he's only been in town about a year." She glanced in Farley's direction. "Did you notice the sadness in his eyes?"

Surprised at her comment, Clint answered, "No, I can't say I did." He pondered what his wife had said, and added, "but now that you say it… *maybe*. You pick up on things like that better than me. I suppose we all have our stories to tell. Don't we? You and I do."

"Yes, we do." She touched his shoulder. "Not everybody gets a second chance at love, like us." She patted the table. "Better get Farley's breakfast tea before he recants his fine opinion of his waitress. I have a reputation to uphold you know," she said with a wink.

Placing Farley's meal on the table, along with a pot of hot water with an additional tea bag on the saucer, she asked, "Is there anything more I can get you?" She figured there was by the expression he held, but for some reason was reluctant to ask.

"No, not really. Thanks," he replied politely. "This'll do fine."

Jules's expression switched to a solemn one. "You look like you want to say something but are holding back. Are you sure there is nothing more? We have wonderful Danish!"

"No, thank you. This is more than enough food," Farley replied politely, not knowing if he should ask what weighed heavily. "You seemed to have read my mind." He smiled.

Jules's curiosity was piqued. Instinctively she sat down across from him. "We can talk right now if you'd like. I've got a few minutes if you'd like to talk." She scanned the diner. No one was looking her way or showing signs of needing anything.

Farley hadn't been expecting Jules to join him, as he previously imagined. Shocked, he promptly said, "It's a simple question, really. I was wondering if cougars roam these parts?"

Jules was astounded. She leaned back in the booth. "Cougars? No, not that I know." She rechecked the diner, turning back to Farley. "Why do you ask?"

"Because I'm pretty sure I saw one–the most gorgeous, green-eyed creature I've ever seen. I got the impression he might be tame, a domesticated cat that possibly escaped from a zoo. I know that sounds absurd, but he–she–behaved that way."

"Do you mind describing what you saw?"

"Sure," he answered quickly, "pitch-black, not the normal tan color you might expect. Resembled a mountain lion. Something you'd see out west. This guy was sturdy and had the most piercing eyes." Farley couldn't help but notice Jules had turned strangely observant.

He continued describing his situation, "The cat's been hanging around my place for over a week. Normally I'd feel nervous about something like that, but I'm not, oddly enough. This guy appears harmless, tamed even. I wasn't certain if I should alert the authorities, is all. But before I did, I wanted to make certain this wasn't cougar territory. Because of the forest and all. I'm fairly certain it's not. Bobcats, yes, but not cougars or mountain lions."

Jules noted Farley's intense stare, realizing something other than this animal was gnawing at him. "As far as I know cougars have been extinct around here since the start of the twentieth century. Mountain lions and cougars are the same animals, assigned different names depending on which part of the country you're from. Black ones were reported in southern Indiana, but rarely before 1900. Sounds like a panther or leopard, but not in Salzburg. Maybe an exceptionally large house cat?" She suggested lamely, a remark that didn't fly.

Farley frowned. "Well, like I said, sounds looney. I'll keep an eye out, and if I see it again, I'll call animal protection services. Must have escaped from somewhere. Hopefully it wasn't a private owner's good sense gone bad. Thank you for listening." His weak smile drooped.

"My pleasure," Jules responded, sliding out of the booth. "I'll ask around to see if anyone else has had a sighting. It's noteworthy that you did."

She made her rounds with the coffee pot, and then headed to Clint's table. He was thumbing through the newspaper. Anxiously she stood by the table, needing to tell him what Farley stated. "Clint," she said in a concerned voice, surprising him.

He looked up, "Jules, you look like you've seen a ghost. What's wrong?"

She wasted no time getting to the point. "You are not going to believe what Farley just asked me."

"Uh, okay," he replied curiously, "and that would be?"

"It's a good thing you're sitting down, Clint, because Farley asked me if we had cougars around here."

"What?" Clint said, shocked by what he heard.

"Yeah, that's what I thought. He described it as a gorgeous black cat with green eyes. It's been hanging out at his place near the forest."

Clint dropped his fork. "*Jules...*"

"I know! Maybe you should make an excuse and go over there. You can say I mentioned it to you, asked if you knew of anyone else reporting one. I did tell him I'd ask around." Jules looked worried. "He took me by surprise. He had to feel perplexed when I suggested it might be an oversized house cat."

With her last remark, Clint's face turned comical. "Really? He tells you he's seen a black cougar and you suggest it's a house cat? Jules, there is a big difference between the two!"

"You think I don't know that?" she said flippantly. "What else could I say? I know this animal? He led my husband to the Reno Gang treasure?" Her questioning eyes widened. "Why don't you just go over there. I've got orders up. We'll talk later. At home."

"Good idea. I need specifics anyway. It'll be a chance for us to get to know each other better."

Clint watched Jules disappear behind louvered doors that separated the kitchen from the seating area. Folding the newspaper, he stood, took out a five-dollar bill and placed it on the table under his plate. He wrote a short note knowing Jules would find it since the diner didn't have bussers. *I love you!* it read.

With the newspaper dropped at the bench by the entrance, Clint turned to walk Farley's direction, noticing he was being observed. Farley had a close eye on Clint's movements.

"May I?" he asked pointing to the empty bench opposite Farley.

"Please." Farley nodded, glad for the company.

"Jules tells me you've seen a cougar out at your place. Can we talk about that for a minute?"

"Certainly. I was hesitant to bring it up, thinking I must be wrong, but I know what I saw. I regret not taking a picture when I had the chance. I'll have my camera handy next time."

"That's a good idea. They say a picture is worth a thousand words," Clint grinned, intending to keep the conversation light. "Where did you say you saw this guy?"

"In the woods behind my house. My place borders Hoosier National Forest." Farley looked in both directions. "I've been on the mend for about a year." His faced looked pained, not certain how much more he wanted to say, but then the words spilled out. "From a heart transplant."

"Whoa. That's a big deal." Clint replied in surprise. "How's it going?"

"Better. Not so great at the start but I'm slowly getting back to normal."

"I've never met anyone who's had a heart transplant before. You look great, by the way." *What do you say to someone who's had their heart replaced, other than they looked healthy,* considered Clint. "I'm glad to hear you're doing well."

"Thank you. I'm feeling fit," Farley assured Clint, "It's been a long time coming, but I think I've arrived." A broad smile swept across his face, framing his distant eyes.

"Okay, let's talk about the cougar you saw. Jules said it was black?"

"That's correct. Hangs out at the edge of the forest, not far from my back door, which I find extremely unsettling. But like I told her,

I'm not overly concerned, because he appears uncharacteristically docile."

Wanting to extract more detail and fueled by his suspicions, Clint said, "Can't believe you were close enough to see his green eyes. That's amazing."

"You wouldn't say that if you'd seen them. Deep emerald-green, they were... couldn't miss 'em if I'd tried. In the dark they appeared to glow, but you know how cat's eyes reflect. It was a menacing thing to see from my window." Farley looked past Clint, thinking about that night, and then said, "Yet kind... isn't that weird? It was late at night both times I saw him. He comes to the same spot. Just stands there, doesn't sit or move around."

Clint's heart thundered in his chest. "So, you've seen this cougar twice?"

"Yup. He's a beauty. Sounds hard to believe. But, Clint, I know what I saw. The only thing I can imagine is he escaped from one of those petting zoo type places. I remember reading about a leopard that did that once." Farley's eyes met Clint's. "I can tell you what it was not! A large, domesticated cat."

Farley smiled and Clint laughed, "I understand. Not like you could confuse the two."

"I thought I must be mistaken. The animal was so out of place." He stroked his chin. "You'll think I'm crazy, but I swear to God he acted like he wanted to be seen. Even gazed up at my window when I was looking down at him. That was last week."

Clint had never been tongue-tied in his life, but at this moment, he was, certain Farley had encountered the exact black puma he had dealings with two years prior. What was he going to say? He couldn't tell Farley the truth, that the cougar he saw was an apparition—a shadow from the past. He punted and kept the discussion on the light side.

"By the way, I live by the forest also. My place is off US 150, about a mile in from junction East CR 350S and South CR 250S. Been there a little over seven years now."

"Is that right?" Farley delightedly responded. "We're neighbors. I live in the same location. Pretty soon you'll be telling me you've seen this cougar roaming your yard," Farley laughed but found it curious Clint did not. He saw only a hint of a smile.

"I'd rather you have all the fun," Clint replied as a joke, but Farley picked up on something more behind Clint's smile. Clint assured him, "I'll be on the lookout. Spotting a cougar in our area is a big deal."

"I'm glad we had this talk," Farley remarked folding his napkin and placing it beside his plate. "I have some materials to return to the library." He took a pen from his jacket and wrote something down on an unsoiled napkin. "Here's my number," he said, handing it to Clint. "If anything does come up, or you spot the cougar, would you please give me a call?"

"Absolutely," agreed Clint cordially knowing he'd never make the call. He reached for Farley's pen. "Do you mind?" he asked, taking the pen from Farley to write his own number at the bottom of the napkin. "Sooner or later, we're bound to run into each other. It's always best to exchange phone numbers. That's what neighbors do."

After Clint had left the premises, Farley followed suit. He stepped out into the street and a smile graced his lips. He now had *three* friends in Salzburg.

Chapter 6
Radcliff's Children's Home

Late that afternoon Clint and Jules drove to the orphanage with the intention of inspecting the floor above what most people considered the uppermost level, a place they had only been to a few times. Initially the buildout for that area wasn't scheduled until the middle of next year, but Clint had other plans and had decided to move the date up. Construction would start right away.

The long, winding paved road to the children's home was always a pleasure to travel. The front entrance gave the impression of a country manor while the lengthy, deep wraparound porch conveyed laidback charm. The second-floor porches had a lovely view of the gardens which were beautifully shaped both in front and at the side of the building.

Chairs and swings on the porch were rustic, live-edge, locust wood with exposed bark and varying wood grains, hand crafted as one-of-a-kind furniture and strategically spaced around the structure. A pair of French doors faced a courtyard lined in mature trees, which opened into a park area with additional seating and a playground. Stone fountains, strategically located, were especially pleasing but turned off until spring.

"Don't you love this place?" Jules commented, wrapping her fingers in Clint's. "We did such a nice job designing it. From the outside no one would ever guess its purpose. The children live in comfortable surroundings until we can find the perfect parents for them. If we can't, it's a splendid home to live in until they go out on their own."

The first thing on Clint's agenda, after liquifying the Reno Gang bounty in 2003 had been to allocate funds according to their priority. The government, of course, was first in line to take its fair share. After that he returned any marked precious metal bars and coins as well as verified descendant claims. This was an ongoing open claim opportunity set to end in 2006. Surprisingly, other than the government, claims were minimal. Most of the gold bars recovered were unmarked and were considered Clint's under the Finder's Keeper's law. The first thing on his agenda was to design Radcliff's Children's Home. Construction began as soon as the funds were available, taking top priority above all else. To fulfill his lifelong dream, Clint appointed a general manager to oversee the project. By the first week of November 2003, interviews for critical positions had begun.

The focus of Clint's attention, until the last brick was laid, and board nailed into place, was to finish the project to partial capacity by Christmas 2004. The doors were opened by Thanksgiving of that year. Clint had thought of nothing else, other than how to serve warm meals to homeless children for the holidays. After countless late nights, and toiling long hours, Rod's Children Home opened its doors on November 19, 2004, ahead of schedule, although not complete. One year from the planning stage, the home was able to house residents in one section of the edifice. With more to complete, the structure would not be fully operational until spring of 2006.

Shortly thereafter, the last of the remaining personnel was staffed. He had engaged an executive recruiting firm to search for people best suited to fill critical positions prior to opening and spent many long, exhausting nights reading through résumés and performing background checks, until, finally, he'd hired the last person.

Clint knew firsthand from living in an orphanage as a little person, how crucial teachers were in helping orphans deal with their lot in life. He passionately considered backgrounds and circumstances on an individual basis. Counselors could offer a world of good to alleviate a distraught child's fears like Clint had experienced when he sat in sessions after entering Vincennes Orphanage at age five.

He had hired social workers to coordinate adoptions and foster care. Next came qualified therapists to lead group talks and private one-on-one discussions with children who held deep-seeded problems. Identifying the warning signs of those not coping well was of major concern. Not all children adjusted to their new environment, so he brought on a behavioral health associate. Clint easily recalled the days ensuing his father's disappearance and his relocation to the children's home. He knew full well how difficult the transition was.

Next, a nutritionist was brought onboard to manage dietary needs, hired to provide the kids with whole food and organic-based meals. Then came the cooks, janitors, and cleaning crews. At last, Rod's Children Home was up and running, although far from completed, supported by a staff of twenty-eight people. Every time Clint witnessed the goings-on inside the home a sense of pride enveloped him.

Occasionally, in the stillness of night, he felt overwhelmed with emotions. He was brought to tears with emotions because his lifelong dream had been fulfilled. The orphanage he'd dreamed of building had come to fruition, no longer a pipedream. His benefactor, Rod Radcliff, Sr., had made it possible for Clint to provide care to youngsters bearing heartbreaking situations.

Aware of his distraction, Clint answered Jules. "I do. Coming here makes me happy."

Gazing through the windshield at the house on the hill, he said, "I can't express my appreciation in adequate terms for the gift and responsibility I've been afforded. Our money is used wisely, never on frivolous things. To the contrary, we are making a difference in the world."

"It sure is," agreed Jules. "We have more than our fair share. How much is enough. Right? Let's roll it out to those less fortunate."

Clint anticipated getting the ball rolling on his attic project. Grinning, he said, "I'm excited about creating my man cave. I feel like a kid in a candy shop." Clint laughed, picturing what his office in the attic would look like. "I don't think I've grown up."

During the construction stage, Clint had fantasized what the area at the top of the building might look like with an oriental rug, window coverings, and plank flooring. Presently the stucco walls were straightforward, the floor plyboard, and the windows without appeal. That was about to change. He pictured his personal belongings from Rod's Apothecary in the room, creating his own hideout with treasures of a different sort.

They entered the orphanage, hand in hand. After spending a short while speaking with the receptionist, they proceeded directly to what would soon be Clint's secret office. Instead of using the elevator, they climbed the stairs to the fifth floor. As they passed workers, they acknowledged them with genuine courtesy.

Disturbed by what he had heard from Farley McDougal earlier that day, Clint found himself fretting over what this development implied. He had no choice except to wait for what came next. One thing was for certain, he'd walk the forest, if for no other reason–out of curiosity. He'd search for paw prints, anything to show Farley's story was true.

Though he hadn't said as much, Clint felt an undertow of turmoil roiling through his body. If the puma was indeed in the woods outside Farley's place, something was terribly wrong. The last time he'd seen what he knew to be *the black puma* was the night of the treasure hunt party in September 2003. Over two years ago.

Could it really be the same wild animal that led Clint to the shack where Rod, Sr. awaited, and ultimately to the discovery of the Reno Gang treasure. The problem was, the cat died fifty years earlier, by his father's side in the bowels of Goss Cave. So, what was he doing walking the forest again? Clint believed the strange events of that affair were over and done, a one-time eccentricity. Still, if the cat was back and walking the forest, there had to be a reason.

Clint recalled Farley's claim. "I think he wanted to be seen."

If that's true, pondered Clint warily, *something awful is going on.* The reality of that thought made matters worse. He cringed, *Why would he return?*

Clint could think of nothing else for the rest of the evening.

"You seem distracted. It's the black cat Farley told us about. Isn't it?" Jules asked, aware Clint's mind had traveled elsewhere.

"Yeah, I can't explain why, but I know it's him, Jules. The same black puma we had dealings with before. Tomorrow I'm going to walk the woods," he said with an air of concern.

"I'll come with you."

"If you don't mind, I'd rather go alone. I'll have my antenna up this time and won't ignore anything that elicits my attention. I've learned a lot more is going on than what our eyes detect." His brows furrowed, as though to say, *I've experienced the truth, and have seen behind the veil.*

Jules nodded, discerning his meaning. She too had a better perception of the larger picture.

"If it is him, there's a purpose." Clint's face grew grim. In truth, he didn't want to be involved with anything that came close to his last encounter. The chaos and uncertainty of that time had affected Jules and him deeply. He wouldn't let that happen again. The uncertainty Clint felt was intense. *If there is a next time, I'll hold nothing back. I'll put all the cards on the table and totally confide in Jules.* Although he prayed it didn't come to that, something deep down told him his black cat had returned and was carrying a message.

He looked at his wife, thinking how much he loved her. He shook the premonition from his thoughts, and mentioned in an upbeat tone, "I'm going to bring the things from the store over as soon as the floor is laid. Should be next week. We'll convert the antique room into something more useful. What do you think about an employee lounge?"

Clint moved to the tall, thin, elongated window on the far side of the room that overlooked the estate, declaring, "This window turned out perfect." He pulled Jules closer. "We did good, kid. You can see for miles from up here. The scenery is spectacular."

Then he joked, "These windows look like something you'd see in a horror film. You know where someone is watching you from pulled back curtains but vanishes the second you look at them."

The window was patterned after a German medieval castle they'd seen in a magazine. "It's ideal." Turning to face Jules, he teased, "If you can't find me, you'll know where to look."

"Yeah," she said, "here, or underground in your ancestor's hide out, in the shack, or Goss Cave. Take my pick!"

He roared, knowing she wasn't far off the mark. Clint put his head on her shoulder, "I'll have one additional hiding place now," he chuckled, tugging on her sleeve. "Come on, we have things to do."

At home, Clint changed into what he described as his foraging clothes–hiking boots, flannel shirt, heavy overalls, and thermal socks. Before setting out for the barn, he gave Jules a peck on the cheek. "I'm going to find something to replace the foyer mirror. The antique mirror is going to my new office. Vintage décor matches what I see in there."

Clint moved toward the back of the house.

Jules called down the hall before he was out of earshot. "Hey, make what you hang in the foyer something pretty. Entry worthy!" The thought occurred to her she should shop for a wall hanging that matched her taste as much as Clint's did him.

The mirror held a certain lure over Clint, although she would never tell him she thought that. When he glanced at it, she saw it in his eyes. Admiration maybe, but Jules saw something more, something unidentifiable. A special bond between him and the antique mirror was real, as well as profoundly uncomfortable. The strange thing was the darn thing shouldn't exist, having been purchased in a store that also didn't exist, yet there it was hanging on the wall. A step further beyond the *unexplained*.

If Clint wanted to take his prized mirror off the wall and rehang it in the attic at the orphanage that suited her fine. If truth were told, the thing gave her the creeps. The grandchildren's treasure hunt items–which also defied explanation, bought at the same nonexistent bookstore–were also in Clint's possession. As far as she was concerned, he could house them anywhere he wished so long as they weren't in their home.

She tried not to think about it too much, but down deep, it bothered her. The weirdness of the whole ordeal that brought this into Clint's possession was creepy. He had replaced the gifts given out at the treasure hunt with similar items. No one argued. She suspected the grandkids didn't want them any more than she did. The objects weren't sitting out in the open, but she felt their presence as she moved through the house. To have them in the attic at the orphanage would be a relief.

A half hour later Clint carried in from the barn a farmhouse scene. "Will this do until we come up with something better.?" His dark brows knitted, not convinced Jules would like the picture. "I don't remember this one, but I like it."

Jules answered lovingly, "That's because it's mine." She had all but forgotten the painting she picked up at a garage sale in Beech Grove a decade ago. She was glowing. After sitting in storage, all but forgotten, seeing it again made her happy. "Couldn't bring myself to toss that one out when I moved to Greenville."

Later, they ate a simple dinner of beef barley soup and warm crescent rolls. An hour after that they were in the living room eating cake and sipping coffee, going over the events of the day. Farley's name came up right away.

"Clint, it must be a mistake," Jules stated logically, feeling better after having adequate time to consider her conversation with Farley that morning. "A feral cat. A large one, maybe, but feral, nonetheless. Our eyes have a way of playing tricks on us. Farley said he saw it at night. Right? I think he was overly tired."

"I agree," Clint responded candidly, thinking about what his wife proposed. "Maybe it's unnecessary but I'm going to walk the woods tomorrow. I'll call if I discover anything that seems strange."

Together they settled on a new motif for the lounge at Rod's Apothecary and Sundries. To make it employee friendly, they'd bring in an interior designer to create a reasonably modern environment. She would take the reins first thing in the morning. Maybe set a meeting with the employees to get their input.

Clint, on the other hand, would hike the forest in search of a cougar.

Chapter 7
Truth or Dare

After his meal at Josie's Farley headed to the library to return Bonnie's materials with an appreciative handshake and an apple Danish. When asked about any cougar sightings in or around Salzburg, Farley was told none had been discussed, leaving him to be the only one to have seen this elusive creature.

Besides the feral animal in close proximity to his dwelling, his troubled heart had found its voice and was trying desperately to invade the quiet layers of his solitude. No longer could he deny what he knew to be true, a *stranger* shared his mind and was forcefully trying to take center stage.

The following morning Farley would traipse through the deep forest. As good a time as any to explore regions he had yet to trek. Besides, time alone would do him good. He had found hiking improved his attitude, offering him a less cloudy perspective. To walk the woods, without the dogs, cell phone, and especially the heightened chatter he dealt with would make for a welcome change.

A while back Farley realized that stepping one foot inside the forest shut out the other person's discourse. It was as though the forest created some type of sound barrier between him and the additional dialogue. For reasons unknown, the problem he wrestled with daily couldn't reach him inside the national forest.

That night Farley had a horrific dream, awakening him in the middle of the night. Panting, a cold sweat beaded his brow. Shrouded in darkness he had been standing at the mouth of an alleyway. Two men were quarreling, leaning into a brick wall. Farley collided into something, causing both men to whip around and break apart. One of the men lunged at Farley, his hands covered in blood. Farley gasped as he watched the other man escape down the dark alley disappearing into nothingness.

The shock caused Farley to roll out of bed, waking him up on the floor. The dream had been so real he remembered the smell of whiskey on the larger man's breath. After his heart slowed, resuming to its normal pace, Farley couldn't shake the surreal feeling he had, so he walked downstairs, grabbed his coat, and went outside.

The chilly air on his exposed skin was a welcomed contrast to the clammy dampness that lingered on his brow. For a long while he sat on the steps, elbows on his knees, head cupped, breathing deeply. He was disturbed by what he saw in his dream. It was evident someone was badly hurt, possibly killed. Farley would have sworn before the Almighty and a court of law, he had been teleported somewhere and saw a real crime taking place.

Getting up from the step–his heart rate steady–Farley moved indoors to the liquor cabinet where he downed a shot of bourbon. A fitting response to the nightmare. Sitting by the woodstove, he stared into the flames, worried about his mental stability.

What is happening to me? he fretted, feeling the dream and the voice were somehow connected. Never had Farley been more aware that he needed outside help. The problem was he had nowhere to turn. *A thread runs through these separate events,* he told himself. *The black cat, the dreams, the voice... who talks gibberish. And who is Charlie, the only word I've ever understood.*

An hour later he trudged back upstairs, a weary man. In the restroom he splashed water over his face and pressed a steaming hot washcloth against his eyes. The bourbon had done its job. Cocoa and Winston, wagging their tails, followed him to bed.

Friday, November 18

The next morning, after a quick cup of Columbian brew, Farley set out to explore the mysterious parts of the forest he had yet to wander. His thermal-lined jacket made the weather more tolerable, along with gloves and the cap with wings he'd pulled down around his ears.

He locked the house and set out. The brisk morning air felt invigorating, his breath forming vapor trails as he progressed down an animal corridor where sunlight penetrated the bare branches, defining the forest floor–a dramatic contrast to the blue sky. The passage was uneven and rough, made by forest wildlife, taking him to parts of the woods he hadn't ventured. His compass showed he was headed east which had been his intention.

I think Clint said he lived east of me, Farley contemplated as he moved further up the trail, noticing pockets where smaller animals bedded down for the night, in decaying trees that had fallen and in cavities dug into the earth. *If I go that direction I might possibly run into his place. Get a better feel for how far apart we are.* The thought of finding Clint and Jules's house brought a pleasant smile—two of his three newly formed acquaintances.

Thirty minutes later he sat down on a branch in a small clearing to catch his breath. Relieved to have a clear head for a change, with nobody clamoring for attention, Farley closed his eyes. Listening to the sounds of the forest, he realized how fatigued he had become. Although he had regained much of his strength over the past year, walking a mile had hammered home just how far he still had to go, and he wasn't anywhere close to one hundred percent.

An unexpected sound grabbed him, bringing him out of his reverie of savoring forest noises. His attention darted in all directions, expecting to see an animal, or even a person, since the sound was so substantial. It occurred to him a tangible presence was nearby. A few minutes passed. Then, just as he was convinced it was nothing, he saw something. The black cat that frequented his grounds stood in the shadows clearly waiting on Farley's eyes to see him.

Farley jumped to his feet. He stared at the cougar. "What do you want?" he asked, not expecting a response. He waited for whatever came next.

Green eyes bore down, as he stepped one paw closer. Then another.

Farley thought his heart would leap out of his chest. *Is he going to attack me?*

When the black cat's piercing green eyes turned away, disappearing into the shadows, Farley cautiously followed. A sixth sense telegraphed this animal's actions had purpose.

Twice the cougar pivoted, waiting for Farley to catch up.

Somewhere, about a half mile later, the cougar abruptly stopped. Pausing to make certain Farley was nearby, he methodically moved out into an open space. Beyond, at the far side of the opening, Farley observed a rundown shack. The cougar silently walked inside.

Am I supposed to go in there? When a wild animal is in there? Am I nuts?

Farley's face contorted considering the insanity of the notion. For several minutes he waited, wondering if the cougar would exit the small quarters, but he did not. Gradually Farley stepped out into the clearing directing his attention toward the shack's apparent entrance. Sucking in a deep breath, he bravely ambled to the side of the structure to see if a window existed. There was none.

He swallowed hard, took a deep breath, and stepped inside. To his amazement, the cougar was nowhere to be seen, only an empty room. The structure showed signs of major repair. To his right, a closet that had been badly damaged, chipped, scraped, and gouged, like a bear had ripped it apart, had a bucket with tools and nails lying next to a tool belt.

Can't believe this is out in the middle of nowhere, thought Farley, uncomfortably aware the feline that had led him to the shack had vanished into thin air. Farley became confused, turning to leave but was taken aback when he found Clint Reeves standing in the doorway with his arms folded.

"Farley, what are you doing here?" he asked curiously.

Farley was embarrassed, dumbfounded, and utterly speechless.

"Are you alright?" Clint asked, seeing the bewildered look on Farley's face.

"Man, I'm sorry. I have no idea what I'm doing, or why I ended up in this structure."

"Hey, don't sweat it. I own the place. Been working on it." Clint looked around. "As you can see… when time allows. Thought I'd do a little work since I'm back this way. You'll laugh, but I decided to walk the forest to see if I could identify any cougar markings, or pawprints."

Farley's thoughts traveled to the cougar he'd watched move into the shack. His stomach tightened. "I'm a little lost for words. I think I need to go home."

"Hey, it's alright. To be honest, I'm glad to see you. Stick around if you like." Clint pointed to the closet, and the space to the left of it where a shelf had once been. "You could hold those boards for me while I secure them to the wall. I still have a lot of unfinished repair work around this place. Could use an extra hand."

"Clint, I swear I've lost my mind," Farley declared, not elaborating on his meaning. "Maybe some other time." Then he mumbled under his breath. *When I'm not hearing voices or seeing things that aren't there.*

"Sure," Clint responded with concern, trying to reconcile Farley's odd behavior. "Please," he implored, "I'm a good listener. I'd like to hear what's bothering you. I can tell something is."

"You'll think I'm mad!"

Clint nearly erupted in laughter but held back for Farley's sake. "I know all about crazy. I promise to keep an open mind." He gazed into Farley's worried eyes, "You apparently don't know much about me, or you wouldn't hesitate on that subject. I'm a safe bet." He chuckled. "Trust me."

Farley desperately wanted to spill the beans, take a weight off his shoulders, but he didn't know where to begin.

"Take a load off," Clint encouraged, reading Farley's mind. He pointed to the folding chairs where he and Jules usually sat.

Dragging them to the doorway so they could look out into the trees, Clint watched as his new friend lowered his lanky body onto one of them. He felt relieved, thinking if Farley didn't sit down soon, he'd fall. "Hey, I'm all ears."

"Just remember," Farley joked, without a smidgeon of humor, "you asked."

"That I did," replied Clint, careful not to make light of what disturbed Farley. "Proceed, please."

"You know that cougar I told you about?" Farley observed the intensity of Clint's face. "Well, I saw it come in here. Then it disappeared. I swear to God, I saw that animal walk right through this door." His eyes followed Clint's.

Now it was Clint's turn to look startled. Taking a minute to let Farley's word sink in. "Man, that is strange. Are you certain?" Clint lowered his eyes, knowing the answer to his question, and sorry he'd asked it.

"As sure as there is breath in my lungs, it's the truth." Farley spoke decisively–one word at a time. "I saw a large, black, green-eyed cougar walk right through the entrance," he claimed. "Quiet as a mouse, I trailed him through the forest right here. I told you I'd sound like I was off my rocker."

Clint's eyes narrowed. *Should I tell the truth of what I know, or a partial one?*

"I believe you. Zero question about it," he said, "I just don't know exactly how to respond." Clint leaned back in his chair, "It may come as a surprise to you, but I know this creature. I know him well, in fact." Clint looked uncomfortable. "There's a backstory surrounding him that exceeds any amount of time we have right now. Someday I'll explain." He looked out the door into the forest. "Few people know about the cougar you described, but apparently, you've had an encounter with him that also defies reason, like I did a while back."

"I'd like to hear about him. Clint, I need to hear about him. I want answers. Truth is I've seen him several times, besides today, like I mentioned the other day. That's why I came into the woods. I wanted to find a pawprint to cast a mold of to show you. I have a small jar of plaster and water in my backpack. Plus, I had in mind to locate the distance between our two homes. Odd, isn't it, that you would be out here doing the same sort of thing?"

"I'm going to say something that may surprise you. I don't completely understand it myself but believe me… it's a fact. I *believe* you were supposed to see this cougar. I'm positive he would have kept showing up until you came here to my property. To *my* shack. We're speaking by design."

Strangely, Farley felt comforted by their honesty. "At this point, I'd believe anything. My mind isn't all there half the time, anyway," he lamely joked. "I've been hearing and seeing things that defy reason. I have issues that are stranger than you can imagine." He turned away and softly muttered, "And to think I was getting ready to make an appointment with a physiatrist. Maybe it's not necessary."

A wave of intrigue rippled through Clint. "We may have more in common than you think, Farley. You won't appreciate it in this moment, but you were supposed to reveal whatever is troubling you. I'd lay money on it."

Farley sized Clint up, overwhelmed with gratitude for a chance to come clean. The serious nature behind this man's kind eyes was profound. A story lay waiting. Giving a slight nod, Farley gestured his approval with glistening eyes. "I'm going to tell you everything, my friend because it feels like the right thing to do. No matter how opposed I am, and at the risk of making a complete fool of myself, I'll do it."

"Before you do, though, I have a suggestion." Clint displayed a charismatic smile. "There's somewhere I'd like to take you first. A place few people have seen. Would it be okay to talk there, safely and without distraction? Believe me, it's the only secure place to disclose deep secrets like we're talking about."

Chapter 8
Epiphany of Counterpart

A handshake confirmed in forty-five minutes Clint and Farley would rejoin forces. Clint gave directions to his residence, off US 150, before the two men went their separate ways.

They both needed a change of clothes for the *dark zone* climate of Goss Cave. Clint knew, firsthand, that the temperature below ground was a steady fifty-five degrees, entirely too balmy for heavy coats, gloves, and skullcaps. Outerwear would be kept topside until the two men resurfaced through the closet's secret passage. A simple hoodie would suffice for where they were going.

Clint made a quick call to his wife. Voicemail picked up on the fourth ring. "Hey Jules," he said, "something's come up and I may be late this evening. Farley and I are getting together this afternoon." He wavered, and then added, "I didn't want you to worry if I'm not home when you get there. I'll explain later."

When the call ended, he quickly made his way down the hall to the bedroom. A jolt of adrenaline raced through his body as he changed. A mystery was afoot. Clint had not been in Goss Cave in a year and the prospect of seeing it again, under such weird circumstances, sent goosebumps up his arms but felt right.

In the kitchen, he filled a thermos with hot coffee and grabbed four chocolate chip cookies from the covered plate sitting on the table. He latched the door behind him and then set out to the barn to grab the Fenix flashlight. Clint learned early on never to go into Goss Cave without a heavy-duty flashlight and a pocketful of extra batteries.

Clueless what Farley might reveal, Clint instinctively knew it was significant. Otherwise, why was he drawn into the mix. The black cat was the linchpin, a link between them—a calling card. Why he returned after the last affair was supposedly put to bed was an unsettling riddle that would soon, hopefully, be made clear.

Farley parked his Land Cruiser on the road in front of Clint's modest home. He knocked on the door and turned to face the field across the street, waiting for Clint to answer. When he moved down to the first porch step, he noticed Clint walking out of the barn at the side of the house.

Crossing the gravel driveway, Clint called out, "Hey, pal." The lettering on Farley's sweatshirt made Clint chuckle loudly. DREAM BIG, it read. A black and white, long haired, chihuahua triumphantly had pinned down a humongous bone with one paw, a silly, undoglike grin on his face.

Farley prepared himself for the usual teasing he received when wearing his favorite sweatshirt. A gangly, six-foot-three man donning a chihuahua sweatshirt wasn't exactly the description of masculinity.

"Oh, that's funny," laughed Clint. "I take it you are a dog owner." He was cautious not to make fun of the half pint on Farley's sweatshirt.

"I am, indeed." Farley proudly grinned. "I have not one but two of those guys. Devoted brothers that fight like siblings. They play equally as well," he declared. "They protect me with everything in them, especially Cocoa. You should see how they can switch to attack mode in a blink of an eye. It's hilarious." Farley beamed affably. "How about you?"

"Nah," Clint confessed. "I'm not sure why. I suppose I prefer cats. The second he said *cats*, the cougar came to mind. He could tell Farley was of like mind.

Farley had kept in reserve the reason he owned a pair of chihuahuas. They were sweet and loving and he didn't want to diminish their value by dragging the ugly past into it. They were unwanted, like him, and no one wanted to air dirty laundry.

The two men strolled to the back of the property shoulder to shoulder, disappearing into the forest down a footpath Clint knew well. Wandering through the winter woods was a stark comparison to the full trees of summer. Clouds drifted, visible through the bare treetops. A ghostly warm light cut through the branches as the house disappeared from view.

"It's magnificent back here," said Farley. "I'm an explorer at heart. The smell of the forest intoxicates me. I'm strongly drawn to it. Probably a trapper in a former life."

Clint spoke over his shoulder, "I totally agree. We have much in common, it would appear. This place is like a second home to me. The land has been in my family for more than a century." A moment passed. "I played here when I was a kid when my father and I came to visit my granddad."

What he had said was a bit of a stretch, nonetheless, Clint enjoyed what he *imagined* to be true. Bits and pieces of visiting his granddad at the shack was sketchy at best. At the time Clint thought the man lived at the shack. Later, the real story surfaced.

"We're almost there," he said, knowing the shack was within a few yards. "It's right around the corner. The journey we are about to take will surprise you. It's a secret entrance into Goss Cave. I hope you're not afraid of the dark because its pitch-black down there."

"Nothing scares me. Not anymore. I'm impervious to the boogeyman," Farley proclaimed speaking boldly.

Farley's comment did not go unnoticed. "That's a brave thing to say. So, you've checked behind the curtain, and concluded the boogeyman doesn't exist?" It was framed as a question but there was an edge to his voice. Clint related to Farley's claim, having been stuck in a quagmire of turmoil after finding his father's corpse in the cave where they were headed. Clint closed his eyes, feeling the weight of Farley's stare.

"Sounds like we have a few things in common," Farley admitted, glad to hear Clint agreed.

"I believe we do my friend." Clint stood aside, letting Farley walk inside the shack.

Farley took in his surroundings. "I can't imagine anyone living here. It's rather small compared to living quarters today. Your grandfather must have been a humble man. I'll be glad to help you with the repair work. Did you remove any furniture?"

"No, there wasn't much here when I stumbled on it." Clint grinned thinking there wasn't anything in the shack. A shelf and a closet made up the interior. Otherwise, the room was bare. As a child, he recalled his grandfather rocking him on the porch and reading stories, but he couldn't bring up much more than that.

Clint pointed to the closet. You're a head taller than me, so being in the cave could be a challenge. The opening to it has been enlarged so that should help. A couple of years ago, we widened it.

"I'm ready," Farley declared enthusiastically, "I can't recall the last time I was in a cave, so I'm excited."

Clint got on his hands and knees, crawling through the closet. He turned and said, "Follow me."

They climbed down the ladder to the cave floor. Farley tapped Clint on the shoulder. "I feel like a ten-year-old. I haven't had this much fun for eons. Thanks for the invite."

"My pleasure," grinned Clint, "I have a perfect location for us to sit and chat. I have a few things I'd like to share. Likewise, I hope."

Cautiously the two men moved through the cave, a worn path Clint helped form. When they reached the area where his father, Eli, had died, Clint stopped. The opening to where the Reno treasure was discovered was a hairsbreadth away.

"This is where I wanted to bring you." Clint looked down. "Where we are standing is noteworthy."

Farley combed the area with his gaze and said, "Interesting place."

Clint nodded. "I found my father's body… right here. He died in 1953."

Farley's jaw dropped. He looked down at his feet.

"When I was five, my dad walked out and never came back. On Christmas Eve of all things," said Clint, sorrow written on his face. "I thought he abandoned me. I lived in shame my whole life until I was shown otherwise." Clint placed his weight against the cave wall, directly where his father's dead body had lain. "I was raised in the Vincennes Orphanage west of here. A man named Rod Radcliff, Sr., showed me the truth about how my dad died and why he didn't come home."

Farley frowned, the wheels in his head turning, "Isn't that the same person the orphanage is named after?"

"Yes, it is." Clint grinned in acknowledgment. "I consider Rod Radcliff, Sr. my benefactor." From his backpack Clint unwrapped an Army blanket and spread it onto the ground. "Please," he said pointing to the ground.

"I get the feeling you are preparing me for something considerable," declared Farley, lowering his long legs to sit on the heavy blanket beside Clint.

"I am," he admitted believing since the cougar led Farley to the shack it was time to tell his new friend the full story. "I want you to trust me because you look like you could use a friend. Your secrets are safe with me, Farley." Clint said, "I have boo-koos of my own. Most originated at this very spot."

Other than the light illuminating from the flashlight Clint had laid between them, beaming against the far wall close to where the treasure had been found, the darkness held no features. Dripping water streamed down the walls and a moist current carried through the air. Minerals from the earth registered strong.

"Let's play a game," Clint suggested holding a watchful eye. "I'll start."

"Alright," Farley agreed smilingly, amused by Clint's strange antics.

"The first time I was here," Clint observed Farley's face closely, and then claimed, "I followed a ghostly spirit who died in a fire the same year my dad disappeared, back in 1953. A man my dad trusted murdered him, so it turned out my dad was wrong. Luke McCauley, my father's partner killed Rod Radcliff, Sr. because he knew too much about my father and Luke's affairs. Although I didn't know it at the time, my father died by the same hand–Luke McCauley's. He murdered them both."

Farley stared ahead, "Holy cow! And you saw Rod Radcliff's ghost?"

"Sure did." Clint pursed his lips. "I also saw my father die. In a vision." He watched Farley's reaction. Seeing he was engaged thoroughly, he declared, "I was shown the truth. Like I said earlier, I believed my father deserted me. It wasn't so."

"I don't know what to say," exclaimed Farley, lacking any adequate words to express his surprise. "If I had heard that from anyone else, I'd say they were out of their freaking mind. But you..."

"I know. Me too, but it happened," Clint stated, cleverly adding, "Your turn."

A flash of reluctance sparked in Farley's eyes. "Me? Oh, God."

"Please, I'd like to hear what is bothering you. Obviously, something is."

"Where do I start?" admitted Farley, rewinding back one year. "I suppose it began not long after my heart transplant."

A long minute passed. Clint waited patiently for more information.

In the dim light Farley's fixed stare locked with Clint's. "I've been hearing things that aren't natural. A guy's voice pops into my head, but rarely can I decipher a word of what he's saying." Farley looked away, out into the shadows, "He's getting more and more vocal all the time. Clint, he's driving me crazy. He wants something from me, but I have no idea what that is."

It was Clint's turn to look dazed. "Really? What do you *feel* is his intention?" Clint didn't bat an eye with his next question. "Is there a chance it's the donor's spirit trying to connect?"

"Good Lord! That's exactly what I've been thinking," professed Farley, relieved to have told Clint and able to let go of the fear he'd been carrying around. "I can't make heads or tails out of what he's saying. It sounds like he's mumbling all the time. That's not all. I hear children, they are singing an old-time nursery rhythm. Do you know it? *This old man, he played one, he played knick-knack on my thumb…*" Farley grinned sheepishly, feeling silly.

"I do, we sang that when I was a kid," he chortled. "This old man he played two, he played knick-knack on my shoe, with a knick-knack paddy whack, give your dog a bone, this old man came rolling home." His face brightened. "This old man, he played three, he played knick-knack on my knee…" Clint burst out laughing, "I can't believe I remember that rhyme so well."

Farley wagged his head. "Me too, Clint. I recognized it straight away. Another time, I heard the name Charlie. I don't know anyone named Charlie." His countenance showed deep roots of confusion when he turned away, turmoil roiling beneath the skin.

Clint conveyed his suspicion on why their paths might have crossed. "Look, the cougar brought us together for a reason. I was meant to get involved in your issues. Don't know how, but I believe I'm supposed to help you unravel this. Let's work together to find an answer."

"The cougar you've been seeing around your place?" A peculiar facial expression accompanied Clint's next words. "He's a magnificent creature. In fact, he led me to the shack, and ultimately to Rod Radcliff, Sr."

Clint eyes narrowed. "He's a puma who died in 1953. He curled up next to my dad after he had an altercation with Luke McCauley. Luke had returned to this very spot to gloat over the treasure my dad had unearthed. That's when Luke killed him. The only problem was the puma was lying in wait when Luke returned. There was a fierce fight. Both sustained fatal wounds."

Clint studied the patch of ground where his father was found and the small bones tucked beside him. "The cat crawled over to Dad before it succumbed to its injuries. Forensics noted multiple puncture wounds around the puma's neck and torso. Later, they were deemed the cause of death."

"Good grief! That's wild, but it's the true story behind how you located the Reno treasure? Wow, that's amazing. The newspapers didn't really offer much detail other than you lucked out. You said in an interview that treasure hunting was in your family history. If I remember rightly, you found the treasure by happenchance."

"I did. Now you know the truth behind the discovery. Like I said, *walking the walk* makes a person appreciate things like what we're discussing—straight-up paranormal activity, and, for the record, I wasn't always a believer. A diehard doubter is more like it. I was forced explore the possibilities. After what I witnessed, I had no choice but to accept what I didn't understand." Clint's words revealed a secret, few, other than Jules and a close friend at the police station, Scott Edwards, knew. "Bizarre dreams turned relevant. That's how it all started. Farley, I tapped into a realm I had no idea existed. Some would call it a sixth sense."

"Truly?" he responded with a startled expression. "You didn't believe in that sort of thing beforehand?" The tension around his eyes lessened. He was relieved to be able to confess the strangeness he'd been shouldering. The timbre of his voice told volumes. "I'm having unusual dreams too. Usually they're short snippets, or shadows of things. Sometimes I see a hazy man's face with sunken eyes in an alley."

Uncertainty lingered between them. What did these recent events mean?

"Still, the other night I had the most vivid dream to date. Two men were in an alley. They appeared to be arguing. Next thing I knew one of them was standing in front of me, his hands covered in blood. He was pleading for help right before he dropped to the ground. I can't get his haunted, icy eyes staring up at me out of my head."

Farley's set jaw telegraphed the tension he held as he waited for Clint to react. A lock of hair lay damp against his forehead. Dark circles under his eyes, revealed lost sleep, or maybe something more. He was a man too young to own such deep expression lines around the corners of his mouth and eyes. Incomparable hardship lay in the contours of his face that even a person of limited intuitive powers would have noticed.

"Do you think the man in your dreams could be related in any way to your transplant?" asked Clint, thinking there could be a connection.

Farley considered what Clint suggested. "Possibly. The guy saw me and asked me to intervene, like it was possible. But it was a dream, so I couldn't. Right? It felt like I had teleported or was remote viewing the incident."

"So, it's your belief, the voice you hear all the time is not the man you saw in your dream?" Clint pondered a moment before finishing his thought. "I've been wondering about that. Have you heard him since we've been talking?"

"The strange thing is, I haven't," Farley admitted with a sigh. "I walk the woods to escape the madness. For some reason when I'm hiking, the voice fades out. It's as though the forest blocks transmission. It's become my place of refuge. The cave must have the same effect. Nothing is as tranquil or healing as aimlessly walking through the woods. Until I met you and read some articles Bonnie gave me regarding heart transplants, I thought I was going off the deep end. I'm relieved to know I'm not."

Clint absorbed Farley's theory that the forest possessed unique qualities. Clint was of the same accord. The forest felt like a living entity to him too. A melody ran through it like flowing water. Even Clint became part of the orchestration when held by its gentle embrace. A tangible, living-breathing connective organism with a vibrational heartbeat.

"Plants generate an energy field. Did you know that? They possess a unique intelligence known to them. They communicate through an integrated signaling response system. They produce chemicals comparable to neurons. Amazing, huh? Their magnetic field is measurable. With fifteen to twenty senses, they have human-like abilities to hear, see, smell and taste through a vocabulary of three thousand chemicals. They relate in ways that are beneficial to the entire organism, and environment. Like I said, the forest works in harmony for its greater good."

"I knew plants respond to positive reinforcement. I read once that a scientist performed an experiment where he spoke harshly to one plant and lovingly to another. The neglected one quickly died, where the plant that had been nurtured, flourished."

Clint became reflective, thinking back two years. "Pine needles whispered acoustically in the wind the day I heard my first voice. Wraithlike it said, *He's here.*" Clint glanced to the side as though recalling the exact moment he heard the voice. "I had been leaning against a Sycamore tree, enjoying the sounds of nature." Clint looked back at Farley, "Turned out he *was* here. My dad that is." Clint patted the ground, "Right where I'm sitting. It's weird, but I still feel his connection in this recess."

"I can't imagine how painful that must have been," said Farley. "To lose your dad at such a young age, I mean. You must have missed him terribly. I had a healthy relationship with my father. Unlike some men, I always wanted to be a dad. Have a house full of kids, you know?" He drew in a deep breath and turned away. "Wasn't meant to be, I guess."

"So, you don't have children? I have two boys, Wade and Rusty. They've been everything I could have ever wished for. Their mother died in 1997. I struggled for a long time, until Julie and I met. She was a lifesaver."

Farley's tears pooled, streaming down his face. "I had kids. Two of them." He lowered his eyes so Clint wouldn't see the deep sorrow they revealed. "That's another story for a different time, my friend. Don't want to talk about it right now."

Clint recognized Farley was having difficulty keeping it together. "When you are ready to talk, I'll have a listening ear."

"My story runs deep, like yours," said Clint. "Rod revealed every sinister step Luke McCauley made—in a vision. Later, I assisted the authorities in solving a double murder. Turned out Rod Radcliff, Sr. died in a fire at his general store. Luke set that fire. Unjustly, Rod, Sr. was blamed for his death and store destruction. They said he was smoking in bed which caused the blaze, but it wasn't true. Luke needed to silence Rod because he was planning to tell the police what he knew about the connection between him and my dad's disappearance. Luke killed them both."

Clint put a hand to his mouth, recalling the first time he entered the cave. "I found the Reno treasure over there," he said, pointing to where a stack of quartz crystals and geo rocks were once piled.

"Is that right?" replied Farley with a huge grin. "That must have been a sight for sore eyes."

"I found it behind that wall of crumbled rocks there." They both looked at the crevice. "It looked a lot different when I first happened upon it," Clint claimed, remembering the tight fit. "A fissure so small, only a skinny person could have squeezed through. I enlarged the space. Otherwise, I couldn't have wedged my body through, but it was clear someone else had been chiseling away at the rock and had reached the other side before me."

"People were thinner in 1953," Farley contended, "if we can believe what we're told."

"The team that moved the treasure pretty much destroyed the natural setting where it was initially hidden. I wish I had taken a picture for posterity's sake." Clint grinned. "The discovery absolutely flipped my life on its head."

"Rod showed you all of that. How incredible." Farley stated shocked at what Clint had told him.

"He did. Made everything crystal clear. Luke wanted the keep the treasure at any cost and wasn't willing to negotiate. Enough to kill for it. He'd do whatever necessary to keep all of it for himself. He didn't plan to share, but the one thing he didn't count on was the puma my father fed in the evenings. Luke met his match when the puma got involved."

Clint got up; Farley followed suit.

Farley put a hand on Clint's arm. "One last thing I think you should know. I believe it's important."

The depth of Clint's stare was piercing, "What?"

"*Ease my pain...*" Farley said softly, "I heard the voice say those words. My feeling is the man is haunted by something tragic, and his soul is not at rest."

Those words sent chills up Clint's spine, remembering Rod Radcliff, Sr. and his restless soul. "This man has a history. We'll dig into it," Clint promised with conviction, assuring Farley they would uncover what was fueling the aggression. "You and I will delve into his death. Find out more about him."

Together they made their way back to the hole that led to the closet. As Clint moved pass the tunnel that burrowed toward his great-grandfather's hidden quarters, he affectionately patted the wall knowing he'd be in that underground section soon.

They squeezed through the gap, forcing their bodies back into the shack. Clint had started to put the structure back to its original condition, the state it was prior to the excavation crew and police investigation damaging it. It was comforting to see the shack returning to the condition his father and grandfather would have recognized.

The men reached an agreement to meet the next day at Farley's place at 7 a.m. Over coffee they would map out their next plan of action.

Chapter 9
Knowledge Shared

In the wee hours of Saturday morning, strangeness occurred.

Doubled over in bed, Farley gasped for air. The instructions were so exact he had no choice but to take notes. He grabbed the pen and paper off the bedstand and started scribbling, as fast as his fingers would allow.

Charlie—Grayson Hospital, June, Ann, Spirit Sisters!

"Go to the hospital?" Steepling his hands, he pleaded for understanding. "I'll do whatever it takes but you'll have to help me... help you."

In pitch darkness Farley tugged on his corduroys, buttoned his flannel shirt, and pulled socks over his ankles. The digital clock on the nightstand showed 3:15 a.m. The energy in the room was palpable. He could have touched it, the lingering pulsation had shaken the furniture, walls, and floorboards. The urgency Farley felt was intense. The message was strong and undeniable.

Within minutes of combing his disheveled hair, brushing his teeth, and splashing a dab of Égoïste cologne on his neck, Farley was out the door in the car driving to Louisville. Whoever this June was, he figured she must be a conduit in authenticating Charlie's unfolding message.

Driving faster than advisable, within the hour Farley pulled into the hospital parking lot. Outside, in his vehicle, he stared up at the enormous building, not having any idea what he was doing there. June was the answer, but what would he say if he located someone by that name? Where would he find her? Was she in there? He moved through the revolving doors, without a clue what to do when he got inside.

At the receptionist desk, he politely inquired, "Which floor is Intensive Care?" Why he asked that, he had no idea. Just seemed like a good place to start. His knees shook as he awaited an answer.

"That would be the seventh floor, sir," the twenty-something blonde responded. "What name are you looking for? I'll look them up for you."

Farley froze, not expecting the question. "No, that's okay, I have family here in the waiting room. I'd like to join them, is all."

The receptionist examined Farley for a moment, and then pointed down the hall. "I see. Take the second elevator on the left. Turn left on the seventh floor. Someone will show you to the waiting room and your family."

Scurrying away rapidly so she couldn't say anything more, Farley looked down at his feet until the elevator doors closed behind him, relieved to have escaped the watchful eye of the receptionist.

When the elevator doors opened to the seventh floor Farley turned left as instructed. He pressed the plate that allowed entrance to the ICU floor and proceeded to the partitioned reception desk. No one was there. The semi-dark hall seemed ghostly. Multiple scenarios ran through his mind as he waited, thinking about how he would go about asking for June.

Soon, a short, older lady with her back to Farley opened a file cabinet on the far end of the room. She started to file the armful of folders she had laid on the table beside her.

He cleared his throat.

Looking up, she apologized as she moved his way. "I'm so sorry sir. I didn't see you there. How may I help you?"

With his heart pounding, he answered hoping he was guessing right, "I'd like to speak to nurse June, please."

She frowned as though confused by the request. After a moment she inquired, "June Johnston or Bennett? We have two Junes."

Ecstatic that he had hit the jackpot with the right floor, Farley understood he had a fifty-fifty chance of answering correctly. He made a split-second decision and blurted out, "Bennett... June Bennett."

"You have good timing. She just walked in. Can I tell her who's calling? And the nature of your visit?"

Another hurdle. "I'm sorry, ma'am. It's of a personal nature." For reason unknown, he added. "Tell her Charlie sent me. She's expecting me." After saying Charlie's name, Farley cringed, thinking. *Why did I say that?*

"I see. I'll let her know you're here. Please have a seat through there," she pointed to a small glass enclosed room. On the door he saw Consultation Room.

Five minutes later a woman walked through the door. "Charlie? You said Charlie sent you?" The woman cocked her head to the side, suspiciously eyeing him. "I only know one Charlie and he's no longer with us. What did you say your name was? And don't say Charlie!" Her brows lifted.

"What about Ann?" Farley asked quickly, afraid June would rush away.

June's face drained of color. "What are you playing at?" she demanded. "That's Charlie's wife. You must know they are both dead. You need to tell me what this is about before I call security."

"I can't," Farley responded frantically, so fast it shocked even him. "I've been instructed to find you. Since 3 a.m. I've been stumbling around in the dark. I had no idea you worked on this floor or that I'd find you. I was told to come to Grayson Hospital. That's all I know."

June appeared frightful. "What? I'm sorry but I must ask you to leave." She stood, yanked on the door, and left the room. She walked over to the receptionist's desk, and a discussion passed between the two ladies. Both turned in Farley's direction as they conversed, one with her hand on the phone.

He jumped to his feet, flung himself into the hallway, not willing to be dismissed so easily. He declared, in a desperate response to her rejection, "Spirit Sister!"

June spun around fear written over her ashen-white face. "What did you say?"

"You heard me," Farley boldly replied. "I told you... we need to talk. It's urgent." He searched the other woman's stance, who appeared ready to make the call. Behind the glass partition, her eyes revealed her discomfort, possibly scared at the boisterous way Farley had swung the door open and charged into the hallway. He prayed she wouldn't notify the authorities.

"In private," he courteously requested. "Please indulge me with a minute of your time, June. That's all I ask. Then I'll leave."

June faced the woman she'd been talking to a moment earlier, her intuition demanding her to hear this man out. "It's alright, Clarice. We'll be in the cafeteria if I'm needed. I'll only be gone a few minutes. Would you like a latte?"

Clarice tilted her head, surprised by June's about-face attitude. "No, thank you. Are you sure? I thought…"

"I changed my mind," June said with her hand up. "I'll be back in a few." June signaled for Farley to walk with her.

They stepped behind the adjoining doors that separated ICU from the corridor leading to the elevators.

"What is your name?" she asked immediately after the doors closed.

"Farley McDougal."

"How do you know Charlie and Ann Hill?"

"I don't. Not personally." Farley thought about the heart that he could feel beating in his chest. More like thumping in his chest.

"Then why are you here?"

"I'm acquainted with Charlie."

"I thought you said you didn't know him, or her," June fired back, drilling for answers from the stranger she'd just met.

Farley stopped. "Please, we must stop here. Not converse in the cafeteria with people around. I was given your name, and I believe," he faltered, trying to find the right words, "with all my heart, you are the sole person who can help me."

June saw the frantic look in Farley's eyes. She pressed the nearest floor. When the doors opened, she instructed him to have a seat pointing to the chair closest to the window on the sixth floor. "You'd better tell me what this is about? Earlier you said, *Spirit Sister.* You have no idea how special those words are to me, absolutely none." Her eyes filled with tears. "They're the one reason I didn't have you escorted out."

"Forgive me, June. I didn't mean to frighten you. I heard them this morning, after I the name Charlie and Grayson Hospital. The voice said, *June, Ann, Spirit Sisters.* I came immediately because I felt led to do so. I felt strongly it was important. I had no idea what the words meant or that they would upset you."

Farley pleaded his case to the woman sitting beside him. "I must know the truth." He put his hand on his chest. "The heart that beats here is a transplant. Something terrible is going on and Charlie is at the bottom of it."

Farley closed his eyes, feeling his heart's rhythm. "How did Charlie die?" he asked without opening his eyes. "You said his last name was Hill?"

June started to sob, crying uncontrollably. "You believe Charlie's heart is in your body?" She turned away, facing the window. With the back of her hand, she swiped tears away that streamed down her cheeks.

"Ann Hill was my best friend. We were like sisters." June looked deep into Farley's forlorn eyes. "We often referred to ourselves as spirit sisters. SS for short. We wrote it on cards, texts, everything." June moved closer to Farley. With a smile, she proclaimed, "Only Ann and I knew what SS meant. I never told anyone, neither did she… that I know of. It was an affectionate phrase we used for one another. Our special code."

June thought back on her childhood. Remembering what it was like performing household duties with her mother. "I never had a sister. Had I… I would have wanted her to be exactly like Ann. I loved Ann so much the grief was unbearable when she died. Didn't know how I could go on, a life without her was empty." June glanced back toward the windows. "Especially how it happened. It was too much to endure. I had to see a therapist to help me handle the sudden shock of it."

Farley got to his feet, "Please, I need to know how they died?"

"Gunshot!" June grimaced, thinking Farley surely knew more than he was saying. "Charlie was shot point blank in a coffee shop. Can you imagine? They were the nicest people you'd ever meet. Ann died from a ricochet bullet from a Glock 9mm handgun."

Farley walked away, the fires of fury simmering to a slow burn when he became distracted by the snow that had accumulated outside the windows. The Land Cruiser was covered in a blanket of snow. Condensation streaked the window glass, as if tears were falling.

Enraged, he questioned, "They were intentionally singled out? Or was it a random shooting?"

"Based on the police report, Charlie was killed purposely. I don't believe Ann was, but who knows. I have a friend on the force. He believed foul play was involved but, that theory was not pursued. The worse part, as if that wasn't bad enough, is the Hills had their son with them. The poor kid."

Overwhelmed by the powers of evil in the world, June slumped in the seat, drawn and unable to describe the horror of that night. "Can you imagine? The child, only seven years old, witnessed the brutality of his own parents gunned down in front of him. He saw it all, Farley, blood splattered on the wall where she hit. My friend said they rushed the boy out, but it was too late. I work in Intensive Care, so I am used to this sort of thing, but this hit hard."

Snow blew sideways outside the window. A winter storm had moved in. "No one else was hurt, thank the Lord," she shuttered, again wiping tears aside.

Layering his hand over June's, Farley told June what he suspected. "I strongly think Charlie wants me to find his killer."

June looked shocked.

"Someone's voice is in my head, trying to communicate. Been there for a while. Since the transplant, last year, but only recently was I able to decipher small blocks of what was being said. It comes so sporadically, I'm never prepared. It's as though Charlie homed into on a frequency he alone could use."

Farley grew distant, turning inward. "It's him, I'm sure of it. He gave me your and Ann's secret code. Who else could it be? So, you'd listen to what I had to say, and not reject me."

He gazed at June with troubled eyes. "Until I walked in downstairs, I had no clue what I was going to do." Farley looked knowingly, "Ann must have mentioned *spirit sister* to Charlie. Revealed its significance. I had no idea where my donor heart came from. I do now–it belonged to your Charlie Hill."

June smiled thin. "I'm glad I was able to help. For what it's worth, I believe you. I've seen strange things working in the Intensive Care Unit. Some defying explanation." June glanced into a space only she could see. "You know the last time I saw Ann… I gave her a London blue topaz ring. She had given me an UNOde50 blue topaz bracelet a few months earlier. We were so much alike, it was uncanny.

"Thank you for sharing," said Farley. "For the longest time, I thought I was losing my mind. Truth be told, I feel compelled to follow this through, no matter where it leads. That's if I want my life back." He thought about the painting of a coffee shop he had drawn. "Thanks to you I have a place to start. Next thing I need to know is the day Charlie died. I want to be certain about the dates. I'd also like to know who the attending physician was."

June stood, pushing up slowly with her hands, ready to return to the ward. With a heavy heart, she said, "I wish you luck. God knows, I hope the person, or persons, who did this are apprehended. Brought to justice." She weighed her next words carefully. "Don't take chances, Farley. An evil person murdered Ann and Charlie. They'll not think twice to do it again. If you start snooping around, you could be setting yourself up." She embraced him. "Keep in touch. Please let me know if anything develops."

"I understand, believe me, and I will," Farley agreed without hesitation. "Going to law enforcement is out of the question. They wouldn't warm up to how I ascertained the knowledge I possess about Charlie. They'd lock me away." He sniggered humorlessly. "I do have a colleague willing to join me in this effort."

June viewed the empty chairs in the seating area. The floor would soon be filled with visitors. "The last time I heard from Ann, she said, *my bracelet connects me to you. Hope to see you soon, my sweet spirit sister.* I loved her accent. She was born overseas, in Ireland or Wales, I believe." June smiled, viewing into the past. "Ann could have been targeted, as much as Charlie, considering you were led here to me." She took Farley's hand. "Please, please be careful."

"I will," he said, and then asked for a second time. "The night the shooting took place? It's imperative the timeframe matches up precisely with my transplant."

June's brow creased, haunted by the dark shadows that accompanied that evening. "Sunday, December 21, 2004, 7:32 p.m.—a day I'll never forget. Snow was coming down in buckets. The streets were treacherous. So close to Christmas. What a heartbreak! My heart still aches for her."

Farley nodded. "Now that you say that I recall the weather was extreme the night they called me to come to the hospital. I've forgotten so much about that evening. When the call came in, I was a nervous wreck. I was shaking like a leaf because I only had a half hour to get to the hospital." His eyes met hers. "This hospital. I was prepped and in surgery in no time. After that, most everything is a blank."

"I'm going to do something I've never done in my life," June admitted, her face beautiful, like an angel's. "I made a copy of Charlie's and Ann's Declaration of Death. A death certificate. And his transplant donor card."

"Are you saying you'll make me a copy?" asked Farley.

"Yes. It feels right to turn it over."

Just then a brilliance of pure energy whooshed through the room, Farley saw it in his peripheral vision. He turned his head just in time to see a being of light rise and disappear through the ceiling. Farley's breath arrested, not believing what he had witnessed.

Energy cannot be created or destroyed, rung in his head.

Charlie had been in the room, listening, directing, pushing for action. His presence dangled in the air. June felt it too, Farley could tell by the alarmed expression on her face. A recognition passed between them. Words needn't be spoken for what they both perceived.

Farley moved to the window, observing the weather, and thinking about Charlie and his insistence to be acknowledged. "I can't thank you enough for the information you've provided. You put me on the right track. Next, I act. What that is I don't really know, but I have faith Charlie will."

"You're welcome," she returned his smile, a question on her mind. "What cologne are you wearing?"

Mystified, Farley had to think, "Uh… oh, I bought it when I was in Louisville. I went to pick up a nice suit at Dillard's for my aunt's funeral a while back. To be honest I was surprised at my reaction to it when I smelled it in the aisle. I'm not normally a cologne kind of guy, I followed this fella who passed by and asked him what it was he was wearing. It's called Égoïste by Chanel. Why?"

June stepped closer. "I thought I recognized the fragrance." June's eyes grew wide. "Farley, Charlie wore that. It's an older fragrance. I'm surprised you found it. It came out in 1990 and has an unmistakable scent."

Farley replied in disbelief. "You must be kidding!"

"Nope, he wore it all the time. I even asked him once what the name was, and he told me the same as you. Égoïste." She laughed, and then said, "Ann told me it was expensive but worth every penny."

As they departed, Farley clung tightly to June telling her not to worry. He assured her he'd keep her informed.

Charlie walked alongside Farley back to his car. Farley felt his presence.

Chapter 10
When One Door Closes…

Yapping dogs welcomed Clint's arrival in lieu of Farley.

On the steps Clint waited, thinking soon Farley would answer, especially with all the commotion exploding on the opposite side of the door, absurdly loud for 7 a.m. and before the sun had fully risen. He waited patiently, and then, at the risk of stirring additional upheaval, he rapped again, this time with less aggression.

Must have overslept, Clint considered, surprised Farley hadn't answered the door. He knocked again, only this time, louder than the first two times, which caused the dogs to freak out. Clint could have lived without the shrill sound.

He waited, and then stepped back into the yard, calling up to the story above. "Hey, Farley, you there?"

He saw no signs of life inside the house, other than the unhappy dogs ready to charge at a moment's notice. Clint went to his truck and leaned against the hood, putting distance between him and the clamor that had erupted inside.

I wonder if there's a problem, he fretted, not expecting for Farley not to be home. *Why wouldn't he have called and left a message if he couldn't keep our appointment? At this hour, why isn't he home?*

Clint walked to the back of the house. He gazed into the woods to where he imagined Farley had spotted the black cougar, a preposterous notion to be certain. What was the likelihood? Yet, it appeared he had seen the feline. He strolled back to the truck, started the engine, and headed toward town.

Chugging along US 150 at a steady pace, the sun pierced the snow laden clouds, manifesting a sliver of a warm glow atop an offshoot barn structure miles from the road. Over outlying meadows, a herd of cattle grazed on sundrenched glistening pastures.

Clint had worked himself into a tizzy by the time he arrived in Salzburg, torn between going back and pounding on Farley's door until he answered or heading home. He decided to do neither. Instead, he rumbled through town and pulled in front of Josie's

Diner. Worried as to why Farley hadn't answered his phone, Clint flipped his cell phone open for a third time and dialed Farley's number. Still no answer.

Sliding into a booth two spots from his usual, Clint put a hand up for Ivan to take his time with preparing the breakfast he had ordered at the counter when he walked in. A deviation from his norm, rarely was Clint at Josie's this early, not since his gal was typically at home.

Patrick walked over and sat down across from Clint. He asked, "How's it going? You're here early." He noted Clint's expression. "Is something the matter?"

"A little perplexed is all," replied Clint honestly. "I was supposed to meet Farley McDougal at his place, but he's not there." Clint frowned. "You know him, right?"

"Sure, he's new in town," Patrick responded, curious where this was leading.

"Yeah, that's him," Clint acknowledged with a quick shrug. "We've struck up a bit of a friendship and were going to have a cup of Joe at his place this morning. Only he didn't answer his door. Therein lies the problem. He doesn't seem like that kind of guy. One who wouldn't call if he couldn't keep an engagement."

"Yeah, you'd think he would have called you. Seems a little flighty. Don't you think?" Patrick joked, trying to lighten Clint's mood.

"I suppose, like I said, not sure what's going on."

Just then Farley walked through the door, his face drawn. He searched the diner until he found Clint. He noticed the owner sitting with his new friend.

Clint waved Farley over. "Clint, I feel like an absolute idiot. I'm so sorry. Not my normal MO to make plans and not keep them." Farley glanced over at Patrick, who waited for more of an explanation.

"I saw your truck when I was driving through town and remembered. I don't know what to say other than I am very sorry. I forgot to put your number in my wallet. It's sitting on the table at home. My phone was silenced."

Clint waved his hand in dismissal, signaling Farley to never mind. "Don't fret, man. It happens to the best of us. I'm just glad you're okay. I must admit I was a tad bit worried." He saw in Farley's eyes that a story waited to be told, but not here.

"I'd better get back," Patrick chimed in, watching a party of five standing by the door. "Duty calls."

When Patrick was out of earshot, Clint asked in a low voice, "What's up? Clearly something has happened. Your dogs went ballistic." He hooted, recalling the commotion generated when he knocked on the door.

"Something sure did," Farley's eyes expanded. "We need to talk. Are you good to come back to the house? I'll put that pot of coffee on that I promised."

"No problem. Let me pay my bill first. I have a slice of pumpkin pie coming, I'll get you one too if you like." Clint slid out of the booth as he talked. "I'll have Ivan toss an extra slice in the bag."

"Sounds good, I'll see you at home," Farley said, turning to leave.

When Clint got into his truck he sighed with relief, pleased nothing of consequence had occurred. He phoned Jules to ask her to inform the movers to transport his things from Rod's Apothecary and Sundries over to the new location at the children's home. Everything should go, except what he had set aside to hand carry personally.

At the kitchen nook in the cabin overlooking the dense forest, Farley poured coffee from the carafe he had placed between him and Clint.

"At three o'clock this morning, something amazing took place," Farley started out the conversation on a sober note with new insight. "Because of it, I will be taking a different course." Farley's attention refocused beyond the pane to the spot where he had first seen the cougar. The animal had not been seen since the day he followed it into the forest and ended up at the shack.

Their eyes locked, Farley's wide when he announced, "I know his name." He waited for his words to register. When he was certain they had, he said, "It's Charlie Hill. Technically, it's Charles. The poor man was gunned down at a coffee shop in Louisville—Beans a' Brewin'." He shifted his position on the bench. "I say poor, but honestly, I know nothing about him, other than what June Bennett told me at Grayson Hospital."

He looked away, internalizing a frightening realization. "Clint, the creepy thing is I have a watercolor upstairs I painted of a coffee shop. I titled it *Beans to Brew*. That's awfully close wouldn't you say? I saw the shop in my mind in explicit detail before putting it to canvas. Like a scene I had committed to memory, it felt so real."

Clint grimaced. He leaned in on his elbows. "Farley, that's uncanny. You know I have a thousand and one questions. For one, why would you go to Louisville at such an ungodly hour? Second, why would this nurse be willing to supply the name of your heart donor? I believe that's personal information. She must realize there are ramifications associated with releasing that sort of information. Why would she do that?"

"Look, Charlie Hill is trying to connect. Before daybreak a precise message came through, although I didn't know what it meant at the time. I heard Grayson Hospital, and then the name June, followed by Ann, and *spirit sisters*. Suddenly, I felt an urgent need to drive to the hospital, not knowing what I would do once I got there. Turns out June is a nurse on the seventh floor, in ICU. I was given a choice of two names. I guessed right."

Farley sat silent for a moment, and then said, "I started at the ICU floor. After my transplant was performed, they took me there. It felt right, as good a place as any to begin my search for someone named June. I hit the lottery. June Bennett happens to be Charlie's wife, Ann's, best friend."

Clint remained quiet, absorbing what Farley relayed. He took a sip of coffee and cleared his throat. "So, Charlie was killed, and he wants you to know. But to what purpose? How are you supposed to rectify that kind of injustice? If that's what it was. Maybe your man was caught up in the underworld, snitched on somebody or didn't pay his dues and they came after him to settle a score."

Farley fidgeted with his napkin. "That never occurred to me. From what June said, Charlie was an ordinary guy, a painter. Nice guy, in fact. But you could be onto something. We can't tell what someone is like from appearances alone–or a book by its cover?" he said, forehead creased.

"Look, I know this might not be easy to hear, but I want you to promise not to go back to the hospital or contact June again. Let me do some investigating before you move forward with any more inquiries. I have a friend who's a cop. I'd like to be given some rope to investigate the circumstances behind Charlie's death. If the wrong people find out you are snooping around, you could put your life in danger. Not so if it's the authorities."

Raising a questionable eye, Farley amiably agreed, "Probably best. I didn't really think about consequences, other than finding out who my donor was. I felt somewhat pressured to followed through now that I think about it. Who knows if this Charlie guy is on the up and up. I've wondered if he could be seeking revenge."

"Good, that makes me feel better," admitted Clint. He had been processing different scenarios that could be behind the insistent voice Farley had been dealing with. "Honestly, I believe we'll get to the bottom of this, in time, but we must go through the proper channels."

Farley didn't like the idea he could be harboring someone's vindictive heart. He'd hold out hope that Clint would discover a more uplifting motive, nothing as vile as he described. "Sounds good. I'll stay put until I hear from you. I'm in no hurry to rock the boat. In the meantime, if anything noteworthy surfaces here, I'll contact you."

Clint reached out a hand, "Deal!"

Farley smiled, mirroring Clint's words, "Deal."

A hollowness in his eyes and smile concerned Clint. Perhaps, it was the dimness of light, but for the first time Clint saw a trace of sadness in the lines on Farley's face he hadn't seen before. What Jules had seen that day at Josie's. Clint saw exhaustion and age, yes, but behind that lay the weight of the world, deep in the folds around Farley's eyes and mouth.

Farley had indicated he was eager for a fresh start. But, with both feet planted firmly in yesteryear, it was difficult to imagine a future without emotional burden. The loss of his children had kept him stuck in a quagmire of pain, but it was his wife's rejection that pushed him over the edge. To live without Gloria was to live without meaning.

The two friends walked to the door with Cocoa and Winston at their heels.

Clint reached down and scratched Winston's tiny little head. His long hair and small frame made him look more female, than male. With Cocoa, however, his male gender was not in question. Cocoa had short hair, his stature broad, sturdy and protective.

Cocoa's ears were taut, his eyes peeled, with one leg lifted, ready to pounce if Clint made one wrong move.

Clint dashed out the door before Cocoa had a chance to make his move.

Chapter 11
If Dinosaurs Could Speak

By early afternoon Clint was standing inside the orphanage lobby, Clint took in the many smiling faces bursting through the glass doors. A busload of children had disembarked from a fieldtrip to Santa Claus Land, Indiana. He saw gifts, packages, and lollipops along with beaming, happy smiles.

"Hi…" one boy blurted out, running full speed ahead toward Clint. Casey crashed into Clint's thigh, hugging it with all his might with a strength greater than his size would indicate.

"Well, hello there. Did you have a nice trip?" Clint inquired, watching the other children move single file into the banquet hall where dinner was being served.

"S-u-r-r-e d-i-d," the youngster stuttered, separating himself from the other children.

Each time the lad saw Clint, he'd cannon into him, which was totally out of the norm. On the spectrum, a high functioning autistic child, Casey interacted with few people. Clint was an exception.

Rarely did Casey make eye contact. His attention was usually drawn to the floor. He showed little emotion except when Clint was around. Speaking in a monotone voice, his interests were contained in the secret spaces of his mind. He had no friends, and his comfort level around the kids was limited.

"What do you have there," Clint asked the dark-haired, blue-eyed boy while trying to decipher what he was holding.

In this singular occasion, a big grin crept onto Casey's face and his eyes looked clear. "Pen-cils. Co-l-or-s. Dr-a-w."

"Wow! May I see it?" asked Clint, waiting for the child to hand it over. Through trial and error, Clint had learned not to take anything from his blue-eyed friend until he was good and ready to hand it over. Otherwise, a screaming fit could develop.

Slowly Casey relinquished his treasure to Clint, eyeing it the entire time until it was back in his hands, safe and sound.

Clint bent down on one knee at eye level. "Would you draw me a picture? Something I could hang on my wall in my new office?" Clint took a step away when Casey's face turned reflective. "I have a secret. Do you want to hear it?" he asked with smiling eyes.

Casey's head bobbed up and down as he took another step further away.

"Okay but what I'm about to tell you has to be kept under your hat." His heart swelled with love for the little boy looking up at him. Casey didn't speak to anyone, only Clint, and for that he felt honored. "I'm moving my office to the attic, and I need pictures to hang."

The child's face radiated with delight. "D-d-d-din-osaur. B-l-u-e."

"Oh," Clint chortled, pleased to see Casey so excited, "that'll be perfect. I was hoping you'd draw me something. A blue dinosaur is a wonderful choice." Clint patted Casey on his head, not sure if he'd withdraw, but pleased when he didn't. "I'll see you soon. Can't wait to see my picture. Those are beautiful drawing pencils you have there. And… I see you have a sharpener. Very nice."

Walking away, Clint's heart ached for the child. The joy he added to Casey's world brought him immense satisfaction. If he were a younger man, he'd consider adopting Casey and take the boy home. Since that wasn't the case, he interacted with Casey as much as possible while at the orphanage attending business meetings or retreating to his office.

The child had been at the orphanage since day one. Sadly, no perspective parents were ever interested in the boy due to his special circumstances. Six other children were admitted that same week, and five were adopted right off the bat due to the hoopla of activity from Clint's advertising. Casey's outbursts and lack of communication skills posed a hindering roadblock for those planning to adopt. Moreover, foster care had restrictions that excluded special needs such as Casey's.

The weather was bitterly cold the night Casey graced Rod Radcliff's Children's Home. Bundled up from head to foot, wrapped in a blanket, the child was left on the doorstep without a note, letter, or piece of identification. Any attempt to find out who he was proved futile, met only with silence when General Manager, Tom Sanders, put forth inquiries. Painfully clear, the boy was abandoned.

Clint moved to the elevators, ready to inspect the start of his new office. Just as the doors opened, he turned and saw Casey staring at him, his look withering. Clint waved. Casey gestured back. Then the doors closed, and Clint disappeared behind the metal cage that lifted him to the top floor and his new hideout.

There appears to be a theme running through my family, he thought with a grin. *A need to become invisible.* He was chuckling when the doors opened to the fifth floor. He stepped out into the hall and walked a few feet. At the door on the left he stopped. It led to the attic and required a code for privacy. He took the steps two at a time until at last he was standing on the highest floor in the building.

Surprised to see Jules putting a few of his things on the shelves, he walked over and gave her a hug. "I didn't expect to see you," he said, a handsome smile gracing his lips.

"Packing your stuff went faster than anticipated. The guys brought the curio cabinet over first, and the rest of the furniture will be here around four." Jules turned to continue her task of dusting and placing each of Clint's most treasured pieces on display in the lighted cabinet. "How did your meeting with Farley go?"

"Thought-provoking," he said with arched brows. "Weirder than anything you can imagine."

"That's not the answer I expected," Jules responded, turning to sit down on a stool. Curious as to his meaning, she waited to hear the rest of the story.

"He wasn't home, so I drove to the diner. Then, within the hour, here came Farley walking through the door. Imagine my surprise, after standing me up. He appeared worried, Jules, and apologized the second he saw me. Said he recognized my truck out front. He didn't tell me what was going on until we were back at his cabin."

Clint wore a boyish smirk. "That pumpkin pie at Josie's is to die for. I swear, Patrick is off the charts with creating desserts that taste a thousand times better than anywhere else. His pie dough is amazing."

"You crack me up with your bottomless pit for a stomach." Her eyes narrowed. "Did you get a piece for your lovely wife?"

"Oops," chortled Clint.

"So, when you got there at seven, he wasn't home. How odd."

Clint nodded. "Some strange stuff is going on with him. First, he sees the cougar, which by the way he hasn't seen since, and then this morning he's persuaded to drive to Louisville at three a.m. He went there to decipher a message he received. How's that for disarming? He heard the name Charlie, and a few other words."

"What?" she exclaimed, confused by his answer. "I don't understand. Why would he drive into Louisville that late at night? I don't understand."

"You know that voice I told you about?" Clint watched for Jules's acknowledgement. "Well, this time it was explicit. Plainly, it referenced names, and places. Farley said it was like seeing signposts with all the markers pointing the same direction." Clint snorted, "I will say, he didn't come up empty-handed, he uncovered some vital information that needs to be explored."

"What does that mean?" she asked with a scowl, suspicious of Clint's reply.

"I told him I'd do some probing. Talk to Scott, see what his thoughts are about the situation."

"About what… situation?"

"Oh, sorry," Clint apologized, realizing he hadn't finished his story. "The night his donor died. A man named Charles Hill was killed in a coffee shop. That dead guy's heart is currently pumping in Farley's chest. Jules, Charles Hill was murdered and he's a troubled soul, reaching out to make contact."

"I don't like what I'm hearing, Clint," Jules said with alarm. "This has *beware* written all over it. We've been down this road before." Thinking back on the dangers of Goss Cave and the dead bodies found therein, she continued giving her two cents. "These things can go sideways six ways from Sunday. Not necessarily in the right direction."

"I know," he concurred. "That's why I'm going to run it by Scott Edwards. I'll ask him to do some leg work on this Hill guy and the night he died. I instructed Farley to stay put. I figure he's not out of the woods with his recovery, not by a long shot. Honestly, I'd rather Farley not traipse around Louisville at 3 a.m. asking questions about a dead guy."

"You're right about that, sounds ill-advised. Especially if the man was killed. Do you know how he died?"

"Farley said *gunned* down. That's all I know. The nurse at Grayson Hospital gave him a copy of the death certificates, both Charlie's and his wife Ann's. Ann apparently worked at the coffee shop. Farley showed me the certificates. Cause of death: Gunshot wounds in both cases."

Clint's sadness reflected in his voice when he said, "This situation is especially dangerous for Farley, and he needs to be careful. There's a possibility he could be in danger. I feel it in my bones." Clint took his wife's hand and squeezed it. "Look, I have no idea why I was dragged into this, but I can say, I believe it was intentional. I need to figure out why."

She groaned. "Please be careful, Clint. Something about this feels wrong." Her eyes grew large. "Besides the fact someone dead is speaking to Farley. As if that's not bad enough, now in essence, you're involved."

"I understand," he said. "The puma lured me into this. I'll wait and watch for other signs. I know how this works. Signs can be anything from a phrase, a book, song, dreams, manifestation, anything." Clint accepted he had limitations in the matter. "All I can say is there is a reason I'm entangled with Farley, in essence… Charles Hill. I intend to find out why."

The door buzzer sounded, workers on the other end were waiting access from the lobby, requesting permission to carry furniture to the attic. Clint had jumped to his feet like a fire alarm had gone off. Answering it, he instructed, "Yes, yes, come on up, I'll meet you on the fifth floor," he instructed, practically screaming into the intercom.

Jules grinned. They both did. "A little loud, wouldn't you say?" she mocked. Tension had been building and it showed on their faces. "Good God. I'm not sure I can deal with this sort of thing, again! We're already on edge!"

"You're not alone…" Clint commiserated, his afterthoughts dangling between them in the silence.

In the empty attic space where Jules remained, she wrestled with the ramifications of Clint's predicament while he raced down the staircase to the landing below.

Only Clint and Jules knew the code that opened the door. Holding it widely so the movers could carry their cargo up the steps, he watched as they raised a rocking chair and desk up the narrow stairwell. With everyone moving about in his soon-to-be office, Clint found the tightness and activity claustrophobic.

"Hey, would you be okay if I split?" he asked his wife. "I'd like to speak with Scott today, if possible." He looked around the room of scattered boxes, displaced items, and handymen. "It's a little crowded up here."

"No problem." Jules smiled, aware of Clint's uncomfortableness in tight spaces. "I've got this. See you tonight. Tell Scott I said hello." She requested, diverting the conversation away from what was at the forefront of their minds.

"Thanks." Clint grinned. Based on his limited touchstone of knowledge regarding personal paranormal involvements, he had business to attend to. "See ya." He distractedly charged out the door.

When he arrived downstairs, he saw Casey sitting at a side table scribbling away with his new colored pencils. He clenched the sharpener tightly as he shoved one of the pencils inside. Papers were scattered around the tabletop. Engrossed in his newly assigned undertaking of penciling a picture for Clint, Casey barely noticed his admirer move closer.

Clint sat down, across from Casey at the table. "So, is this my picture?" he inquired, waiting for permission to turn the image around to face him.

They exchanged glances. "Yes."

"May I have a look?"

"Yes," Casey replied, not moving the sketch.

Slowly Clint rotated the picture toward him, his pulse quickening. He was staring at two dinosaurs, not one–or blue. The dinosaurs were in battle. Red squiggly lines were scrawled viciously as if angrily penciled on the paper. Clint was tongue-tied, not knowing what to say. The red lines undoubtedly depicted blood. The triceratops was an amazing rendition of Trixie from *Toy Story 3*, but that was where the similarity ended. It was not a feel-good image.

Once again, their eyes met. "Is this for me?" Clint asked, wishing to avoid what the drawing represented.

"W-a-n-t it?" asked Casey with downcast eyes and drooping shoulders, which spoke volumes. Childhood normalcy was interwoven with inner rage, suppressing obvious resignation of a tragic past.

"He-r-e," Casey stammered, pushing the picture away as though it had suddenly become distasteful, his eyes filling with stifled tears as he looked down at his pencils.

Clint didn't have to be a mind reader to see what was written on Casey's face. The boy's hurt expression revealed all the ugliness of an unwanted child, a history unbeknownst to Clint.

"I noticed you have a slight drawl." Clint affectionately pointed out, poking Casey's ribs. "Your voice has a Portuguese ring to it," he joked with a silly face. "I bet you're someone famous. Aren't you?" He lifted the sketch and walked to Casey's side of the table. "I want you to know something. I plan to hang this in a very special place in my private office. That way, every time I see it, I'll think of you."

He looked down at the image and tried very hard not to alter his expression. "You did an amazing job. You're a talented young man. I'm proud to own one of your drawings. I sincerely thank you for taking the time to create it for me."

Casey's face took on a haunted countenance, though he uttered not a word. He stood abruptly, gathered up his colored pencils, and paper, and shuffled away. Looking over his shoulder, only once to consider the sketch Clint was holding at his fingertips, Casey turned quickly, his chin quivering. "Make a-nu-ther..." he mumbled loudly enough for Clint to hear.

Positive reinforcement was especially vital when it came to traumatized children. Clint knew, since he'd been one himself. Thanks to the nuns who encouraged him, Clint worked through his pain and landed on his feet and solid ground. His desire to encourage

Casey was the same. To stay open, not to be afraid to express his most guarded feelings. Getting the boy this far hadn't been easy, but that didn't discourage Clint. He would continue to work with him while providing a safe, loving environment.

"I look forward to seeing it, son." he replied in a raised voice. "You have a nice evening, okay? See you soon."

Recollecting his painful past, a curtain of damage hung undraped, trapped in Casey's mind.

Chapter 12
Unlocking Pandora's Box

Salzburg Police Station was nearing a shift change when Clint entered the building. Fortunately for him, Scott Edwards was still on duty when he asked for an audience without an appointment.

By the windows he waited for the okay to head up to the second floor where Scott's corner office was located. Once he was given approval to proceed, he was standing outside Scott's office door within a minute, waiting until Scott wrapped up the phone call he was on.

"Sorry about that," Scott apologized, indicating Clint should have a seat. "You know how it is." He grinned. "Luckily that was a two-minute conversation."

"No problem, I'm glad you could accommodate me. I wasn't certain you'd be here on a late Saturday afternoon."

"Typically, I'm not, but I had some paperwork to catch up on. Thought I'd clear my desk before Monday since next week is Thanksgiving. I plan to take two days off, before and after." Scott noted Clint's body language and could tell something was up. "Good to see you, but why are you here… not to be rude."

"I need your help. A situation has been brought to my attention that I'd rather not tackle alone. With your resources I felt I might bypass some awkwardness that's sure to surface."

"Oh brother, that'll need some clarification. Are you in trouble?" probed Scott with uncertainty, not knowing where this conversation was headed but hoping his guess wasn't right.

"No, of course not," snorted Clint surprised at Scott. "Are you kidding? I'm too old to get into trouble. I just need information. The background of how someone died. Could you see what the police report shows?"

Scott couldn't wipe the astounded look from his face. "Died? That's a rather unusual request. Who?"

"A guy named Charles Hill from Louisville, a heart donor. Farley McDougal, one of our new residents in Salzburg, has Hill's heart."

Clint watched Scott's expression turn even more surprised than with his first remark. "Seems he's experiencing a few irregularities. Maybe Hill's cause of death could shed some light on the issue." Clint left out the core of the story not wanting to get into the weeds with Scott.

"Come on, Clint, you'll have to do better than that," Scott curtly retorted. "If this fella, Farley, wants to ask questions about his donor, why isn't he here? He needs to go through the proper channels or talk to his doctor. Why are you asking, on his behalf?" Scott frowned. "Besides, that's confidential. A donor's name is kept private for obvious reasons. I shouldn't have to elaborate on that point."

"Alright, Scott," Clint exasperatedly replied. "Because he's not a typical case. You, of all people, should know if I'm asking for insider help, its founded. I plan to explain but would prefer not to discuss it here at the station. Maybe over drinks at Aces & Eight? Do you have a small block of time?" Clint shrugged, waiting, aware of how vague he sounded.

A glint of humor flashed in Scott's eyes. Their relationship had always been askew, in a good kind of way. "You betcha! Give me five to lock up. I'll meet you over there."

Before another word was exchanged, Clint was out the door and on his way to the town's newest bar and grill, built after 2003's clamor and onslaught of traffic through town. Since then, the establishment had been giving In a Pig's Eye, another local eating establishment, a run for its money.

Walking in, Clint stood at the counter waiting for his favorite waitress to return from seating customers. "Hey, Trudy," he greeted her, "Scott Edwards and I are going to need a table and a couple beers, away from the main area. Anything available?" he asked, eyeing the crowded bar.

"Your usual spot is open," she indicated, signaling for Clint to follow her. Trudy pulled on a paneled door, widening it a bit to expose a festively decorated motif on the wall of card playing, whiskey-drinking, cowboys in a Western saloon. The wall mural showcased gunslingers, rowdy goings on, dead men, and scantily clad dancehall girls. This section was reserved for privacy–Clint's usual spot. Few individuals were escorted to this room, and it came at a cost. "Will this do?" she inquired, pointing to a table he used most often for business and solitude.

"That'll do perfectly," Clint pleasantly answered, handing her a ten-dollar bill. "You're a doll."

"I'll tell Jules you said so." She winked with a smile. Everyone was aware of how devoted Clint was to his wife.

Clint chuckled. "You do that, and she'll hit me with that frying pan again. I must mind my p's and q's around that woman. She's not as she appears, all sweet and charming. Don't be fooled, Trudy." Grinning, he tossed out, "Are you aware p's and q's stands for pints and quarts, referring to a customer's tab, a drinker told to watch how much they're consuming?"

Trudy guffawed, matching his joke with one of hers. "Jules looks like the type that could keep the likes of you in line with one hand tied behind her back."

"What a hoot. You're not far off." As she walked away, getting ready to pull the door closed, Clint called out, "Scott should be here any minute. If you don't mind showing him to the table, I'd be much obliged."

Trudy put one hand in the air to indicate she had heard his request.

The two men frequented their favorite establishments, but Aces & Eights was where they went when privacy was of the upmost importance. Too many of the town's locals stopped at In a Pig's Eye to feel confident of not being interrupted or overheard.

Since the Reno Gang treasure discovery, Salzburg had been listed in a handful of travel journals as a place to tour in Indiana. Clint had received considerable notoriety, earned by fame and fortune. He was Salzburg's local celebrity. Albeit, accustomed to the attention that surrounded the affair, it drove him to seek places to conduct business without infringement of privacy.

Clint phoned Jules to inform her where he'd be, and to invite her to come join them if she had the time. "Over here," he called to Scott as he slid sideways past the partition. Clint laid his cell phone on the table, in the event Jules returned his call, and stood.

Trudy had already placed two ice cold Modelo Amber beers on the table in preparation of Scott's arrival. Lately, both men had acquired a taste for dark beers, as Trudy well knew, not asking before putting in their order. She also set a large basket of tortilla chips along with bowls of salsa, and queso on the table.

"I'm dying to hear what you have brewing," Scott confessed, having thought of little else since their office conversation. "Feels like shades of another time, just with a different spin." Scott cocked his head. "So, what's this about? What do you hope to uncover?"

"Insider knowledge, like I said," stated Clint. "I'm driving somewhere to shake a few bushes. Didn't want to do that until I had a little more info about Charles Hill. Truthfully, I don't know if I'm walking into a hornet's nest or not. Who knows, but the guy was targeted for some apparent reason."

"Are you serious?" Scott rifled back, concerned for Clint's safety. "Why are you involved in this anyway? Why isn't Farley McDougal pounding the pavement if he's so interested? He should be doing the leg work."

"Scott, you don't have the full picture. Not yet. Relax, man!"

"Then enlighten me. Won't you?" Scott snapped, not comfortable with Clint's involvement with anything surrounding a corpse, shooting, or foul play. A no-nonsense kind of guy, he wasn't the type to beat around the bush or spare Clint's feelings.

"I plan to, but you'll need to take your cop hat off for twenty minutes. Can you do that?" With a sideways glance at the door when Trudy passed by, Clint asked, "Will you put your friend one on for me? Like in 2003. Because we are talking the same type of situation."

"Holy cow," scoffed Scott, "not another one of those?"

"Afraid so…" the corners of Clint's mouth curled subtly at Scott's reaction "And this one is a lulu! Believe me, like nothing I can wrap my head around. You won't either. It's way outside the normal lines of weird."

"Alright then, start talking." Scott leaned back in his chair, waiting.

"I'm glad you're sitting down." Clint declared not sure where to start, he collected his thoughts before articulating them precisely.

Clint proceeded to catch Scott up on everything that happened earlier in the day.

When he'd finished, he grimaced realizing how crazy he sounded. He took a swig of beer. "So, Charles Hill is the entity behind the voice Farley's been hearing." He set his mug down and injected for clarity's sake, "June Bennett enlightened Farley with specific details that connected the dots."

"I hear what you're saying, Clint," Scott reacted with a questioning eye. "But I have heartburn with a registered nurse freely disclosing information when a stranger walks up to her with a story like that. And says what exactly to get her to break hospital protocol?"

Clint didn't like the way Scott phrased his question and pondered it a moment before replying. "Well, that's the thing, Ann Hill and June Bennett had a secret code they alone knew. The voice that broke through at 3 a.m., Charles Hill, said that code."

"And that would be... ?" Scott scowled, cocking his head, and briefly closing his eyes, thinking Clint had been reeled into a cockamamie story.

"Spirit sisters," Clint exclaimed with conviction. "Again, according to Farley, when he said, *spirit sisters,* to June, her whole demeanor changed. Literally did an about-face and immediately agreed to speak with him in private. June was visibly shaken, Farley said. I guess she and Ann used that term to describe their relationship. SS for sort."

"Uh-huh, and then what happened?" Scott shifted in his seat, sitting sideways and casually stretching his long legs out in front of him.

"June kept a private diary, chronicled the shooting. Farley said she'd struggled terribly with Ann's death, even went to a physiatrist for professional help after her friend on the police force suggested it was a contract killing. This was off the record, of course."

Scott sat quietly for longer than Clint was comfortable. He wasn't sure how to respond. What to believe, or how much to believe. He finally conceded. "No wonder she talked so openly. Especially, if Farley knew something no one else knew. That's hard to reconcile."

He straightened, took a sip of his now lukewarm beer. "So, you are convinced Charles Hill is influencing Farley through their shared heart?" Scott looked incredulous but continued his train of thought. "My question is what exactly does Farley think he'll accomplish by pursuing this?" Scott noticed Clint's face hadn't changed. He remained somber.

"That's where you come in. Farley isn't healthy enough, nor should he investigate anything pertaining to this case. If Charlie Hill isn't at rest, Scott, there's a reason; otherwise, he wouldn't be reaching out from the grave."

Clint folded his arms, thinking, "I'd like to know if the Incident Report shows any anomalies. Also, what the officer on duty that night summarized in his report. No matter how slight, it could lead to an explanation as to why Charlie hasn't moved on. If Charlie, by chance said anything of significance before he died, it could turn useful. I owe it to Farley to try, so the man can find peace of mind."

Scott closed his eyes, and then slowly opened them. He looked pained when he said, "Clint, this is outside my jurisdiction. You're asking a lot. I work in Salzburg, Small Town, Indiana, not Louisville, Big City, Kentucky! Yeah, I can pull up the report."

Moving his plate to the side, and rearranging the utensils on the table, Scott admitted, "If it was you, buddy, that'd be a different matter, but when a person we don't really know says he hears voices and wants you to believe his heart is the driving force behind investigating a crime, that's an entirely different matter. My guess is Farley needs a shrink."

Scott looked straight across the table at Clint. "Everything except the *spirit sister* thing... well, I'll give you that one. How bizarre. Gives Farley's story merit, enough that I might read the report."

Clint released the breath he had been holding. "Thank you, Scott. I figure it can't hurt to scan it. If nothing stands out, fine. We'll drop it."

"Makes sense." Scott nodded, of like mind. "It's what I do. Which means I'll dig a little deeper. Not you, do you hear? Come Monday morning, *I'll* see what pops up and then get back to *you*. Only when I have something to report, not until then."

Scott glared at his friend, seeing the wheels in Clint's head turning. "Do I have your solemn oath not to go hound dogging around. You'll stay out of it." He waited for confirmation but wasn't convinced that Clint was even listening. "*Do not* get involved. Do you hear me? Or stick your nose anywhere it doesn't belong!" Scott lifted a brow, "I suspect you told Farley something similar. Did you not? I'm doing the same! You came to me for help, so the only way I'm going to honor your request is if *you* back off."

"Alright," Clint complied, reluctantly, fully understanding Scott's terms. "I'll not rock the boat. Or probe around."

"Good, don't get involved in police business, Clint. That's an order."

Clint agreed, "I brought you into this, I'll do as you ask."

They stood, shaking hands, an oath between friends. But then, just as Scott and Clint were leaving, Jules walked into the room, closing the panel behind her.

Seeing the two men walk her way, Jules grumbled, "Oh no, I'm too late. Scott, I was hoping to have a chance to spend some time with you."

"I'm so sorry," he said, giving her a quick hug. "I would have enjoyed that, but I need to get back to work. Maybe next time." He looked at Clint but directed his comment to Jules. "Keep an eye on this one. He's a shifty character."

"Mi amigo, estoy de acuerdo." She giggled knowing Scott knew some Spanish and he'd figure it out.

Scott laughed. "Does your husband understand what you just said?"

"Probably. He didn't come in on the noon balloon, ya know." She looked at Clint and translated her comment. "What I said was, *my friend, I agree.*"

Clint winked, "I knew that..." he chuckled, not knowing any Spanish.

When Scott was out the door, Clint asked Jules to hang around, thinking dinner at Aces & Eights would be fun. He was relieved to have solicited Scott's assistance and felt like celebrating.

Clint promised not to stick his nose into police business, that was true, but he did not promise he wouldn't drive to Louisville for a quick peek at the general area that surrounded Grayson Hospital to get the lay of the land where Farley's transplant was performed.

After they finished their dinner, Clint and Jules took a quick drive to the orphanage to check on the progress Jules had made. Clint felt guilty for not spending more time on the project or helping Jules with the decisions concerning his office. Farley had thrown a curve ball that had sidetracked him all afternoon.

When they got to Radcliff's Children Home, the lobby was empty, short of the receptionist sitting behind the desk reading a book. They waved on their way to the elevators. On the fifth floor, used for storage and administrative purposes, Clint and Jules moved to the second door on the left and punched in the code.

They climbed the tight spiral staircase to the attic. Jules walked in first, excited for her husband to see the new arrangement and décor.

"Holy smokes!" he said enthusiastically when he saw his furniture from Rod's Apothecary & Sundries arranged perfectly in the room. "This couldn't have been better. I love it!" he said, turning to give her a pat on the back.

"I hoped you'd feel that way," Jules beamed, enjoying Clint's animated reaction to her handiwork. "Figured if you didn't care for it, you could push things around to where you wanted them. I tried to achieve a comfy working environment and think I succeeded. The rocking chair by the fireplace looks so nice."

Clint scanned the tight space. Window coverings hung floor to ceiling over the elongated panes that overlooked the three-hundred-acre estate where the orphanage was situated. A moss green leaf pattern printed on slubbed linen of uneven texture, trimmed with cream satin rope, grabbed his attention right away. The presentation of the tall, slender window was nothing short of breathtaking. It was everything he had hoped for, and more. The fabric fashioned the elegant room into what he had envisioned to a tee. The place would take him back in time to the turn of the century. The drapes looked like they had hung on the windows for decades not hours.

His attention diverted to the corner of the room where a handcrafted five-foot upright wooden frame and mirror dominated the left wall. Displayed, suspended unimpeded from the center top was Clint's antique mirror hanging freely by a puffed gold mariner chain. Clint felt his past envelope him.

He turned with a shocked expression, and commented, "Good Lord, how could that mirror be any more beautiful, especially in that presentation. Where did you get the mariner chain and frame? It's incredible. What a surprise. Jules, I can't say thank you enough!"

"A guy I met at Josie's," she answered proudly. "He does wood carvings and general carpentry. I described what I wanted. He was excited to oblige. I snuck the mirror out of the house so he could measure it." Jules grinned big, "That was a challenge. I was afraid if he came to the house, you'd surprise him, and me." Her face brightened with delight at her deviousness. "It was finished months ago. I wanted to surprise you. It appears I have."

"Reminds me of when I first saw the mirror hanging at Rod's New and Used Books." Clint stepped back, fully appreciating his prize possession. The room seemed to expand in its presence. The two-sided glass mirror became larger than life, one side displaying his image, the other side facing the wall. This mirror had a history.

Clint moved closer, just as he had done the first time he viewed it, touching its smooth surface, eyeing the label, *Hand Crafted from Variegated Andean Walnut*. The difference, this time, was the man with sunken cheeks and haunted eyes, Rod Radcliff, Sr., was not peering out.

A wisp of a memory clung to the fringes of Clint's mind. An essence passed through the room.

There is power in magic.

Chapter 13
Every Picture Tells a Story

"So, what are you up to today?" Jules asked, pinning her hair into a bun, and fastening it with butterfly clips. Dressed in her fifty's diner attire, she was ready to leave.

"Not much," confessed Clint. "I left a message for Farley to call me. I'm thinking about stopping by his place later today. I'd like to bring him up to date, let him know Scott is looking into Charlie Hill's death. After that, I have chicken feed to pick up and a dryer vent hose to buy at ACE Hardware. I pulled the hose out too far and can't get it back on," he grinned sheepishly. I'll have to buy an elbow connector to reattach the hose."

"Why did you pull the dryer out?"

"There was water on the floor. I thought the washer was leaking. It wasn't, and now I'm paying for being a dutiful husband," he chuckled cheerily. "I've never been a handyman. We'll see if I have the aptitude to put the darn thing back together. If not, I'll be calling a plumber."

They both laughed knowing Clint was not a do-it-yourselfer.

"Sorry I won't be here to witness your expertise," she joked as she walked out the door. "Tonight will be a late night," she called back, "I'll grab a bite at the diner. Leftovers are in the frig."

Clint waited until Jules had pulled from the drive before checking his messages. Sure enough, Farley invited Clint to stop by, whenever convenient. Clint grabbed his hat and keys and was out the door. On his way to Farley's he'd phone Scott to let him know he would be updating Farley about their conversation and would not mention that Scott questioned Farley's mental stability.

On the first knock the door opened. The chihuahuas were barking nonstop, Cocoa growling and nipping at Clint's pant legs.

"Sorry about that," Farley apologized. "Cocoa, Winston, stop it! Go upstairs! Take Rudy with you," he yelled at the troublemaker of the two.

Cocoa, the high-strung brother of the two, always carried his beloved Rudolph the reindeer toy with him—his security blanket. They watched Cocoa scamper to the woodstove where he snatched his stuffed, battered toy and charge up the steps, lickety-split without a second thought. They knew the drill. In an instant both dogs had vanished into the room on the right.

Clint walked to the far side of the room where a canvas was displayed, a light shining over the painting. "Farley, I didn't know you were a painter. This is amazing. Who's the subject?"

Farley blushed. "Don't really know. I often see her and every line on her face. Her porcelain skin is so vivid in my mind, I decided to put brush to canvas, hoping to capture her beauty. She is beautiful. Isn't she?"

The woman in the portrait looked as though she were alive. Her porcelain skin was radiant. Ruby red buds adorned a leafy green, embroidered pale cream silk scarf that swept across her bosom wispily as though tousled by the wind. The face of an angel with tendrils of blue-black strands gently caressing ocean-blue eyes, intensified by her dark arched brows.

Clint was so stunned by her magnificence, he stopped abruptly, not saying a word. When the shock passed, he questioned what Farley had claimed. "You've never seen this lady before?"

"Nope," was Farley's immediate response. "Only in my mind's eye. I've had her image upstairs in my drawing room, the problem was, it felt like every time I walked in there, her eyes watched and followed me. Figured I might as well hang her on the wall down here." He snickered. "I can't believe I'm going to say this. She makes me feel like I'm not alone. With her up there, I have company. No offense to my guys, but a lady's presence livens the place up a little." Farley blushed slightly but enough for Clint to notice.

"I understand," commiserated Clint, thinking of the antique mirror and his reaction to it. "Sometimes inanimate objects feel real as real can be. They take on a life of their own."

Farley's eyes drifted over to the painting. "This one does. I can't describe it in words, but it's like she's here in the cabin. The weirdest thing is her stare doesn't bother me. Quite the opposite. Gazing into those deep blue eyes generates a sense of belonging. Like she's my girl."

The portrait, the expression on the lady's face, and her come-hither look had transfixed both men. Alluring body language embodied European charm with an air of frolic behind a hint of turned lips. Exquisite bone structure seen in a painter's eye, and, of course, the fertile imagination that had brought her vibrant image to life.

"Well done, Farley," Clint finally said, still stunned by the portrait's realism. "I had no idea you were so accomplished. Did you ever think about selling your artwork?"

Farley belly laughed. "Clint, I developed this talent *after* the heart transplant. Before that, I promise you, I could not paint the broad side of a barn. I have no idea where this ability has come from. I feel drawn to art in a way that has no narrative."

"Are you kidding me? You didn't paint at all? Until after the transplant? That's remarkable."

"Correct. I had not a lick of talent. Zip."

"Oh my God, Farley. Do you think it's possible that Charlie could have been an artist?"

Surprised by the question, Farley quickly responded, "Certainly, I do. It's crossed my mind many times. How could it not? If he was, he must have been extremely gifted because I had no artistic ability at all, and now I do. New heart, new skill. There can only be one explanation in my book. Wouldn't you agree?"

Farley waved a hand, inviting Clint to the upper floor of the cabin. "Wait till you see what I have in the studio. If you think that lady is amazing, you'll most assuredly be impressed with what's up there. Gallery worthy pieces, all of them."

Climbing the steps, they kept an eye on Cocoa and Winston, who were waiting at the top of the stairs ready to spring into action if Clint made one false move. Farley gave them *the eye* and pointed back down the hall from which they came. They instantly obeyed, tucking their tails, before scooting off to the last room on the right.

"When I first moved here, I painted nonstop. Constantly had a brush in my hand." He shook his head, expressing his disbelief. "It took so much will power to overcome the compulsion. To this day, I'm still fighting the urge. I force myself to walk away."

Farley leaned over the railing to look at the downstairs furniture. He pointed at the woman's portrait, "She's part of it," he said with a knowing eye. "I can feel her essence in every inch of this place."

Again, Clint was taken by surprise. "You had this cabin built, right? No one lived here before you?"

"True. I'm the only one who has ever lived here."

Farley's life was nothing short of a Pandora's box with clues dropping in Clint's lap at every turn. Like a jigsaw puzzle with the border now framed, the question was what pitfalls lay inside the unassembled likeness of Farley's story?

Farley opened the door to the studio, standing aside for Clint to move past and waiting, knowing full well what Clint's reaction would be.

Inside the small area, Clint calculated somewhere near a hundred canvases, all leaning into one another against the walls, also stacked in the middle of the room. Nothing short of masterpieces were arranged everywhere, works of art that were indescribably unique, as well as diverse. Disciplines of every style imaginable graced the room.

How is it possible a guy like Farley could have painted all of these? Clint weighed, perplexed by the sheer number of paintings generated in a year's time, during recovery from heart surgery. *No way does a guy who can't paint, produce this kind of work.*

Farley waited for Clint to absorb the extent of the collection laid out before him. "I told you, Clint, I'm just a regular *Joe Blow.* Not a Claude Monet, or a Pablo Picasso, that's for certain. Although, you'd never know it by all of these. Call me a *wannabe* Picasso!"

Clint gasped, swinging around so fast it startled them both. Drained of color, Farley's reference to the famous painter, Pablo Picasso, triggered a flashback.

"What's wrong?" Farley asked after seeing Clint's shocked expression.

"I remember that name–Picasso!" Clint said darkly, thinking back in time to when he was a five-year-old.

Farley thought, *Doesn't everyone know that name?*

"It's the name my dad called the black puma that walked our land when I was a kid."

"What?" Farley reacted, suddenly understanding Clint reaction.

Clint stared into a past only he could see, the small world of a young boy listening for Picasso's large paws to cut through the thick forest undergrowth. Out of the shadows, Picasso arose from a place he was often seen sleeping, a tree branch deep in the forest. Clint could feel the creature moving through the back pages of his memory.

"I have a question," Farley said, putting a hand up. "So, is this the same animal you mentioned in the forest last Friday? You said a puma perished alongside your father."

"Yes, it must be. The pathologist determined the bones belonged to a puma. It was an astonishing discovery. Poor thing was stabbed multiple times in the neck and chest, yet still had the strength to drag Luke McCauley's body off to a remote location. Then he crawled back to my dad, where he eventually perished. None of it made sense at the time I discovered my dad's body, but it sure does now. Especially in light of dad's relationship to Picasso and how loyal he was to that cat, and Picasso to my dad. Evidently so, to have shown up to do Luke in." the corners of Clint's lips turned up, thinking how cool, yet fatally tragic the affair had been. A big grin crept onto Clint's face. "Dad would talk to that big guy like he was a kitten. And what was funny, Picasso reacted to dad the same way. Like they were brothers from an alternate reality."

Putting his head down, in an undercurrent of emotion, Clint said, "I remember that gorgeous black, velvety creature like it was yesterday, checking us out with those intense pools of green eyes. He was our feral pet, leery of humans, but appeared every night, like clockwork, for our table scraps. There were these times –I would have sworn–when he'd close the distance between him and my dad, I heard him purr."

"Normally wild animals won't let you come anywhere near them. The fact he did is unfathomable." Farley's eyes grew wide, "And you called him Picasso?"

"Yes," Clint sniggered, "that's the name my dad assigned him." Clint felt awed by the memory. "Farley, I'd forgotten his name until now. Not until you said, Pablo Picasso. Not even two years ago when the Reno Gang discovery was in full swing, did it occur to me! I always did think there was something more at the edge of my memory."

"Do you know what I think?" Farley postulated, putting one finger up. "We are talking about the same animal. My cougar and your puma are one in the same. Picasso!"

"I need a drink! Something stronger than coffee if you get my meaning. And, yes, before you say it, I know it's early. I don't know about you," Clint grinned anxiously, "but my throat is parched." His smiling eyes took in Farley's. "What'd say? In a Pig's Eye? I haven't even told you what I came over here for. I have an update. Scott is looking into Charlie Hill's death. We need to talk about that."

Farley glanced out the window behind his place, giving a swift response. "You're on! It's never too early for a cold one."

Chapter 14
Broken Promise

On his way to Louisville, after having a drink and early lunch with Farley, Clint found himself running scenarios and dialogues through his mind that would explain his behavior–if it came to it. After Scott Edwards specifically instructed him not to get involved in Farley's affair, Clint's trip to somewhere he wasn't supposed to go, might get awkward if the subject arose. Jules, he assumed, would be fine with it, and even inquisitive. Scott, on the other hand, was a different matter.

It was vitally important to Clint to keep his word and not lie to Scott. He'd keep the promise he'd given at all costs. His intention was to merely scope out the area where Farley McDougal had once resided, check out Grayson Hospital, and do nothing more. He'd speak to no one. Stop nowhere.

Motoring over the Sherman Minton Bridge, an arched double-decker road used by I-64 and US 150, connecting Indiana and Kentucky, Clint gazed down at the Ohio River and its exceptional mightiness. Rarely did he travel to Louisville but when he did the river was a pleasant sight.

Clint checked his phone. He had sufficient time to achieve his mission. He'd be in and out in no time. More curious than anything, he had convinced himself the sole purpose to come to Louisville was to have a boots-on-the-ground experience.

Simple enough, he reasoned. *I'll be here no more than forty-five minutes. A quick turnaround. When Farley talks about Grayson Hospital the next time, I'll know precisely where it is and what it looks like.*

Key landmarks Clint wanted to check out included Grayson Hospital, and Shelby Park–a seventeen-acre park where Farley used to jog prior to his operation. He mentioned his old residence was near the Germantown establishment in an historic section of Louisville where in the early 1900s German immigrants settled. The park was named after Isaac Shelby, Kentucky's first governor. The area catered to working-class people. Farley described it as artsy and vibrant with loads of energy and a diverse blend of individuals from every corner of the globe.

Clint liked what Farley had to say about his former neighborhood and felt compelled to check it out–mostly cottages and camelback homes constructed between 1900 and 1910.

Farley talked about visiting Thomas Edison's home in Butchertown that had been turned into a museum. "Edison lived in the area from 1866 to 1867 in a shotgun duplex built in 1850," Farley boasted. "He got fired after spilling sulfuric acid on his boss's desk when he worked at Western Union," he howled.

Turning onto Bank Street, off Business 60 and US 150, Clint took South Preston Street and then turned left on East Oak Street., south to Germantown. Farley had said Grayson Hospital was a short distance from there. That would be his starting point.

Clint found Germantown delightful. Quaint cottages lined the streets, reminding him of a trip he had taken through Columbus, Ohio, a few years back where German immigration presence was strong.

Slowly he cruised the streets, taking in the historic buildings and monuments that boasted of German heritage. Driving north, he located Edison's enchanting home. He got out to read the plaque that stood in the yard by the door.

Thomas Edison

Butchertown House

Edison (1847–1931) rented a room in this house. As a young man he conducted experiments, often all night and then walked to his job as telegraph operator at 58 West Main Street. Experimenting at work, he spilled acid and was fired. He left Louisville and later developed over one thousand patents for such devices as the phonograph and microphone.

Clint smiled at the irony of Edison losing his job then going on to achieve great success. A warm admiration seized him along with an understanding why Farley enjoyed visiting Edison's home and this old-world village. Clint walked the streets for a better feel of what it was like to live here and to be Farley McDougal.

Parked at the curb, his turquoise Camaro–after so many years –still caused his heart to flutter when his eyes rested on it. It was a gorgeous day to drive a classic automobile. He climbed inside, turned the engine over, and sat for a moment. Before pulling away, he listened to the roar of the engine, appreciating its power. Never a day went by that this treasured gift didn't elicit memories of his best friend, Gary who had willed the vehicle to him.

A minute or so later, he was in the parking lot of Grayson Hospital east of Germantown. Clint let the engine idle, trying to decide his next move. He knew he should leave but felt compelled to stay. He had the lay of the land down, so he didn't have a good reason to stick around. Compulsion demanded differently.

Although he did his best to squelch the urge to walk into the building, it didn't work. The only purpose for going in was to put a face with a name. No big deal. That way when Farley talked about June Bennett, the next time, he'd know what she looked like. No different than driving by his old house and neighborhood.

Acquainting himself with the things that comprised Farley's world made sense. His long-term intention was to step up as a pal. If June happened to be on duty, and walked outside the ICU into the hall, or took a seat in the waiting area, presuming it was outside the ICU doors–no harm, no foul. He had a reasonably good idea what she looked like from the description Farley had given. Clint's curious nature was aroused.

In the elevator on his way up to the seventh floor Intensive Care Unit, Clint thought better of his plan, telling himself to turn around, get back in his car, and go home, but his feet kept moving in the wrong direction.

Leave. You shouldn't be here. What about your promise to Scott? he chastised himself, thinking he was taking his probe a little too far. Then the double doors opened. Clint had a decision to make– turnaround and go back to the lobby or ask to see if June was there so he didn't waste time. If she wasn't working, there'd be no purpose in staying. The doors shut behind him.

Nurses and attendants moved through the hall, in conversations. No one paid him much mind. That was until a tall, black man in a lab coat walked up and asked Clint if he needed assistance, stating he appeared lost. "Are you alright, sir?" the man inquired.

Clint was tongue-tied. He wasn't expecting to engage in a conversation. Sweat beaded on his brow. Thinking fast on his feet, he blurted out, "Me? Oh, I'm fine. I climbed the stairs rather than taking the elevator."

"I see," said the man, feeling relieved Clint wasn't ill. He looked at the elevator Clint stood in front of and had obviously disembarked from. "How may I help you?" he asked, scratching his chin.

Again, Clint froze momentarily. "I don't need anything. Not really. I have a friend who works here is all, and thought I might stop by to say hello, but I realize now that wasn't a good idea. Not during work hours." A guilty grin covered his face when he joked, "No social calls on the ICU floor... what was I thinking? I'll be going. Thanks, though."

Clint turned, hurriedly he walked away down the hall to the door he'd seen, hoping it led to the stairwell. He felt like a kid caught in a lie. For a man who prided himself in honesty, he'd been lying a lot lately.

Not finding a sign to the stairwell, he came back, prepared to push the elevator button and leave. Waiting on the doors to open, he noticed the orderly, nurse, technician, doctor, or whatever the medical man was that had spoken to him, was keeping a close eye.

Uncertain what to make of Clint, the man sensed something wasn't right. Not everything was as it seemed—a friend taking the time to stop by the ICU and then deciding it was a bad idea didn't sound plausible. He appeared to be lying, but why? Figuring there was only one way to find out, the man asked, "Sir, what's your friend's name? I could see if he or she has a minute. I'd hate for you to come here and miss whoever you wanted to see."

Reacting to the stranger's request, Clint wanted to hightail it off the floor anyway he could but was afraid security would be notified to escort him out of the building by the time he reached the lobby.

He'd also be asked questions he wasn't prepared to answer. For a split second he visualized the scene as it played in his mind, paralyzed by the ramifications.

"No, it's okay, really. Never mind. I'll ring her."

Not liking Clint's answer, the man's eyes narrowed suspiciously, repeating his question. "I'll ask again, sir, what is your friend's name?"

Caught in an inconvenient conundrum with no way to retreat, Clint stammered, "June Bennett!"

The man's face relaxed back to normal, not nearly as tense. "June Bennett? We have two Junes that work this floor, but today is your lucky day, Bennett is in the staff room," he jovially proclaimed. "I'll get her for you."

"No," Clint protested vigorously, "*please*, don't bother her. Like I said, I'll give her a call when I get downstairs. If she has the time, she can meet me in the cafeteria."

Clint scurried toward the elevator button, pressing it hard several times. He hoped to slip behind the metal doors before the man could push the issue further.

"Wait," the man demanded, holding a hand up for Clint to stop. "Like I said, she happens to be in the break room. Your timing is perfect." He took a step forward. "I'll get her for you." His eyes reflected his humor at Clint's unorthodox behavior that was beginning to look like a stage show. "I said you were lucky," he teased, noticing Clint didn't look relieved Bennett was on duty. "Give me your name?"

Oh, good grief, Clint bellyached, *how am I going to get out of here? I promised Scott I would not speak to anyone. This is not what he had in mind.*

Realizing he had no other choice but to patronize this person's persistence, he delivered a reluctant, "Clint."

Taking a step closer, the man cocked his head with an expectant look. "Clint...?" the man asked. "Does Clint have a last name?" He was ready to burst out laughing yet wondered if he had made a mistake by not notifying security in the event Clint was carrying a concealed weapon and had intentions of hurting June. *Maybe a jilted lover?* he considered.

Clint exhaled in defeat, "My name is Clint Reeves."

"Stay put I'll let June know you're here." Dr. Jackson, the man in the lab coat, had no intention of letting June Bennett meet this man until he was one hundred percent certain Clint Reeves wasn't a lunatic.

"Great!" Clint hissed under his breath.

The man broadly smiled as though he'd won the battle of the wills, "You're welcome."

Seconds later June Bennett stepped out from the break room and into the hallway, escorted by the man Clint had been talking with. When June saw Clint, and not Farley as she had expected–even though she'd been given the name Clint Reeves–she became befuddled. She assumed Farley had used an alias to protect his identity, and she readily agreed to meet him.

She felt concerned until she searched Clint's forlorn eyes and saw an expression she'd seen on Farley's face when they met. Dr. Jackson had said the man was acting strangely, which also led her to believe Farley had come to call.

Her eyes met Dr. Jackson's. Then she turned to the stranger, wondering how to react to this odd man. She and he were definitely not friends–as the stranger had indicated. However, having been through this once before with Farley McDougal, June would not underestimate the importance of the encounter.

The handsome, dark-haired man standing in the hallway looked exposed and terribly uncomfortable, shifting his weight from side to side and looking everywhere but at her. Her consensus... he was harmless.

"Thank you, Dr. Jackson," June politely said to her colleague. "I'll only be a minute."

Jackson circled Clint, patting him on the back. "Aren't you glad you didn't give up? That would have been a shame."

Clint was dumbfounded, shocked at how everything had turned out in his favor. "Yes. Yes, I am, thank you," Clint swallowed hard. All this time he'd been talking to a doctor. "Thank you, Dr. Jackson," he said politely.

June pointed to the area where she and Farley had spoken only two days prior. Clint followed obediently. Sitting across from him, she inquired, "So, who are you? Why are you here, and what do you want with me?"

Relieved not to have been called out for the imposter that he was, Clint offered, in a way of an explanation, "I'm not certain where to begin. Farley McDougal and I are friends. He confided in me the discussion the other day, and to tell you the truth, I had no intentions of asking to speak to you. I simply wanted to see where Farley used to live and the hospital where his operation was performed. And, out of curiosity I came up here to ICU on a whim. I got cornered into this."

He sat quietly for a moment. Hands folded in his lap like a child who had been caught in a fib, waiting to be reprimanded. "Farley told me you knew the Hills."

June connected deeply with Clint, believing he had good intentions. "I did," she replied, "Ann was a dear friend. After speaking with Farley, I've thought of nothing else. Ours was a strange meeting." She grinned. "That's an enormous understatement. Farley seems to be directed by an otherworldly agent."

Clint nodded, mirroring her thoughts exactly. "Something is awry with Charlie's death," he proclaimed, finding his voice at last. He spoke his mind without holding back. From what he knew about June Bennett, she was a safe bet. "For whatever reasons, Charles Hill's soul is wayward and has not moved on. He isn't at peace, and is reaching out, using Farley McDougal as a conduit due to their unique circumstance. Don't ask me to explain, but I am positive Charles Hill is begging for help."

June lightly touched Clint's arm. "The other night I remembered something Ann once told me. I didn't mention it to Farley on Saturday because I'd forgotten about it, until after he left."

The elevator dinged, an elderly couple got off, one with a walker, the other guiding their way to the ICU doors. When they passed, June spoke in a low tone. "Ann told me Charlie had seen a man killed in an alley. Charlie ran into the coffee shop where she worked, worried he was being followed. He used the establishment's phone to call the police. Ann said Charlie was extremely agitated."

Clint took a step back, "Is that right? He witnessed a murder?"

"It seems so," June replied, sorrowfully. "When the authorities got there, Charlie informed them the attacker ran away but would take them to where the body lay. He said the injured man struggled to his feet and reached out with blood on his hands. But here's the thing. Before he died, he gave Charlie something. The worst part?" June said tearfully, "Charlie believed the killer saw his face."

Clint felt like the life had been sucked out of him. What June relayed sounded an awful lot like the dream Farley had recounted at the cabin. "In other words, Charlie witnessed a crime, and the killer might have recognized him."

"Exactly," concurred June, "but here's the weird part. When the police arrived and were taken to the place Charlie said the crime occurred, no body was found, nor a drop of blood anywhere. It made no sense. They even accused Charlie of concocting a story, *crying wolf, wanting attention,* and warned if he ever did anything like that again they'd arrest *him*. Charlie was humiliated, mortified because he was adamant about what he witnessed." June became pensive. "That was in the late afternoon."

"And that same night a random shooting takes place? Charlie and Ann just happened to fall victim?" Clint pointed out, mindful neither of these two people could tell their side of the story. "June, it wasn't random. You, Farley, and I all know that. The guy was probably lying-in wait."

Clint rubbed his chin, processing the chain of events. "But why kill a person in a congested area where others could easily identify the shooter? That doesn't make sense."

"Beans a' Brewin'... Ann worked there. She was a barista and shift leader." Tears welled as the memory of that night brought the walls closer. "Whoever killed them must have been hiding somewhere nearby for Charlie. The shooting took place toward the end of her shift."

June's faraway eyes roiled with emotion as rage churned. "Charlie went home after the police left the coffee shop but came back that same route to walk his wife home. She clocked out shortly after seven." June shrugged. "Charlie and Ann's place wasn't far from the shop. "They lived maybe three-quarters of a mile from there. I remember the weather was unseasonably cold that night, even for December. Flurries fell in the afternoon. Several inches had fallen by the time Ann's shift ended."

June recoiled from the intensity of her memories. "Charlie's body was transported here within minutes." June looked excruciatingly pained, miserable even. "Charlie's heart was transplanted too quickly." She saw Clint's eyes show his surprise at her claim. "They want them to be as fresh as possible. I'm sorry if that sounds gross."

Mirroring Clint, her face too turned equally grim. "I've read hearts transplanted too soon after a person is declared legally dead can hold certain memories, even of how they died." June considered Charlie Hill's tragic death, speculating on other reports she had read, from first-person accounts of transplant recipients.

"Don't know, but I've heard stories that would make your skin crawl," she said.

Clint thought long and hard about what June had proposed. "So, Charlie saw someone murdered and the perpetrator removed the body before the police arrived." Placing two fingers to his lips, Clint groaned. "Good Lord! The killer must have worked super-fast to pull that one off. Bodies don't just disappear into thin air," remarked Clint trying to understand how that could be, especially since Charlie reported the crime directly.

"Here's the really weird part," June eagerly disclosed, still surprised by what she had later gathered about the affair. "Witnesses said the man that shot Charlie bent down and started rummaging through Charlie's pockets, hightailing it out the rear door when an off-duty officer came through the door requesting to have a word with the owner. As witnesses described, it was as though the killer was looking for a specific thing."

"So why did an officer drop back by," queried Clint, confused why an officer wanted to talk to the owner of the establishment when the police had already determined Charlie was *crying wolf.* Was he patrolling the neighborhood?"

"No," June shot back quickly, "from what I was told, the cop had returned to speak to the manager on duty." She hesitated, her mind straying to a place Clint couldn't follow. She turned to Clint and said, "If I'm not mistaken, the owner's name was Mark something."

"A friend on the force told me, in confidence, that the original report Charlie Hill called in from that coffee shop, was incomplete. That's why the policeman returned. Before filing his report, he needed a few details explained. They had Charlie's address incorrect. He had gone to the wrong house. So, he returned to the coffee shop and walked in on the crime. My understanding is he wasn't as convinced as his partner that Charlie was unstable, pretending, or an attention seeker. Charlie's report had omitted his wife worked at Beans a' Brewin'."

Clint's brow wrinkled, "So what happened?"

"The officer ran after the shooter, but was met with a bullet, shot in the head at close range the minute he flung the door open in pursuit of the shooter. My friend mentioned the police officer was a rookie and his response wasn't standard protocol."

"No wonder Charlie is unable to move on. This cold-blooded murderer killed four people in a twenty-four-hour period: the man in the alley, Charlie, Ann, and the policeman who tried to do the right thing. But why such extreme violence? Charlie must have had something the murderer wanted badly. But because of the officer, the killer couldn't get his hands on."

"That's my guess as well," June concurred, having no doubt Charlie was in possession of something valuable. "I've had a lot of time to think about this since Farley came here. Charlie must have had something on his person that tied the first murder to the second, the object must somehow identify the killer."

Dr. Jackson suddenly walked through the ICU double doors, startling them both. He casually strolled over to June, scrutinizing Clint closely before speaking. Jackson remained leery of Clint's intentions, especially since June did not return as quickly as she had indicated. "I hate to break this up, but we need you back on the floor, asap."

June apologized, "So sorry, we were wrapping things up, anyway." She saw doubt in Dr. Jackson's eyes when his locked with Clint's. June volunteered, "Clint is my second cousin's husband… from Tennessee." She hoped her lie wasn't too transparent. "I'll be right there." She glanced at her timepiece. "Oh my, I did lose track of time. Didn't I? I am so sorry!"

"No problem," Dr. Jackson said, his voice sounding sincere. "Turns out we are short-handed. Susan went home sick. Truthfully, I think she's feeling burned out from the long hours. It's best not to push our new employees so hard." He looked at Clint. "We lose good people that way."

"I understand. I'm on my way." June assured Dr. Jackson, watching him stride off through the automated doors and return to the ward.

June turned to Clint. "Look, Ann and Charlie's death hit close to home, and I prefer this exchange stay between us. The killer is still at large. No arrests were ever made. I've tried to stay up on any developments, but there really aren't any."

"You have my word," Clint assured her. "Truth is I'm not supposed to be sticking my nose into things, but this case seems to have taken on a life of its own. I don't think anyone is directing it. It's directing itself, taking us where it wants us to go. Without trying to explain, just know, I was drawn into this. We are both part of a bigger picture."

Right as June was about to leave, she paused as though remembering something more. "Charlie said the assailant in the alley didn't remove his victim's wallet. Don't you find that odd? He told Ann the guy's wallet was in plain sight, right there on the ground. Charlie almost picked it up but thought better of it. He was afraid it might implicate him.

June's brow wrinkled. "A staged robbery. Do you think? But even at that you'd think he'd grab the dead guy's Rolex. Charlie said he was wearing one. Ann told me after the incident, when we were talking, Charlie didn't touch a thing. Can you imagine Charlie saw someone kill a guy, who then leaves all guy's valuables, and then removes the body before the police arrive? Clint, there is a huge problem with that scenario."

Clint watched June returned to ICU, wondering what cards lay on the table of this unraveling mystery, cloaked in Charles Hill's *telltale* heart.

What was *he* going to tell Scott?

Chapter 15
Another Disembodied Soul

Bonnie and Jules sat at the diner waiting for Jules's shift to wind down. Jules was never fond of driving home in the dark when winter shadows grew long. By the middle to late November, daylight faded by five o'clock, making it appear later than it was. By seven it felt more like midnight than early evening.

"I thought Clint would have called by now," Jules rambled on. "Maybe he's out in the barn." Jules noted Bonnie's empty cup. "Can I get you another cup of tea?"

Bonnie cased the room, as though checking to see if anyone was listening. "I know you only have a few minutes, but I have something I'd like to share. Yes, I'd love another cup if you can sit a bit longer. This should set you on your heels. If not, I can come back tomorrow on lunch break."

"Are you seriously going to play that card?" Jules laughed aloud. "Sit tight I'll be back in a shake."

"Thought you'd feel that way. I dangled a carrot you can't resist." Bonnie laughed knowing Jules couldn't turn down a juicy piece of gossip.

That was part of the attraction of working at Josie's diner. Scuttlebutt was always flying this way or that with Jules in the middle of it.

Bonnie watched Jules's conversation with Patrick behind the counter in the kitchen. He glanced over at Bonnie, noticing her. She quickly turned away but kept an eye on Jules's hands, as they did her talking, waving them around like an orchestra conductor.

Back at the table, Jules set a hot mug of tea on Bonnie's side of the table and a hot cup of cocoa on hers. Then she sat down across from her friend. "Pat said I could leave early. I strongarmed him and said I had to visit with you before I took off for the night. The place is dead anyway so what's the point of sticking around?"

"A convincing argument!" Bonnie laughed, thinking she couldn't hold her news a second longer. "Let's get down to brass tacks, girl."

"Fire away," encouraged Jules, anxious to hear what Bonnie had up her sleeve. Working at the library had its advantages, Jules was keenly aware, just like Josie's Diner.

"Well," Bonnie started out, "Farley McDougal is more complex than either of us could have ever imagined. He seems reserved, sure enough, but I had no idea the depth of his sorrow. That man is carrying a heavy burden, Jules."

"Why do you say that?" asked Jules, sincerely concerned, not expecting Bonnie to talk about Farley, of all people. "I've never met a more pleasant man." Her face drooped, worried about him. "But I see resolve in those steely gray eyes of his. He's a strong man. The creases around his eyes speaks of laughter. Sadly, they are contradicted by the deep furrows that bracket his mouth. Those are deeper than they should for a man his age."

Bonnie's face turned solemn. "Jules, I bawled my eyes out when I read what happened. I don't know how the poor man survived a tragedy of this caliber. I hope someday he'll feel comfortable enough to talk to one of us. I'm glad he's moved to Salzburg, and we get to be his friends."

"So…" Jules eyes widened, tossing her hands into the air, "give it up, Bonnie. I can't stand this any longer."

"Alright." Her expression turned grave. "Here's what I know. Farley was married. He and his wife, Gloria, had a set of twins, a girl and a boy, Violet, and Vincent." She took a sip of her cooling tea and then dropped the bombshell.

"Jules, they died! The article stated Jackie Lovecraft left the children in her daughter's care while she went to the grocery. While she was gone, the children drown in her backyard pool. The article didn't go into any real details other than to say the toddlers slipped into the pool and were found face down."

Jules put a hand over her mouth, gasping. "Oh my God, Bonnie, no wonder I see sadness in his eyes. What a thing to have to live with." She had paled from the news. "I wonder if the children's accident contributed to his heart failure. People in their late thirties don't normally need a heart transplant. If I'm not mistaken, Farley will turn thirty-nine soon, February 2, I believe. I was thinking about throwing a small dinner party for him." Jules wiped a tear away. "His torment must follow him always. Poor guy."

"If that's not bad enough, I found a divorce decree. Gloria filed nine months after the accident." Bonnie reached out for Jules's hand. "Within a year, he lost two children and his wife left him. I'm shocked the guy is still standing."

"I have no words," Jules spoke softly, still stunned. "We all need to step up to support him. We can be his family." Jules glanced at the clock in the kitchen. "I've got to go. Clint will be wondering where I am."

"Sure, me too. It's getting late and I've had a long day," said Bonnie. "I put in an order for takeout. We'll finish this chat later."

"Just checking…" Jules mentioned as she slipped her coat over her shoulders. "Are you still coming over Thursday for turkey day?"

"Wouldn't miss it for the world," Bonnie answered pleasantly, a look of excitement appeared on her face. "Are the kids coming?"

"Some of them. Wade and Coleen can't make it but Rusty, Molly and the boys can. Clint invited Farley, Ivan, and Patrick. It should be a fun day." Jules gave her a hug and was out the door.

Bonnie went to the counter to have a word with Patrick. Signaling she was ready to pay, she waited at the register for her takeout order.

When Patrick laid the container on the countertop, Bonnie said, "Patrick, I love your Chicken Divan, but you need to let up some on the curry! It's one of my favorite dishes here, no matter how heavy handed you are with that spice. It'd be better if you cut it down a notch!"

Patrick looked put off. "It's fine! Customer's love it."

"Excuse me," Bonnie interrupted, "not all customers like it, I think it's a little strong. I thought you'd want to know my opinion. It might help improve the dish." Bonnie's flirtatious conversation was genuinely charming, but irritated Patrick to no end that she had the audacity to criticize his flair for the exotic.

He retaliated with a quip of his own, "If it's good enough for Paula Deen, it's good enough for most of us. I suggest you order something else, more to your liking if Chicken Divan doesn't fit your palate," he said irritability, not agreeing with Bonnie's assessment of a dish he ranked at the top of his menu, thinking it heavenly.

"Whatever, Patrick," she flippantly replied. "I thought you'd appreciate my opinion. Apparently not. Forget I said anything."

"I already have!" Patrick spat, swinging around, halfway to the kitchen before Bonnie lifted her takeout bag from the counter.

She waved her hand in the air, annoyed, as if to say, *Whatever…*

Jules left through the back door. Her Volvo streamed passed the front glass just as Bonnie walked out onto the sidewalk into the brisk night air. She had used her key fob to start the engine of her new Infiniti from inside Josie's. When she laid her takeout on the seat, the thought occurred, *Boy, does that smell good.* She grinned knowing Patrick was in the back spitting nails over her suggestion. *He'll get over it! I was only trying to help!*

Driving down US 150, Jules phoned Clint and was surprised to learn he was on the road heading home from Louisville… talking a mile a minute, he went on and on scarcely taking a breath. He was royally wound up and jabbering faster than she could listen.

"Slow down," she fired back. "Clint, you've got the pedal to the metal. I can't understand a word you're saying." Her laughter was infectious. She thought he'd laugh when she said, "I know which car you're driving. How far out are you?"

Clint took a needed breath. "Fifteen minutes, at best."

"Let's talk when you get to the house, then," she suggested, noting an edge to his voice. Clint didn't comment on her reference to his big block Camaro. That spelled trouble.

Later that evening, Clint brought Jules up to date on the latest. What June Bennett had made known, and how gracious she had been to sit down with him. How she expertly diverted Dr. Jackson's skepticism, which in turn, gave them time to share notes.

On the flipside, Clint was dumbfounded to hear Farley had lost two children and his wife divorced him soon after. What a shocker that was. Clint felt eternally grateful to have found love a second time and couldn't imagine the pain Farley must have endured during those horrendous days. Like most people, Clint figured Farley harbored some regrets. Hopefully, Farley would feel comfortable enough to confide the story behind his losses. Until then Clint would bide his time, moving forward with his private investigation, on Farley's behalf.

The focus of his emphasis, after chronicling the events that had transpired, was to seek more information on Charles Hill. Who he was... really. He'd dig deeper, turn over every rock, until he had a better understanding of the man. However, Clint had made his mind up not to share his findings with anyone, until he had a full picture of what had gone down. At some point he'd circle back with Farley.

Charlie's tormented spirit demanded to be heard. Clint planned to give him an audience. A mystery hung in the air, and Clint heard its call. Thanks to Picasso, who had continued to make himself known, he'd explore the undercurrent surrounding Charles and Ann Hill's premature deaths.

I shouldn't have involved Scott in this, Clint grimaced, regretting discussing the matter with him. *It was a mistake but now it's too late to ask him to back off. If I did, it would put red flags up. I hate lying to him.* Clint scowled, not feeling comfortable with partial truths. *I have to research this situation on my own. Until I have something more concrete to go on, I'll not bring it up again.*

Jules had a bad feeling when she saw the all too familiar look in Clint's eyes. "So, what are you thinking?" she asked.

Clint stared directly at his wife, surprised by her question. "That Charlie Hill is a disembodied soul, very much like Rod Radcliff, Sr. was. Radcliff had been tethered to this town for fifty years before his soul finally found peace. Hill's ghostly presence is getting stronger and more persistent. I can almost feel him, very much like Rod."

"Something happened to you back there, surrounding Rod and that situation. It changed you from a soul perspective. On a core level."

"Jules, you're spot on. It's as though I sense things I never did before." Clint's attention was drawn to the foyer where the mirror once hung. "Farley said something that made me take notice. He said since he and I met, Charlie isn't as vocal as he had been. He's tapered off to almost nothing." Clint raised a brow. Words unspoken hung in the air between them, and volumes were left unsaid.

"If I'm honest…" Jules reached across the table to grab Clint's hand. She pulled it close, putting it on her chest, above her heart. "I'd like you to stay out of this whole affair. But I know that's not possible. You can't do that and probably shouldn't take my advice," Jules admitted painfully, worried where the path was leading, "I also understand you'll not rest until you get to the bottom of why you were dragged into it."

She pushed her chair back from the table and walked over to the kitchen counter where she refilled her cup slowly. Standing with her back to Clint, she voiced her concerns cautiously. "Why Picasso steered Farley to the shack and then to you is cryptic, at best. Why would he do that? Not to mention… how can he return from the grave, not once, but twice? I thought he found peace after the Reno Gang chapter found closure. The same as Rod Radcliff, Sr. Why is he back? Twice the cat shows up, both times, centered around a murder." Her expression tightened. "Pardon me, *murders*! That's creepy on all kinds of levels."

"That's the point, Jules. Why? He has returned and he coaxed Farley to the shack. There *is* a purpose behind his return, I can feel it. I feel compelled to understand. Bear with me. I promise not to get too deep into the weeds on this one. Not like I did with Rod Radcliff's murder."

Clint appeared lost in thought, not saying anything for the longest while. "I don't know if I told you this, but after the ordeal two years ago I read up on black pumas. I found it odd to *ever* have one here in Salzburg. Something about that seemed off." Clint leaned in. "Did you know in some cultures black pumas represent death? They are associated with casting doubt, surveillance, and scrutiny. In the wild, they have been observed staring at an object–unmoving–for hours, remaining still, showing incredible patience before pouncing."

Suddenly, Clint became aware of his wife's unreadable green eyes. "I'm sorry," he said. "I got carried away."

She reached out, laying a hand over Clint's, and said with a grin. "Thanks for enlightening me. Was that supposed to make me feel better?"

Feeling bad that he had bridged the subject, Clint repeated, "I'm sorry."

"I will say, anyone hearing voices sounds possessed. If it was anyone other than Farley, I'd tell you to run and never look back. But the poor man needs us. After all he's been through? And now this. I have no idea what to think."

Clint's eyes narrowed, worried. His wife's underlying message was easy to translate. "It could be dangerous to nose around. I give you that. Ann Hill died along with her husband. It makes me ill to think about it. What did Charlie know or have that triggered their deaths? Or what had he done to incite the killer?"

"To your point," Jules concurred, aware Clint would not rest until he knew the answer, "something wicked lies behind this whole affair."

"Charlie is trying to communicate. It's scary to think I've been added to the mix, but I can't turn my back on him, or Ann. I will do my best to unravel what happened to them."

Jules lowered her eyes. "I understand and support you one hundred percent. Look, I knew when I married you something otherworldly was behind the treasure mystery. For a man to go from a disbeliever of anything supernatural, or even a higher power, to solving an investigation using paranormal intervention, is nothing short of mind-blowing. Of the highest level," she smiled tenderly. "Clint, I'm suggesting those same forces aren't done with you yet."

Clint glanced out the window to where darkness filled his vision. "Jules, I do feel I'm being summoned. Picasso turned the frequency dial up to where I was in 2003 when I didn't understand anything except to follow my intuitions. You see where that ended up. I will follow the breadcrumbs. See where it leads."

Jules leaned over and gave him a hug. "I'm with you no matter what. We are a team too. We will work as *one*! I'll keep my antenna raised and pass along anything out of the ordinary. Bonnie will be a great resource as well, and so will Farley. I want that man protected at all costs. To think he houses Charles Hill's heart and the secrets it shrouds. Let's call it a day!"

When Clint crawled into bed, sliding beside his *dream come true, angel of a wife*, the dark tendrils of grief reached out to him. Jogged by a memory of abandonment, Clint revisited a time when he didn't believe in forces greater than himself. That no longer was the case.

In the distance, a faint, methodical drumbeat sounded. Tears filled his eyes.

"I'm listening," he mumbled as he drifted into dreamland, behind the curtain that separated night from day, reality from the unchained.

Chapter 16
Disclosure

Thanksgiving week had given Clint and Jules plenty to do. At lunch Clint planned to invite Farley and his two chihuahuas to join them for Thanksgiving dinner tomorrow. He realized it was late notice but figured it couldn't hurt to ask. Clint wanted to introduce Rusty's family to their new friend.

Wade, Clint's oldest son, and his wife Coleen, and granddaughter, Lily couldn't make it this year since they were overseas with Coleen's family. However, Rusty, his youngest, and his wife Molly, with his grandsons, Trey and Dylan, excitedly accepted Jules's invitation when she phoned at the start of the month. It had been a while since the family had gotten together, so everyone was looking forward to a fun day of activities. To make the occasion more festive, they'd invited Bonnie–same as last year–and she readily accepted. And, new this year, were the owners of Ace Hardware and Patrick. Adding Farley would make it that much better.

"Farley should feel at ease with Bonnie here." Jules imagined as she wrote her menu and grocery list at the kitchen table. "You know? Plus, Patrick, who Farley also knows. All you need to do is convince him to come."

Clint and Jules had built an additional sitting room off the rear of the house with French doors leading to a heated swimming pool with a retractable awning last March as a wedding gift to Jules. In the summer, and fall, they used the pool heavily. It was Jules's place to unwind, day or night, under the sun, and stars. At one end was a jacuzzi, designed for year-round use.

Coming into a windfall of extra funds had its advantages. Their lives had been enhanced substantially but never as much as when the orphanage was erected, standing stately on hundreds of acres off Grandview at the edge of town, where its main entrance was located. Clint and Jules had an extensive list of charitable contributions they had distributed over the year, all directed to the homeless and children.

The bulk of settled funds were managed by Jeremy Sullivan, Clint's lawyer in Paoli, who coordinated the Reno Gang treasure transfer from under the shack in Goss Cave to Evansville. They'd created a slush fund to allow them access to ready cash on an as-needed basis until the dust settled.

Cash liquidity had been redirected into investments, equally divided between mutual funds, money markets, stocks, bonds, and the like. Clint and Jules lived a comfortable life but not an excessive one, considering the money in the various accounts. Theirs was not an extravagant lifestyle. Initial upgrades to the house easily fell into the category of maintenance and repair, other than Jules's outdoor impressive pool area.

Later, Clint would extend an invitation to Farley to join the Reeves' family for a Thanksgiving feast tomorrow early afternoon. He and Farley had plans to meet at twelve thirty at, In a Pig's Eye. Agreeing to have lunch in town, now and again, today was one of those days. After hearing what Jules had repeated regarding Farley's past, Clint was more inclined than ever to convince him to dine with them on this upcoming family holiday.

Relieved to have Jules's support, Clint relaxed into his decision regarding Charles Hill. He would not drag his feet but move ahead full force. His first stop of the day was at the Salzburg Police Station to inform Scott to drop the matter, the information he had requested was no longer required. Clint wished he'd never told Scott. Like a dog with a bone, Clint knew his friend would not drop the issue, unless he had a good mind to.

Clint strolled into the building, assured of a no before asking. Scott was predictable as the sun rising in situations such as these. Clint waved at the receptionist as he passed her desk having been instructed, by Scott, to come on up.

Taking a quick glance at the landing above, Clint recognized David Andrews as he headed downstairs.

"How's it going?" inquired Clint. "Nice to see you. Been awhile." They shook hands as acquaintances do, but in David's case, he had turned friend. That was not always the case.

At the beginning of their relationship, things were bumpy. David was not a fan–leery of Clint, to be exact–due to Clint's unorthodox way of reporting his first dead body, found in Goss Cave. He had omitted many details of his discovery. David was a by-the-book kind of police officer and didn't warm up to people telling half-truths, as Clint had done. It made him suspicious.

"It has," David agreed, stopping on the steps to converse. "Same ol', same ol' I'm afraid. The town had its day in the sun, relating to your bombshell that is. It's somewhat normal, again. As far as people causing a ruckus in the bars and home. If anything, I've found, people are excitable!" He laughed. "Including you!"

"I'm not going to argue that point. By the way, my wife would concur," Clint grinned big. "She's the anchor in our household. The level-headed one," he kidded. "These days I can sit down to a meal in a public restaurant without interruption. How nice is that." Clint's face turned comical, "I'm not the social type, so notoriety wasn't my cup of tea. Not like my Jules who talks to strangers like they're longtime friends."

David was fully aware that Clint enjoyed his solitude. "Since marrying Jules, you've come out of your shell, from what I've observed," noted David. "I see you more now than I ever did. Before Jules, you acted like a hermit!"

"She's behind my change," admitted Clint with a smile that matched his love for her. "Nothing like having my own table at Josie's to lure me to town." Clint moved to the next step. "Bet you can't say that."

"You lucky dog!" David laughed, thinking Jules had brought a special kind of sunshine to the town. "I, for one, am grateful she moved here. Salzburg needed livening up." David guffawed. "Lunches are easier, but you must admit, it was fun while it lasted."

Clint patted David on the shoulder as he moved away, heading up the steps to the second floor. "We'll have to do lunch sometime. Catch up."

"You're on," David agreed. "Have a good day, Clint." A sudden grin plastered itself on David's face. "And stay out of trouble."

"I'll do my best," responded Clint, wondering if Scott had talked to David about their latest conversation.

Standing outside Scott's open door, Clint cleared his throat. "I need only two seconds of your time, and then I'll be out of your hair."

"No rush," replied Scott indicating Clint should come on in and have a seat. "What are you up to today?"

"I'm on my way to have lunch with Farley McDougal." The moment felt awkward, the thought occurring that maybe he should invite Scott to join them, but that idea was instantly squelched by Scott's response.

"It's good for Farley to get better acquainted with Salzburg. We're a small-town, filled with good folks. After living in Louisville, we might have an appeal. Once he's fully recovered, he'll feel right at home like the rest of us."

"I'm so grateful he came into Josie's that day and Jules drew him out. She's the one who introduced us."

"Your wife is a friendly one," Scott cited. "I'm glad you're trying to help the guy. Speaking of charming wives, I'm taking mine to lunch." Scott grinned broadly, teasing Clint. "An upscale restaurant you might not have heard of… Josie's Diner."

For the most part, everyone in Salzburg migrated to Josie's Diner, no matter the season or weather. In a rural community consisting of farmers, blue collar laborers, and housewives, the town's watering hole was a noisy, high-spirited joint. Friendly faces packed the fifties diner with an appeal of genuine people.

"That's nice. Tell Wende I said, hello," Clint responded, his mind distracted with how to open the discussion to drop Scott's inquiry into Charles Hill's death.

"I'll do that," replied Scott. "Truth be told she'd rather go to Josie's Diner than anywhere else."

Bridging the subject before he lost his nerve, Clint expressed what he had come for. "You know that favor I asked?" He instantly detected a change in Scott's countenance. "You can forget about it. I talked to Jules," which Clint thought sounded good, and in fact was true. "Maybe it's best to back off."

A suspicious glance appeared on Scott's face. *What is that about?* he wondered. *Last Saturday it was top priority and now it's pull back?*

CHAPTER 16

"It's a dead issue," Clint lamely joked, hoping Scott wouldn't ask his reasoning for not checking into the situation. Although, he would like to withdraw his inappropriate reference to the matter.

"That was especially crude, even for you." Scott barely laughed. "You're too late, I've already done some digging. I've uncovered some interesting facts."

Clint couldn't help himself. Filled with curiosity, he replied, "You're right, I shouldn't have said that." Clint made a face, disgusted with himself. "But I'd be lying if I said I wasn't interested in what you found."

"It turns out a cop was killed at the scene that same night. Tony Moretti made a cardinal error an experienced policeman would never make. He surprised the shooter in the act and then chased him out into the alley where the assailant was waiting and opened fire. Tony was shot in the face for his well-meaning efforts."

Having already heard this account from a different source, Clint tried to show his surprise. "I'm sorry to hear that. Poor fella. I hope the young man didn't have a family." This was his response when first hearing about the officer. He thought it the most *natural* reply.

Captain Scott Edwards, on the other hand, who was good at detecting the smallest of *tells*, picked up on Clint's split-second delayed reaction. "Who said he was *young*?"

Clint responded fast. "You stated he made an uncommon error. I assumed he was young since seasoned officers wouldn't make that kind of mistake. Right? That's all!"

Scott examined Clint's face for *tics*. "He did, as a matter of fact, three little people, and a wife. A sad affair to be sure. Losing new officers is always tough but those with families is exceptionally hard. Most of us carry that fear. It's rarely mentioned." Scott paused in reflection before adding, "Like I said, you're too late, my friend. And if you approve or not, I'm up to my eyeballs in this. I have a feeling something's not quite right."

Clint sat down, defeated yet relieved to be able to speak freely. "Then you won't like what I'm about to say but believe me it wasn't intentional. I didn't mean to go against your orders."

"What is that supposed to mean?" asked Scott tersely, not liking the sound of what Clint said.

"I went to Louisville. Only went to see Farley's old stomping ground prior to moving to Salzburg. That was it, nothing more. I promise."

"Oh, good grief, Clint. Tell me you didn't speak to anyone." Scott wagged his head, knowing the answer to his question before hearing it.

"Uh… that's the thing. We need to talk but not here." Clint glanced at his watch, "I'm supposed to meet Farley in five minutes. Can we have this discussion later?"

Scott threw his head back, staring at the ceiling and wondering where this was leading and how much trouble Clint had gotten himself into. "Yes, later." His eyes were direct. "Today! No excuses. I don't care if it is Thanksgiving Eve, I'll meet you at Aces & Eights at 5 p.m. End of discussion. Got that?"

Clint squirmed in his chair. "Alright." He stood, ready to leave, "Like you said, *you'll want to know what I learned.*"

He walked out, not happy.

On his way to In a Pig's Eye to meet Farley, Clint felt like a trapped animal. He was irritated at himself for doing what he was determined not to do… keep Scott involved. The exact opposite had happened. Now, he was assured, without a shadow of a doubt, Scott would be jumping head-first into the matter, *no holds barred!*

After his talk with June, Clint struggled with how much to say to Farley, or Scott for that matter. Part of the decision had now been made for him. He'd been backed into a corner by his friend. Truth was he should have guessed Scott would see right through him. He'd never been a good liar.

He would not come clean with Farley. Farley didn't know him like Scott, he'd not see through him so easily. The verdict was still out on how much disclosure he'd share with Scott when they met at 5 p.m.

On the other hand, Clint needed Farley to stay clear of the entire mess, other than telling the truth about meeting June. In the off chance she encountered Farley in some unexpected future event and brought the subject up, Clint felt it was important for Farley to know. The last thing Clint wanted was for Farley to doubt him. He felt forced to tell him about his trip into Louisville, but when that would be he wasn't sure.

Clint walked into the bar and grill. Jamie, the hostess, greeted him with her usual broad grin and lovely disposition. "Want your same booth?" she inquired. If Clint was anything, he was consistent with his choice of seating.

"That would be nice, Jamie. Do you know Farley McDougal, by chance?"

"No, can't say I do," she fired back "Will he be joining you?"

"Yes, he will. He's a very tall, thin man with light brown hair. I thought he might already be seated."

"Oh!" Jamie squealed. "Yes, a man by that description came in a few minutes ago. He said he was waiting on someone. I'll show you to his booth."

"Hey there," Farley said when Clint slid into the booth across from him. "I always carry a book with me." Pushing it aside, he stated, "If you haven't read, Genesis Awakening by Ron Radisson, I highly recommend it."

"Thanks for the suggestion," Clint replied, looking over at the book cover of an eagle, spread-winged, soaring over the Grand Canyon with a sunrise in the background edging over the rocks. Shades of yellow and orange dominated the scenery.

"I don't read much these days, but I do enjoy a good book now and again. I think the last one I read was Bid Time Return by Richard Matheson." Clint's face brightened, remembering the fiasco that surrounded the book. Trying to read Elise's favorite book turned out to be a convoluted affair at best although he thoroughly enjoyed the story, as Elise predicted he would.

"Isn't that a surprise," declared Farley. "I've read that book too. Wasn't the movie Somewhere in Time based on the book?"

Clint chuckled with reservation, not wanting to dive too deep into the subject. "It was. Did you see the movie?"

"I found it a fascinating read. The movie was excellent. I like both the main characters, Christopher Reeves, and Jane Seymour."

"Me too," laughed Clint, remembering the movie well, but not elaborating. "I'm glad to see you, my friend," he said, hoping to change the subject. "How's it going?"

"Doing fine," Farley replied in an upbeat tone. "I'm still finding subjects to paint. That shouldn't surprise you." He grinned.

"Is the voice still around?" asked Clint, afraid to hear the answer.

"It's not! It started to dissipate a few days ago. Out of nowhere it simply stopped." Farley breathed deeply. "I can't tell you how relieved I was not to have my thoughts competed with. All day yesterday I walked around afraid it would start up again, but I didn't hear him *once* and haven't today either. Isn't that something? For months I've been tormented by it, and then the voice simply stops. I pray I'm free of it forever."

Farley turned serious, "You have no idea what it's like to have a voice in your head that isn't yours. I honestly thought I had lost my mind." His eyes shifted, thinking about how different things were. "Until you came along."

Clint found Farley's revelation as odd as Farley did. "That is strange," he consoled Farley. "Miracles happen, and positive thinking works. I say, you are rid of the voice–permanently."

While Farley mulled over Clint's prediction, Clint leafed through several explanations as to why Charlie Hill would have stopped communicating. The answer that popped into his head was because Charlie had someone else doing his bidding. It seemed the most plausible explanation.

"Let's hope so," Farley admitted, exuding hope for better days. "A quiet life sounds heavenly." He shook his head, "Mine hasn't been these last few years."

Clint saw his opening to ask Farley about his past and jumped on it. "Is that right? Are you referring to the heart transplant. Your fall? The one you mentioned in Goss Cave when we talked?"

"Yeah, those for sure. Like I told you, when I climbed the utility pole that night, I had no idea the direction my life was going to take. It's been a whirlwind since then."

Disappointed Farley didn't go into more detail, Clint commiserated with the man. "Truthfully, I can't imagine how you survived everything that followed."

Farley laughed abruptly, shocking Clint. "That was a cake-walk compared to what came before." Farley's expression appeared as though he might cry. "Clint, may I speak of a personal matter with you and not have it go outside us… other than Jules, maybe? I would never ask you to keep secrets from your wife."

Sitting back in the booth, Clint countered fast, "Absolutely. I'd like to think we are becoming the best of friends. Please, speak freely."

"I was married once." His lips broadened into a full-face smile, the wrinkles around his eyes growing deeper than his age would indicate. "I can still see her face, so vividly. I'd melt every time I gazed at that lovely woman. I could never say no to her," he grinned, "She was the light of my life."

Farley's gently gray eyes beamed from the memory. "The last time I saw Gloria her train case was sitting by the front door. I still can hear her high heels clicking on the tile. See her burgundy coat tossed over her arm with her hand on the doorknob."

Clint was shocked, not knowing how to react. He watched as Farley tried to collect himself, a weary, painful expression carved into the folds of his face. "She left me for a better man," he choked out, his voice wavering.

Clint's eyes grew wide, trying to find the right words that refused to form. Jules had provided a version of what he just heard from Farley, but he wasn't about to reveal his prior knowledge. Instead, he'd let Farley speak uninterrupted.

Farley scanned the bar, wanting to make certain their talk remained private. "After our two children—twins—died in a gut-wrenching accident. They were at the babysitter's house at the time. There because of me. They drowned." Farley's voice faltered, on the verge of tears again. "They were the cutest little things, nearly three years old. Oh my God, what a heartbreak." Farley looked away, not wanting to make eye contact, "Almost didn't survive losing them. Even thought about ending it myself."

He took a deep breath and in a quivering voice, said, "We tried for four years without success to have Vincent and Violet. When we received the good news, we literally jumped up and down in the doctor's office." Farley grinned. "I still remember the doctor and his expression when he told us the fertility treatments had worked, and Gloria was pregnant. I've never seen such joy on a woman's face in my life. She glowed from head to foot. She was so happy, Clint." The memory of her joy caused him to feel sick.

Then he sighed with admission, "I talked Gloria into dinner and a movie that afternoon. She wasn't keen on the idea, didn't want to leave the kids with anyone when we were having our hands full with the terrible twos. They were just shy of three and getting into everything. Babies at that age are always curious about stuff, ya know? They were continually getting into our cabinets and drawers. We had to secure them with safety devices." His eyes twinkled, remembering the days when his house was alive with laughter. "Oh, my Lord, what a pair they made. What one didn't think of, the other one did."

Swallowing hard, Farley said, "Gloria was uneasy about leaving the kids with anyone, so we asked a close friend of hers, Jackie Lovecraft, if she'd babysit them for the afternoon. She happily agreed, and Gloria relented." With his eyes closed from the agony he felt, he said, "Jackie made a grocery run. Put our babies in her daughter's care. The daughter was on her phone when the accident happened. Vincent and Violet wandered outdoors through the sliding door. They toppled into Jackie's uncovered pool." Farley's shoulders slumped.

Clint felt paralyzed with grief for the poor man sitting across from him. "I'm so sorry, Farley, I had no idea," Clint said, not having heard the story with this much detail. It hurt to realize Farley was so in love with Gloria when she walked out on him. Clint was aware she had divorced him, but this version of events put a whole different spin on things. Overwhelmed by Farley's admission, Clint bowed his head. Under the table, his hands trembled. He tried desperately not to lose it, feeling for his friend. "What a terrible thing to have happen. I can't imagine."

"It's something a person never gets over," Farley admitted with quivering lip. "To this day, I replay that horrific nightmare. The scene at the restaurant… oh my! When our names were announced over the intercom at dinner, we knew." He struggled to get the words out. "When the news was delivered, Gloria fainted, collapsed on the floor. They rushed her to the hospital where she stayed for several days, kept under observation, on suicide watch."

His skin turned sallow. "She wouldn't see me, Clint." His head fell. "My heart was broken a thousand different ways, and my wife wouldn't allow me in her room. She was eventually discharged." He shrugged, "But even then, she refused to let me come anywhere near her.

Nothing was the same after that. Her loathing glare bore her feelings. It was undeniable how she felt. The hatred and despise. That was late May of 2001, by the following February I was served papers." He snapped his fingers. "Nine years of marriage down the tubes just like that. One day I was in bliss, and the next I was tossed in hell. She moved in with a guy almost immediately. I suppose she felt comforted. By the time the divorce was final, she'd left him too. I have no idea where she is now. We don't keep in touch."

Clint's stomach churned. "I can't imagine being in Jackie's shoes, either. She must have carried terrible guilt. How is she? Do you know?"

"Not good. None of us fared well. She and her daughter went to therapy. Don't know how that turned out. We never really talked about it. Gloria doesn't keep in contact, and neither do they. How do you recover from something of that caliber? You don't! All you can do is try to hold on to your sanity." A frighteningly sinister look appeared in his eyes. "It's that, or the alternative."

Clint swallowed hard. "Just saying I'm sorry falls way short of how I feel. No words could convey my deep regret. I'm here for you if you need me. I can't erase the past, but I can promise a brighter tomorrow if you stay open to that promise. I've found talking things out is healing."

"Look, I wouldn't have told you all that if I wasn't willing to climb the mountain of a new tomorrow, lift myself out of the quagmire I've been wallowing in. I've been hiding from the world way too long. What I'm doing isn't living, Clint. I assure you. That's why I never came to town. A part of me wants to crawl in a hole and never come out."

Farley reached his hand across the table, a gesture of friendship, when he announced, "On December 21, it'll be one year since my heart transplant." He manifested enormous pride. "After six months I was considered a survivor! Grant you, with some baggage, but I'm now headed to one year. Still alive and kicking, the gods haven't given up on me yet."

"That's amazing," congratulated Clint, happy to change the subject. "From what I see, you're in excellent condition. I won't have to twist your arm then." Clint chuckled, glad to take the dialogue in a different direction. "Thanksgiving on Thursday, my place. Two p.m. sharp. I won't take no for an answer."

Taken by surprise, Farley had no choice but to accept Clint's gracious invitation to Thanksgiving dinner with him and his family.

His eyes glistened with gratitude. "Then I guess I'll see you on Thursday."

Chapter 17
An About-Face

ACES & EIGHTS

Glaring across the table, Scott was not happy. "What were you thinking, Clint? What part of *don't get involved* didn't you get?" He drummed his fingers on the table. "I don't care if the pope, in the flesh, spoke to you and told you to do it, I said *not* to stick your nose into this, and under no circumstances, speak to anyone, which is exactly what you did. Against my advice."

Scott's anger was palpable. Under his breath, but distinctly discernible, he mumbled, "You can't fix stupid!" Although he didn't intend to make a scene at Aces & Eights, he felt like throwing down the gauntlet.

Without making an excuse, or offering a farewell, Clint purposefully got up from the table, calmly set his soiled napkin beside his plate and reached for his coat that was laying on the back of the seat next to him. He bit his tongue so as not to let the words that had formed at the tip spill out.

In that moment, Scott realized he had crossed the line. Insulting Clint wasn't wise or professional, friend or not. From experience in dealing with Clint, glimpses of his *will of steel* would surface when backed into a corner. This was one of those time.

What Scott observed during the inquiry into Clint's father's death had come around in spades. Clint was more alert and attuned to coincidences than ever. This strange situation, swathed in Farley McDougal's remarkable dilemma, had triggered something deep inside Clint. Cognizant of his intuitive side–more pronounced than before–Rod Radcliff, Sr. had ignited Clint's inner being of sentience. There was no turning back now. His antenna was on high alert, and Scott could see it in Clint's cold, dark, cautious eyes that seemed to have changed color.

"The crux of the problem, as I see it," Clint curtly articulated, "is we're not on the same page. You will always be the cop. I, on the

140

other hand, am the inept amateur." Speaking with barely contained anger, his words poured forth, out of him, without restraint. "I'm not as simpleminded as you believe."

"C'mon, Clint, come back, sit down. We need to talk this out."

"No, thanks," Clint replied, walking away without turning around nor intending to further the conversation.

"For heaven sakes!" Scott yelled, running after Clint and pulling on his sleeve. "Don't you get it? This closed case isn't cold, not any longer. I'd never forgive myself if you collided with the person behind it, who seems to be minus a conscience. Out of ignorance or from you playing amateur sleuth, if he killed four times, he'd have no qualms pulling the trigger again. Don't you see? How could I live with myself if I didn't try to stop you from getting involved? This isn't like last time. The murderer is still alive and out there."

Clint whipped around. "Look, I said I was sorry. What more do you want from me? Nothing was intentional. Quite to the contrary, I tried to weasel my way out of speaking with June, but this Dr. Jackson simply wouldn't hear of it. If I hadn't complied, he would have alerted hospital security, and that, my friend, would have made matters even worse. Sometimes a person has to pick their battles."

"Come on," Scott implored. "Let's discuss this civilly. I need to hear it a second time, especially what the nurse had to say." Scott reached out in apology leading Clint back to the table.

The two men walked back to the table where they had been sharing a drink. Clint stared stoically over at Scott. "June Bennett, as I mentioned, was a good friend of Ann Hill's. She was on duty the night of the shooting and ultimately the transplant. She was outside the operating room the night Charles Hill's heart was placed in Farley McDougal."

Over the next half hour Clint summarized, step-by-step, every move he had made while in Louisville and at Grayson Hospital— *except one*. He didn't tell Scott about June possessing Charlie and Ann Hill's declaration of death and a copy of an unauthorized transplant donor card. She had asked him not to reveal her secret. Having an unauthorized document would place June's employment at risk. She didn't want to jeopardize her job. It was a promise Clint intended to keep.

Standing on equal ground, Scott and Clint agreed they would mutually examine this new case from an entirely different angle–Scott as an off-duty cop and Clint as an involved outsider. As friends, they had delved into a previous complicated cold case, unraveling the mystery of Clint's father death, Eli Reeves, coupled alongside Rod Radcliff, Sr.'s demise and true cause of death. Those cases came to light in 2003, over two years ago but remained close to the surface for both men.

After a discord of wills, Scott elected not to attempt to force Clint to stand down, or backoff in the least. Instead, he encouraged him to dig a little deeper into the narrative surrounding December 21, 2004 through the lens of a bystander only. Not to turn paranormal investigator in disguise, which would surely send up red flags to any criminal with an ear to the ground.

Using whatever intuitive means Clint tapped into, like he had done during the Goss Cave incident, would present a proper line of inquiry. Scott had witnessed Clint's impressive investigative skills firsthand and wouldn't underestimate his instinctive ability going forward. Together they would walk the fine division of proper investigation without stepping over the line.

Conversely, unbeknownst to Scott, Clint's harbored secrets had started to mount. Keeping promises was paramount to Clint, but to keep information from Scott, after their exchange felt misguided. However, in June's case, he had no choice.

Scott and Clint parted ways in a better mood than when their conversation started. They finished their drinks and promised to stay in touch.

Shadows marked the trees and ground from drifting clouds moving past a late-day sun, fading in and out like time hurtling away as he walked the street, thinking. Introspectively, Clint thought about how life ran through cycles–from childhood when everything was fresh and new to the very old, where people wore wisdom and scars as badges of honor, forging over the decades in the continuous classroom of peaks and valleys.

Clint felt perplexed by which direction to take. Should he ask Bonnie to assemble news articles from the night of December 21, 2004 so he could read more in depth before going into Louisville where he would potentially talk to the owner of Beans a' Brewin' and walk the pavement to get a better feel of the streets Charlie walked? Or did he relax and wait for the next sign he knew would present itself? Patience wasn't his strong suit, but he was getting better at staying still until compelled to react.

Unclear as to when or where to start his probe, Clint settled on driving to the orphanage to help clear his mind. He'd walk the manicured estate and reconnect with his place of solace. To him, when he moved through the woods there on the grounds, he felt strange vibrations in and among the trees along with a sound that prevailed no matter what time of day or night. He felt connected. Where at his place that feeling had dissipated. At times he would have sworn Rod's spirit walked alongside him when he was at the orphanage. That was especially true when the building phase of Rod Radcliff's Children's Home was in full swing.

Pulling into the orphanage drive, he phoned Jules to let her know Farley would be joining them the next day. He had stopped by the orphanage and would be home in a short while.

Jules knew that meant Clint had some thinking to do. Besides, she was busy setting the formal dining room table and preparing tomorrow's menu.

"Hey, Casey!" Clint called out when he saw the boy sitting on a bench in the hallway, his feet dangling. "What are you doing?"

Casey's eyes twinkled with delight, "Th-i-nk-ing."

"Really?" fussed Clint. "What are you thinking about?"

"Stu-ff!"

"Me too. Would you like to join me for a turn around the property? Maybe a half hour?"

Casey jumped to his feet like a jack rabbit. "Yes-s-ssss!"

"Alright, let's do it then," declared Clint reaching for Casey's hand but not sure if he'd take it. "You must stay close and not run off. Understood?"

"Ye-s. Cas-ey c-lose," he said.

Outside on the lawn, after checking Casey out of the building with the desk clerk, Clint let go of his hand. They walked together, neither saying a word, until they came to the children's playground.

"Would you like to take a spin on the merry-go-round?"

Casey looked up with endearing eyes. He was nearly in tears but said nothing.

Clint translated his expression to mean, yes. "Okay, well then, that's what we'll do. Be careful and hang on tight to the bars." He helped Casey onto the wheel and placed his hands directly on the rounded surface of the bars attached to the center of the spinning disk. "You ready?" he asked with smiling eyes.

Casey replied in the way of a screech so loud Clint had to put his hands over his ears just to tease him. He started acting silly.

Casey joined in, chuckling as robustly as Clint. "Go, go, go, go, go!" he commanded.

With both hands on the u-shaped bars, Clint gave the mighty metal spinner a huge hurl. The wheel began to move. Slow at first, but in a flash it was whirling like a top, forcing Casey to hang on. Until finally, Clint pulled on the bar to slow it down and help Casey step off. To his surprise, Casey hugged him like he'd never let go, clinging to his pant leg for dear life.

Casey lowered his body to the ground, surprising Clint. He was wobbly but his expression happy.

"What are you doing down there? I thought you wanted to walk with me. Are you sick to your stomach from spinning?" Clint asked, assuming Casey might be dizzy.

Burying his head in his hands, Casey started to whimper.

"What's wrong, Casey," Clint asked, putting a hand on the child's shoulder.

At first Casey pulled back, not wanting to be touched, but then he relaxed into Clint's side again. It took several minutes before words were spoken but when Casey did speak, Clint was flabbergasted. In a weepy voice, Casey said, "Da-d-d-y."

Stunned to his core, Clint replied, "What do you mean? No one is here but you and me, Casey."

"No-o-o," was his final word of the day. With his head low, he began to cry again, a sound like that of a wounded animal.

Not sure how to respond to Casey's outlandish claim, Clint did what came naturally. He coddled him until his crying subsided. Not backing away from an uncomfortable situation, Clint asked, "Casey, we've not talked about your family before. Would you like to?"

Getting to his feet, Casey's small frame waited for Clint to lift from the ground and join him. He spoke no words but simply pointed to a grove of beech trees some fifty feet away.

"Okay, we can walk that way. That's fine with me." Clint tried to soothe the boy, but quickly got the message to let him be when Casey stepped away. He had made such huge strides with the introverted boy he didn't want to push too hard. No one in the facility had reached the closeness Clint had with Casey and he wasn't about to endanger his progress by taking too much for granted.

"We still have some thinking to do. Don't we?" Clint stated in an optimistic tone. "It's nice to have company. Don't you think?"

Casey nodded, lifting his hand to be held in Clint's.

Dusk had settled in when Clint suggested they return to the building. "I enjoyed your company today," he told Casey as he checked him back in. "Maybe we can do it again sometime. Would you like that?"

Casey didn't answer but did nod.

After the merry-go-round incident, Casey had become withdrawn and non-responsive. Whatever had happened out on the lawn had affected him profoundly. Clint was aware that most children had overactive imaginations, including imaginary friends, but this seemed more than pretend. Frightened by what he had seen, Casey's hands shook violently and his face distorted.

Later, Clint would call to make certain Casey was all right and had recovered from the episode. He'd request an orderly to check in on the boy before bed as an extra measure.

When he walked in the door at home, Jules's lovely smile greeted him. She kissed him on the cheek while helping him with his coat. She hung his hat and coat on the hall tree in the foyer.

"You look rough around the edges," she commented, quick to observe. "You're concentrating awfully hard."

Holding a freshly poured decaf espresso, he replied, "You could say that. I'll explain later, but for now I'd like to spend time with my favorite girl." His shoulders relaxed. "What is that awesome smell? Brownies?"

"Nope, death by chocolate." Jules snickered. "My favorite cake, especially when coupled with rich, bitter coffee. Thought I'd make it while you were out. It falls easily. The slightest jarring causes it to topple."

After dinner, Jules went upstairs to wash her face and change into her nightgown. When she returned and sat next to Clint, who seemed to be transfixed by the fire, she asked, "So are you going to tell me what happened today that has you disturbed?"

Turning, he explained, "Casey thought he saw his father today." He watched Jules's expression shift to panic. "It happened while he and I were out walking. He was on the merry-go-round at the time. Everything was great until he called out, "Daddy," and started crying. I swear to God it looked like Casey was listening to him, but I saw no one. Jules, it freaked me out. The first thought that came to mind was he was going to kidnap the boy. I'm terribly frustrated. How did he manage to get past security without detection? That's a problem. For all the children. I told Tom Sanders to keep an eye out and put security on alert. I'm concerned the man is still somewhere on the grounds."

"Oh my. That is a problem. Do you think he wants Casey back? Why didn't he just approach you and Casey? Why hide?"

"Jules those are the same questions I've been asking myself. Why? Why not just go inside and wait for us? Unless he didn't want me to know he was there." Clint frowned, unhappy with the situation. "Can you imagine dropping your kid off at an orphanage without a word of explanation? What circumstances would cause a person to do something so cruel? Has guilt driven him back here?"

"As distressing as this might sound, maybe the man wasn't able to adequately care for an autistic child and felt desperate." Her eyes drifted in thought. "What do we know about Casey, other than he was dropped off the night our doors opened? We have no records?"

"Honestly, we don't have a clue. He calls himself Casey, so we followed suit," Clint admitted shamefully. "I'm going to reopen his file, do a more thorough search. Especially now that he thinks he saw his dad. That man isn't going to just waltz into my orphanage and out with Casey." Clint showed his irritation. "He's too special to let that happen and deserves better."

Clint breathed angrily, "I remember being told Casey had a trench coat on and was wrapped in a blanket when someone opened the door and found him on the step, shivering. That was it, nothing to identify him, and to make matters worse, Casey wouldn't speak. Not to anyone during those days. His lips were sealed like a steel trap. He wouldn't let people come anywhere near him. It would turn into a screaming fit if they tried."

He touched Jules's hand. "Not until recently has Casey let his guard down and only with me. The sad thing is we don't know any more today than we did a year ago."

"That's why you built the orphanage, Clint. To take children in and give them a safe environment and good home. Food on the table and a roof over their heads."

His eyes softened. "Exactly. I've accomplished one thing. Casey draws me pictures now. Grant you, they are strangely bizarre, disturbing even if I'm honest," he chuckled, "but the point is he does."

"Poor kid," said Jules. "Carving extra time out of your schedule for him has made a noticeable difference."

"It has, and I'm not letting some bozo undo my efforts. Casey is happy. It's going to stay that way. The man gave up his legal rights when he dumbed his kid on the porch like discarded trash. Casey isn't going anywhere!"

Chapter 18
Thanksgiving

Thanksgiving turned out to be a lively affair, both at the orphanage and at home. A big Thanksgiving spread was laid out for the staff, families, and children at Radcliff's Children's Home. Clint made a point of stopping in early to make certain everything was coming along smoothly. The aroma when he walked through the door was delightful. Turkeys roasting in the ovens reminded him of home. When he left the house Jules was standing in the kitchen wearing a decorative pumpkin apron, peeling potatoes.

Clint singled Casey out. He'd brought him a small gift. A pad of colorful paper. The child was ecstatic and ran to his usual table to start using the pad right away.

Jules and Clint entertained eight guests at their home. Macy's Thanksgiving parade played while Clint and Jules cooked and baked. Clint lit a fire and turned-on Christmas music when the parade ended.

Clint's twenty-three-pound turkey was cooked to perfection and Jules's twice baked potatoes vanished before her eyes after sitting down to dinner, a huge hint she had chosen the right potato dish. Patrick brought tiramisu topped with strawberries, drizzled with chocolate fudge icing, just as he had done for Clint and Jules's wedding.

Farley came in carrying a bottle of zinfandel, and one of merlot plus Cocoa and Winston at Clint's insistence. Bonnie supplied party favors for each plate, plus flowers for the table. Terence, from Ace Hardware, and his wife, Carrie, came empty handed, apologizing profusely for not bringing a dinner gift.

Rusty's family transported their Maltese pooch, Bobo, to the affair. They'd quarantined a section at the back of the house for Cocoa, Winston and Bobo's arrival and play. At the beginning, ceaseless barking yelped through the house, but then, after a short while all three dogs became best of pals. Jules baked homemade dog treats as a special surprise and served them when dinner was put on the table, which she assumed would keep them busy.

Farley and Bonnie hit it off immediately. Having met one another prior to the gathering, they sat side by side at the dinner table, interacting like old friends catching up on current events. Terence, Carrie, and Patrick discussed food and business affairs; labor costs, supply issues, and the red tape created by bureaucracy.

Rusty, Molly, and the children brought Clint and Jules up to date on school activities and farm issues while dessert and drinks were served. The hot apple pie topped with vanilla ice cream was a winner, along with Patrick's tiramisu.

A game of Tripoli monopolized the remaining evening hours. Everyone had been requested to bring jars of pennies for wagering. No one had played Tripoli except Clint's kids. It was a huge success. When the evening ended, vows to play another round of cards were on everyone's minds. They tossed out a date near Christmas, and everyone gladly agreed.

That night after everyone had departed for home, Jules brought up something Clint hadn't noticed during the dinner hour. "Did you notice Patrick staring at Bonnie at dinner? He seemed overly attentive to that side of the table. Kept looking at Farley and Bonnie."

Jules rubbed her jaw, grinning conspiratorially. "Farley and Bonnie did get along well. Didn't they? It was gratifying to see Farley engaged in conversation. No loss for words between those two. She really brought Farley out of his shell."

Clint wore a lopsided grin. "Farley had a good time, I could tell. It's the happiest I've seen him," he said observantly.

"Did you notice Patrick try to sit next to Bonnie at cards, but she waved Farley over before he could sit down?" Jules questioned.

"Julie Eileen Reeves, are you pretending something is going on with Patrick that isn't there?" Clint chortled, amused at his wife's commentary.

"Of course not," she protested unconvincingly. "Are you kidding. Those two are like oil and water. They fuss like cats and dogs." She chortled impishly. "I guess that's why I found Patrick's attention to Bonnie so odd."

"What's on our agenda for tomorrow, may I ask?"

"Changing the subject, are we?" Jules teased knowing her husband better than he knew himself.

"Maybe," he grinned, acknowledging she had hit the nail on the head. "I need to speak with Bonnie is all. I'd like her to look up some information for me. See if she can pull up newspaper articles or any other reports that might be associated with Charles Hill."

"I have more redecorating to do at Rod's Apothecary. Thought I'd run into New Albany to Hobby Lobby and check out the Black Friday sales. I've set a meeting at four with the staff, asking for feedback on the new lounge. Wall plaques are on order. They are beautiful. Remodeling your old office will make for a relaxing employee environment when breaks are taken."

"I might stop by. I haven't met the new girl you hired yet."

"That'd be nice," Jules replied and then asked a question she knew the answer to. "Do you want to ride along to New Albany?"

"Nah, don't think so. I'm not good at shopping, I'd be a thorn in your side. After the library I have a few errands to run. I could stop by the gift shop for the meeting, though."

After pouring a nightcap, Jules and Clint went to the living room to appreciate the last of the fire's dying embers and let the evening grind down to a halt. Tired to the bone, setting their crystal wedding shot glasses aside, they shuffled off to bed, feeling good about the fine day they had extended to their friends and family. They were out the minute their heads hit the pillows.

Before dawn the following morning, Clint slipped out of bed and went to the living room to layer kindling and logs to start a fire. He emptied the ashes into the copper bin and then struck a match, watching the kindling go up in flames and igniting the firewood into a heavy blaze.

In the winter Clint typically arose first to prepare a nice fire in the hearth ahead of his wife awakening. Coffee finished brewing and bacon lay in the skillet sizzling when Jules, a late sleeper, fumbled out of bed, not fully awake. Although she wasn't fond of her early morning bedhead appearance, Clint, adored her tousled auburn hair and sleepy green eyes. It was one of things he adored most about her.

Early mornings were Clint's favorite time of day. He gazed into the flames with holding a mug of coffee while relaxing in his oversized leather chair. The mug warmed his hands as he sat quietly reflecting on what had transpired over the last few days and week. Not sure where to begin, in respect to Farley's situation, Clint pondered his next logical move. The library. He'd only scratched the surface of investigating, considering his unskilled status. Inexperienced in such matters, Scott was right to warn him to tread lightly. Grateful for the advice, he'd let his instincts guide the way. Asking too many questions in Louisville could turn ugly if not handled well.

He thought about his new office in the attic of the orphanage. It was everything he had imagined it would be, right down to the curtains covering the windows. Moonlight hit the windows exactly right, he had noticed when he stopped by that first night, streaming across the oriental rug Jules had placed in front of the fireplace. She had done a masterful job. To finally have it ready was a relief. She had put his Treasure Island copy, the one his dad intended for him in 1953, on the fireplace shelf. He was thrilled to see it sitting on the mantel. It would always remind him of his father and the peace Clint carried after locating his remains.

Presently, the home housed thirty-two children. Clint couldn't be prouder. When he worked in the attic, they would be studying, reading, and playing. One big happy family. The idea of working above all the activity brought a smile to his face.

But then a feeling of sorrow arose. Most of these children had been dropped off by their own parents, often too poor to care for them. Some children had learning disabilities or an illness that was overwhelming to their parents, making it financially impossible to care for them. Living in poverty, unable to provide basic needs for their child, was a desperate circumstance. Eighty to ninety percent of the kids at Radcliff's Children Home fell into these categories.

The remaining children were from situations much like Clint's. A parent, or parents dying, abandonment, or someone simply un-willing to take responsibility, with no relative to step up.

Kids like Casey left on orphanage's doorsteps without a clue to his identity, were exceptions. The facility knew nothing about him, other than the name he called himself... Casey. No one had been able to ascertain even a scant piece of information. Casey's plight in life felt particularly heartbreaking.

Clint made a mental note to stop by the home again today. He had a sudden urge to pay the children a visit and see how adoptions were coming along for the third quarter. The prior week had been exceptional. Clint assumed the increase in activity was due to the upcoming holiday.

Fridays were normally quiet days, a day when he often took the reins to read during story hour. This was one of those times. Clint also wanted to inspect Casey's file for potential overlooked clues. He had reported the incident concerning Casey thinking he'd seen his father. No paper trail existed that he knew of, but he felt compelled to take another look.

"Good morning, sleepy-head," Clint said when Jules walked out into the living room, her hair uncombed.

"I smell bacon..." she blissfully mumbled.

"You do," he grinned, pleased to have fried it an hour ago. "I put a plate in the oven to keep it warm until you got up. Meet you in the kitchen in fifteen," he suggested, watching his wife shuffle down the hall to the restroom.

"That sounds heavenly," she muttered walking toward the bathroom in her pink chenille housecoat.

When Jules returned, she looked like an entirely different person. Her auburn hair had been clipped with a fancy jeweled claw and she was wearing a forest green top, long beads, and black jeans. Her midnight blue mascara lent color to her fair skin.

In his eyes she looked radiant. Stunningly beautiful. Clint put blueberry pancakes on the table, awaiting her arrival, along with the bacon and orange juice. It wasn't a huge breakfast, but certainly a tasty one.

After finishing breakfast, she got into her Volvo, slipping her coffee mug into the cup holder. She tossed her purse onto the passenger seat ready to head to Hobby Lobby. She waved as she pulled out of the drive, and the plan was to hook back up at 4 p.m.

Clint went inside to grab his coat and wallet, lifting his keys from the wall rack that he had made so he'd stop misplacing them. He had trained himself well, and these days they were always where they ought to be. Fifteen minutes later he was at the Salzburg Library. He went inside, homing in on Bonnie's location. She had told him at Thanksgiving she'd be at the library from 9 a.m. to noon. Clint didn't want to address his request during Thanksgiving. He preferred to speak to her in private.

"Hey, stranger." She laughed. "I've been watching for you."

"You have? he replied, returning her smile. "I hope you don't mind me coming here rather than phoning. I need a personal favor to ask and didn't want to talk business yesterday with everyone around."

"No problem. By the way, that meal you two served was to die for," she complimented Clint. "I was so stuffed when I got home, I could hardly move. For breakfast, I ate a slice of the pie Jules sent home. And seeing your family again was wonderful." She pulled out two chairs at the nearest table, indicating Clint should have a seat.

"It was," he replied, sitting down beside her. "I'm happy everyone could make it. I've never had an apple pie better than hers. You're lucky she kept a slice back for you. The rest of that thing was gone in no time flat. And Patrick's tiramisu was out of this world. He has a magic touch!"

"He does. That man is amazing!" Bonnie watched the front door as two people walked in, reading the message on the door of short hours. Okay, let's change the subject. You're making me hungry."

Clint searched Bonnie's inquiring eyes, his face taut and lips wafer thin. "I have a favor to ask."

"Okay," she replied, curious about his reserved nature. "Happy to help."

"You know about Farley's condition. He told me he came in here looking for information and that's how you two met," Clint started off.

"That's right. I learned a lot about transplants by simply putting that material together for him. There's a lot more to it than most people would imagine, very complicated proceeding. Not all recipients make it past six months. Farley is one of the lucky ones. He seems to be doing quite well at the end of year one."

"That's true. Farley is an amazing person," he agreed, thinking Farley fit, and remembering what Jules had said about their attraction.

"The favor I need is related to his situation. I'd like to know more about the night of his transplant, which was December 21, 2004, around 7:30 in the evening. Was wondering about accident accounts corresponding to that timeframe?"

Bonnie expressed her disapproval. "Don't tell me you are trying to figure out who his donor is? That would be next to impossible because names aren't released in initial news reports."

"To be honest, I already know who the donor is." His eyes narrowed, "I want death reports and obituaries that line up with that night. In addition to what is already known."

"Hum," she muttered, holding her stare on Clint. "Should I be concerned? What are you wanting this material for if you already know the donor's name?" Intelligent, brown eyes steadily awaited Clint's answer.

Clint was in a pickle, realizing it would be an exercise in futility to lie. Wryly, he replied, "I want to know who killed the donor." He could see the shock on his friend's face. He had rendered her speechless.

After a long pause, Bonnie inquired, "And what will you do with this knowledge when and if you receive it?"

He knew Bonnie talked to Jules about community affairs. She had divulged Farley's family trauma in a side chat with his wife at the diner less than a week ago, which gave Clint heartburn. He blatantly asked, "Can I trust you? I mean really trust you?"

"You know you can, Clint," she replied, visibly insulted. "You are asking me to look for a needle in a haystack. I'd like to know why."

"What I'm requesting is extremely sensitive, Bonnie. Scott and I are working together to gain insight on that specific night. Nothing more. He's done some legwork and I'm following suit. We are working in tandem. Charles Hill, the donor, and his wife were both killed that night if it helps. The man who shot them got away scot-free. I'm wanting you to help me fill in the missing blanks surrounding the crime."

Bonnie leaned back in her chair. Her arms folded and a forefinger pressed against her lips. "For the record, something of this magnitude would never be discussed with anyone. You do realize, I've worked with the police on many occasions. In all that time, I'have never whispered a word or breached a confidence. Just so you know."

"This isn't going in the right direction," he admitted feeling uncomfortable. "I didn't mean to offend you, Bonnie. I have to be very careful. My being here cannot be discussed with anyone, which includes my wife or Scott, for that matter. It's not like they aren't aware of my actions because they are. Talking about this in a public setting, however, could turn disastrous."

"Look, working at the library often puts me in a position of secrecy. Jules is the only person I share knowledge with, so don't judge me. The stuff I tell her isn't life threatening. Yes, I told her about Farley, and maybe that was a mistake. It didn't feel wrong at the time since he's our friend, and I thought by telling her, it would help us understand him better. But, if I'm told to keep a confidence under my cap, I do. As I will with this. I'll research the night this man, Charles Hill, died, and any corresponding incidents that might tie to December 21 around that hour."

"Thank you, Bonnie. I'm sorry if I crossed the line. Truth is, I'm nervous because Charles Hill's murder directly pertains to our friend. Farley's had a mountain of problems to deal with over the last two years. At some point I'll fill you in on what brought me to you, but for now I'd like to keep my cards close to the vest."

Prying into a cold case file was risky business, and Clint was an amateur snoop at best having never done anything on this scale before. Two years ago, that was different, he had been urged to solve a major mystery, all pertaining to his personal family history. Farley's affair wasn't the same. Clint was shooting in the dark, and other than Picasso showing up, he was on his own. The last time he didn't have to follow his nose. He was directed, even pushed into making discoveries. In Farley's case, Clint felt duty-bound to become a fast study in undercover work.

With a boyish shy grin, Clint asked, "We still friends?"

"Certainly," Bonnie responded leaning in for a hug. "Be careful, Clint. I'll call when I have something of value."

Bonnie walked Clint to the door, and out into the street. Coming back indoors, she wondered how smart it was for her to assist Clint in his efforts. Although he'd said nothing specific to lead her to believe Clint was walking into danger, she believed it was possible.

Chapter 19
An Inner Message

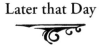

Later that Day

Snow was coming down hard when Clint entered Radcliff's Children's Home. Overcast skies commandeered the frosty vanilla morning Jules and he had enjoyed, unexpectedly converting it into a snowstorm. Having called Jules, he was relieved to know she was on her way back home and would miss the heaviest weather moving in.

When Clint strolled through the lobby, the place was buzzing with excitement. Children were heading into story hour, where he too was headed. He carried in his hand, *Tommy's Hot Air Balloon Lands on Forbidden Island*. When he first noticed the book, its title reminded him of Treasure Island, a tale full of adventure, same as the book he was carrying.

Figuring he had enough time before the event commenced, Clint took the elevator to the fifth floor. As he walked into the administration office, the office manager greeted him.

"Hi, Mr. Reeves, good to see you." Greg said standing to his feet to shake Clint's hand.

"You, too, Greg," Clint responded pleasantly.

"Is there anything you need?"

"No, I'm going to look through some of the hard files. I'll be in and out in no time. I'm reading to the kids today in ten minutes."

Greg relaxed back into position. He had been balancing the company's October bank statement.

Clint thumbed through several files before he found what he was searching for, Casey was written on the file folder with no last name, in Clint's own writing, written on the front of the file. He remembered the night well when he first laid eyes on the lad. A feeling of sadness engulfed him. Cold and shivering, Casey reluctantly stuttered his name after coming indoors and drinking hot cocoa in the dining room. When asked his age he held up six fingers. Now at age seven, not much had changed in his autistic demeanor since that night.

At the desk he opened the file and read every word of the one paragraph describing Casey's arrival. Next to nothing, no parents, or indication of where Casey lived prior to the orphanage. His accent gave a slight clue to a foreign ancestry. Clint's best guess suggested Casey wasn't from southern Indiana. He closed the file, knowing no more than he did when he sat down. Clint felt frustrated from having so little to go on. He was hoping, at the very least, by now they'd have found birth records, or family that might have surfaced inquiring about the boy, but that wasn't the case. In the true sense, Casey had been, in every aspect of the word… forsaken.

Taking the elevator back down, Clint walked out into the lobby searching for the object of his attention. Casey was not in the reading room or cafeteria. Clint checked his room and bathroom before returning to the main entrance. Both places showed no signs of the boy. Casey's bed was neat as a pin. A toy triceratops sat on the nightstand alongside a tablet and a box of colored pencils.

Clint gave up looking and went to the reading room/library, taking his place at the front and greeting the crowd of attendees. The chatter in the background was pleasant to hear when Clint opened the book he planned to read.

"Good afternoon, everyone," he said with a welcoming smile. "I'd like to read from a book that reminds me of one I particularly enjoyed reading when I lived in an orphanage west of here. The title is *Tommy's Hot Air Balloon Lands on Forbidden Island*. Does that sound good?"

The group exploded with chatter, voicing their approval.

"Super. Let's get started."

As he started to read, his attention was momentarily drawn away from the words on the page when Casey walked in. The child stood at the back of the room, near the door for easy retreat.

Clint noticed Casey's fingers twitching, although he looked at the floor, a sign he was aware of Clint. The nervousness in his facial twitches telegraphed his discomfort.

Story hour went by quickly as Clint read with extra enthusiasm, aware Casey was listening. When he closed the book, the children clapped excitedly. Clint promised to read the next several chapters the following week since the book was larger than most.

Two children approached. They began discussing the book and the adventures it held. Clint politely interacted with exuberance, glad to see they were interested in the story but disappointed when he realized Casey had left the room. A short while later he was standing outside in the lobby readying himself to leave and wanting to have a slice of pie at Josie's before the meeting at the gift shop with Jules started.

He was pulling his coat over his shoulders when from his peripheral vision he saw a small dark silhouette coming closer. He turned just in time to see Casey slipping into the reading room. Oddly, he eyed Clint before turning the corner.

At the desk where Clint had been a few minutes earlier, Casey sat erectly with his hands folded as though expecting Clint. Silently he opened a folder he was holding and waited.

"Whatcha doing?" asked Clint standing at the front of the room. "A picture for me, I hope. I've been waiting for another one to hang on my wall."

Casey didn't speak. He did, however, point to the picture he had drawn.

Clint was astonished at the precision of exactness to detail. Before him was a beautiful flower garden under a butterscotch sky. Brilliant colors graced the paper canvas. The opposite of bloody dinosaurs. To the right was a bench under a white canopy trellis where a woman sat gracefully attending to her needlepoint. Blue birds were perched on the branch behind her. Cardinals had landed in a weeping willow tree.

"Casey, this is amazing. I don't know what to say. It's beyond anything I expected." He looked at the wide-eyed boy. "You have some serious talent, young man Do you know that?"

Casey grinned, prideful of his work. He pointed to the woman. "Th-at's mu-mmy."

Clint's chest tightened.

"P-re-t-ty?" Casey stuttered with eyes bright.

"She is! It's such a lovely picture." He handed the picture back after taking a closer look.

"For y-o-u." Casey said handing it over.

"Casey, are you sure?" responded Clint, shocked Casey would offer him the picture of his mother. "Don't you want to hang it in your bedroom so you can admire it?"

Casey patted his chest, "I ha-ve on-e."

"You do? Great, I feel honored," boasted Clint, proud to be regarded so highly. "I can't wait to show it to my wife, Jules. She'll love it as much as I do."

Casey abruptly stood, marching to the door with purpose. He turned, speaking as he never had. Clear, precise, intelligible. "*Daddy said you would.*"

Before Clint could respond, Casey was on the elevator, headed to his bedroom or some other place of seclusion. A safe hiding place where others couldn't find him.

Clint gazed at the image, floored at Casey's words and the clarity with which they were delivered. His blood pressure rose from the thought Casey's father had spoken to him and was still around. The picture he held was masterful, especially for a little guy.

Confusion set in, *Should I follow Casey to ask him when he spoke with his dad, or is it possible he's pretending to have talked to him?* The thought never occurred to Clint, until now, that he might have underestimated the power of the child's imaginative mind. *Casey wants a mom and dad, so he invented them,* Clint deliberated. *The facility's security system did not malfunction. Casey imagining parents makes a lot more sense. Rather than his father, in the flesh, appearing on the grounds, not once, but twice undetected. With the grounds under surveillance twenty-four hours a day, that's highly unlikely.*

He recalled the staff security officer's words, "Nothing out of the ordinary on the cameras last Tuesday." A huge weight was lifted from Clint's shoulders when he walked through the problem in his mind. He couldn't believe he hadn't factored in Casey's fertile imagination before.

He went to the supply cabinet and took a large envelope out, slipping Casey's artwork inside for protection. When he returned to the office, he'd pin it to the wall beside the first picture Casey had drawn for him.

On his way to Rod's Apothecary to join his wife for their staff meeting, Clint stopped in at ACE Hardware to pick up a few household supplies, including the hooks required to hang Casey's second picture. He had decided to put both drawings in matching frames above the fireplace. A perfect place for the young boy's creativity to be appreciated.

He waved at Carrie when he turned the corner headed for AISLE 3. The smell of DIY handyman supplies sitting on the shelves was intoxicating. Clint loved wandering through the hardware store. The scent of lumber, tools, leather, oils, gadgets, nails, and fasteners was a heavenly scent.

Terence, stood at the end of the aisle he walked down. "Hey, guy!" he said, setting an armful of containers down. "Glad to see you, I was going to call. Thanksgiving was loads of fun and I want to thank you again for the opportunity to be included in your holiday festivities. The wife and I thoroughly enjoyed ourselves. Thanks for the invite. Your family is delightful! Those boys, Trey and Dylan, were hilarious. So full of energy. And the dog racket was lively."

On the way out, Clint extended an invitation to dinner, suggesting the four of them get together soon. Terrence gladly accepted, suggesting a Christmas get-together at their place.

The staff at Rod's Apothecary and Sundries was bustling when Clint and Jules walked through the door with armfuls of samples. The couple had met outside in the parking lot and talked a short while before coming indoors. Clint offered to help carry the bulk of Jules's other supplies consisting of refreshments, cupcakes, bakery croissants, and folders, one for each employee. She had printed out employee guidelines and benefits for years of service, a generous package for those with longevity.

Customers mingled in the aisles, eyeing the store's hodge-podge of eclectic goods. Rod's Apothecary was a cross between an old-fashioned general store, counter eatery serving basic menu items such as hamburgers, hot dogs, tenderloins, onion rings, French fries, draft root beer, sodas, hot tea, and coffee.

Unlike most retail establishments, the store permitted patrons to carry drinks with them as they roamed the aisles in search of necessities and novelties. The exclusive shopping hampers, stacked by the entrance with the logo, Rod's Apothecary & Sundries, gave the place a unique downhome charm. The store's reputation was known far and wide as always having an uplifting atmosphere. He and Jules felt good about what they had achieved.

When the meeting adjourned, the employees were energized about what they'd discussed, bringing up several brilliant ideas on how to make the storefront and breakroom more attractive. On their way out, Jules and Clint greeted every worker, showing their support and appreciation of their devotedness to the store's growth.

"So where now," Jules curiously asked. "Home?"

"It's early yet, but we could head that way. Would you want to do our normal Friday night pizza? If so, I could stop by that new pizza joint in Palmyra, Pietro's Pizzetta Pies, and get us an assorted half dozen." Clint's brow creased. "Don't you love those little deep-fried pizza crusts? The flavor and texture are so addictive!"

"That sounds fantastic. I'll get my bath out of the way. By the time you get home, we'll be ready to sit down to a movie. I heard *The Core* is outstanding. A sci-fi movie! Right up our alley! I'll grab a copy at Blockbuster if you're interested. It's early so hopefully they'll still have a copy."

Noting the excitement in Jules's voice, Clint readily agreed. "See you at the house in about an hour, or soon thereafter." He opened her car door, waiting for her to slide into the driver's seat. After a quick kiss, she pulled from the parking lot, headed for home and a hot bath.

Another idea crossed his mind as he walked to his truck, something more important than pizza selections. He had sufficient time to hang Casey's drawing in his new office, which he'd like to do before his first of the week visit.

It'd be nice to see them hanging on the wall together when I visit next, he thought envisioning walking through the door and seeing both above the fireplace. Pleased to be Casey's only friend, he considered taking the boy to his office to let him see how nice the artwork complemented his room but thought better of it. He didn't want his conduct to be misconstrued.

He phoned his order in and headed to Radcliff's Children's Home. The yearning to return to the orphanage overrode all else. The idea of Casey's picture with his mother sitting in a garden followed Clint all the way to the orphanage, waylaying all other thoughts.

Chapter 20
Manifestation

When Clint entered the orphanage, he detected an unmistakable energy. He attributed the sensation to his excitement of placing Casey's second drawing next to the first and putting them both in frames. The second drawing he had been given was a hundred-and-eighty-degree flip from the first creation. Clint compared them to darkness and light.

He clutched the Ace Hardware bag tightly as he waited for the doors of the elevator to open on the fifth floor. He went to the second door on his left and punched in the code before proceeding to the winding black iron staircase on the other side that led to the highest level of the building.

When he unlocked the door, he sensed an undercurrent thrum and felt its vibration. He intuited the same frequency when he identified the cluster of quartz crystals piled at the mouth of a fissure in Goss Cave. Later they served as a marker indicating the location of Reno Gang treasure.

On the desk Rod's quartz crystal shimmered, glistening in the late afternoon sun.

What's going on here? Clint questioned. Fretting, he neglected to flip on the overhead light. His trembling hands caused him to drop the bag, and the frames, hooks, and nails clanked hard against the bare wood slats.

Although the hour was not excessively late, the winter sun had already moved behind the trees, ushering in a bridge to midnight. The floor was dappled by the fading sun and the appearance of pale moonlight rising.

His knees buckled from the force of energy flowing through his office. Clint reached for the desk chair, startled, and confused. He combed the space but saw nothing out of the ordinary, until the antique mirror caught his attention.

A flicker of illumination danced against the dark wall generated from the reflective backside of the mirror. The reflective front side that faced Clint looked perfectly normal. Yet, on the reverse side, there was movement. Clint locked his attention on that side, cutting through the shadows in the room and trying to make out what was causing the glints he saw. Nothing in the room could explain it.

The room suddenly went cold. The temperature had dropped. Clint knew to stay put, having been down this road before as an undeniable presence filled his office. Getting to his feet, he inched closer to the mirror, his heart racing.

Carefully, he swiveled the mirror, turning it around to the backside. What he saw defied explanation. He fell into the rocker, spellbound by the scene it projected. In disbelief, he observed snow flurries captured inside its glassy surface, floating, swirling, drifting wildly in all directions.

There in the mirror, to the right, Clint saw what appeared to be a brick-and-mortar wall. Unable to discern much of the image, other than bricks, he leaned forward in the rocker, slowly standing. Moving closer did not make the image clearer. It remained out of focus.

Bricks! A wall of bricks, he thought, puzzled by what lay inside the mirror.

He scanned the room. "Rod? Are you here? Are you behind this?" he whispered nervously.

Unlike the cave, Clint saw no silhouette of a figure standing near, yet a presence was evident. He could feel its strong vibrational frequency.

Perplexed, Clint demanded, "If you want to show me something, do it. I'm not a mind-reader."

The image disintegrated into a powdery poof of particles, leaving only a reflection of Clint looking at himself with a rocker and blank wall as his backdrop. He bent over, hugging his body, feeling unstable and falling apart from the inside out, making a mockery of his false courage and response to it.

When his cell phone buzzed, he nearly jumped out of skin, returning his attention to the ordinary. Jules was on the line wanting to know where he was, and when he'd be home. She was finishing her bath.

Clint didn't know how to respond. "Sorry, honey, I should have called." Quickly constructing an alibi, he added, "They are backed up, as usual. A typical Friday." Clint remembered the last time he ordered on a Friday, and said, "They're always slammed with orders on Friday nights. I'll be there soon. The calvary is on its way," he weakly joked.

"I'll hang tight and tell my stomach to find something else to do, other than scream, *feed me*," she teased. "By the way, I got the movie. It looks like a goodie!"

Ending the call, Clint took several deep breaths. He needed to calm down and turn on the lights. He glanced at the mirror but saw nothing to indicate the features it had exhibited just moments before.

"God, help me," he uttered, stepping further away from it.

No wiser than before he entered the office, Clint turned the lock, securing the door the old-fashioned way, with a key, before making his way down the steps, less certain of himself than ever.

The depiction displayed in the mirror was beyond reason. All he could do was wait to see what happened next, if there was a next time. A state he was all too familiar with, seemed to be advancing toward him. The trigger to its onset was his involvement with Farley McDougal, and he felt convinced there was a connection.

After having been exposed to this phenomenon two years prior, Clint did extensive research about sound and its relationship to light. He read atomic sound collisions, created light. He learned words spoken travel out into the cosmos to distant stars, in the form of adapted infrared light. In turn, sounds generated by other star systems bathe our earth. An invisible force, sound permeates nature. It encases everything in a vibrational energy, including the seven primary chakras aligned along the spinal cord of the human body. This was what he found most intriguing. The pineal gland, often referred to as the third eye, can transmit and receive sound.

Could this be how Rod's messages were transmitted? he pondered, deducing the pineal gland, if highly in tune with the environment, could be responsible for what science referred to as a sixth sense.

Clint was convinced the material he had found explained his clairvoyant episodes where unexplainable things materialized.

According to what he had read, the golden quartz, which was sitting on his desk, contained a rare energy. Quartz frequency had the ability to stimulate the third eye chakra, empowering the crown chakra to activate profound clarity in a human, which Clint found especially thought-provoking considering he'd experienced this strange phenomenon firsthand.

What I saw in the mirror must reference something specific or a place I'm meant to find, he decided. *But how can I find a location I've never seen and was as vague as that was?*

On his way to Pietro's Pizzetta Pies, he deliberated on the image in the mirror. The shock had been so great only temporary mental notes lingered. By the time Clint walked through the door at home his head ached.

He had irrefutably experienced something he couldn't explain or share with Jules. He made a deliberate decision not to tell her what happened in fear of alarming her. The last thing he wanted was for Jules to worry or become fearful of his progress in Farley's case. Until he understood the magnitude of the image the mirror projected, the incident would remain unstated.

While the evening was pleasurable with the couple thoroughly enjoying the movie Jules had selected, Clint was mostly distracted. He couldn't get the antique mirror out of his head nor the image it had portrayed.

Those bricks must have been part of an existing structure, Clint reasoned. He continued thinking about the incident, not absorbing much of the movie.

As the night wound down, Clint became steadfast in his desire to return to his office the next day. He would hang Casey's picture, as intended, and not allow the incident to deter him. The predicament it posed did alter his attitude about the space and his enjoyment of it. With the mirror there, he'd have to adjust to the idea anything was possible.

"Don't know what you have planned for tomorrow, but I'll be stopping in at my new office for a bit." Clint conveniently omitted he had been there. "I really want to get Casey's drawings hung. After that, I expect to stop by the police station to call on Scott and have lunch with him if he has the time. I thought about inviting Farley, but I haven't made my mind up yet."

Jules chirped a reply, "Bonnie and I have plans, too."

"Is that right? Clint said with a frown, still worried about Bonnie saying too much to his wife about their conversation.

"What's with the look?" questioned Jules curious at Clint's reaction to her remark.

Clint recalled his and Bonnie's exchange and prayed she'd keep her promise. Fast on his feet, Clint realized his expression must have given him away. "No look, I had considered stopping by the library but will wait until I know she's there, is all."

"Oh," Jules said, aware Clint had been visiting the library more regularly of late. "She and I are going into New Albany to a new restaurant. Lizzy's Closet is a tearoom that focuses on lunch, offering a wide selection of teas. It also has a shop."

Clint's face contorted, thinking how boring.

"They serve meals on fine bone china plates and teacups." Jules raised a brow as though to indicate the specialness of the restaurant was exquisite. "We heard the eatery has an old-world charm."

Jules easily registered Clint's expression. "Okay, it's not a guy place, but it's our type of place. The way Bonnie described it I believe it might have an L.S. Ayres Tearoom flavor, a place my mother and I frequented often when I was a kid. Downtown on the circle, in Indianapolis, they served lunches on delicate dishware. That place brings up wonderful memories. Besides, Bonnie and I haven't spent any quality time together for quite a while. Today's the day."

Again, Clint cringed realizing his wife and Bonnie were about to spend the best part of the day together. Letting the feeling pass, he had no choice but to trust Bonnie, and taking her at her word was easy enough, especially after their in-depth conversation.

"Did you know bone china was originally made of bone ash from slaughtered animals? This guy back in 1743 had a porcelain factory in East London and started adding crushed bone to make his porcelain stronger. He termed the product, 'fine porcelain.' It didn't fly, for obvious reasons. I assume people must not have warmed up to the idea of drinking from bone ash from slaughterhouses once they found out his secret ingredient." Clint snorted. "Later this other guy tried the same process in his factory, adding a higher percentage of crushed bones, and the formula proved successful. He labeled his creation fine bone china."

Clint snickered. "A superior marketing plan boasting a 'high-end' product. It had a nice ring to it that people warmed up to. His wares became a successful story."

Now it was Jules turn for face contortion, "Clint, I'm so glad you shared that with me."

"Just saying…" Clint hooted, reaching into the fridge for his nightly bottle of cold water. Clint had a habit of sitting water on the nightstand next to his side of the bed.

The next morning, they went their separate ways, neither having any idea when they would see each other next.

Saturday, November 26

Following Jules's example, Clint phoned Farley as soon as he got into the car after talking to Scott, who said he didn't have time for lunch. He invited Farley to join him at In a Pig's Eye for a quick bite and was pleased to learn Farley was of the same mindset. Clint's invitation was readily accepted.

Sitting quietly beside the window, with his hands folded on the table, Clint waited for his friend to arrive. He chose his words carefully so as not to reveal the underlying reason why he had extended a lunch invitation. In truth, Clint was on a fact-finding mission. Before sunrise, the thought occurred to him that the dream Farley described when they spoke in Goss Cove sounded uncannily like the one Ann Hill conveyed to June Bennett on the phone hours before the shooting. The two stories were oddly similar. Clint suspected they were one in the same.

"Good to see you, man!" Farley said with an outreached hand and generous smile, genuinely glad to see Clint. Thanksgiving, and the great time he had while at Clint's home, was at the forefront of

Farley's half of the conversation.

The first half hour they engaged in small talk, chatting about family, friends, and Salzburg. Then Farley referenced Louisville and June Bennett, triggering heavy emotions. Farley confessed the voice he'd mentioned seemed to have taken a sabbatical. He rarely heard the man anymore, only now and again when trickles of jabbering broke through in the wee hours.

"Mind you," Farley claimed, "he's still restless but no longer bothersome like he once was. I know it sounds crazy but it's like… he's gone elsewhere." Farley grinned, "Thanks, buddy! Because of you, he seems to have retreated."

Clint thought about Farley's comment. He suspected he knew where the man's attention had shifted to. The mirror immediately came to mind.

Charlie had witnessed a murder in an alley not far from *Beans a' Brewin'*, the coffee shop where they were both gunned down. Farley, too, spoke of a man being murdered while he stood at the mouth of an alleyway.

Before Clint could ask, Farley said, "Worked at United Alliance Electric for all of my adult life. Who would have thought I'd end up in this lovely little town with friends like you and Jules? My mom died in 2003. Then, after Gloria left, I was pretty much on my own. Until now."

Knowing not to stray too far from the subject and understanding the importance of the information Farley was sharing, Clint asked, "Is your father still alive?"

"Nah, he split when I was a kid. Took off for the sunshine state." Farley pulled a face. "Never heard from him after that. Can't say I blame him. They were only seventeen when I came on the scene in sixty-seven. He did the right thing though to marry mom, but it was a constant uphill battle, according to her."

Doing the math in his head, Clint said, "That'd make you thirty-eight, right?"

"Yup! Getting old. Found some unwanted wrinkles around my mouth and eyes. I've lived a lot in my time." He laughed, grinning big. "Makes me about the same age as your oldest, Wade, if my math serves me right."

"That's true," Clint acknowledged with a nod. "Wade was born in 1967, December 30. I thought you two were about the same age." Right away Clint realized he and Farley's father were also close in age. *What a strange coincidence*, he considered, realizing how important his role in Farley's life could turn out to be. "January 21, 1948, is my birthdate, so I'm a shade older than your father."

Soft thoughtful eyes examined the lines on Clint's face. "All in all, I've been fortunate. My Aunt Becky left me a sizable fortune," proclaimed Farley. "I bought the cabin with the inheritance she left my mom, which I received when she passed." Farley turned toward the windows. "I'm not complaining, mind you, lots of people have it worse than me. Aunt Becky's money was a huge gift which put my life back on course."

"Sounds like we have a few things in common. I thought my dad had abandoned me. And, like you, the unexpected Reno Gang treasure rocked my world! Set my life on a whole new trajectory. I came here in 1997. The crazy thing is, I lived here when I was a kid but didn't remember. Anyhow, my wife, Elise, died a week after we purchased the house where I now live. Later I met Jules but was reluctant to admit I cared once I found out she was twelve years my junior!"

The humor on their faces was comical. "Looks like it worked out in your favor," Farley teased. "She's a doll!" Making a conscious effort to force the devils of his past back into the crammed box where they had been locked, the last thing Farley wanted was to sound like a pity-party. "I'm sorry to hear about your wife, Elise. It must have come as a great shock."

"It was, but Jules brought me back from the brink of despair. She's been a ray of sunshine. Every day is an adventure with that woman." Clint too wanted to turn the subject around, asking, "So no voices, that's good. What about dreams? Have you had any more of those or are they settling down as well?"

"Odd you would ask. I had one the other night that made no sense at all. Still, it felt real as real can be." Farley repositioned his napkin and took a sip of beer. "I was in an art studio that resembled a warehouse. All kinds of canvases were sitting around. I was attaching an envelope behind the lining of one of the paintings. Isn't that weird? It felt like I was concealing the envelope, as a security measure."

"Did it feel as lucid as the dream you had about the guy moving toward you with his hands dripping with blood?"

"Oh yes, just as real, only not as disturbing. I still can't get that one out of my head. Those two fellas acted like they were friends until the one lashed out at the other. It was so dark and disturbing. Tough to see any real features though."

"Do you think it could have been somewhere near here?"

Farley gave Clint's question some thought. "Not around here, no... but in a large city. The one guy was leaning against a brick wall." He thought back on the scene. "It might have recently rained because the alley had puddles scattered in places."

"So, your best guess is it was a city environment?"

"Oh, yeah, for sure," Farley's attention drifted upward as he recalled what he witnessed. "A door on the left looked like it might have been the back entrance to a restaurant or bar because a trash bag had been tossed there."

Farley walked through the dream as best he could remember. "At the other end of the alley I could see a broader street like you'd see downtown Louisville." Farley clasped his hands. "The impression I had was the alley was narrow and grimy, like backstreet cities would be. Where you'd go to exchange drugs? Maybe? Which could have been the case because I think the one guy was taking something or handing something over to the other, fighting over what he held, before he was knifed. Both of his hands grabbed for his chest and then his stomach."

A sickening expression appeared when Farley stated, "I'll never forget his eyes. Surprised lookin'... ya know?"

Clint was tense. What he saw in the mirror around the bricks had the same dark, seedy texture as what Farley had just portrayed. *Where is this place?* he pondered. *June said the alley where Charlie saw the murder wasn't far from the coffee shop. That's where I'll begin. I'll check out the streets near Beans a' Brewin'.*

"Do you remember if it was raining, snowing, or if it was day or night?" asked Clint.

"Now that you say it, yes, it was snowing. I remember now. How weird," declared Farley. "Why did you ask?"

"I don't know, just trying to picture the scene more vividly, weather, things like that," which was a fib because Clint wanted to pin down the specifics and see if they matched what June had said.

The two men continued their talk on a lighter note. Then, somewhere in the bar a clock struck, and the hour tolled two. "My, the time has flown," Clint made note. "I'd better be getting. Let's do this again, soon."

"You're on!" Farley said, standing and grabbing both tabs.

Clint grinned. "Thanks, next time it's on me, partner."

Chapter 21
Beans a' Brewin'

2:15 Saturday

Crossing the lobby, Clint noticed two children standing in the administrator's office, waist high to the social worker who was speaking with Clarissa Jackson, the home's admissions director.

He made eye contact with Clarissa, who communicated a faint nod, indicating the two youngsters were processing in.

"Who do we have here?" he asked looking down at nearly identical faces. Clint knelt eye-level to speak with the children. "My name is Clint Reeves. This is my house," he said as an introduction. With a warm smile, he asked, "Who might you two be?"

Both looked down at the floor, the youngest child standing behind the older sibling.

"I'd like to welcome you. We have lots of fun things to do around here. We are happy to have you join our family."

The boy looked at the girl, up at Clint, and back at the girl, his eyes swollen but showing a twinkle of interest.

"Most of the year we have outdoor activities, and we take fieldtrips in the summer. Places you'll enjoy like Brown County and the Indianapolis Children's Museum. We have Easter egg hunts in spring and wiener roasts in the fall." Hoping to elicit a reaction, he added, "I hope you'll consider me a friend."

The boy spoke. On the edge of crying, he softly said, "Thank you."

Clint stood to his feet, patting lovingly the unwanted. He noticed a bruise on the side of the boy's face but quickly redirected his glance. "I'm pleased to meet you both. We'll be seeing a lot of each other. Never hesitate to approach me. I'm here for you."

He heard a small voice behind the older child. "I'm Josephine," a tiny voice said, tears glistening on her lashes.

Clint turned to see the face of an angel smiling up at him a girl no more than eight years old. She turned to her brother, who then volunteered, "My name is Joseph. I'm her older brother."

"I'm very happy to make your acquaintance," Clint said in an uplifted tone while searching Clarissa's response. "My friend here will take very good care of you." He smiled gently. "If I'm not mistaken, we are having spaghetti and meatballs for dinner tonight. Do you like spaghetti and meatballs?"

Joseph nodded, clutching Josephine's hand, "Yes, we do, sir."

"Call me Clint, please. Well then, you have a fine dinner to look forward to. But anytime you don't like a certain food, all you have to do is tell the person on staff and they'll bring a different choice. No problem! No one is forced to eat things they don't like." Clint made a silly face remembering a dish he hated. "Like turnip greens!" The children both giggled, which, in turn, lifted Clint's spirit.

Moving to the elevator, Clint tried to keep his emotions in check knowing how lost and scared the two children were feeling in the moment, having been in their shoes when he was their age. It was a scary place in a little person's life to be alone in the world, without parents, or people who wanted you. That's why he always made every effort to show his appreciation of the children at the home.

When Clint reached the elevator doors, he stopped. The doors opened and closed without Clint climbing on board. Swiftly he made an about-face. Waving at Clarissa on the way out, he motioned for her to call him.

Climbing into the F-100, his thoughts, busy with questions and details, Clint placed his to-go coffee into the console retrofitted for the truck's interior, and gripped the wheel, trying to decide if now might be a good time to drive into Louisville. Figuring he could hang Casey's artwork later when he got back, a quick trip southeast seemed timely.

Light traffic moved steadily over US 150 going toward I-64, heading out of town. Not knowing where he would end up, Clint wanted to get back on the road no later than four thirty to avoid heavier traffic on his return trip. The sole purpose in going to Louisville was to locate Beans' a Brewin' and walk the general neighborhood.

Checking his phone Clint noticed he had a voicemail. He played the message while keeping a close eye on the road. Scott had requested Clint call him back. On his way home he'd return the call. If his whereabouts came up, a quick sidestep maneuver would do, but for the time being he planned to keep his activities to himself.

Without a license, detective work at a bare minimum was risky business. Private citizens didn't typically run around involving themselves with the complexities of cold case files. Tiptoeing around criminality associated with Charles Hill's death, should be handled judiciously.

Confident Bonnie and Jules's time together would consume the better part of the day, Clint knew several hours of daylight remained before he had to return home. Crossing the bridge over the Ohio River into Louisville, Clint aimed his vehicle in the general direction of Grayson Hospital, ground zero.

The trip was a basic exploratory mission, to map out the area where Charles Hill died while familiarizing himself with the streets and alleyways near the crime scene. A possible location where the first man fell victim, the one Charlie saw killed, was a crucial part of the puzzle. Clint wondered how the killer tracked Charlie down a second time, figuring he must have been lying in wait, or uncannily lucky.

Efforts to uncover facts as a private citizen was next to impossible. Investigating as a Private Investigator could open doors not accessible to an amateur like him. A scant bit of online research revealed a license was attainable through limited training. An idea he found attractive and would pursue in the future.

A large metropolis, Louisville with its skyscrapers, highway traffic, and jets flying over, could swallow Clint's town many times over. Motoring through crowded city streets, he recognized Grayson Hospital when it came into view.

The truck rumbled back and forth through the streets, traveling in all directions. Up and down every side street and neighborhood that circled Grayson Hospital. Methodically, he searched, but came up emptyhanded. Expanding parameters further out, he examined residential areas with great care, looking for a coffee shop that fit the description he imagined. Making a U-turn, he cruised back toward the hospital on a narrow street no one appeared to travel. Clint was about to throw in the towel when he saw it.

He hit the brakes. Through a murky windshield, at a dark cross section, shielded from the bright overhead sun, the coffee shop appeared. He paralleled parked the F-100 next to the curb, ahead of a Volkswagen Beetle. A sliver of blue sky shown through the tight adjoining buildings, shedding little light on the street.

Clint was surprised to see a shop filled with customers, meandering, holding drinks, sitting at computers, reading, and talking. He watched staff crisscross behind the counter, giving latitude not to collide into one another.

A dark complected, older man with a manager's air, stood at the one end of a glass display case examining his phone. For a hole-in-the-wall operation, the place was remarkably busy. It was a neighborhood hangout, a destination.

Do I dare walk in? weighed Clint, unsure if venturing inside was wise. *What would it hurt to sit down to have a cup of coffee and take a five-minute break?* The streets were void of pedestrians, and very few cars were parked on the street, presumably allowing him leeway to move about without notice.

Buildings towered overhead, giving no indication as to their frontage side, other than typical inner-city establishments. A small edifice, it was sandwiched behind. A local bakeshop sat adjacent the coffee house. He didn't see any other retail shops.

He stepped out of the truck, locking the door. The sound of his boots clacked against the uneven pavement as he crossed from one side of the street to the other. A mind sown with questions and curiosity, Clint's need for insight outweighed the little voice inside his head warning him to stay in his truck. Leave.

Hypothesizing brought him only so far. From here on out, boots on the ground were the only way forward. He could only excavate answers by placing himself where the incident occurred, not from reading articles and reports. Maybe not this visit, but the next one he'd find sufficient nerve to speak with the manager or one of the employees. Nothing else could propel his query to the next level like paying a quick visit to the place where the shooting occurred.

Turmoil occupied his thoughts as he walked through the door, finding a seat close to the restroom and hoping he'd not be noticed. A need to get to the bottom of why Charles Hill was not at rest, making effort to be known through Farley was one thing, but the image he saw in the antique mirror had taken his plight to a whole new level of uncertainty. Pulling back the curtain of wrongdoing could reveal darkness he'd never experienced.

Thinking about Picasso and how his involvement had lured him into regarding Farley's problem as his problem, Clint pondered. An internal compass has highjacked my life. The cougar's presence implied I was to get involved and now I am… up to my eyeballs.

Sitting patiently watching customers come and go, Clint got up and walked to the counter to order a large coffee. He waited to the side pretending to decide, until the older man, he assumed was the manager, covered the register.

"What would you like to have, sir?" the man asked. The normal greeting.

"A large black coffee is all," Clint responded pleasantly, searching the less crowded shop for a better place to sit. Moving down to the area designated for order pickup, his eyes observed the backside of the man as he filled a polyethylene paper cup advertising the coffee shop's logo set in a holiday design. The man gave Clint's drink to a young woman, who in turn walked it down.

"Thanks," Clint said taking the cup from the barista's hand. "Is that the manager?" Clint asked casually, pointing to the older gentleman, as though the question didn't matter.

"I am." A nod verified Clint's guess when the man turned around. "Going on twelve years now." A coy glance passed between them. "I also own the joint!" A broad grin softened the man's ruddy complexion, making him appear younger than his years, the man's pleasant disposition was a refreshing change. Gray sideburns, longer than fashionable, and a cap with the logo, Beans a' Brewin' to cover his balding head, he wore dark casual jeans and a matching red logo shirt that complemented his cap.

"Nothing like a coffeehouse to brighten your day. People who come in here are a certain breed. They thoroughly enjoy hot drinks and pastries, a great combination." Watching for the desired response, he pointed out the window. "The bakery ties in nicely with a java shop. We feed off each other, sending customers in both directions."

Faint voices, penetrated and animated, drifting in from street as they blended and moved closer. Clint watched as a small cluster of people crossed the street.

Extending a hand, Clint quickly introduced himself, "Clint Reeves," he offered. "You serve a mean cup of coffee, easy to see why you do a good business. Your specialty blend is superior." He took another sip. "Medium to dark roast holds body, strong, with more flavor and aroma."

"Mark Carlson. A pleasure to make your acquaintance, Clint," he responded good-naturedly while eyeing the group filing in. Signaling one of his employees to take the new orders, Mark finished his sentence. "Hope to see you around. Is this your first time in?" With a nearly imperceptible furrow of his brow, he stated, "I don't recall seeing you before."

"That's because it is my first visit."

The pressure of phrasing his words exactly, prior to other patron's filing in, forced Clint to cut his chat short. "Hopefully you'll be around next time I stop by. Your coffee is worth driving the distance. I'll not take up any more of your time. I can see you're busy." Graciously Clint walked away.

He pivoted toward Carlson who had stepped to the far end of the counter away from customers. "I may be wrong, but you and I look about the same age. We probably have much in common being from an older generation. Sixties, that sort of thing."

Not accustomed to patrons so laid back, let alone someone interested in him personally, Mark replied, "Don't know, I'm not good at judging ages. Pushing sixty, not born in the sixties, I am. Doubt you have bragging rights," he replied, cracking a smile.

"Born in 1948," Clint guffawed, "I was referring to music! Beatles and the like. I confess, I've not reached sixty yet, but I'm looking down the barrel," he kidded, hoping his joke wasn't politically incorrect in a coffee shop.

Enjoying the banter, Mark chuckled, "You're two years my junior. I thought we looked about the same age, but you never know. The Botox factor makes it tough to tell, even with men." He chuckled. "Where are you from? You said the distance was worth driving."

"Indiana side of the bridge. Salzburg, I doubt you've ever heard of it. It's a small town with lots of charm, as most rural towns are."

"Is that right? How coincidental, most folks around here have been to Josie's Diner at least once. That place has a reputation." Mark stopped dead in his tracks. "Wait a minute, I thought you looked familiar, you're the guy that found the Reno Gang treasure. I'm right. Aren't I?"

"Guilty as charged," Clint chuckled, shocked that his fame had reached this far.

"Well, I'll be a monkey's uncle," Mark said, slapping his thigh, "I can't imagine what it feels like to be in your shoes. If I recall, you established an orphanage out that way."

"I did," Clint proudly said, pleased his name was associated with Radcliff's Children's Home and not just the treasure. Unaccustomed to talking about his orphanage or the incident that happened in 2003 outside of Salzburg, he stated, "Discovering the treasure put me in the limelight, a place I'm not very comfortable with, but it didn't last long. The orphanage was a lifelong dream of mine. One I still can't believe I'm living."

"So, what brought you in here? If I may ask. You're a long way from home. An hour and fifteen minutes, and that's if traffic flow is in your favor, I imagine. Beans a' Brewin' isn't a Josie's Diner where reputation precedes it. Neighborhood folks are my bread and butter. That's about as far as my place goes. Good cups of coffee aren't that scarce."

Cornered into speaking the truth, Clint fumbled for an answer. While talking, Mark had stepped away from the counter to converse with Clint one on one. The discussion changed direction, pushing for an explanation why Clint was so far from home, at a coffeehouse off the beaten path in Louisville, Kentucky.

He decided on an honest answer in lieu of a lie. "Someone I'm acquainted with knows about your place. A guy he knows used to come here. His wife, I believe worked for you. I was in Louisville and thought I'd look you up. It wasn't easy to find your place. I was curious, is all."

"I swear, you are full of surprises, Clint Reeves. What was his name? I will know hers if she worked for me. Names I never forget. Faces, maybe, but not names or phone numbers. Don't know what it is about numbers…" Mark appeared thoughtful.

Again, Clint held his tongue, cautious. He was fearful of the reaction he would surely receive, as he fidgeted with his coffee cup, wondering if he should cough up the reason he had driven so far. "Not an easy topic, I'm afraid. His name was Charles Hill, but his friends called him Charlie. Ann worked for you."

Mark stepped back, staring at Clint. "An understatement," he admitted. Pointing to the table, he said, shakily, "Please, have a seat."

The distress on Mark's face was unmistakable. He sat down, lifted his fresh poured coffee, and took a swallow, like it possessed liquid courage. Revisiting a nightmarish event that had befallen Beans a' Brewin' was a subject he never breached. The silence was palpable. A one-word reply was delivered, "Yeah…"

"Look, I didn't want to lie, and you asked, so, there is it. Out in the open, let's leave it at that. I'll take my leave. Sorry if I upset you."

The torment, guilt, and pain Mark suppressed registered in the profound depth of agony captured in his eyes. "I prefer you didn't. You apparently came here for a reason. I'd like to discuss why. If you don't mind."

Settling in, Clint said, "It can't be an easy subject to address. I'm sorry you had to experience a tragedy of that scale."

"When you lie down with dogs, you get up with flies…" Mark muttered. "Owning a coffee shop in the heart of Louisville brings in all sorts of people."

"I don't understand."

Lifting his eyes to connect with Clint's, Mark stressed, "That dreadful day has gnawed at my conscience nonstop. Always there under the skin like a cancer, eating away." He shook his head scornfully. "Things I didn't say that should have been said." Deep in the recesses of a past time, darkness fell. "How does a man retrace his steps and then do the right thing?"

CHAPTER 21

Clint studied the man seated across from him. He'd been cheerful when their conversation began, but now his dark eyes stared into oblivion, turning darker as anger crept into their depths.

The question was to whom the anger was directed. At him, or someone else?

Chapter 22
Confession of Fear

"A month or so after the shooting, this man comes into the shop." Mark eyed the empty table at the far side of the room. "And I notice he's staring at me, right?" His eyes narrowed. "I thought it was odd but then it occurred to me I'd seen him before. Imagine my shock when it dawns on me, he's the guy who shot Charlie and Ann. When it sank in, it must have shown on my face because his expression changed too. He must have seen my worry because he motioned for me to come over to his table."

A grave ambiguity passed over Mark, "So, I did." Shrugging, as if to say, *what other option did I have,* Mark further remarked, "I can tell you that was a long walk."

Waiting to see if Mark was going to tag on anything more, Clint waited. When it became apparent he wasn't, Clint asked, "So what happened?"

Seconds lapsed while Mark collected himself. "I swear, I saw the devil himself in those black eyes when he asked if I knew who he was." Mark relived the encounter, his heart pounding. "He knew I knew. Ain't no question about that. I played it smart, though and kept my mouth shut. Granted, when he pulled his jacket back, exposed a Glock 9mm strapped to his side, I stiffened, and my knees went weak. He claimed I had two choices, not tell anyone he was the one who ran, or die right then and there."

"Good Lord," exclaimed Clint, "I assume you placated his wishes, or you wouldn't still be here."

"Must have spit out the right words, but honestly, it was a blur after that. Don't remember what I said. Most of it I've forgotten. Didn't remember any details later, other than what resurfaced when I started talking to you. Wishful thinking if I thought I'd ever forget that face and those malevolent eyes. That man was evil!"

Recalling the event brought up painful memories. Mark quietly said, "Charlie was unconscious. Just lying there on the ground, his eyes looking up at the ceiling. Ann was against the wall in a pool of her own blood when the ambulance pulled out front. They were here three minutes after my call. How do you erase a scene like that from your mind? When the police arrived, they wanted a statement. I told them everything I knew, including a vague description of the shooter, which by the way wasn't anywhere near accurate after seeing him a second time."

"I'm so sorry, Mark," Clint said with sincerity, "Nobody should have to endure anything so tragic. And to have one of your employees die. I have people working for me at the orphanage. I feel your pain."

Mark sneered in distaste, "That creep questioned me, wanting to know if the paramedics removed any items from Charlie's clothing. Was anything put into plastic bags, and if so what where they? I was too dazed to remember how the paramedics handled his body, which was what I told him. I didn't recall them bagging anything. He asked for the names of the ambulance staff and anyone else associated with the retrieval. Then he asked about the paperwork from that night, assuming there was a record."

Mark shamefully dropped his eyes. "I can't believe I handed over what was in my files like it was of no consequence." Chastising himself for his decision, he said, "I was too *damned* scared of dying to do what was right. Which was call the police, take a bullet, but at least try to the set the record straight. Take my chances and hope he'd be caught this time. Then to make matters worse, I should have phoned the police the second he left the building, but I turned coward, too afraid he'd find out. Some dirty cop on his payroll would tell him what I'd done. Ya know? My welfare came ahead of bringing Ann Hill's murderer to justice. Charlie's, too."

The shop owner's manner clearly conveyed his dismay. The affair had cut deep, a residual scar Mark was condemned to wear through life.

"Don't be so hard on yourself," Clint stated, feeling pity for the man. "None of us know what we'd do in any given situation. The guy had already killed three people, he'd proven he'd kill again if he was cornered or threatened. Your employee and her husband are gone, you can't bring them back. Your death would only compound the tragedy."

Mark closed his eyes. Dejection lined the features of his face. "I understand. I tell myself that all the time, but it doesn't seem to help." He calmly folded his hands, glancing out the window into the empty street. "Never saw him again after that, although he's out there. I kept my mouth shut all this time afraid what he'd do if I didn't. Scared he'd waltz right through that door," he turned toward the coffee shop entrance, "and put me out of my misery."

Clint leaned forward. "Look I hate to leave, but my wife will be wondering where I am if I'm not back by dinner. I could stop in again if that's alright with you. I never got a chance to explain why I came here. The real reason, that is. I'm afraid I haven't been completely honest with you."

Clint saw a flicker of fear flash in Mark's eyes. "Don't worry, we are on the same side. What I have to say pertains to additional background information you might find of interest."

Mark was curious as to Clint's meaning but elected to let it drop. "Absolutely. I know this sounds crazy, but I feel better, lighter even, than before we talked. So, thank you. Please feel free to drop in anytime." He cordially stated. "Shoot me a text when you're headed this way. That way I can make a point of being here. I'd like to hear more. It feels like we've known each other forever, rather than have met only an hour ago. Strange, huh?"

"Like I mentioned, I'll explain more later, but I couldn't agree more. Mark, we were supposed to meet. That's the way my life rolls…" Clint laughed deeply. It was an inside joke Mark would never understand. "We could make a difference if we work together. Every piece of this story I collect could help it to have the outcome you hope for."

Through a recently washed pane, Mark watched his new acquaintance cross the late afternoon street, staying put until Clint had disappeared. He decided Clint was a messenger to help lighten his heavy burden. Lighter on his feet, he walked behind the cash register feeling renewed. As Mark stood there, staring outside into the fading light of day, he pondered what Clint had held in reserve. Intrigued as to the nature of their next conversation, he relinquished his powerlessness over the situation. He'd someday know why Clint had entered his life.

Clint, on the other hand, drove home with the waning sun that matched his mood, astounded to have learned so much in such a short time. Reluctant to enter the coffeehouse at the start, Clint grasped the serendipitous advantage it had afforded himself by facing *his* fears.

He tucked away the words they'd exchanged, anticipating his and Mark's next encounter. Easier than the first now that they were acquainted. Clint didn't know when they'd see each other, but he'd pencil something in, soon.

Before heading home, he'd make a quick stop at the orphanage. Casey's picture wasn't going to hang itself and he wasn't going to rest until the chore was complete. With all that was going on inside his head, he had forgotten to phone Scott. It was now past work hours and he figured Scott was at home with his family. The call could wait.

Forty-five minutes later Clint was back in Salzburg, poking his head inside the reading room where Abby Harper was sitting with a book on her lap waiting for other children to file in. Clint waved at her on his way to the elevator and the top floor.

The elevator doors opened to the fifth floor. When he punched in the code to his office, he hesitated, remembering his last visit. At the top of the steps, he opened his office door and walked into the dim light. The room appeared normal, unlike the last time Clint was here. His eyes scanned the room and specifically the antique mirror. Everything seemed normal, as it should be. He saw what he wanted to see–nothing out of the ordinary.

Clint progressed to the fireplace and lifted the Ace Hardware bag from the ground. He felt an urgency to finish the task of hanging Casey's artwork. Soon Jules would be back from her day trip with Bonnie and he planned a hodgepodge of leftovers for dinner, remains of the last couple nights which suited him fine.

Using a stud finder, Clint hammered nails into the wall, stair-stepping Casey's two drawings. As he stood back to admire the pictures, a smile graced his face. One drawing was violent, which he found disturbing. It was the first Casey had drawn for him and a hundred-and-eighty-degree turnaround from the peaceful garden scene that came later.

A sense of ownership rushed over him when he closely viewed them. They'd seen such wonderful progress with this young man. To have Casey's handiwork on Clint's wall brought him pleasure. The next time he saw Casey, he'd let him know he'd hung the pictures.

A pace further back, his attention was drawn to the dipping leaves swaying in the wind past the elongated windows that faced the backside of the orphanage. The hour was closing in on six o'clock. He needed to leave, but something seemed out of order besides the chill that accompanies darkness and a paint-brushed sky of blues and blacks. Standing at the window, Clint observed an indeterminate black shadow on the grounds. Then he saw him…

The black feline moved into the light, sitting erect and looking up to where Clint stood looking down. Beyond the shadows the untold story he had embarked on was unfolding. Evening wrapped itself around Clint, as several minutes passed. Finally, the animal slipped back into the trees, leaving Clint to decipher the meaning behind its presence. A plethora of unanswerable questions swept over him. One specific, provocative thought rose above others. *Most murderers know their victim.* He let that notion simmer, pondering if the murderer knew Charles Hill.

At the mirror, he stared into the depths of nothingness, thinking about Picasso. He didn't expect anything to occur. Certainly not a repeat of his last visit. He waited, staring at his image. Why… he didn't know. A second later the answer became clear.

Pillowy swirls of smoke stirred inside the mirror. The bricks he had seen on his previous visit became visible, only this time with a sharpness not seen before. A solid wall of bricks on the right side of the glass blocked out his image.

Dropping back, Clint's legs hit the rocker. He stumbled to his desk and put his hand on its surface to find his bearings. Turning around, he leaned against the desk, facing the window. After a while, he slowly moved toward it.

Out on the lawn, larger than life, Picasso's green eyes met Clint's. A knowingness passed between them. A strength Clint had never felt before came over him, surpassing normal concentration. The mission he'd embarked on, was his destiny. After a moment, the large cat placed his paws slowly and deliberately until he was absorbed by the shadows.

Clint knew what he had to do. Returning to the mirror, he waited. Again, he watched the inner bricks appear. This time they began to shift, pulling apart horizontally, making an opening wide enough for a person to enter.

That's intentional, thought Clint, convinced it was an invitation.

His heart thundered against his ribcage. "What am I supposed to do?" he asked, afraid of the answer. Without explanation he placed his hand on the mirror. It gave way, curving inward, allowing his hand to pierce its rubbery surface. Clint pulled it out, away from the glass, as if he'd been burned.

"God help me," he whispered, staring into the darkness on the other side. He flinched, afraid to consider the consequences of what he knew he was about to do. Glancing at his phone, he saw the time was 6:23 p.m. He should have been home by now. Jules would surely be there.

It felt like the mirror was waiting on him. Reluctantly he gazed at it, shocked to see a man standing a good distance back. He wasn't moving, his dark silhouette still as the night.

He asked, "If I come with you, can I get back?"

The man nodded, putting his hand out in invitation.

Again, Clint looked at the time. *I need to call Jules.* He went back, picked his phone up from the desk, and dialed her number.

She answered on the third ring. "Hey, honey. I'm so sorry I'm late. Bonnie and I were having so much fun we lost track of time."

"No problem," he responded, relieved she wasn't home. "I'm running late as well. I'm over at that orphanage. Take your time and enjoy your trip. I'll pick up a sandwich here. You guys might want to do the same thing. Maybe stop in at a restaurant on the way. I know you had lunch but its nearly dinner time."

Jules was ecstatic. "That's a great idea. I'm glad you don't mind. We've had a blast. Bought too much, but hey, it's not every day we get to spend the entire day together." Pleased Clint wasn't at home waiting, Jules said, "Okay, sweetheart, I'll see you in an hour or two."

"Sounds good," Clint sweetly said.

He turned the phone off, laid it down, and remained seated at the desk. Picasso was an agent, a sign signifying he was where he should be, doing what was expected. Which included delving into what lay inside the mirror.

Clint got up and walked back to the mirror where the featureless, dark shadowy figure was waiting. His hand was raised, signaling for Clint to walk through the glass and join him. The brick opening was larger than when he'd first seen it.

He took a deep breath and pushed his arm through the mirror, and then his torso, finally his legs until his entire body was on the opposite side of the antique mirror. He viewed his office, desk, and door. The room was dark, as though he had never entered.

Clint turned to where the faint figure had been but saw nothing other than blackness. Across from him on the right the brick wall he'd seen earlier had reshaped itself, only this time it was distinctly outlined. Weather-beaten, crumbled chunks of bricks formed an entire wall, displaying an elongated opening in the center. He observed the mysterious figure who had lured him through the mirror slip into the bricks to an undefined location.

Clint moved to the jagged barrier, putting his hand on its coarse surface. On the far side of the gap, he saw a cave-like space where the mystery man stood waiting.

There's no going back now, Clint told himself. I've come too far. I was told I could return, so I'll see where this takes me.

Clint pulled his body up and climbed through the opening, just as the man had done, dropping to the floor on the other side. Looking through the slit, he could see the place he'd been where shady dark hues lingered in a vacuum of flowing vapor.

The man indicated Clint should follow. Through the cave, along a dirt path, he led Clint until finally they arrived at a sizable opening in the stone. The man walked out into the light.

When Clint got to the spot where the man advanced into brightness, he saw nothing but another wall. No man, no light, no features. The figure had closed off the light and replaced it with a dark alley, capped at both ends by city streets. Clint moved into it, confused why he had been brought to this place. He felt a cold chill pass by him. He waited for an explanation.

"What have I done," he asked, thinking about Jules and his life on the opposite side of the mirror? But then, abruptly, a scene manifested.

Two men were angrily shoving one another. To Clint's surprise, the shorter of the two dropped hard to his knees. From his peripheral vision Clint saw a bystander appear at the opening to the backstreet. The man looked startled by the physical confrontation taking place. A tin can rolled over the bricks, unknowingly kicked by the stranger. The sound was distinct, causing the other men to stop quarreling.

The man who had fallen struggled back to his feet while the other man dashed away, running into trash bags as he rounded the corner. The escaping man glanced back at the two people still in the dark alley–one who struggled to stay upright, and the man who had witnessed the conflict. The assailant fired a warning shot before disappearing into the night.

Clint noted the hurt man lunged at the onlooker, blood covering his fingers and wrists. Through a wool coat his wound spilled, pouring from his chest. The injured man grabbed the passerby's sleeve, right before collapsing in the grime at the man's feet.

The man who had witnessed the crime staggered. Frozen until he guardedly bent down and whispered something into the victim's ear. Then he scurried off, but not before clasping an object the dying man had tucked into his hand, wrapping his fingers tightly around it.

With adrenaline pumping wildly, Clint moved cautiously toward the wounded man. With glazed eyes, the dying man stared hard at Clint, trying to bring him into focus. Then, as though he recognized Clint, a hint of a smile appeared on his lips.

"Axel," he breathed, exerting tremendous effort to articulate the name he wanted Clint to hear. He enunciated it slowly as he focused on something beyond Clint. The man refocused his attention, eyes filling with tears at whatever it was he saw. The man's heartbeat suddenly hastened, and then stopped. His Rolex marking the time of death, his arm rested on an open wallet.

June Bennett had stated the man Charlie saw in the alley was wearing a Rolex. Still on his wrist, the crime could not have been robbery motivated. Not only that, but before running for help, Charlie witnessed the fallen man's wallet lying on the ground.

Clint grasped the importance of why he was here, aware that he had seen exactly what Charles Hill had lived through. Something else registered with Clint, Charles Hill had been in possession of an object the dead man passed to him, and the killer wanted it back. Badly enough to kill.

I wonder what he handed Charlie.

Chapter 23
A Flawed Murder

Ready to return to the cave and back to his own life, Clint came to a quick halt when he saw the man who had killed the other coming back down the alley toward him. Clint slipped in the shadows even though he knew he couldn't be seen. He remembered what happened next. No body was found at the scene. Charlie had declared a murder had taken place but couldn't prove it. Instead, he'd been accused of concocting a fictitious yarn.

Within minutes of fleeing, the killer returned to dispose of the person he had knifed. The cold-hearted assailant worked fast and furious. He approached the body, looked down and quickly turned away. The hands atop the body were folded as though the man were simply asleep, except blood pooled on his chest, which was quickly covered.

In the shadows the large man stuffed the corpse into an abnormally heavy unzipped bag, dragging him feet first to the opposite end of the alley where his truck idled. Not easily managed, the stranger flung the body into the bed of the truck. With calloused intention, he lingered, and then ran to the driver's side, jumped in, and sped away.

Clint had seen time turn back on itself, to the afternoon of December 21, 2004, when Charlie Hill had witnessed a murder. Except in this instance Charlie Hill also had a witness–Clint Reeves. He heard the dead man's final word–Axel.

The antique mirror was an instrument of truth, revealing to him a terrible injustice. The man in the mirror had opened a door for Clint to see what had transpired that fatal afternoon, hours before Charlie and his wife were brutally slain.

Clint denoted a sound that originated from the street. He stepped back, his body leaning against an unknown structure and waited for whomever was closing in. To his surprise, a stray camel-colored, long haired matted mutt trotted into the alleyway. The dog cautiously strutted to where the dead man had lain, sniffing the ground before finally advancing to where Clint was standing.

The hound inexplicably smelled the ground, and then Clint's leather shoes.

He eyed the dog, shocked by its behavior. Curious if the animal detected his presence, Clint shifted his stance only a little. When the animal sniffed the hem of his pantlegs Clint was certain. Soon the dog lost interest and pranced away, turning the corner with his head held high, having found a worthy prize. He trotted to the end of the alley carrying something small in his mouth and disappeared down the street.

Time had come to retrace his steps, through the cavernous area, beyond the brick wall to where he had obediently tracked the figure. He had seen all he needed to see. With a handful of empty blanks filled in, Clint could step back into his office, beyond the antique mirror, a wiser man. The ammunition he had acquired would assist him on the next leg of the journey. But now, his mission was to return home.

He had no idea how much time had lapsed, but the hour felt late. He was preoccupied with what excuse he could manufacture to suffice for his absence when something grabbed his attention. Just as he was about to reenter the cave, Clint noticed a glint in the alley.

What is that wedged by the building? Unsure he was seeing an actual object, he moved closer. Maybe he saw a paper wrapper pulled from a pack of cigarettes or nothing at all. Upon examination, he decided whatever it was, the thing was indeed shiny, elongated, and pointed. Bending down, he put his face as close to the ground as possible without touching the filth he knew coated its surface, straining to make out what the object was.

Whoa, that's not something you see every day.

Putting his fingers into the stone crevice where the item appeared lodged, Clint finagled until he was finally able to pry it loose. He held the small item in his hand. A gold toothpick? Polished as though brand new.

Well, that is odd. What are you doing here? he wondered. Clint knew not to disregard what could be a significant find. He aimed his attention at the end of the alley where the truck had been only minutes before. Could this have belonged to the killer?

Clint carefully placed the toothpick inside his top pocket. Painstakingly he buttoned it, making certain it didn't slip from his possession as it had the person who originally owned it.

Later, when time allows, I'll check to see if anything is stamped on its surface. Providing the toothpick is pure gold, as I suspect it is considering the weight of it, there might be a maker's mark to identify where it originated and eventually shipped. If I can establish that, I could possibly track down a receipt with the name of the person who purchased it.

Snow began to fall. Lightly floating in the air, wisps of flakes touched his face and hands. June Bennett had mentioned bad weather had moved in the night of the shooting. Light snow now but conditions were soon to change.

As he edged his way through the darkness of the cave returning to the hollowed space in the bricks he had earlier accessed, Clint felt weakened by what he had been shown, one man dead, another about to die, and a criminal who got away.

Pulling his body up and over the brick wall, he entered a blue mist. Through it, Clint managed to find the backside of the mirror. It was weird seeing his office from the reverse side of the antique mirror, where a world no one could ever imagine existed. When he turned to look at the brick wall for the last time, he watched in amazement as it gradually disintegrated, creating a cloud of dark red smoke swirling through the air where the wall had once stood.

Clint closed his eyes, thinking he must have reached some insane level of madness to have witnessed what he had seen on both sides of a wall no longer there. Just like Rod's New and Used Books and how it had vanished.

When he placed his hand on the mirror, it undulated, rippling like a gelled substance. Hoping against hope his body would remain intact and unscathed, Clint pushed through the reflective glass one leg and arm at a time, poking his head and entire body through.

When the weight of his body became lopsided, he fell through the mirror out onto the office floor, landing hard on his side. Sitting in silent lucidity, he reached for his head. Something didn't feel right. He felt a pain above his right eye. "Merciful Jesus, thank you for keeping me in one piece," Clint cried out, sincerely relieved to have survived the ordeal. He tried to lift himself from the floor, but his limbs gave way, caused by buckling knees. Geez, he thought fearfully, this better be temporary.

Sitting still for a minute or so, he tried again, this time with more success. Even with the tingling in his extremities, he managed to stand upright. He took a deep breath, steadily moving toward the desk. He sat down, picked up his phone, and turned it on. Checking for a message from Jules, he was surprised to find none. Then he noticed the time display. Thinking he must be mistaken, Clint glanced at his watch. His eyes had not fully adjusted yet, so he raised the phone closer to his face.

"What?" Clint reacted, not believing what his eyes saw. No time has passed. That's not possible. He checked his watched again, 6:23 p.m. It felt like I was gone for an hour or more. How can that be?"

Clint couldn't think straight. With his head in a fog and his brain like mush, he decided the only place he could go to reset himself was outdoors on the widow's walk. Didn't matter if it was freezing outside, the platform he had built at the very tip top of the building was the answer. He crawled through the hatch out into the wintry night.

Standing in the refreshing evening breeze looking up at the stars, he turned. He climbed the four-prong ladder to a small cupola belfry area above and sat down. When the orphanage was built Clint insisted on a 19th century design, including a turret space he had converted into an observation tower. Sitting in a foldable rocker he specifically had made for the tower, with a cabinet to store it in when not in use, Clint rocked, thinking about what he'd experienced.

Is there any chance I didn't go through the mirror? he questioned feeling somewhat disturbed, uncertain if, where he had been, what he had seen, or done, was real at all. He reached for the spot on his forehead that ached and realized it was bleeding. A bump had risen and stung when he touched it. *Did I fall, hit my head, and pass out on the floor. Could I have dreamt all that stuff? Charles Hill has been on my mind constantly.*

Aware he should head home, Clint closed his eyes and listened to the sounds of nature. Peace engulfed him. The orphanage was his refuge, though he never thought he'd feel so attached to a place that represented what he despised as a child.

He made his way down the ladder and back through the hatch. Navigating the dark office, Clint aimed his attention toward the door, ready to leave, but then remembered his billfold and keys were sitting on the desk. He backpedaled.

Something felt off. Moonlight streamed through the tall windows, casting light on a dark beige envelope lying on the floor. It was sealed tightly, with no writing on the outside. Clint lifted it. Having not seen it before he stepped outdoors, he pressed his thumb under the seal until it gave way.

Thinking clearer, Clint remembered something important. He had placed an object inside his shirt pocket. Running his fingers along the inside seam for what he hoped was there, if in fact it wasn't a dream, he was disappointed to find the pocket empty. He sat down in the rocker, resigned that he had taken a fall and hit his head.

The envelope fell through the armrest of the rocker. He lifted it wondering who had left it for him. No one had access to his office other than Jules, Tom Sanders, and the security guard. He cautiously removed the contents. Adrenaline was pumping wildly when he lifted out a tiny black velvet pouch with the initials A.A.D. stitched in gold lettering. He unfastened a double fold, looped through a strap to secure the bag's contents. He took out a small, folded piece of paper.

He leaned back in the chair, his hands laced behind his head. "Well, well, well, how did you get in there?"

Tucked inside was a gold toothpick, identical to the one he had picked up in the alley and slipped into his shirt pocket. From what Clint could ascertain, the miniature bag was handmade and had been detailed specifically for this object. The paper inside revealed a tiny round sticker–**24K Gold**. Scripted words at the bottom of the paper read, *Evidence.*

For a long while, Clint considered what he had in his possession, having trouble believing he was looking at the gold toothpick from the alley. He glanced up at the mirror, seeing his own reflection sitting in the rocking chair. Somehow the toothpick had transferred to the envelope, except now there was a black pouch with the initials, A.A.D. on it. A clue greater than the toothpick alone, he had a person's initials to consider, evidence that might be critical to solving the case.

The phone's shrill ring gave him a jolt. Jules was calling. He collected himself and answered, "Hey, babe."

"Okay, I'm home. Where are you? Thought you'd beat me here."

"Truth is, I wasn't in a hurry. I figured about an hour or so. It only takes a few minutes to run home. I didn't know for sure when you'd get back. Did you have a good time?"

"Sure did. I couldn't put another bite of food in my mouth if my life depended on it. Do you want me to whip something up for you? Did you get a sandwich? If not, I can put a potato in the microwave, or fry bologna."

"Heavens, no!" Clint responded without hesitation, aware that his wife had to be dead on her feet after a full day of shopping with Bonnie.

"If I want anything I'll pick it up here and eat it on the way home," he replied. "It's too late to eat heavy. Especially a fried bologna sandwich."

"Alright." Jules's voice sounded delighted not to have to cook.

"See you in a few," he said, picking up the envelope. He slipped it into his coat pocket, knowing not to overhandle the envelope or its contents. If he could find a serial number, it could trace back to the manufacturer, and then to the seller. Hopefully, by a receipt, he could find the person who had purchased it. He wondered if the trail would end with A.A.D, whoever that was.

Clint was in ownership of an item he had no choice but to share with Scott Edwards. An alarming thought surfaced. I saw him! The guy who killed the man in the alley. The one Charlie could have identified had he lived. The same man who paid a visit to Mark Carlson months later. Contrary to logic, Clint was ecstatic with the idea of bringing a killer to justice. It was risky to attempt an explanation on how he happened upon fresh, vital information. Who would believe him? Other than Jules. Clint figured his investigation could turn deadly if he didn't use extreme caution from here on out.

Twenty minutes later he was in the kitchen at home leaning on the doorframe, watching his wife prepare two cups of hot tea.

"Did you have a nice day?" asked Jules turning from the counter to pour half and half in a pitcher before setting it on the table along with a bowl of sugar. When she sat down, she was shocked to see a gash above Clint's right eye. "How did that happen?" she asked, examining the puncture.

Clint reached for the spot, now more pronounced and sorer than at first. "Oh that, it's nothing. I was clumsy, lost my balance. Fell into something sharp."

Thinking his answer terribly vague, she asked, "What was that *something sharp*? It's a deep gouge, Clint."

Do I tell her the truth now? Or wait until later?

Chapter 24
The Plot Thickens

Clint agonized over the position he found himself in. Did he tell Jules what he had been up to? What about Scott? Or Farley for that matter? How much did any of them really need to know, considering he didn't have but a few pieces to splice together.

Finally, after considerable mental grappling, Clint broke down, giving in to his conscience. Jules should be told some of what he'd learned. She wanted to know what the sharp object was he encountered, he told her the edge of the mirror which was close enough to the truth.

However, Scott was owed a broader explanation since Clint required his input and assistance. Farley, conversely, would be kept in the dark.

After a restless night, Clint awoke to a spectacular Sunday morning. Temperatures ranged close to forty degrees with plenty of sunshine and blue skies. His mood had lifted. They were traveling to Greenville to visit with Jules's brother and sister-in-law, Randy and Anna, their boys, David, Chris and Walley, along with several extended family members.

Randy enjoyed whipping up recipes known only in his head. By two o'clock, he had a feast laid out on the dining room table, which was used only for special occasions. As usual, they had enough food to feed an army. On the buffet, Anna arranged three pies, a fruit bowl, and a carafe of coffee.

The visit was long overdue. Over drinks and dessert, they organized a Christmas trip up north to Beech Grove to see Clint's father-in-law, Walter, and Jules's other sisters, and brother and sister-in-law. Jules's baby sister, Faith MaDawn, lived less than a mile from their father. She had graciously invited everyone to her home for the holidays, including overnight stays if anyone was inclined to accept.

Clint and Jules accepted her invitation and had arranged to spend the night of December 23 in Beech Grove. They would visit Rusty, Molly, Trey, and Dylan on Christmas Eve. They planned an overnight stay there as well. Then, they planned to drive home late Christmas Day. They were both looking forward to the trip.

When they pulled into the drive at home after their visit to Greenville, Clint left the engine idling. He sat in stillness, without opening the door.

Jules turned. "Why aren't you getting out?"

"I'd like to speak with you. Here if you don't mind."

Her heart fluttered, thinking Clint's remark didn't sound good. "I thought you seemed a little distracted. What's wrong?"

"Oh… nothing's wrong. I don't mean to scare you." Clint stated, reaching out for her hand. "I never want to hide anything from you, and I will be if I don't tell you something that happened yesterday."

Clint formed his words carefully, his intent to voice what he'd been up to, without causing Jules needless concern. She had always been supportive, and he didn't want to abuse that trust. Being upfront in his marriage was paramount. At the same time, until he knew more, he didn't want to put up any red flags. He struggled with how much he should disclose?

"Last week was busy, and this one will be too," Clint started out, his inner wall of strength making it clear what he needed to say. "We have two new residents at Radcliff's Children's Home, Joseph and Josephine. The cutest things you've ever laid eyes on."

In the dark, Clint could see the outline of his wife's pretty face against a backdrop of light radiating from a streetlamp.

"Is that right? How nice we can provide them a safe home. Is that what you wanted to say? You could have told me that indoors, where it's warmer. Unless you are suggesting we adopt them." She cocked her head to the side with a witty expression, as if to say, Tell me that's not what you're thinking.

"No, but if we were younger, I might," he conceded, grinning slightly. "A couple of things happened I'm still trying to wrap my head around. One of them is, I went to Louisville yesterday while you and Bonnie were out. I had extra time on my hands, figured a quick trip wouldn't hurt. I wanted to acquaint myself with Farley's old residence, in relation to the hospital, and to walk Shelby Park."

Jules thought about what her husband had said, "Did it turn out to your advantage? I mean, do you feel you relate better?"

"I do," he nodded. "I found Beans a' Brewin' coffee shop as well." He waited for his words to sink in, then added, "And, I talked with the owner about the night of the murder."

Jules turned, her face showing her surprise. "What? You spoke with the owner of the coffee shop? How did you manage that? It doesn't make sense he'd speak to a total stranger about something so personal."

"All I can say is, the subject came up unexpectedly. We hit it off right away. Not only did he describe what happened that night, he also told me about a visit he had later from the man who killed Charlie Hill. The guy threatened him. Showed him a Glock and told him to keep his mouth shut, or else."

Jules couldn't believe what she was hearing. "So why did he return? Did the guy think the owner had seen his face?"

"Maybe, but that wasn't the full reason. He demanded to be given the paperwork from the incident. Wanted to know if anything was removed from Charlie's body by the police, or anyone else."

"So, he was searching for something. Something he thought Charlie had?"

"Exactly," Clint responded quickly, not sure how much more to tac on. Information had mounted, not all of it needed to be discussed. "Look, Charlie was given an item from the dying man. That object is what the killer is trying to find."

Clint thought hard about the recent developments that had arisen. "I figure they may have been fighting over that very thing when Charlie arrived at the scene. He saw one guy pushing the other into the wall. The killer came back to collect the body—before the police could authenticate Charlie's claim."

"Holy cow, how are you so knowledgeable about this?"

"It's starting to piece together, like a jigsaw puzzle. The point is, I'm telling you what I know so far, or suspect. Tomorrow, I'll try to hook up with Scott. Ask him for guidance. I want to know what was on Charlie's body the night he was taken to Grayson Hospital. In his personal effects I think we'll find what is at the root of these murders. I want to search through those things and will need help from Scott to make that happen."

"I'm not sure how to respond," Jules admitted, worriedly. "Seems like we are headed to a new level on Farley's case. Clint, you must be extremely careful. You're using the word, I, a lot. This is police business." She sternly inserted, "I hate to break it to you, but you're not a Private Investigator. You are a regular family man with kids and a wife."

The conversation had become intense. "Look, I wanted to talk to you about that. I'm considering applying for a license. That will open doors easier. Inquiries only, I understand, but a license will facilitate my efforts, rather than snoop around like a bumbling gumshoe."

Clint grimaced, uneasy about spiraling deeper into the subject. "It would be impossible for me to articulate this, but I was summoned into this affair. A PI license might come in handy. It won't hurt to have one in my possession."

Jules frowned, pushing the ramifications of his remark to the corner of her mind. "Look, I'm no fool," she said candidly. "This is a wild supposition on my part but are you inclined to walk this path because you believe the powers Rod Radcliff, Sr. instilled in you will help resolve this issue? Clint, could you be a puppet, and someone not so benevolent, is pulling your strings?"

Clint was taken aback by Jules's directness, not having seen this side of his wife before. It made him think about the issue from a different angle.

They sat in stillness, neither one willing to say something they'd regret.

"Jules, I know that's not the case. The reason I know is because Picasso is involved. He's an integral sign in what has unfolded. Nothing sinister came from the events in 2003."

Clint leaned back on the headrest, looking up at the headliner above him, struggling to find the right words. "When Rod departed Salzburg something deep inside me was activated. A sixth sense I didn't know was there. A knowingness I can't articulate. The awareness I feel is impossible to describe, but I've changed. Some might call it clairvoyance."

"You've never mentioned this before," Jules said, surprised by his confession.

He turned her face toward him. "I know. Until now it wasn't that important. And, as far as me being a family man, I get that. One hundred percent, you're right. There is nothing more important to me than you and the kids."

"The other side of that coin is," he continued, "Picasso would not have shown up if I wasn't supposed to be involved in Farley's predicament. A level of protection surrounds me, that is a true statement. Someone has my back. And I can tell you this mystery has more facets than you can possibly imagine." He touched the bump on his head. "This wasn't a clumsy accident."

Jules stared at him, and his swollen eyebrow area, weighing his words. Darkly, she admitted, "Honestly, I can't believe we are having this conversation. We're talking about murder… and you diving in headfirst. I suspect you are up to your eyeballs in the investigating and are only telling me key points you deem necessary."

Clint started to speak, to defend himself, but Jules put her hand up, stopping him. "I'm not finished," she said firmly. "Two years ago, incredible circumstances arose that neither of us, to this day, can explain. During the whole affair you were led one step at a time until you reached resolution. Clint," she said, laying her hand on his arm, "I don't understand any of this, and I won't pretend to. Still, one thing is clear, Rod Radcliff, Sr.'s soul stayed in Salzburg, waiting, even luring you here. So, you would help him unravel his own murder, and your father's. He directed–you followed. Through coincidences, dreams, signs, and intuition."

She stared out at the blacktop driveway, absorbed in thought. Heaviness hung between them until the silence was broken with her what she thought was her final statement on the matter. "That's good enough for me. None of us have guarantees about tomorrow. You are right, Picasso is a messenger, and whoever they are, they wouldn't entangle you in this affair knowing you'd be harmed. You have in mind to execute their bidding. Honestly, I question who is really behind this. Rod Radcliff, Charlie Hill, or someone else."

She glanced at him, her face serious, "That's not to say, mind you, that you can go traipsing around like nothing bad can ever happen. Because it can if you don't use your head. You are not invincible, Clint. It would be exceedingly stupid of you not to tread lightly. And I mean every step of the way." She raised a brow, "But you know that, right?"

Clint sighed with relief. He'd told her how he felt, and she was standing behind him, challenging him, even. Giving advice. "Okay, here goes nothing," he bravely announced. "If you can wrap your head around that much, and accept it, you're going to love this next part."

"Oh, good grief," she squealed, seeing a grin appear on his face. She shook her head; not sure she was ready for the next part. "Go ahead, Clint, fire!"

"I walked through the antique mirror. Or, at least, I thought I did." His lips pursed, waiting for her response to his extraordinary claim. He watched as her eyes grow large and her face change.

She couldn't have heard him correctly, she decided. A scowl appeared, "I must have misunderstood you."

"No, it's true," he said rubbing the bruised area. "I saw the full murder. Inside the mirror. I was coaxed into it." Clint realized how crazy he sounded but went on. "I followed a man through a brick wall, into a cave, then out into the alley where the first murder occurred. Jules, I saw everything, including that object exchanged between the dead man and Charlie Hill. Charlie put something in his pocket when he left to call the police for help."

"Clint!" Jules's mouth flew open. "I'm speechless. If it weren't you telling me this story, I'd say you were out of your freakin' mind." She took a deep breath, "So, what you are telling me is: you…walked… into… your… mirror… ?"

Again, she gasped, "That's not remotely possible." She scowled. "But considering in 2003 you saw your younger self walk out of it after the grandchildren's treasure hunt, then led you to the shack and Rod Radcliff, who revealed where your dad's remains were and the Reno Gang treasure, how could I doubt you?"

"Yeah. It's not the first weird experience with that mirror. It shouldn't be possible, but it happened. After I got back from talking with Mark Carlson, the owner of Beans a' Brewin'." Clint hesitated; not remembering if he had mentioned the owner's name. "Anyways, a brick structure appeared in the reflection, then, out of nowhere, I saw a shadow standing in the distance. A person's shape. He indicated I should follow him," Clint splayed his hands, "which I did. Through the mirror and into an opening that had expanded in the brick wall. Only I had to crawl through sideways because it was a horizontal slit."

His eyes rolled when he saw his wife's face contort. Clint wagged his head, "Truthfully, I can't say one hundred percent that it wasn't a dream because I found myself on the floor next to the mirror, bewildered, and dazed."

"Do you think that's when you hit your head?"

"I figure that's when it happened though I don't really remember," Clint considered, then added, "I didn't notice it at first. Everything felt so surreal if you know what I mean."

"Either way, a while after that, something even more weird happened."

Jules butted in, shocked at his revelation. "Really, Clint? As if what you just told me wasn't weird enough. Please, continue. Enlighten me!"

"Alright, smart aleck," he chuckled, feeling the comic relief typical of Jules. "I found an envelope. That was shortly after I went outdoors to the roof to clear my head. When I came back in, there it was."

"And it wasn't there when you went outside? You're certain?"

"Absolutely positive. A 24K gold toothpick and a black pouch with the initials A.A.D., stitched in golden thread, was inside. Plus, a note. In the vision-like thing I experienced," his brow lifted, "I saw the exact toothpick in the alley, on the ground. I put it in my pocket. Somehow it made its way out of my pocket and inside the envelope. I told you this part was bizarre." His expression was telling. "I feel like a character in a Twilight Zone episode!"

Jules's face turned ashen. "What have we tapped into, Clint? I'm sorry, but the word bizarre… that's not strong enough."

"Believe me, I'm still trying to make sense of it, that's why I believe a higher agenda is involved. I'm tracking breadcrumbs. Who knows where they will lead. But I promise you, I will not be foolish, nor will I allow myself to be led down a perilous path that has even a hint of jeopardizing us. I don't understand the why me part of this equation, but for whatever reason I've been selected to do some investigating. Not Farley. Me!"

Clint walked around the truck to open Jules's door. He extended his hand to assist her, trailing her inside envisioning a slew of scenarios.

Once indoors, Jules plopped down into a kitchen chair with a suddenness that telegraphed exhaustion. "Don't you wonder at times how we ever found time to hold down jobs?" she asked, intentionally changing the subject.

"No joke," Clint chortled, relieved she had taken their conversation in a different direction. "It's been a minute. I can't imagine working twelve-hour days like I used to at the sawmill, in Seymour. Those were long and hard. Didn't mind my seven-to-seven schedule, but when evening rolled around, I was ready to go home."

"Working only two days a week is the perfect number of days," Jules declared, standing, ready to take her purse to the foyer. "I've graduated to semi-retired status. I work the days that fit my mood better," She glanced over at him, "That's better than before. If you recall, I was the one Patrick always called when staff didn't show. I even filled in for the cook once or twice." She grinned, "Ivan is rarely off, that was a disaster. No one can outcook him."

Jules's dimples deepened. "I never really minded it back then, but things are completely different today, aren't they sweetheart?" She took a long gulp from the bottle of water she was holding. "We have the orphanage, the Apothecary, and other things to attend to these days. Who would have thought life could take such a hard right turn."

She chuckled at the irony of their situation, from getting by, to no worries. "Patrick has been such a great boss, always was, but since we got married, he bends over backwards to accommodate me. My schedule depends on what's going on with us, not the other way around."

"We have the best of all worlds, you, and me," Clint affably agreed, pulling a chair beside her. He squeezed her hand, "We have more good memories to make." His tone turned mindful, recalling Charlie and Ann Hill, and how their last day was faced without warning. He lowered his head. Sadness filled his heart.

"Why so glum?"

"I was thinking about the Hill's. How their child witnessed his parents shot." Pensive, a jogged memory came to mind. "No family member can ever fill the shoes of a mother and father. No matter how sincere and loving they are. But thank God for those who try. They are the angels among us," he claimed thinking about the nuns who had raised him despite his behavior and lack of appreciation. Clint knew firsthand the pain that came from being unwanted.

Clint closed his eyes, wondering what Casey was doing at that very moment. Had he seen his father since he and Clint last talked? In his heart, Clint believed his orphanage would take better care of the child than a father who elected to abandon his child on their doorstep.

"I'm ready for bed," Jules said, recognizing Clint's tired expression. "A penny for your thoughts," she suggested, seeing his far-off look.

"I'm not thinking about anything in particular," he lied, ready to call it a night as well.

"Normally I don't work Mondays, but I am this week. I'll be going in at eight tomorrow for a change. Thought I'd help out. Darla won't be able to handle it on her own. We've been overly busy these last few days. I'll get to sleep in a little."

She tugged Clint out of his chair, pulling him to his feet. "Follow me!"

Chapter 25
A Force to Reckon With

The start of the week ushered in cloudy skies and cold temperatures. Overcast fit Clint's mood as he drove into town, formulating in his mind what and how much to tell Scott about recent developments. They'd set an appointment at 6:45 a.m. at Josie's Diner rather than at Scott's office, per Clint's request. He preferred to discuss Farley's case in a less formal setting than the Salzburg Police Station.

Surprised by Scott's quick response to his text message before the sun broke in the east, Clint felt anxious about their meeting. When he walked through the diner door, a new face greeted him. Patrick was behind the counter ringing up an order and Ivan was cooking frenziedly, setting plates on the window ledge that divided the kitchen from the dining area. Clint was shocked how many people were already eating and finishing their meals.

"Good morning, Mr. Reeves," Darla Thompson said with a generous smile and lots of teeth. In a uniform more exaggerated than any Jules ever wore, Darla showed Clint to a table two booths up from his usual one.

Not fully awake or ready for conversation, Clint informed his waitress, "Scott Edwards will be joining me in a few. Do you know him?"

"Oh, yes sir, he's Salzburg's police captain. Really cute… comes in every now and then for a large, to-go, coffee." Her face brightened. "Patrick will open the door early to let Captain Edwards in if he's standing out there before we open at 6 a.m."

"Great," Clint grinned, thinking inwardly that was more information than he needed to hear. "We'd like not to be disturbed." When Darla's face drooped, Clint added, "any more than necessary. You know, private police business."

"Oh… thank you. I understand," Darla replied enthusiastically. "I'll set a carafe of coffee on the table so's as not to interrupt you. Will you be having breakfast?"

"Toast is all, thanks," answered Clint with a pleasant smile, feeling older than his years.

Darla scurried away in a jiffy, ready to diligently fill his order and prepare their coffee.

When Clint glanced up, he noticed Patrick staring at him. They exchanged hints of humor that expressed everything needed to be said. He pulled the newspaper close, thumbing through it and noticing The Vincennes Sun-Commercial was thicker than usual. He figured the holiday season contributed to its bulkiness with ads and upcoming events around southern Indiana. His eyes stopped on one headline he found especially newsworthy.

November 28, 2005: Shadows of Venus

> The planet Venus is growing so bright it's casting shadows. Few people have ever seen a Venus shadow. But they're there– elusive and delicate—and, if you appreciate rare things, it's a thrill to witness.

In his peripheral vision, Clint detected movement. "How's it going?" he asked when Scott slid into Clint's booth across from him.

"Fair-to-middling," mumbled Scott, knowing he had a full schedule awaiting him at the office. He had two messages yet to be heard. "Mondays are always a pain with chaos from the weekend." In a dreaded tone, he explained, "You know the drill. You've heard me complain about Mondays before."

They laughed in unison, recalling numerous times where Monday issues made their way into their conversations. The two friends drank coffee in silence before Scott finally broke the ice. "I was thinking on the way here, you didn't return my call last Saturday."

Clint suddenly realized he'd spaced Scott's voicemail. He had meant to return the call on the way home from Louisville, but it was too late and he didn't want to bother Scott afterhours. "Sorry, things got a little crazy last Saturday."

Scott studied Clint's countenance. "No worries… turned out to be a busy day for me too. I was checking in, is all." Scott chuckled. "As I was driving over, I was thinking how I enjoy our tit for tats."

Clint scowled, questioning what Scott was referring to. "Why did you say that?"

Scott lightened the mood when he clarified his remark. "The last time we were together, I swore, and you got mad as a wet hen. And here we are getting ready for another round of me listening to what you shouldn't have done. That's my guess, anyway." His face colored with the humor that defined his and Clint's relationship–Clint pushing his buttons and Scott reeling Clint in. "I suspect this time we'll be a bit more civil than the last go-round at Aces & Eights," he comically stated.

An amused expression crept onto Clint's face, remembering how they quarreled. It wasn't exactly a friendly conversation, at least at the start. "I sure hope so," he joked, "but you'd better hold onto your hat. The way things are going, anything is possible."

Scott got up, grabbed the pot from the machine, and topped off their cups, waving off the waitress that was approaching their table, having forgotten the extra coffee Clint had asked for. "Just so you know, my cop hat is in the Interceptor. This is your friend sitting with you now."

"A good thing," Clint chortled, "because what I uncovered is going to shock you. I don't even know how to describe it in terms that won't make me sound like a lunatic."

Scott became curious. "Really?" Looking down at his watch, he realized his time was limited. "Look, I've only got about twenty minutes. Maybe the gist of it, or an encapsulated one. Can you do that? We can set up another meeting for later when my schedule frees."

"Sure," Clint grinned, deciding he'd put the black velvet pouch that held the toothpick on the table before saying what it was or how he happened to be in possession of it. "Without going into the details, I've talked to the owner of Beans a' Brewin' in Louisville. Mark Carlson, had information no one else knows."

Clint pushed the pouch to Scott's side of the table. "Take a look."

"What's this?"

"Just open it."

Scott lifted the bag, opened it, but still didn't understand. "What am I looking at?"

"Unfold it," Clint eyes gleamed. "There's a small object inside. Check out the stitching on the flap."

Scott unwrapped the cloth, this time he saw what he was supposed to see. "A toothpick?" he said, "That's rather unusual."

"It is. You still want the abbreviated version?"

"I do," Scott replied, narrowing his eyes, holding a policeman's countenance.

"Long and short of it," Clint took the bag from Scott. "The toothpick belongs, I believe, to Charlie Hill's assailant."

He watched Scott's expression shift. "There was a sealed envelope on my office floor last Saturday night, with this inside." He pointed, waiting for Scott to absorb his words.

"Mark Carlson told me the man who murdered Charlie and his wife came back to the coffee shop and threatened him days later. He wanted to know if the police removed anything from Charlie's body before transporting him to the hospital."

Scott drew a picture in his mind of what Clint had described. "Medics wouldn't dare remove anything from a deceased person," stated Scott, "it would be considered evidence."

"You and I know that, but it would seem the killer didn't. He was searching for something he didn't find the night of the murders. Witnesses said earlier that the man was rummaging through Charlie's clothes when a policeman caught him off guard. This officer wasn't as convinced as his partner that Charlie fabricated the story of seeing someone murdered in the alley."

Scott's mind filled with questions he didn't have time to ask, other than, "Where are you getting all this information?"

"A number of sources," answered Clint with a crooked grin and a shrug of his shoulders, thinking of the mirror, and the trip to Louisville, although he wasn't ready to broach those subjects yet.

"Scott, the guy who paid Mark Carlson a visit was there to retrieve what he had shot Charlie for." With a hand on the table, Clint offered, "I have a theory. Do you want to hear it?"

"I suppose it's best considering you're the one holding all the cards."

"Deduction, the guy who murdered Charlie is the same person who killed the man in the alley. Charlie witnessed the two men fighting. One man dropped; the killer ran. Between the time Charlie went to phone in the incident, and the police arriving at the crime scene, the killer returned and removed the victim."

Clint took a moment to let that part of his theory digest. "The problem was the dying man had given something to Charlie, and the killer wanted it back. Later, the killer went to the coffee shop and shot Charlie, assuming that something was still on Charlie. But the shooter was interrupted when the off-duty policeman showed up. The killer escaped out the back door, not having adequate time to find what he had come for."

"Pray tell, Clint, how did you arrive at these assumptions?" questioned Scott skeptically. He believed Clint could be on the right track, but what he had described rang of a first-hand account.

"June Bennett, the nurse at Grayson Hospital. She has a friend on the force. He told her the cop who was killed must have been a rookie because he didn't follow protocol." Clint looked down at his hands to avoid eye contact. "You said he had a family, wife, and children."

"Geez, that's quite a revelation," Scott said, taken aback with information overload. I suppose you'll get around to telling me the rest of the story, and how you happened on so much insider information, instead of trying to convince me June Bennett was your lone source, or this Mark Carlson."

"That's fine, somewhere more private works for me if you have the time," Clint agreed, glad their conversation was moving in a different direction.

"I need to put what you've said in chronological order. Try to sort this out. Charlie Hill's personal effects should be with the executor of his estate. That's where the deceased's belongings are typically taken."

"Look," declared Clint, "Charlie saw a man knifed. The reason they didn't find a body is the man who killed him came back to dispose of him. He removed his victim and all traces of evidence." He held up two fingers, "My first question is, where is the dead guy? And, secondly, what did the dying man give Charlie?"

Scott reached for the pouch, taking out the shiny toothpick from its sleeve. In his palm, he turned the diamond-dotted cap at the thickest part of the shaft, from side to side, examining it. He glanced over at Clint. "Says 24K gold." Pointing to two tiny circles near the head, he noted, "A mark, and gold purity stamp. This thing isn't cheap. The fact that it has initials stitched in gold on the outer cloth is telling. Could lead us to the perpetrator. Don't know, but it sounds reasonable if we find A.A.D., we find our guy."

Of the same mind, Clint nodded. "It's the killer's, I'm certain of it." He noticed Scott's keen eye, interpreting what he'd said.

Deeply focused on the initials, he wondered why anyone would want a 24K gold toothpick. Scott theorized a possibility. "Maybe it's a gift from a lover? Could be the killer thinks carrying a gold toothpick around gives the impression that he's cool? Or rich. Sexy, or simply a hot-shot personality!" Scott thought about the character he was describing and felt convinced he had pegged the person who had previously had the toothpick to a tee.

"Wouldn't there be an actual receipt for Charlie's effects somewhere?" asked Clint.

"Absolutely, there would be. I'll look at my calendar. We need to schedule another sit-down. By then hopefully I will have been in contact with the executor. Do you need to tell me anything else before I take off?" he closed his eyes afraid Clint would insert another hand grenade into the conversation.

"I asked the librarian, Bonnie Woodlock, for an obituary listing for December 21, 2004, and anything out of the ordinary surrounding death reports. I told her you and I were working on a case. I also mentioned Farley McDougal's donor's name was Charles Hill so when she saw his name, she'd know. So far, only four people know about this, Farley, Bonnie, you, and me. Oh, and Jules, of course. That makes five."

"Honestly, that's three people too many, Clint." Scott frowned, pulling his keys from his pocket. "Maybe four!" His face showed his disapproval. "We need everyone to pull back. Tell Bonnie to drop the request. Say you found what you were looking for. Tell Farley absolutely nothing. This could set him back and undo what he's achieved so far. The stress could weigh heavy on him. We need to remember his heart transplant was less than a year ago."

He stepped aside, and then back again, "You do understand the risk involved. Correct? No more information-sharing, with anyone." Scott leaned down, close to Clint's ear, and extended a warning, "Lives could be at stake. This isn't a game we're playing. It's not cops and robbers. This is the real deal, Clint. People died for whatever the killer wants, and more could if he gets an inkling someone is sniffing around."

"I understand," responded Clint. "From here on out its just us." Clint's expression showed his determination. "Let me know when you're available. In the meantime, I'll speak to Bonnie."

Scott gave a subtle nod. "Hang tight until you hear from me," Scott said on his way out.

Chapter 26
The Red Herring

December 21, 2004

Murder Spree

At his new, shiny black, Super-Duty F-250, Axel Drako reached behind the tailgate for the handle to release the safety lock mechanism, opening the door. He took out a body bag he had wedged under the bedliner. It could be used for anything Axel killed–animal or human–though he never dreamed someday he'd need one for Thaddeus.

At the opposite end of the grime-laden alley, lined with garbage, rats, and human waste, Axel unfolded and unzipped the bag. Shamelessly he filled the cavity with his cousin's corpse. He proceeded to drag Thaddeus's unwieldly body over rough, fluid-filled ruts and filth back to his truck.

There, he hurled the body bag over the edge and into the truck bed. Vacant eyes faced skyward as Axel hastily dug through his cousin's pockets, inside Thaddeus's wool coat, heavy trousers, and elsewhere. Axel frantically scrounged but came up empty-handed. Frustrated when he didn't find what he was searching for, he cursed vehemently. Under his breath, he seethed. What did you do with it?

As he did, he recalled seeing an exchange between Thaddeus and the passerby who happened into the alley just as Axel did the deed. The moment Axel pulled his switch blade to settle the disagreement, the stranger appeared. Axel hadn't hesitated to end the argument. Now, he felt angry with himself for running like a scared jack rabbit the second the witness showed.

With tempers flaring, both lives had been on the line. Axel's if he didn't get what he wanted and Thaddeus's for being plain stupid. Enough to think his cousin wouldn't kill for what Thaddeus had. All Thaddeus had to do was hand over the goods and keep his mouth shut. His cousin gave him no other choice.

Why did I run? Axel chastised himself. Could have handled the situation just as cleanly as I did with Thaddeus. That mistake could cost me. Big time. He shoved his hands into his pockets. How stupid could I be? Thaddeus must have given it to him.

Hurriedly, Axel got to work stuffing Thaddeus's body inside the heavy plastic bag. He zipped the bag and wrapped it with duct tape, and then covered it with weighted blankets to keep the bag from shifting. Before motoring away, he made one last mental scan. The area where Thaddeus first dropped and the spot he crawled to after being stabbed. No blood, or signs of disturbance, were left in either place. An irritation arose when he realized Uncle Dorian's watch wasn't lying on the ground or next to Thaddeus. When we left the bar, Thaddeus had it in his hand, Axel recalled. And was holding it when we resumed our argument outdoors.

Although Thaddeus's sweater was soaked in blood, none of it flowed to the ground. His body lay face up with his bloody hands resting on his chest. Thaddeus hadn't been there long before Axel bagged him, and then dragged him to the truck. It was a clean, precise puncture wound he'd performed producing little outwardly blood. Internal bleeding mostly, enough to do the job in short order.

Axel thought about the passerby who had observed Thaddeus and his argument. His shoulders tensed, not knowing exactly what he should do about that situation. As he drove out of town to discard Thaddeus, the thought occurred to him that his only option was to lie in wait, in the event the man showed up again.

If he was there once, he may be back, thought Axel. Where I'm going shouldn't take more than two to three hours, plus turnaround time to get back to the alley. I'll stay nearby. Hopefully I'll see him. My guess is he lives nearby or possibly works around here.

An alibi for himself, and an explanation why Thaddeus wouldn't be in touch with his family and friends was next on the list to manufacture. Cookie Crenna, Axel's ex-girlfriend, could be his alibi if enough money changed hands. Money is a great motivator with women.

When he had little funds, Cookie wasn't nearly as interested. But when he flashed around a windfall of dough, she flirted more, making him feel like royalty. It cheapened her in his eyes. He found

Cookie pathetic and her behavior repulsive. But because she was great fun to toy with, he played along. Then Alice Gregory came on the scene. Cookie needn't know, he'd figured. Two girls were twice the delight.

It had been three months since Friday night, October 31–during a costume party on his uncle's yacht, docked on the Kentucky side of the Ohio River, where Axel made his move. He'd seamlessly executed a long planned-out scheme that had been in the works for months.

Axel rather liked being a thief. After cleaning out his uncle's safe and walking away with the goods, his pockets full of cash, he felt exhilarated. A new high. Being a close family member, Axel figured his absence would not be spotted, and he was right. Anyone who knew him would presume he was in pursuit of a lady friend. A rugged man, Axel never lacked female attention, although he was picky with the ladies. Long legs and big bosoms were his preference. Blondes were his favorites.

When the robbery was discovered, he wasn't considered a suspect nor questioned to any degree. Afterall, Axel was his uncle's favorite nephew. A business tycoon, Dorian Andersen, was a stately man who made a grandioso appearance wherever he went. But with Axel, he was a kind, generous, playful surrogate father.

Axel's mother Irene, and her brother Dorian, grew up privileged, never wanting for anything. Theirs was old money passed down through the generations. A respectable family, Andersen was a recognizable name in the finance world. Dorian took over the family business when his father's died from a heart attack at age fifty-two.

The same could not be said for Irene Andersen's choice in a husband. Jay Drako was a blue-collar man with no means. He came from a poor background and his family lived paycheck to paycheck. Jay didn't wear fine clothes or smoke Cuban cigars like Dorian, but he could sing. Irene was smitten from the start. Jay's seductive eyes, and fun nature made Irene an easy mark.

No matter the family protests, Irene married Jay Erik Drako despite their objections. One Monday morning, after the couple eloped, they surprised the family with matching wedding bands.

In the wake of his sister's marriage, Dorian found Jay a serious thorn in his side. Repeatedly getting into trouble, Jay presented a respectability problem to his family's honor, but even Dorian grossly underestimated the complications and baggage, associated with Jay Drako. The Andersen patriarch never accepted Irene's marriage. He warned his sister Jay was a bad apple from the start, but she didn't listen.

Three years into the marriage, Jay Drako was given a life sentence for drug trafficking. Dorian Andersen stepped up after the arrest, taking Axel under his wing and raising his nephew as his own. Although Axel and Thaddeus co-existed under the same roof, Axel was never an easy child.

When the safe was found empty, with the door swung open and its contents missing, everyone was shocked, but no one more than Axel, who pretended to be stunned as well.

Having no clue to the hour the robbery went down, it was evident the items were lifted by the hand of a professional. The lock was damaged, however, the mechanism appeared easily manipulated, which elicited doubt. It was as though the lock was jiggered purposefully to give the appearance of robbery.

The idea that Dorian's code was applied to gain access to the safe was broached but quickly dropped after Andersen told the police only a handful of people knew the combination, and they were above reproach. No one he knew would have done such a thing.

The family believed the break-in happened afterhours while the party was winding down, around 3 a.m. or so. Attendees departed at the latest, 3:45, Andersen recalled. With the hour late, clean up was left for the housekeeping staff the following day. It was presumed the safe was broken into after 4 a.m. and when the staff arrived the next morning. No one could be certain of the hour.

Andersen had shelled out an enormous fortune to secure the yacht safe. Its precious contents were in a sequestered spot where the bulk of his time was spent, always close by, especially the pocket watch. On the water, or lounging in the captain's quarters, Dorian traded and negotiated contracts as he wheeled and dealed through life.

Devastated beyond words, of all the things missing; gold, sizeable cash, collectible coins, etc., Andersen's antique pocket watch pained him the most. Presented as an heirloom, inscribed by his father when he graduated from Stanford, Andersen was visibly broken. Though he was never seen crying, he was clearly holding tears back. He demanded everyone leave the room and didn't come out until nightfall when he was more collected.

After a week of no police results, or even the slightest lead through proper channels, Andersen put ads in all the regional newspapers, offering a sizeable reward for the watch's return. No questions asked, give a location, the money would be there. The problem was the ad he ran had an emotional, desperate undertone, soliciting the wrong type of people, thereby encouraging pranks and charlatans. Not one legitimate response emerged.

The pocket watch was gone.

The night of the robbery, when Axel first laid eyes on the pocket watch, he was instantly enamored with it, having not seen it in his hand before. Uncle Dorian had shown it to him, of course, even told Axel the story behind it, but he'd never let him see it for more than a quick glance. It took a quick second to drop it into his trousers, along with wads of high denomination bills, including several $500 bills no longer in circulation–highly sought after–plus two $1,000 bills. Axel was told his uncle's stash was still legal tender and collectors would fork over big bucks to have any of them.

Axel recalled his uncle telling him the first $500 note was issued in 1780 by the Province of North Carolina followed by Virginia the same year. They were used as confederate currency during the war of 1812 and the civil war. Congress authorized issuance later. In 1934 the last $500 bill was issued. The country's 25th President William McKinley was pictured from 1928 to 1934, and Chief Justice John James Marshall was before that. They, along with all high denomination bills such as the $10,000, $5,000, and $1,000, were subsequently discontinued in 1969. Sophistication of thieves was one of the many reasons the bill was retired. Axel laughed when he heard that piece of the story.

Uncle Dorian proudly boasted to Axel, his $500 bills' face values were tiny compared to their real value. At least worth twenty times more, and the sky was the limit on the $1,000 notes, a prospect Axel couldn't forget or ignore as an adult. He'd entertained the idea of stealing them as a youngster. No longer a kid, the time came to execute the plan.

His Dracula costume allowed him easy movement around the boat, people paid little attention to his whereabouts. He'd created plenty of pockets and secret compartments in his costume for the purpose of toting the goods off the yacht, undetected. With pockets full of coins, big bucks, and the watch, he stopped for few cursory conversations before taking off. The whole while he pretended to be three sheets to the wind. When he walked down the plank, he waved, courting a sassy young thing on his arm. It was what everyone expected. He'd dumped her the moment they were out of sight. Axel had the perfect place to move his newly acquired gains.

He's loaded, Axel convinced himself, not worrying about his uncle's loss or the feelings attached to the things he'd taken. Uncle Dorian has stuff on every continent, toys everywhere. He might not be too happy, but he can buy the bills back, and restock. Then Axel chortled at his luck. Possibly from the guy I'll sell them to. A worry entered his mind. I'd better take them far enough away, to pass through multiple hands, because of the serial numbers.

In the present moment, with Louisville in the rearview mirror, Axel knew exactly where he was taking Thaddeus's body. He'd go to a section of a twelve-hundred-mile stretch of abandoned railroad tracks. Unable to adapt to new-world transport, rail cars were obsolete by today's standards. Technology had replaced railroads that spurred on the industrial age. No longer of use, they made an excellent, convenient location to bury a body.

He had the perfect location in mind, having sought in advance a spot to hide things but never thinking Thaddeus would be one of them. Derelict passenger cars, cabooses, and selected former Louisville & Southern Railway cars were stored in a mothball nostalgia of yesteryear. That was where his cousin would be laid to rest. Axel figured his secret spot was good as any, thinking, Thaddeus might even approve. I'll put cool rocks, stones, and ornamentals to mark the site. I'll put wildflowers on it in the spring.

The next problem was what to tell people when they asked about Thaddeus's whereabouts and why they hadn't heard from him, especially Uncle Dorian, Aunt Jessica, and his mother Irene.

Axel thought long and hard. Nothing was plausible, until he remembered the classic car Thaddeus had been considering in Eureka,

Montana, a 1967 C-2 Corvette L89S that had been disassembled and displayed on the seller's barn floor.

"The owner," Thaddeus had relayed to Axel, "was in the middle of restoring the car when the accident occurred, taking restoration off the table. Some elderly person hit his car broadside, crushing his leg." Thaddeus was enthusiastic at the prospects of owning the parts. "You know how I am with cars, good at restoring them, I'd love to take a stab at a '67' Vette. Can you imagine how cool that would be? Those things are rare."

Recalling the conversation well, Axel connived, he'd give his uncle the Cliff Note version of events. *Thaddeus went up there to check it out, taking a friend. I'll tell Uncle Dorian that Thaddeus borrowed a friend's transport truck to haul it back. The C-2 was being restored but the guy who was working on it had an accident and had to sell it for parts.* Axel thought through his lie for inconsistencies. *I can toss out I offered to tag along, but with a girlfriend going, Thaddeus thought I'd cramp his style.*

Axel rehearsed his story on his way to a secluded end of Young's High Bridge in Tyrone, Kentucky. He knew the neglected bridge was, on occasion, used by kids who dropped things from it. A nearby bourbon warehouse drew people in which was the reason he had run across the location. Out hiking for areas people were less likely to be found, Axel came across the old distillery and thought it exceptionally cool. The ravine area he'd chosen had become his secret hideaway, a stone's throw from rusting, graffiti art décor on abandoned rail cars.

Axel disposed of his cousin's body, and had his alibi wrapped up tight by the time he arrived back at the Louisville alley. All that remained was to await the stranger's arrival. He took a knapsack from under the seat and carried it to the end where the man was last seen, unfolded it, disheveled his hair to appear like a vagrant, and slipped in as any homeless person would do.

It had been a long afternoon. With a gun at his fingertips, he closed his eyes and listened to the sounds of the city and befalling footsteps.

Chapter 27
A Time to Reminisce

On the way to the library, after meeting with Scott at Josie's Diner at 6:45, Clint articulated in his mind just how he was going to retract his request to research obituaries for December 21, 2004 that he'd asked for. Bonnie knew him too well to think he no longer had an interest.

Just tell her the truth, thought Clint, level with her about the seriousness of how things were advancing. I owe her that. Be honest, share Scott's concerns and that he wants no one involved, or snooping around.

"Hey, you," Bonnie called out as Clint walked through the door. She looked around to make sure she hadn't caught anyone's attention, or disrupted anyone, and then lowered her voice. "I found something you are going to find especially fascinating."

When she approached Clint, for a friendly hug, he appeared weary and distracted. She pulled back, "That's not exactly the greeting I was expecting."

"Bonnie, I shouldn't have involved you in this mess." He scanned the room, as well. "Can we talk in private?"

"No problem," she complied, not liking the pitch of Clint's voice. "What's wrong?" she asked, sensing his tight reserve. "We can talk back here." She pointed to a space in the back. "You look worried."

When they reached her office, Clint closed the door. Bonnie poured two glasses of water and set them on her wooden desk, a display of fresh fall flowers positioned under the window.

"So, what's this about?"

"Where do I start?" Clint gazed into her deep brown eyes, "Again, everything stays between us? Right?" He moved around the room, nervously pacing.

"I already signed that contract, and read the fine print, Clint Reeves. Move on."

"Okay." Clint chortled, thinking Bonnie was as direct as his wife. "You remind me of someone," he teased. "Jules can knock my nose out of joint just as easily as you can."

Bonnie cracked up. "There's a reason why we're friends, Clint. We were cut from the same cloth." She grinned. From day one when Jules moved into Salzburg, back in 1998, they had navigated into each other's camp. "The moral to this story is we're independent ladies with minds of our own."

Clint clasped his hands behind him, displaying a generous smile. "That's why I'm drawn to both of you. I like a challenge."

"The truth surfaces," she shot back.

"Just making certain we are on the same page, Bonnie. Especially since I've been informed, in no certain terms by Scott Edwards, to withdraw my request."

"Your request?" Bonnie reacted in surprise. "Why?"

"So much has happened since we last talked, I don't even know where to begin. This situation has become complicated. Very complicated," he confessed without elaborating or revealing his thoughts, certainly not related to his paranormal encounters. "What I can disclose is, Farley's case has risen a notch. It's turned much more problematic than any of us could have imagined."

"That's an interesting comment," she remarked. "I won't ask, since apparently Scott has a bee in his bonnet regarding my involvement. However, I have something to show you that you'll find of interest, I believe. A full-page ad. Do you want to see it? Maybe not connected to your inquiry, but it caused me to pause. Please, sit down," she said pointing to the chair across from her. "Take a load off. And for goodness' sake, stop pacing."

Bonnie pursed her lips, and with her fingers clasped, she suggested. "Just the way it reads seemed relevant. You'll see what I mean." She handed over the piece of paper she'd been holding since Clint first entered the library. "Here. Have a look."

Clint sipped water as he scanned the page, but immediately stopped, his brow wrinkling.

Just as Bonnie had anticipated, the first thing that grabbed Clint's attention on the full-page ad was the words, missing person. Contact

Dorian and Jessica Andersen was the plea. If anyone has information regarding the whereabouts of Thaddeus Aaren Andersen, please reach out. Thaddeus was last seen on December 21, 2004. Three quarters down, in smaller print, it read: Thaddeus failed to show for the Andersen Christmas gathering and on New Year's Day. Please contact Dorian Andersen. His phone number and email address were listed. The newspaper was dated, Friday, January 2, 2005.

Holding his hand up for Bonnie not to speak, Clint moved out into the hall, leaving the shocked librarian sitting at her desk.

This is the man I saw killed in the alley. Thaddeus Aaren Andersen is that guy. The missing man? Clint sat down on the nearest chair, too fast not to be noticed.

Bonnie sprung to her feet. "Are you alright? Do you want me to call 911?"

"No, please give me a second. Nothing is wrong, I can assure you," Clint said decisively.

She put her hand on his forehead, and then walked to her desk and sat down, awaiting Clint's return and an explanation for his bizarre behavior.

"I have a favor to ask," Clint reluctantly said, aware that was the last thing on earth Scott would want him to do.

"Sure, what?" She hesitated. "But before that, would you like to tell me what just happened? And don't tell me *nothing* because I know better." Bonnie's body was resolute, expecting a truthful response.

He glanced up toward the windows, not certain how to put into words what had transpired seconds before. What he had seen or knew. "You remember in 2003, and the things that occurred that were out of the ordinary. Without explanation then, and to this day."

With a nod of her head, Bonnie acknowledged what didn't need said. Jules had summarized events that had taken place at the bookstore on Grandview, the one that didn't exist, although Clint had spoken with the owner and visited the store multiple times. Through the grapevine, she had heard about an eerie presence that facilitated Clint's final discovery of the Reno Gang's hidden treasure.

"You and Jules exchange personal information occasionally. I don't know how much she has shared with you in respect to Rod

Radcliff, Sr. and why his name graces my two buildings, but I suspect enough to recall he's the man my whole life revolves around. You know the story of Rod's General Store and the man's tragic end, but his story doesn't stop there."

"Yeah, it would be tough to live around here and not be aware of Rod Radcliff, Sr." Bonnie studied Clint's face and knew something profound had taken place. "I respect your privacy and the background of the events two years ago."

"Thank you. Trust me when I tell you, I'm not the same guy who moved into Salzburg in 1997 with Elise, my wife who passed away that same year." Clint made an almost imperceptible distraught sound. "She died the same month to be exact."

"I remember Elise," Bonnie said displaying her regret, thinking how pretty and friendly Elise had been when she visited South Creek Assembly of God for the first time, drinking coffee, having dessert after the service, and going around introducing herself. "She came to our church a couple of times. Clint, she was a lovely human being."

Looking deeply into Clint's eyes, Bonnie stated, "I was at her funeral. The way things turned out was truly heartbreaking. Elise was so excited about living in these parts, away from the busyness of I-65 and Seymour. Coming here... then to have died, was tragic. Lilacs were in bloom, that day, I remember. Their fragrance carried through the breeze. They smelled so sweet."

Clint's face turned grave. "Elise was special. She had a beautiful spirit," Clint replied painfully. "Neither one of us could have seen it coming. That she had one foot in the grave when we got here." He swallowed hard. "Life without her was unimaginable after so many years. I dreaded waking up. Thank goodness I had people around me who cared." A peaceful smile appeared. "People from the church dropped meals off for nearly six months. You were probably one of them."

Grateful for how life resumed, and the realization he was supposed to live in Salzburg, he admitted, "Jules saved me, brought me to my senses. I know in my heart; Elise would have given us her blessing. As I would have her if the situation had been reversed."

His face brightened into a sarcastic grin. "Back then, I was so opinionated. Science was my only avenue to what made the universe function. God, a supreme presence, or anything otherworldly? That was poppycock, myth, and fanciful thinking. You know the type." He smiled and she returned the favor. "The start of my transformation, oddly enough, was my fear that Elise was haunting our place. I couldn't explain what I was experiencing through normal outlets. And did my best to deny anything happening as paranormal, but it was."

"Really?" Bonnie leaned back with a surprised expression. "You came to your senses, I suspect."

"Yeah, that other me is long gone. The best part? No longer do I pretend to know anything about anything. I've had my feet put to the fire more than once."

He shook his head. "Suffice it to say, incomprehensible clarity, the same as in 2003 that led me to the treasure, is still alive and well. I don't want to go into it, but what's been happening lately is undeniably more obvious than back then. Tangible, even. Unquestionably transparent."

Holding a tight fist, he exclaimed, "You'll have to take my word for that. You should know, though, the ad you showed me? I believe the fact you saw it in the first place means it has similar threads, just like back then. It's part of a larger picture."

Her eyes grew large, not certain how to respond to his exact meaning. Thinking how fortuitous she was to have stumbled across it, she replied, "I'm glad to be of assistance. I want this situation resolved as much as you. Farley is a super nice guy," her eyes narrowed, "and, he's not at peace. I can tell. You can see it in his eyes."

"I couldn't agree more. That's why I need to get to the bottom of this affair. And I will. That's a promise to all of us who care about him."

Chapter 28
An Unlikely Coincidence

"Looks like we're in luck," declared Scott on the phone. "Are you available tomorrow? If so, I thought driving to Louisville was a good idea. I've taken Tuesday off."

"Certainly," agreed Clint with a ripple of excitement. "Where exactly are we going?"

"To meet David Dunn, Charles Hill's executor, at eleven. We'll grab a Starbucks on the way. I'd like to pick his brains and find out what he knows, plus take a look at Charlie's personal effects."

Clint was ecstatic. "I'm glad. It would appear something he had possession of caused his death. I'd like to find out what that was."

"*We* need to know what that was." Scott corrected his friend in an instant.

"Yeah, right. Sorry. This case is a joint effort." Clint recollected his and Bonnie's conversation. More than you know, Scott.

He felt like he had fallen into a rabbit hole with limitations on how much he could divulge, and to whom he could say it. Jules, Bonnie, Farley, Scott, all had Farley's best interest at heart. However, Scott wanted to close the loop, and keep the rest of the players out.

"I'll pick you up at nine," Scott interjected, breaking into Clint's ponderings. "Hopefully, we'll walk away with more ammunition than we have now. Clear a few things up."

"I'll be ready and waiting," stated Clint aware he had an additional piece of information Scott would find noteworthy. After he hung up, he dialed Farley and asked him to an early lunch. Checking in, every other week had been effortless and enjoyable. Until Farley was out of danger that was the plan. Clint was pleased they had struck up a friendship.

His typical detour to the orphanage would happen prior to his lunch. Clint relished early morning hours, even in the winter. With a bright blue sky overhead and tunes blasting, he headed that way. Driving down the long private road, Clint noticed children playing out back, running like they might be playing tag. Joseph and Josephine were among them. He waved as he stepped out of the truck.

When he walked into the lobby, he was disappointed to see Casey sitting in the corner, alone. He went over to join him. "Hey, why aren't you outside with the other kids? I bet they're having fun."

Casey didn't answer.

Clint spotted the paper on the table, full of mathematical equations. He was thrown off guard, but not shocked by what he saw. "What's this?"

Casey didn't answer.

"May I?" asked Clint.

Casey's eyes drifted upward.

Clint took that as a "Yes."

Holding the paper, he saw equations up one side and down the other. Clint was confused. "Where did you get this, Casey?"

No answer. Casey got up and moved away.

"I'm sorry, Casey, please don't go," he petitioned in earnest. "I'd really like to sit with you. I won't talk. I'll seal my lips and throw away the key, promise."

Stopping midstream, Casey stared ahead. He turned around, coming back. He sat down a distance from Clint and put the paper back inside the table, slipping it into the bottom of the pad. He replaced what had been a page of equations with a blank sheet and then pulled another sheet of paper out from a stack on his left.

Glancing down, Clint said, "Is this for me?" his eyes bright.

Casey offered a slight nod. His answer.

A new drawing lay faceup. A steam engine, weather-beaten, rusted, doomed to be scrapped. Only that wasn't the procedure for extinct railroads, locomotives, and cars these days. Clint was aware first- and second-generation locomotives and abandoned cars littered the entire United States, coast to coast. Stationary, on rails equally lost in time, Casey had drawn a picture of one of them.

Blown away, wondering how Casey could know so much about derelict trainyards, he asked, after promising not to speak. "Casey,

I'm so surprised with this picture. Where did you get the idea for this image?"

Sunlight filled the room, but Clint recognized darkness cross Casey's face. Waylaid by Casey's answer, Clint was taken aback.

"S-a-w it," Casey replied, fixated on Clint's bruise.

With the ice broken, Clint reacted to Casey's revelation. He had learned if he could get Casey to focus, they could manage an abbreviated chat. "You did? Wow, how lucky for you. You did a superior job of replicating what you saw."

"For y-ou."

"Me? Whoa, I didn't expect that. Thank you."

Casey frowned like he was disturbed with the conversation. "S-uppos-ed to be yo-u-rs."

Clint was thunderstruck. "Casey, wait a minute. Did someone ask you to draw it for me?

Without responding, Casey stood and walked away, this time for good.

As he disappeared up the side stairs, Clint watched in awe. He gazed at the image… an expert rendition of what had once been a grand L&N locomotive. He carried the drawing to the receptionist desk and reached in for an oversized envelope, glad no one was there.

On the fifth floor he punched in 7387, hastened up the winding staircase and entered his private office. Sitting down behind the desk he stared at the antique mirror and picked up his phone.

"Farley, it's Clint," he said, leaning back in the chair. "I'm ready to head to Josie's if you are."

Farley's response was chirper. "How about you come here. I just took out a batch of cinnamon rolls. I can whip up a few eggs. Coffee is already made. Didn't think you'd mind."

"That sounds terrific. Thank you. I'd rather sit at your place any day than eat in town," chuckled Clint. "What time? I'm at the orphanage right now. I could be there in fifteen minutes or so."

"I'm buttering the rolls. Need to ice them, but that should be perfect timing."

"Great, I'll see you in a few." Clint hung up the phone, the picture of the locomotive at his fingertips. Did he dare hang it on the wall next to Casey's other drawings. This one unframed?

Feeling a little bamboozled, he did not fully grasp his and Casey's conversation. Rarely did their interactions make sense but this one was particularly awkward. He got the distinct impression the drawing was meant for him specifically. In fact, now that he thought about it, Casey appeared to be waiting on him.

He shook off the feeling. *Poor Casey, always living inside his head.* Opening the drawer, Clint slid the picture inside for safekeeping, patting it gently before putting it in the top drawer.

Glancing out the window at the grounds, his last visit came to mind. He turned to the mirror and wondered if what he thought happened really did.

Clint touched the bump over his eye. It hurt more today than it did last Saturday. It had turned black and blue and was now an ugly shade of yellow. He had noticed Casey staring at it and wondered what the boy was thinking, but he knew those thoughts were trapped in Casey's head, only for him to know.

Glad to get out of there, he looked forward to sitting with Farley, enjoying a pleasant chat. He got in his truck and headed to Farley's.

Clint knocked and waited for a response.

"Knock it off! Cocoa, go upstairs." Winston wasn't named. The door opened.

"Sorry about that," Farley apologized. "Those dogs need chill-pills."

"It doesn't bother me. One of these days, I predict Cocoa and I will be best buddies!" Clint jested.

"I won't hold my breath," laughed Farley. "Please, come on in. The rolls are on the table, along with the coffee. I was waiting for you to arrive before I made the eggs. I had some Canadian bacon, so I fried up a few slices."

"What a pleasant surprise. I didn't think I was hungry until you mentioned the cinnamon rolls, but I am now." Clint patted Farley on the back, glad to see him. "I've been wondering how you are doing and thought we could spend a few minutes together. This worked out great. I love your place. It's very comfortable." Clint observed the beautiful windows that covered the wall, letting a generous amount of sunshine through.

"Thanks, I'd rather be here too. I don't go out that much. I'm a home body, always was, but I think I mentioned that before."

"Yeah, we both are, my friend."

Clint sat down at the table while Farley busied himself.

"How do you like your eggs?"

"Over easy if you know how. I don't. That's why I go to Josie's."

"No problem, that's my preferred choice of eggs. How many would you like? I usually fix three," Farley grinned as though three was an indulgent amount.

"Me too. If you'll excuse me… may I use your restroom, while you're frying up the eggs?"

"Sure, you know where it is. Don't let Cocoa ambush you."

Clint stood, grinning comically. "I'll do my best."

Moving through the living room, he took a quick glance around the charming, spacious cabin. The room was full of light and felt wonderfully alive. He took in the lady's portrait he'd seen on the previous visit, her eyes following him just as before. Then, as he rounded the corner on the way to the restroom, he noticed an unfamiliar drawing on the side table next to Farley's easy chair and backtracked. It was a close facsimile to Casey's L&N locomotive. Slightly different, but pretty much the same image. He couldn't believe his eyes.

"Ready whenever you are," he heard Farley call from the kitchen.

"I'm on my way," he said, rushing to the restroom, "two seconds."

Back in the kitchen, eating his eggs and thinking about the picture, he said. "Those eggs are cooked to perfection."

"I'm a decent cook, not a great one, but good enough. I love eggs," he smiled. But then noticed the strange look on Clint's face. "Wouldn't you agree?"

"Yeah," he replied, not adding anything more, as Farley would have expected.

"You alright?"

"Sure, why?" Clint answered, realizing he was distracted. "I didn't mean to be nosey, but I took a quick peek at that beautiful woman you painted, and I saw the locomotive sketch lying next to your chair."

"Oh?" Farley's face lit up, surprised Clint had seen his newest artwork. Not yet complete but well on its way.

"That's amazingly authentic. Congrats on nailing down the essence of a disgraced beauty. The most innovated technology of yesteryear has been put out to pasture. Literally covered in weeds and overgrowth, eroding, disregarded chunks of junk."

Surprised Clint had found what he had drawn the night before so appealing, Farley replied with a bit of awe. "You like it? I have no idea why I created it, other than I couldn't get the thing out of my head, so I gave up and worked on it."

"It's a stunning depiction. It felt like it might jump off the canvas."

"I knew I had to finish it before I turned in. Otherwise, I'd lie in bed thinking about it until I got up and did. I added more detail and shading this morning."

Clint, who had been thinking about Casey while Farley explained how creating the L&N locomotive came about, said, "It's unusual. That's for sure. Not something you see every day. For your information, I have always loved trains. They bring back childhood memories."

A pleasant smile graced Farley's lips, but behind that smile was a haunted expression Clint recognized. He wondered if Charlie, in the dark recesses of Farley's mind, had stirred.

For Casey and Farley to draw the same picture must hold meaning. One more clue in a list of many, thought Clint, knowing how unlikely it was to see this image twice in one day.

"Farley, I've been wondered about the voice. Are you still hearing it? Last time I asked you said it had pretty much stopped."

Farley thought a moment before answering. He took a sip of coffee and replied, "Not as a voice, per say. But certainly, as a direct influence in painting specific scenes. Like the locomotive, for instance. It felt urgent I get it drawn before the sun crest this morning. Why? I couldn't tell you, but I did. It was though some other person drew it, not me." He looked to the side. "I've grown used to impressions. Thoughts and images, coming and going like Grand Central Station."

"Have you ever painted or etched a train?"

Farley pulled back, puzzlement showing on his face. "Strange you would bring that up. I was thinking about that this morning when it was complete. How unusual to paint a train, a very specific L&N locomotive. I admit, it was fun to draw, but to answer your question… no, never. It's my first."

He leaned forward. "Would you like it? It's not like I don't have enough artwork around here." He glanced toward the stairs. "This place is full to the brim. Soon, I'll have to get a storage locker. Besides, I can draw another. I have a clear image of it in my head."

"Yes, that would be fantastic. I'm very fond of train scenes. Thank you." Clint now had two of the same drawing.

Chapter 29
Confession

Clint thought long and hard about what he was about to do, drive to Louisville on Monday while Jules was at work, the day before he and Scott were to drive over for a meeting with David Dunn, executor of the Hill's estate.

Were there risks involved? He knew there were, with the situation growing more complex by the hour. The purpose of driving there was a friendly chat with Mark Carlson. He'd be working from ten to four. The likelihood that Mark would have seen the toothpick before was next to nil, but Clint figured it was worth the trip.

He glanced at the drawing Farley had given him, a near duplicate of Casey's. A clue. Granted, one that made no sense. Not yet, but he felt confident, in time, it would.

 Crossing the Sherman Minton Bridge, he called Jules to let her know he'd be home close to six o'clock, or thereabouts. She was at Josie's Diner, and he knew she'd be late, which afforded Clint ample time to converse with Carlson and be home before his wife.

Clint turned his truck onto the narrow road where Bean's a Brewin' was located. Like the last time, few cars lined the street. Cloudy skies rolled overhead, blocking any light from entering the tight space between buildings. Although his phone indicated the hour to be 12:47 p.m., the shop showed little activity. Not nearly as packed as he would have imagined for a work week lunch hour.

When the door opened, Mark acknowledged Clint's arrival, turning to the barista beside him to ask her to mind the store. "Glad you had time to drop back by," Mark said cheerfully, holding two cups of brew. He placed them on the table and sat down. "I didn't expect to see you this soon. Yours is a friendly face."

"A small window opened, so I jumped through," replied Clint with a grin, truly happy to see Mark. "We seemed to have hit it off last time." Looking at the Columbian dark roast Mark had graciously presented him, Clint said, "Nothing like a good cup of coffee between friends. How long is your break?"

"As long as I'd like." Mark beamed, "I'm the owner."

"So you are," chuckled Clint, thinking he really liked this guy. They had much in common, both were direct, which made it easier to speak candidly. "I mentioned when I was here last that I wasn't completely honest about how I ended up at your shop. I'd like to explain. I've been looking into Charles Hill's murder. An amateur sleuth, yes, but I know someone in Salzburg who is aware of my movements and supports me."

"So, you were looking for information and thought I might be of help?"

"No, not really, our meeting was happenchance. A nurse on duty at the hospital that night told me Ann worked here. Getting the lay of the land was my intention. Since then, a lot has changed. I know more than I did the day you and I met."

Tilting his head, Mark stated, "No matter the reason, I'm glad you stopped in; hopefully, I was able to shed some light on the matter." His face turned comical, "I was an open book that day. Everything I know about that incident, you know."

Clint reached into his pocket, putting the black pouch with A.A.D on the table, withdrawing the toothpick, he asked, "Ever see this before?"

Mark frowned, "No, should I have?"

"Not really. I think it belongs to the man who paid you a visit." Clint thought back on his discovery, and said, "Just trying to put two and two together, is all. I'm wondering if the man who threatened you, lives around here. Where I found this," he pointed to the toothpick, "is the same alley where Charlie witnessed the first murder. That's my belief, anyway, because he came here to call in the incident."

Mark rubbed his chin. "I wish I could help. No one wants this guy off the streets more than I do. I was here when the police went with Charlie to what he thought was a crime scene. All three men came back frustrated, throwing accusations around right and left."

"I think I'm going to walk this area. The alley can't be too far away. How long were they gone? From the time Charlie and the police met up and then returned, do you think? Approximately?"

Considering the question for a moment, Mark answered, "I'd say ten minutes. Not long. Fifteen max."

"Then it is close. Wouldn't you agree?"

"Yes, now that I think about it," Mark concurred, "that day I never gave it much mind since a body wasn't recovered. There's an alley, about a half block south of here, on the left. The only other possibility is closer to Washington Street, north of here. If I were you, I'd head south."

Clint became absorbed in thought. "Please keep our interactions between us," he requested. "I've been turning over rocks, and who knows what will jump out. The less you know the better. I owed you an explanation, and I've given it. If anything more arises, I promise to keep you informed."

"Thank you," Mark replied gratefully. "Every day when I wake up, I wonder if this clown is going to get trigger happy again." His expression turned solemn. "There is trauma associated with the aftermath of what happened. This guy could decide I'm a liability and stage another random shooting."

Clint realized how tense Mark was, and stated, "Look, I have insider information that I can't share, but rest assured we will find this guy."

"I'm not asking you to disclose contacts or information, but you should know, around here, you'd better be extra careful. Louisville is not Salzburg. This is the big league."

"I know, and I will," replied Clint with conviction. Standing, he extended a handshake. "Better be getting along. Take care, my friend." Clint's words cemented an idea he planned to entertain.

Mark watched him leave the building, feeling worried about the danger Clint could be putting himself into. Probing the back streets of downtown Louisville and asking questions about a closed murder case, could turn deadly.

Crossing the street, heading south on the broken sidewalk, Clint shaped his next move. From the truck, he grabbed the Gambler cowboy hat he'd brought, complementing his boots and duster. The disguise would conceal his identity.

Finding the alley was the priority. Once he found that—a baseline—he'd look for where the two men he'd seen while in the mirror might have been beforehand. One thing Clint was positive of is they were raging mad, deducing the argument probably started elsewhere and continued in the alley.

Another thought occurred to him. The object that was given to Charlie was a huge part of what went down, spawning the fight, possibly. *Why would one man kill another unless whatever that thing was held massive importance*, questioned Clint. "Thaddeus Aaren Andersen," whispered Clint. "Who are you? And what did you do that made your attacker so angry?"

Searching every nook and cranny of the long, dark, narrow street, Clint finally saw what Mark had described, a side road too narrow to be a main access road. Carefully he approached, looking in all directions before moving forward. Clint wasn't one to coward away from a situation, especially when he was certain he was on the right track.

Slowly, and cautiously, Clint moved deeper into the alley, immediately recognizing it as the one he'd seen last Saturday from inside of the mirror. I was here! This is it, right over there is where I stood.

Step by step, he strolled, cautiously searching the ground for more possible clues, while attuned to the slightest sound or movement. Every single cell in his body was on high alert. He walked over to where he'd found the toothpick and bent down.

Where did the velvet bag come from? he questioned. *How did it land on my office floor, with the toothpick inside when it had been in my shirt pocket?* While pondering that thought, he concluded it wouldn't be the first time he had been supplied evidence out of the clear blue. *I need to cut through the madness and connect the bits and pieces that make up the primary points. Patience is a valuable tool. One I'll have to work on.*

Clint's boots clicked against the pavement as he made his way to the other end of the alley. When he reached the corner, he turned left. A blinking neon sign came into view, Cell Block #49, a hole in the wall tavern. Just the sort of place A.A.D and Thaddeus might have been before their disagreement reached its boiling point. Then continued it outdoors in the alley, Clint presumed.

He checked his watch. *Plenty of time before I have to head back,* he assured himself. The time was 1:37 p.m., and hours of daylight remained, although not in the alley where he had been. There, it was dark, damp, and possessing a sinister vibe.

Clint peered through the grime of the dingy bar. Cell Block #49 had few customers. Most sat at the bar stools, their images reflecting in the mirror behind the bartender that showcased high-end liquor bottles.

He reached down to silence his cell phone, making certain it wouldn't ring unexpectedly. Last thing he needed was to draw unwanted attention. Clint would pretend he was passing through town, looking for a nearby watering hole before heading out to some other unknown destination, keeping up with an urban cowboy mentality. A shot or two in the late afternoon before headin' home to the little lady. Staying in character, he walked in, strolling over to the bar to order a drink.

"Do y'all serve Knob Creek?" he inquired. "Figured you might since it's a Kentucky bourbon. Got a hankering for that one. If not, I'll take three fingers of Jack, straight up, no ice."

"Yeah, we've got Knob Creek, if that's what ya want," said a voice, the owner of it, blue-eyed and donning false lashes with bright red pouty lips. Her dark hair flung around her shoulders as she turned to grab the Knob Creek bottle from the shelf, her lithe body swinging back to pour Clint his drink.

"That's ordered most often. When bourbon is requested," she claimed, "Has a smoothness other bourbons don't have, I'm told. Don't touch the stuff, myself. I'm a Disaronno Amaretto and coke kind of gal. Or Frangelico in coffee mixed with Bailey's. Where you from, cowboy?"

What have I got myself into? wondered Clint knowing he wasn't going to drink bourbon or any other type of hard liquor, let alone engage in conversation with a bar maid. She'd called him *cowboy!* For a moment Clint had forgotten how he was dressed.

"We serve good grub, if er' hungry," she was saying. "Steak, potatoes, nachos, finger food, that sort of thing. Nuttin' upscale but better than those fine restaurants that charge an arm and a leg for their fancy surroundings."

"Nah, nothing, thanks. Just a quick stop before leaving town." He picked up his drink and walked over to a table nearest the door, sat down, and wondered what he was going to do for an encore.

For reasons, he'd never fully understand, Clint took the black velvet bag from his pocket and set it beside his glass, pushing it from side to side, observing the weight of it. Full of curiosity, he crossed his long legs and tipped his hat to cover his eyes, planning to leave. He had come in to decide if this might be where Thaddeus spent his final hour. In his peripheral vision, he saw the black-haired beauty leaning against the bar, freeze, her eyes zeroed in on the bag.

I oughta be horsewhipped, complained Clint. *She recognizes it.*

Chapter 30
Truth Be Told

Cookie walked up, pulled out a chair, sat down, and stared long and hard at Clint. "Who are you?" Her eyes narrowed. "Really?"

Clint didn't reply right away, not sure how to respond without trapping himself. His stupidity had blown his cover. All the cowboy words in the world, like *vittles or heading out of town* were not going to get him out of this one. His compulsion to take another look at the contents of the black velvet bag, not considering this wasn't the place to do that, had superseded his good judgment.

Feeling upset with himself, he realized, more than ever, he was out of his league. An amateur trying to support a friend, not a legitimate private eye. It could not have been more obvious than at that moment. Aware a real private eye wouldn't have been so careless with evidence from a murder, Clint had a lot to learn if he planned to move forward with his investigative intentions.

"I don't understand," he stated, trying to buy time. "Are you asking my name?"

"You know I'm not," Cookie replied harshly, put off with the cavalier response.

"Where'd you get that?" She tapped the black bag. To drive her point home, she added on, "I know someone who's been looking for it in case you're interested. So, which is it? The truth or do I make a phone call to introduce the two of you?"

Clint's heart hammered, literally feeling like it might pop out of his chest. Caught between a rock and a hard place, did he cough up the truth or lose any ground he'd gained? Why would the powers that lead him to this sleazy tavern set him up? Unless there was something to learn, otherwise he wouldn't be here. Those were his overriding questions when he answered.

"Look, my name is Clint Reeves. Truth is I can't tell you why I came in here, other than I felt compelled to. I was across the way and somehow ended up here." Thinking that was a good start, he waited for her to respond.

"Good to meet you Mr. Reeves. I'm Cookie Crenna." Her lips curled and eyes sparkled, unaffected by his elusive reply. "As in Richard Crenna, the movie star. Do you remember him? He was in Body Heat with William Hurt and Kathleen Turner." She scooted closer. "Dreamy lookin' guy, don't ya think? Looks sorta like my Axel." Her smile and eyes softened, and then turned pained. "That was silly of me."

She lifted the bag from the table. Clint made no effort to stop her. "How, may I ask, did you come into possession of this?" She turned the bag over, caressing its soft texture. Then, to his surprise, she said, "It was a gift."

The deep contours around her eyes spoke of despair. "About two years ago. Took three years of squirreling every spare dime I had and a lot of finagling on the side." She winked, as though Clint should know her unspoken meaning.

He was afraid he might and looked away, pretending to take a sip of the single malt he'd been served. He put the glass back on the table, and glanced at the dim tavern, silhouettes of bodies tucked in recesses of every corner. Stalling, he bought enough time to fabricate a reasonable story based in partial truth. "I found it."

Cookie's expression showed her disbelief, prompting Clint to swiftly tag on, "In the alley right around the corner." He liked the way his version of events sounded and ran with it. He turned toward the window. "The one that connects this street to the one my truck is parked. It was wedged in a crevice against the bricks. The streetlight must have caught it just right. An easy thing to spot."

He sensed the enormous attachment Cookie felt toward the piece and gently mentioned, "I was stunned to find something so incredibly beautiful." He pointed to the toothpick she was fondling, as if it belonged to her and not someone else." Clint's mind reeled, fixating on the name Cookie had dropped… *Axel*. The first letter of the initial stitched into the bag. Positive of the connection, with dots connecting, Clint searched for clarity.

"Axel… is that your husband?" he watched her face contort distastefully. "Boyfriend?" he second guessed. Cookie's expression grew even darker, her eyes ablaze. Urging him in a different direction, he guessed again, "Brother, dad?"

Cookie's spine straightened beyond what was natural, annoyed by Clint's questions. "Do you think I'd give something like that to a brother? Seriously?" she huffed, spewing out, "It was a gift to my boyfriend. For his birthday. But he ain't that now!"

"I'm sorry. I didn't mean to offend, but I didn't want to take it for granted that it was for someone that close to your heart." Clint walked a very thin line in the next words he chose. "I was so surprised when I realized what it was. I've never seen anything so utterly intriguing. The bag and the 24K gold toothpick are stunning." Clint took the toothpick back from Cookie, inspecting it as though he'd not seen it before. This was, however, the first time to admire it through another lens.

The bag lay on the table between them, A.A.D. in gold stitching was well-defined. "What do the initials stand for?" Clint asked hastily, hoping to catch Cookie by surprise where she'd answer his question without hesitation. Instead, Cookie buried her head in her hands and began to sob. Clint was stunned, taken by surprise. "I'm so sorry, Cookie, I didn't mean to trespass on private affairs. Please forgive me."

"Are you kidding?" she exclaimed, her voice bitter. "These ain't tender tears." She yanked a towel from her belt and wiped the tears from her cheeks. Then, after a few select curse words aimed at Axel Drako, she spat out, "He's a no-good, two-timing, son of a gun. A waste of a human being. I hate him."

She gasped, delightfully. "At least he gave me my dues. For putting up with him all those years. For wasting my time." Her brows lifted animatedly, and her eyes twinkled. "Coughed up some of that dough he kept flashing around here. Big bucks, I tell you. More than I'd ever see in my lifetime." Her spirit hardened, adding, "So's long as I keep my trap shut, he warned." She studied Clint's handsome face. "You got somebody?"

Again, Clint was taken off guard by her brashness, not used to such straight talk from a lady. "Yes, a wife. Lovely, woman. The love of my life." He knew that sounded over the top but aimed to drive his point home. Clint's smile could melt most any woman's heart when he directed his attention their way. He was genuine, and not in the least bit egotistical, never thinking twice about his rugged looks.

Put a cowboy hat and a pair of boots on him, and Clint Walker, the actor in the TV series, Cheyenne, not Clint Reeves, had walked onto the scene.

"Found a soulmate." Grateful to be able to describe his and Jules's relationship so accurately, he grinned. "I'm the lucky one."

"Figured as much," Cookie whined, flipping her hair over her shoulder to show she was put off by his answer and didn't want to hear anymore. "You don't look like the type of fella girls would leave be. You've got what I call them *bedroom eyes*, just like my Axel and his dad. Men with your looks don't stay on the market long."

Clint realized in that capsulated moment that this woman had the potential of *spilling the beans* if he handled her with kid-gloves. He didn't want to take advantage of her circumstance; however, his need to uncover more information, was at the forefront of his thoughts.

Slowly, without specific tonality, Clint inquired, "What does A.A.D. stand for? Undoubtedly the first initial is for Axel."

Cookie eyed Clint closely, leery of the question.

"Please," holding a hand up, "I don't need to know. Just curious, is all. It's so beautifully scripted. Did you do it yourself?"

Relaxing, she replied, "Nah, I ain't that talented. Certainly not with a needle and thread." She cocked her head in a flirtatious gesture. Seeing Clint had no interest in her antics, she offered, "Axel Alrik Drako. An impressive name, wouldn't you say? For a no-good. Sounds more like a lawyer or politician, I think. All of them is just as bad as he is. Middle name's the same as his grandfather's, Alrik Andersen, or so Axel says."

Not wanting to provoke or shut off the valve of information pouring out, Clint suggested. "Since this gift was so special maybe I could have you return it to Axel, or I could, if you don't mind giving me his address." With knitted brow, he inquired, "Why did he want you not speak to anyone about him? Besides, you are talking to me now, so that request must have passed."

His last remarks raised serious red flags, causing Cookie to spring to her feet. She leaned down, and whispered, "Keep it. He doesn't deserve having anything that nice. And it ain't none of your business, cowboy! You can pay up front or lay a worthy bill on the table for my time."

"Man… that was curt. I'm just carrying on a conversation here. Why bite my head off? You brought it up. Remember?" Clint hoped his strategy worked. Acting insulted. "Look, do you want it? You bought it, so rightfully it's yours."

She squirmed, feeling guilty for her rudeness. "Probably doesn't even know it's missing. What a creep." Cookie took a step forward, easing her rigid stance. "Strange you'd find it in the alley." She thought a moment. "I suppose when he and Thaddeus got into their fight, that's where they ended up. Must have come loose." Cookie wrinkled her nose. "Thaddeus is too good to hang with the likes of Axel. They are like total opposites. Axel was born on the wrong side of the tracks if you ask me."

"Are we still friends?" Clint chuckled, trying to lighten things up.

"Sure," she answered with her hands on her hips. "I've gotta get back to work though. Can't sit around talking or I'll get in trouble. Boss doesn't like it. Been nice talking to ya, I suppose this'll be the last time you'll be coming in." She sighed, sorry to have treated Clint so badly.

"Never know where my wanderings will land me," he said wanting to assure her he wasn't upset or put off. "Like coming in here. It wasn't a planned thing."

She eyed the bag in Clint's hand and his untouched drink. "You didn't finish your drink."

"I know, decided drinking and driving isn't smart."

"I don't want any part of that bag of yours. Thanks for trying to give it to me, but I wouldn't touch it with a ten-foot pole. It's got his cooties on it. Sell it, give it away, I don't care what you do." Cookie grimaced… her eyes distant. "Bonehead! Ran off with his latest floozy, DeArra D'Amelio. Blondie in a box, with her fancy name, and expensive clothes. She stole my man."

Down deep it was obvious Cookie still cared–a whole lot more than she was putting on. But she hated him enough to defy his orders. Telegraphed in her every word, was her deep resentment of

Axel. Cookie had shown affection to the bag and its contents, even cried over it, so Clint had a hard time believing Cookie had moved on, forgiving Axel for dumping her. The cut was fresh.

"I'm sorry for all of this," Clint apologized a second time, "didn't mean to touch on a sore subject, but I'm appreciative to know the history behind the gift you'd given Axel. Makes it more valuable to me if that helps." Wishing to know more, he made a guess. Choosing his words wisely, he speculated, "Thaddeus is a friend, I presume. That must have been awkward for you to see them going at it."

Once again, Cookie vehemently reacted, like Clint should have known the answer to his own question. "Thaddeus Andersen, Axel's cousin. Nice guy. Doesn't come in here... ever, but he did that day and was hot under the collar when he walked through the door. Like a raging bull. Paced around like he was circling Axel's camp. Never did understand what he was furious about, but things ramped up fast."

"That's strange, for cousins. Wouldn't you say?"

"That's true in their case too, normally." Cookie frowned. "Axel raked me over the coals, upset because I told Thaddeus at the market the day before about Axel's new pocket watch and truck. Mentioned them in passing, is all and he'd have to come by. Axel was real proud."

A moment of clarity crossed Clint's mind. Thinking quickly, he stated, "I wonder what was under Thaddeus's claw. What kind of truck? Maybe Thaddeus was jealous."

"Doesn't matter, nothing is worth fighting over like they did. An F-250," she answered finally. "Axel was showing off the pocket watch to someone at the bar, Mr. High and Mighty, when Thaddeus walked in. Guess I shouldn't have said anything. Next thing I knew, Thaddeus was hopping mad. I was surprised when he insisted on seeing the watch. Matter of fact, that's what started the fight. That dumb watch, they were tugging back and forth, and started punching each other. Thaddeus was trying to take it from Axel."

Picturing how the scene must have unfolded, Clint commiserated with Cookie. "You're right, Cookie, nothing is worth feuding over like you described. Thaddeus and Axel must have the same last name. Andersen, you say?" Clint deliberately misled her, remembering

Axel's last name. He wanted it to appear like it wasn't that important to him.

"No, they have different last names, Drako is Axel's," she scowled, unhappy. "I told you that, remember? Axel Alrik Drako…"

"Oh, that's right, how dumb of me." Clint smiled shyly, "Not always quick to remember things I ought. Especially names."

Oscillating from one emotion to the next, she softened again. "Oh, that's alright. Me neither," Cookie replied sweetly. "Not good when you serve people for a living. Anyways, it's Andersen… remember I said Alrik Andersen was Axel's grandfather? Axel's mom's name was Andersen though. Irene Andersen is Dorian Andersen's sister. That's Thaddeus's dad. One big happy family, those guys are."

She shifted her weight. "Everyone, 'cept Axel's pop. He's serving time in Kentucky's state penitentiary. Over in Eddyville for drug dealing. He got a life sentence. Was selling heroin to minors and got caught. Been there since Axel was a little guy. From what Axel told me, Dorian raised him, alongside Thaddeus when Jay Drako was hauled off to prison."

Clint was beside himself. This barmaid was a cornucopia of knowledge, giving him everything he needed to climb several rungs up the ladder of investigating Charlie Hill's death and pointing him in the right direction.

"I wish there was something I could say, or do, to make the situation better, but I know there isn't. I've had my own troubles over the years, and know from personal experience, only time helps." Clint looked at her, understanding how broken she was, and what a rough life she lived. "It'll get better. I promise."

"I suppose. Just a working woman trying to make a buck. That's me," she said flippantly, glancing at the black bag one last time. "I'm so stupid. As soon as he came into some moolah, I was dropped like a hot potato. Then Ms. Goodie Two Shoes starts showing up everywhere he is." Cookie lowered her head, shamefully. "I followed him around for a while. Finally came to my senses. Stooping that low didn't suit me. I know the difference between normal curiosity and being sick in the head with love."

"I'm proud of you. No one is worth groveling over." Clint's last stab for information had him ask, "Axel must have come into an inheritance or something along those lines."

Cookie came up for air. "Heaven's no. Nobody died. Not that I know of, but then again, I can't say for certain. All I can say is he turns up here throwing money around, buying rounds, like he won the Kentucky Derby."

She shrugged and looked over her shoulder at the bartender. "Last time I spent the night with Axel, I saw some remarkable stuff, I can tell you. Axel was in the shower, and I went through his drawers and billfold. You are not going to believe this, but he had gold and silver coins and $1000 dollar bills, plus a bunch of $500's, along with wads of $100s.

I was in the bedroom when he walked out of the shower. He slapped me and told me to get out." Cookie's expression was one of defiance. "He has a place under the basement where he keeps stuff. I bet it's all in there."

Cookie's latest revelation was too much to hope for. "Is that right," Clint replied, trying not to overreact.

"Yeah, he's a rich man, now. That's why he started courting blondie, she's a rich man's lady. It's why she clings to his arm like gluc. He's been buying her expensive jewelry and taking her on lavish trips. Don't know where his loot came from, but you can bet on one thing, it's most likely stolen. There ain't an honest bone in Axel's body. That's why he warned me not to discuss what I knew with anyone. But I'm not worried about you, you have an honest face. Besides, I don't care anymore. If he gets angry, so be it."

Chapter 31
Ante Up'd

Looking out the bar's window, Clint sat staring into an empty street. Although he couldn't see the sun, he imagined it sinking in the west, casting long shadows over the land. The clouds of earlier had drifted north and the time had come to head home. Later he'd decide what to say, and to whom.

Feeling numb from the load of facts Cookie had unloaded, Clint wondered if he had the courage to follow wherever this new information took him. Whose paths would he cross? How dangerous would it get before a charge of murder could happen? Not having ever done anything of this magnitude before, he felt nervous at the prospects.

Sure, he'd gotten up to his eyeballs in the Rod Radcliff, Sr. affair, a cold case murder, and had explored Goss Cave to resolve fifty-year-old crimes, but this situation was different. It was a modern-day murder with the killer still running loose–Axel Alrik Drako, the son of a hardened criminal serving time in the Kentucky State Penitentiary.

Doubt washed over Clint. He questioned why he had been chosen, a regular guy with no special skillsets to qualify him for this task. Yet, his fallback position reverted to Picasso's involvement. He slipped his leather duster on, laid two twenties down, pushed his chair under the table, and walked out into the bitter cold of midday December, numb from information overload.

On his way home the tires hummed against the pavement. With the droning sound came the thought Cookie had no idea what she was up against. Axel's threats were genuine. With all her tough talk, she wasn't aware that her ex-boyfriend was a killer and would, in an instant, shut her up permanently if she started blabbing her grievances to every Tom, Dick and Harry who walked into Cell Block #49.

A sudden urge to expedite closure into the Hills' murder felt urgent. If he didn't move with purpose, more people could die, on the heels of Ann and Charles Hill, and Thaddeus Andersen, if he mistakenly lowered his defenses. Clint had drawn others into this affair; Mark, Bonnie, Farley, Cookie, and even Scott Edwards. A rush of fear blindsided him... Jules too. A consequence of Axel catching wind Clint was on his trail, could strike out where it hurt the most.

When he left Cell Block #49, Clint saw suspicious shadows falling behind his footsteps through the alley, and to his parked truck. He had passed it off as a case of jitters, but now he wasn't so certain. He wondered if it was true, and he had been followed.

Paces, matching his, echoed on the street. The shops on the opposite end of the alley, where Beans a' Brewin' was located, were dark. Few lamps flickered light onto the pavement making it hard to see any real distance when he concentrated on the bare street. He was convinced an object in the dark moved suddenly across the road, vanishing into thin air. He had hastened to his truck. He saw Mark Carlson behind the emblemed glass door, closing-up shop.

In his current state of mind, how could he be certain of anything. He was jumpy, and his nerves were on edge when he crossed the river over the Indiana state line, Salzburg less than thirty minutes away. With any luck he'd be back to his place before Jules. It would be close, but he felt certain he'd make it in time to start supper. Preparing dinner for the two of them would help get his mind off the visit to Louisville and the discoveries it had unearthed.

His mind rambled when he pulled into the drive. He got out and walked inside, questions darting in and out of his mind. He'd never seen himself as a bellwether, taking the lead in anything as off the wall as this, yet here he was, hunting down a killer and trying to link him to a crime, and the assassinations he had so coldly executed. Clint's only prayer was he'd find Axel before Axel found him.

I have to live in the moment, or I won't have moments to live. Follow this through and be extremely cautious. Others could get caught in the crossfire, not just me. Shivering under the throes of acceptance, Clint said aloud, "I'm one hundred percent in!"

While behind the wheel of his truck, heading home, he had decided to send money to Cookie. Clint felt extraordinarily grateful for the help she had provided, supplying him with ample ammunition to blow this case wide open. He owed her, it was the right thing to do. He thought about hiring a courier to deliver an anonymous envelope of cash to Cell Block #49, certified, Cookie's signature required.

Headlights flashed against the kitchen wall; Jules was home. Clint had baked potatoes in the microwave for quick cooking and had pork chops frying in the pan.

"Honey's home," Jules called out from the foyer. "Your better half is hungry."

Clint felt grateful to hear his wife's sweet voice, as opposed to the gruff tone of Cookie Crenna's. It was a stark difference when two worlds collided, one innocent and inspiring, the other worldly and seasoned. He walked over and hugged her. "I'm glad you're home. I missed you."

"It's nice to be missed, thank you very much," she cooed with delight, knowing she was loved. "I smell like French fries and the grease I spilled on the floor. What a mess. I changed out the fryer and goofed up, dropped the basket and fries went everywhere. Just as I was getting ready to leave too, cost me a good forty-five minutes." Her face was full of humor. "What a dunce."

"Didn't Patrick help?"

"Oh, he left early. There were only three of us there. No big deal, but that's why I'm running behind. I'll be working again tomorrow, but that's okay. I enjoy the holiday festivities. Thanks for getting things started! Nice boots!" she said, pleased to see Clint wearing his leather boots instead of his normal everyday sneakers.

Jules went down the hall, talking the whole while. When she returned, she was fresh and in lounge pajamas, ready to wind out today's clock beside her husband along with a bit of television. She chatted about her day, before asking him about his.

Clint had been setting the table when she sat down. He added little to their conversation, mostly listening to Jules go on and on about this customer and that. Occasionally he inserted a comment to show he was fully engaged, but he wasn't. His mind kept drifting back to the alley and Cookie Crenna. Was his imagination playing tricks on him, wired after conversing with Cookie, or was someone really tailing him when he walked out of the tavern.

Deep in his core Clint believed somehow Rod Radcliff, Sr. had awakened a sixth sense in his energy field. A connection, that before they met, was not there. Not existing in his everyday life, prior to April 2003, but then again, when his thoughts digressed back to 1997, it distinctly aroused a memory associated with Elise's funeral. A feeling he was not alone after everyone departed the service when he stayed late into the night at the gravesite.

Clint remembered sitting on the ground, close to her coffin, unable to bring himself to leave. A feeling came over him that was tangible, a sensation Clint could never forget. Back then he decided it was due to the heavy stress he'd been under. He determined on his way home that night, that her spirit had been with him.

However, after that, nothing was ever the same. Strange occurrences started happening right away, and on a regular basis. Now Clint wondered about her graveside service and who had truly been there with him. Signs pointed to Rod Radcliff, and not Elise. Since then, Rod had a huge influence on Clint.

Clint decided he needed to tell Scott what he had learned and bring him up to speed. He would share the missing person's classified ad dated January 2 of this year and all of Cookie's conversation.

Tuesday, November 29

Overcast skies ushered in temperatures just above freezing on Tuesday morning. Sitting in his Ford Interceptor, Scott waited for Clint to lock up. Two black coffees sat in the cup holders, steam curling into the warm blowing air from the fan.

"Mornin'," Clint greeted Scott when he got into the car.

"Is Jules working today? Saw you lock the house up."

"I always lock the house when she's sleeping, or home alone when I leave. Can't be too careful." Truth was Clint had become extremely paranoid and was taking more precautions than usual. So far no one had paid much attention to his change of habits.

"Being in law enforcement, I agree. Especially these days. Err on the side of caution."

On the way to their appointment, the two men went over the latest developments. Clint filled Scott in on Cookie Crenna's revelations, causing Scott to literally drop his jaw. The missing person's report brought up another line of inquiry Scott would explore later.

All three lanes of the highway were jammed going into Louisville with the residual of eight o'clock rush-hour traffic. Fortunately, Scott knew exactly where he was going and turned off at an exit Clint was unfamiliar with. Dunn and Murphy Law Offices, located downtown on Liberty and Third Street, wasn't far. Having been there before, Scott made a few maneuvers and quickly parked below ground using his credentials to bypass the attendant.

They took the unground elevator up to the second floor, suite 204. Awaiting their appointment, the two men chatted only a short while before David Dunn walked into the lobby to greet them.

A fair-haired, blue-eyed middle-aged gentleman with a deep tan stepped into the room. Wearing cordovan leather wing tip shoes and a navy pinstriped suit, Dunn extended a cordial welcome. "Hello gentlemen. I'm David Dunn."

Scott was the first to respond. Dressed in police uniform, he was aware of the response his attire drew. "Captain Scott Edwards." Turning to Clint, he said, "And this is Clint Reeves."

The three men shook hands, and then advanced down Carpathian paneled walls, and the plush carpeted hallway to a door that donned David R. Dunn, Attorney at Law, Esq. etched on a frosted pane. They walked into a rich man's office.

"Please have a seat," David said, his finger on a button, ready to alert his assistant. "Can I offer you anything, a soft drink, coffee, water?"

"No, thank you," replied Clint, his eyes sweeping the room.

Dunn sat patiently behind his desk with his hands folded waiting for one of the visitors to state their business.

"We're here on behalf of Charles Hill, and his wife, Ann Hill," informed Scott. "On December 21, 2004, they were murdered. Their personal effects are why I called." Scott, glanced at Clint as if to say subliminally, *at your request*. "We'd like to see them. We understand you handled their affairs, as executor."

"That's right. The Hills are…" he wavered, restating what he'd said. "*Were* my clients. By law their personal belongings are kept at this law firm until their release. They are dispersed accordingly to those named in the Will. What isn't taken possession of is turned over to the state."

Dunn looked off to the side, and then back at Scott. "I suppose I should mention their Will wasn't extensive. Not much of value." Dunn didn't elaborate. "An itemized receipt is in the file, listing what was on the couple when they were admitted to the hospital. Grayson, I believe. Ann was already dead, and they thought they got a heartbeat on Charlie and rushed him to surgery. He died in minutes."

Scott studied Dunn's body language and determined he was open to having an honest dialogue. "Look, I don't have a court order, but I can get one if you wish. You obviously remember the couple well. When they brought Charles to the hospital, he had something on him that could lead to finding his killer. That's why we are here. When I went over the documents from that night, it showed you signed for those items. I'd like to have a look at the receipt."

Dunn leaned back in his chair with puzzlement written on his face. "What are you expecting to find? Maybe I can help you right here and now. I'm not far from wrapping up their affairs. Most everything is done."

"That would be greatly appreciated," replied Clint honestly, a hint of excitement in his voice. "I have several questions about the Hills, but two need direct answering. Most importantly, was there a watch among his things?"

He noted a glint in Dunn's eyes when Clint suggested, "Not just any watch, a pocket watch. There's something special about it." The depth of investment Clint felt from Charlie Hill was tangible, no longer in Farley's head clamoring to be heard, but gaining traction in Clint's mind through insights, art, redirection, and persistence. His face turned grim.

"Something worth killing for."

Moving around to their side of the desk, Dunn supported his weight on the edge, placing his gaze at Clint. "I don't know who you are, but I sense a personal interest in this matter."

"There is," Clint responded without elaborating, "However, I am not a relative or know the man personally."

Dunn's expression turned perceptive when he admitted, "There *was* something exceptional among his belongings. A vintage pocket watch that plays the most amazing melody–Ludwig van Beethoven's Moonlight Sonata. The most haunting tune I've ever heard." Dunn shook his head. "Once I heard it, I couldn't get out of my head. The casing appears to be pure gold, I'd say maybe mid-1800s. It has an intricate old West motif that's certainly impressive.

"May we see it?" Scott requested without missing a beat. Sliding to the edge of his seat. "I'd like to view it. I'd also like your permission to have it dusted for fingerprints." Scott glanced at the folder opened on David Dunn's desk, his mind occupied with the reason he and Clint were there. "They were targeted, you know, and I want to know who pulled the trigger. This case has been sitting in a cold case file for a year with not one viable lead, until now. Considering recent evidence, it's worth taking a closer look."

The attorney didn't respond, instead, he took additional time to weigh what they had proposed. His instinct was to consent to the request, but he had to think through the legalities it could violate. Should he request a court order? he deliberated.

Clint shoehorned himself back into the conversation after seeing the hesitancy on Dunn's face. "My second question has to do with the Hills as a couple. My impression is they weren't wealthy people, yet they hired an executor for their estate and have a Will. Seems odd for two youthful people barely getting by." Clint's confusion showed on his face. "I don't mean to be rude, but from my experience attorneys aren't cheap."

"True, but that's not always the case," Dunn answered, humored by the assumption. "On occasion I do pro-bono work. However, they didn't qualify."

Clint found Dunn's reply curious. "What about the watch? Is it here or kept elsewhere?" Clint hoped the former was the case.

"It's here. My feeling is it's valuable, so I brought it to the office for safekeeping. Nothing else bagged that night appeared consequential. Just the usual credit cards, house, and vehicles keys. Ann was wearing a jade cross. Only the vintage watch held import." Dunn's lips ran a thin line, thinking something didn't add up. He would like a second opinion, specifically from Captain Edwards. "The watch has a history. It's old and has an inscription on the inside cover."

Instantly, Dunn had Clint and Scott's undivided attention. His eyes glinted comically, when he said, "It reads, *You only live once, but if you do it right, once is enough.* That's a saying by Mae West."

"How utterly charming," smiled Clint.

He thought about Thaddeus Andersen and his parents, who were no longer running ads. Sadly, Clint realized the ads would have yielded no results.

He was also aware that the watch had been at the crux of the quarrel's escalation in the alley. According to Cookie, Axel had the watch in the tavern, bragging about it more than once, but it must have initially belonged to Thaddeus by the way he had reacted. A stolen piece was Clint's educated guess, but he wasn't convinced it necessarily belonged to Thaddeus either. It could have been someone else's watch. A person with whom Thaddeus was acquainted.

"I can't imagine its worth, but I'd say a pretty penny," Dunn suggested, more aware of the item's value than the two men sitting in his office. He'd made his decision. "Yes, I'll show it to you. And, dusting it for prints is fine. I'd like to know why this tragedy occurred as well."

"Thank you," said Scott, his sentiments echoed by Clint.

"I understand the couple had a son who witnessed the murders. What happened to him?" queried Clint, obviously more in tune with children's welfare than the average person. Being careful, he asked, "Wasn't he young?"

"They did, and he was. Charlie's half-brother took him in at first, but then, escorted the child to a female family member more suitable for raising a child. She had other children."

"Are you under privacy laws, unable to answer questions about their Will? From what I ascertain, the Hills had no assets to speak of. I find that curious." Scott shifted his position. "Has the Will cleared probate."

Something stirred behind David Dunn's gaze. He knew what was in the Will would explain the couple's need for his services. "Charlie's half-brother, Mac, was named primary." Dunn pondered, and then said, "Since you are in a position of authority and probation is close to ending, I'll make you a copy and hand over the watch for evaluation."

Dunn walked to the door and turned. "Mind you, the estate will not be finalized until the end of next month. Processing takes longer when death comes suddenly like theirs did."

Chapter 32
Meltdown

As Scott and Clint drove back to Salzburg, they discussed what was learned about the Hills and some of the circumstances that surrounded their private affairs. With a copy of the Will and the pocket watch with Scott, they were now on solid ground to further the investigation.

While making a quick stop at the gas station, Clint checked his phone. A voicemail from the orphanage flashed. A message from Tom Sanders requested his presence, saying, "Please stop by, if time allows." It had come through at 11:02. "Not urgent," the message informed; however, the tone rang urgent which gave Clint reason to pause. The call aroused alarm. He would pay a visit immediately upon returning to Salzburg.

Scott, too, had plans for the afternoon leaving no time for a sit-down chat in his office. He and his wife had dinner plans in West Baden.

Before going home Clint would visit the orphanage to see what was on Tom Sanders' mind. He didn't want to jump to any conclusions or assume the worse, but he could sense an undercurrent of frustration, or worry.

At Clint's house the two friends went their separate ways, pledging to hook up the following week to map out a new strategy after Scott had a chance to read over the Hills estate declaration. He would have the watched dusted for prints in the meantime.

Driving the long blacktop road to his second most favorite place, Clint felt an overwhelming sense of accomplishment when he saw children running and taking part in activities designed to release their kind of energy. A broad smile graced his face when he stepped out of the truck onto the path to the front entrance.

"Good afternoon," he called out, seeing three employees huddled at the receptionist desk swapping stories. It did his heart good to know he had provided so many jobs for the local youth and townsfolk.

"Good afternoon, Mr. Reeves," they collectively responded.

"Would you let Tom Sanders know I'm here? I'll be up in five, thank you."

"Certainly," a lanky kid with red hair countered, picking up the phone immediately.

The lobby was bustling, normal for a weekday afternoon. The staff had beautified the lobby with Christmas related decorations, including his favorite, bubble lights. The place looked amazing. The staff had done a superior job. The oversized wreath at the front reflected cheer and goodwill. A homey place for well-deserving little people who lived here awaiting new homes.

He searched the reading room, cafeteria, and every corner of the main area in hopes to find Casey coloring something new. Clint had decided, no matter how many pictures the child created, and handed him, they would be displayed in his office. Disappointed not to see him, he made his way up the elevator to the fifth floor.

"Tom, how's it going," asked Clint as he pulled up the chair across from his general manager fully aware something of importance was on Tom's mind.

"Thanks for stopping by," Tom started out, "I have a situation. One I didn't want to leave in a message. It's about Casey. He's in his room, bawling his eyes out. He shut himself in." He shook his head, perplexed. "No one can get him to come out. If you touch him, as you know, he throws a tizzy fit. Goes into a full meltdown!"

"Good Lord, what happened? Is he alright?"

"Not really. You seem to be the only one who can reach him." A smile appeared on Tom's face, "I've noticed he prefers you. Right now, he needs calming down. That's why I phoned." Tom scratched his chin. "He's upset about his name. I have no idea why it sets him off. The therapist has been trying, unsuccessfully I might mention, to get him to write it. She can't even get him to look at it. She's been so patient. They all have, but nothing is working. He threw a book at her today. I'm not kidding. When he sees his name, he screams at the top of his lungs, starts shaking, and cries like something is hurting him. I haven't mentioned it because what can you do. Right? He only acts this way in therapy."

"I wish you had said something. He doesn't act that way when I call him Casey," stated Clint, feeling upset at himself for not realizing Casey was so disturbed. "What do you think triggers this reaction?"

"Honestly, I haven't a clue. It's not the first time, though. Happens on a regular basis, according to Laura, his primary therapist. They've tried everything under the sun, but nothing seems to work. It's part of his development therapy, helping him to name associate." Tom noticed Clint looked worried, and added, "You know… Casey, this is you… type of thing. When Laura tries to guide his hand, which is pretty much impossible, Casey clams up. This time he went off the rails."

Tom put his pen down and closed the desk drawer. "Let's take a walk."

"Yes, I'd like to see him."

"I'm sorry, Clint," Tom said, "but that kid takes everything our counselors have, and more. He is in another world twenty-four-seven. This time he went berserk, slapping his face and banging on his ears. Screaming out of control. He's in his room now bouncing his head against the wall."

"Look, I understand he's not easy. I also know… you know, I love that kid. There is something about him I relate to. Can't explain it. I just do."

"That's why I called. Figured if anyone could settle him down, it'd be you."

When they arrived at Casey's room, the door was closed. They heard whimpering coming from the other side. Clint tapped, announced himself, and giving Casey a second to adjust, he walked in.

"Hey, I hear you aren't feeling so great," he said in a gentle tone, waving behind his back for Tom to wait outside in the hall.

Casey watched Tom and Clint closely through red, blood-shot eye, his body trembling.

The door was pulled partially closed, leaving just the two of them in the room. Clint sat on the bed, viewing the youngster's forlorn expression. Then, something happened that put Clint in a tailspin. Huddled in the corner, Casey started rocking, his arms around his legs, singing an old-time children's song. Over and over he repeated the words.

This old man he played one… he played knick-knack on my thumb… with a knick-knack, paddywhack, give your dog a bone, this old man came rolling home. This old man he played two… he played knick-knack on my shoe… with a knick-knack, paddywhack, give your dog a bone, this old man came rolling home. This old man he played three… he played knick-knack on my knee…

Somewhere in Clint's memory he recalled Farley telling him he had heard children singing this same tune. Then he remembered, more shockingly, that the man sharing Farley's mind had spoken the word, *kid, or kids.*

Farley said the encrypted message was vague at best. Clint had a strong feeling the message was meant for him and not Farley. One thing he knew for certain was the paranormal world did not operate by the same rules.

Clint stood, walked over to the window, thinking about Picasso, and how Farley and he happened to meet not long after the voice became stronger. He took a serious moment when his heart began to pound like a freight train rumbling inside his chest. Lights were coming on, one by one, the shock on his face was easily read, revealing his insightful moment. The room seemed to illuminate with Casey and Clint's energy.

"C a s e y…," Clint slowly pronounced. When he said the child's name more deliberately, it occurred to him Farley had mentioned the *voice* early on referred to a K, or possibly the word kid.

Clint's eyes widened as he turned toward Casey. Their eyes met. A scope of clarity hit Clint right between the eyes. "My God," he whispered. "Could he be Charlie and Ann's kid?" Clint's breath caught. *Are you K.C. Hill?*

A thousand questions raced through his mind. *I thought the half-brother took the boy. Then handed him over to a more capable relative. David Dunn told us he did. Or,* Clint pondered, *the brother flat out lied. Instead, he deposited Casey on our doorstep, wrapped up in a blanket, on Christmas Eve. Like an unwanted gift–from the giver.*

Clint thought a moment longer, remembering an uncanny, similar Christmas Eve, in his own life. Where he too was abandoned and carted off to an orphanage. *My impression was the child on our porch was younger than what their boy would have been. There was no information on him, his age, name, or anything, and we still don't have any.*

Clint glanced over at Casey, a small child for his age, hugging his ribs tightly. *A special needs child would have been a challenge for anyone,* considered Clint. *He's a handful, even for us.*

Clint took his ponderings one step further. *Farley painted a coffee shop, titled it, Beans to Brew.* So very close to Bean's a' Brewin.' Clint ran with the thread. *Casey, likewise, draws dinosaurs. Blood splattered, representing violence and death. He also crayoned a woman sitting in a beautiful garden under a trellis. Could that image have represented the boy's mother in heaven?*

Goosebumps ran the length of Clint's arms as he let the picture in his mind fully develop. *Casey insisted that he saw his dad, right here at the orphanage. Outside, on the playground.* Clint wondered, *could he have seen Charlie, right here, for real?*

Then, in tandem, June Bennett's words replayed. "A heart, transplanted too quickly, holds memories." Clint covered his eyes, tears rolling down his cheeks. The realization of what he was processing was tangible. That the boy in the corner of this *very* room could be Charlie and Ann Hill's kid. Charlie had been trying to get that message to Clint all along.

After taking a few moments to regain his composure, Clint moved over to Casey's side of the room. He braced himself against the wall and slid to the floor, sitting close to the boy.

Casey didn't recoil as Clint thought he might. Instead, he sat stone cold staring out the window into oblivion.

"I know how you feel, Casey. I do." Clint started out, sad from his own disturbing memories. "I'm truly sorry for how things turned out. I know what it's like to lose parents."

Clint's chin quivered. His words struggled to release from his tongue. "But you are here with me now. You're not alone. I'm not your dad, but I love you." Clint could barely finish what was in his heart and mind. "I'm Clint Reeves, a person who thinks the world of you. Truly I do. I hope you believe me."

Just as he spoke the last word, Clint felt Casey begin to shudder. The boy was crying.

Hustling to his feet, Casey hobbled over to the school-style desk under the window, pulling out a piece of paper from the top drawer. With a black marker, he sat down on the floor next to Clint, gazing up, his big blue eyes wide. He handed the paper to Clint. Then the marker.

Clint took the paper, not sure what he was supposed to do with it. Then, a brainstorm hit. Intuitively he wrote, K.C. Hill. He pointed at the letters.

"Is that you?"

Snatching the paper back from Clint, the boy scribbled best he could. KEELAN.

Clint could barely breathe or believe what he was looking at. He turned, stunned, asking, "Your name is Keelan? And we've been calling you Casey all this time? Laura has been asking you to spell your name wrong?" Daring to ask his next question, in fear of misinterpretation, he made an educated guess.

"Does the C in K.C. stand for Charles? Keelan Charles? Charles after your daddy?"

Tom stepped into the room, surprised by the conversation, having overheard it from the hall.

K.C.'s face flashed his recognition. Tears immediately pooled, spilling onto his cheeks. He turned to Clint and nodded before burying his face, groaning, and rocking in place.

Clint felt K.C.'s pain, lamenting with him. Presumably the boy must have tried to pronounce his name, at the beginning as K.C.– probably the way his parents referred to him. K.C.'s efforts to say his name got translated into Casey. Then, when therapists tried to help him spell Casey, and he knew it was wrong, K.C. didn't have the communication skills to express his displeasure, instead he broke down emotionally.

To Clint's gratification, Keelan laid his head on his lap, sobbing softly. He signaled for Tom to leave them. With the door open, Clint watched Tom step away, waiting at the elevator but not pushing the button. Behind Clint's smile was gratitude to everyone responsible for this moment, Tom, Farley, June, and most of all, Charlie Hill for pursuing Clint believing he would uncover the truth.

Outside, winter winds whispered, triumphantly, *Keelan Charles Hill, my boy. My kid.*

Keelan and Clint's two enlightened souls found peace. The truth had surfaced, at last.

Clint gazed out the window and realized darkness was setting in, ready to replace the afternoon sun. Although he knew better, the hour felt late. December was like that, darkness ushering in late mornings, and clinging tightly to the long nights as the winter solstice fringed the shortest day of the year.

Clint stood, lifting K.C. from the floor and cradled him in his arms as he carried him to bed. A dead weight, the child's small body exhibited exhaustion. Pulling the blankets up around the K.C.'s neck, Clint ran his fingers through the child's hair before tucking him in for the night.

Fast asleep, K.C. stirred, but then rolled over on his side. When he did, Clint studied the boy's silky black mane contrasted by his pale skin. Born with unusually high cheekbones, K.C.'s appearance was unique. He had the bluest eyes Clint had ever seen. From memory, the portrait of the beautiful woman hanging on Farley's wall, whose *eyes followed him*, as Farley put it, came to mind. Farley described *seeing* her European features, face, and exquisite bone structure in detail prior to painting her.

Clint's eyes considered the child lying on the bed and how he strongly favored the lady's image. *Could it be?* he wondered. *That the lady in the painting is K.C.'s mother? The woman Farley couldn't get out of his head until he painted her. She is Ann Hill?* Connecting the dots, Clint remembered how Farley had described his insatiable need to paint what he saw, in painstaking detail.

We both suspected Charlie is the one driving Farley's talent, reasoned Clint. *I'll lay money down that Ann's portrait was in his mind because it was in Charlie's heart memory. That's why he could so vividly draw her. It originated from Charlie's heart!*

Clint pondered his line of thinking, aware that each drawing painted, sketched, pen-and-inked, water-colored, or created… by whatever means, were being influenced by Farley's connection to Charlie Hill. *I bet there are more clues hidden in plain sight on those many canvases sitting around Farley's cabin.*

Clint speculated about how the images could be direct links to the events leading up to the murders. He felt a fissure of excitement when he recalled the *Beans to Brew* painting.

"That was only one clue. Who knows how many others are sitting around?" Then a gargantuan thought popped into his head. "What about that L&N train? The one Farley felt compelled to draw." Clint frowned, thinking about their talk at breakfast the day before. *Farley told me he felt an urgency to finish it before I arrived.*

Believing he was onto to something Clint became more certain of himself. *Love is behind this entire affair,* he measured, instincts pushing him forward. *Funny thing about love, it wears multiple faces. A father's love for his son—*Clint pictured Charlie and the light shed on his son's special condition. *A father protects.*

Then he assessed what he knew of Axel Drako, the killer of three people Clint knew of, so far. *There is love of money, possessions, jealousy. Envy and revenge.*

Glancing down at K.C., Clint softly spoke, *"I'm going to have you tested, young man. I want to know more about you.* Clint remembered the equations K.C. so diligently tried to bury under his artwork. Even then Clint realized there was more to the boy than what met the eye. At this moment, he was positive his assumption was correct.

Lovingly, he squeezed K.C.'s foot, ready to leave. "I think you might be a bit smarter than most of us give you credit for, Mr. Keelan Charlie Hill. But you aren't fooling me." He lovingly grinned. "I'll have a talk with Laura, set things right with her, first thing in the morning. Make sure your therapist calls you by your proper name. You can show her you know how to write K.C." Clint's smile grew broad. "Or Keelan if you wish."

"I'll ask to have you tested," proposed Clint, brushing away a tear that had pooled at the corner of his eyes, while recalling the equations K.C. had scribbled on his drawing pad, before conveniently tucking them away when Clint inquired as to what he was doing. Clint could see there was more to this lad than temper tantrums and a lack of communication skills. *Why didn't I ask more questions about him,* thought Clint sadly?

Proud to have unraveled a mystery, he figured all that mattered now was he knew more about the child than he had. He looked back at the peacefully sleeping child, cuddled under the covers, holding his hands prayerfully at his chest, and said, "I'll follow this through, for you and me. You have my promise."

Outside in the hall, a cascade of likelihoods cataloged themselves as a familiar voice sounded from an accustomed place deep within his being. An action plan was forming. In that one angst-ridden instance, he knew he was going to catch a killer.

Not until this exact moment did Clint see himself capable of such a ginormous feat. As the picture in his mind reeled, his quest for a zero-sum game was paramount. Axel Drako would soon learn which side of the equation he was on.

With fists clenched, Clint's fury raged. He would finish what he had started. For everyone's sakes, but especially K.C.'s. Axel may have woven the threads of deception, but Clint was about to prove his equal.

Before leaving the orphanage, Clint climbed the stairs, two at a time to his office to retrieve K.C.'s drawing and put it into the top drawer of his desk. Given to him as a gift, it was a picture of an abandoned L&N diesel locomotive. Clint was supposed to have it, according to the boy. Oddly, K.C. acted like he didn't know why he drew it, but he did know he was to give to Clint. In his possession, he had two depictions of this same locomotive, Farley's and K.C.'s, nearly identical images. It didn't take a genius to deduce this was a major clue. Where it led, he had no idea, but it was brought to the forefront.

Chapter 33
Chain of Clues
Friday, December 2

Wednesday flew by quickly. On Thursday, Jules worked extra hours. It wasn't unusual for her to clock out late on a day where people received their paychecks a day early. Plus, the diner had been especially busy since Thanksgiving.

Not far from Clint's mind was the situation he'd found himself. A part of him wanted to retreat, wash his hands of the entire affair but he was driven by something much deeper. A desire to expose the unvarnished truth about a man he now loathed. Another trip to Louisville for a brief chat with Cookie Crenna was considered. Only she could provide the answers to Clint's lingering questions.

He walked outdoors into the frigid morning air, his breath pillowing into the air. Since his mind wouldn't relax, he decided to drive to the orphanage to consume his first cup of coffee for the day. He had thoughts he wanted to put to paper. He'd start a fire in his office and jot them down there.

Jules had indicated she intended to sleep in after getting in late the night before. By mid-morning she expected to shop for last minute Christmas gifts and a toaster oven for the Apothecary. She'd told Clint she'd be home around five, which suited him fine.

Clint planned to devote Saturday and Sunday to his wife, starting with dinner this evening at a fine restaurant. On Wednesday he called to make a seven thirty reservation. During the week when approaching the Ohio River, he noticed a highway sign promoting the four-star restaurant's grand opening.

The Water's Edge was a nice place to jump start their weekend. No precipitation was in the forecast, which made it possible for them to drive the Camaro to dinner. They'd crank the tunes and the heater up. Act like the kids they both were at heart. As they always did when driving the Camaro.

When he walked into the orphanage the lobby was empty. He proceeded up the steps to the fifth floor. He opened his office door and smiled. This was a homey room that felt like it was part of him. After starting a fire, he spread the newspaper out on his desk and began to comb through its pages. When he finished, he folded it and took out a tablet from the desk draw. He took a sip of coffee and began to put his thoughts on paper.

An hour later, Clint was in his truck with the engine running. He phoned Jules, asking her out on a date that evening, which she readily accepted. "You'll need to dress fancy," he jovially suggested, "no movie tonight. I'm taking you somewhere special."

She sweetly replied, "That should make my day more exciting. You know how I like surprises."

When he hung up, Clint phoned Bonnie. She answered on the third ring.

"Good morning, Bonnie."

"Hey, Clint! Good to hear your voice."

"I have a favor to ask."

"Fire away, I'm all ears," she joked.

"Would you mind searching the internet for a recent picture of Ann Hill? Plus, see if there have been any new advertisements relating to Thaddeus Andersen." Off-the-cuff, Clint tossed in one more request, not giving Bonnie a chance to answer, "And, if it's possible, to research Charles Hill's art popularity? Find out if it's been gaining any traction."

"I'm beginning to feel like Dr. Watson?" she teased.

"For good reason, only you're Bonnie the undercover Librarian!"

"That sounded so lame, Clint," she countered. "Of course, I'll be glad to. No problem. When do you want this information?"

"Monday, if you can manage it."

"I'll see what I can dig up. In the meanwhile, you and Jules have a nice weekend."

"You too, Bonnie. Tonight, I'm taking my bride for a nice meal at a place called The Water's Edge. That a great beginning, I'd say."

"Oh, I've heard about that place. Let me know what you think. It's a national chain but I hear the food is outstanding."

"Will do. I'll update you on Monday. I appreciate your help. It's not taken for granted. You've had a huge impact."

"You're welcome, Clint. I'm a librarian for a reason," she chuckled.

After making a few stops and running his own errands, including a Christmas gift for Jules, Clint arrived back at the house late afternoon. Jules was already home. When he told her where they were going, she was elated. She too had heard about the restaurant's grand opening from a customer.

At dinner that night, Clint briefly filled Jules in on the progress he'd made concerning his investigation. He told her about the two locomotive drawings and how he thought they were linked to the murders, although he didn't know how, yet. He'd ask to look through Farley's artwork to see if anything else stood out. Albeit he wasn't quite certain how to decipher the relationship between all the different images Farley had painted, he would persevere until he made any important connections.

Jules was particularly surprised by Clint's revelation regarding the lady's painting on Farley's wall and how he believed it to be Ann Hill.

As the evening wound down, they discussed their upcoming holiday trip to Beech Grove and Seymour. All in all, the evening was magical. They were two people thoroughly in love.

Monday, December 5

Although Jules and Clint had spent Saturday and Sunday together, they'd also spend time on Monday since she wasn't scheduled to work. She had errands to run in the morning and so did Clint, so they agreed to meet back at home by mid to late afternoon.

Tonight, chili was on the menu. Jules had challenged Clint to a hand of rummy after dinner. In their standing game, the unending score had Jules twenty-three hundred points ahead. She apparently wanted to widen the gap.

She had gotten up early to start homemade bread. The smell of yeast permeated the house, and the bread dough was rising in a bowl on the stove when Clint left for town. He had calls to make and preferred to place them out of earshot.

He'd tried to forget about the thing that most occupied his mind these days. Truth was, he needed to put distance between him and the narrative that had commandeered his thoughts–how to convict Axel Drako.

Clint had become two people. Clint the investigator, and Clint the husband and friend. Never would he have seen this one coming. Still, he found himself captivated by what Picasso had drawn him into. Nervous to step outside the wheelhouse of the ordinary, the sleuth side of his personality was obsessed with righting a terrible transgression.

Jules would be at work the next day, so Clint intended to drive to Louisville to see Cookie Crenna. He wanted to prod her memory to see if she had held anything in reserve. At some point, he'd have to turn every piece of information he had over to Scott, but for now, digging a little deeper felt right. There wasn't enough evidence to implicate Axel in anything, though Clint sensed the man wasn't as clever as he might think. Axel had made mistakes. Clint's task was to expose them.

In his truck, he dialed Cell Block #49. The tavern wouldn't be open at this hour, he knew, so he left a message to have Cookie return his call after the message machine voice said, *"You've reached Cell Block #49. If you leave your name and number, we'll get back with you at our earliest convenience."*

Clint was both shocked and pleased when his cell phone rang five minutes later, and it was the tavern. He certainly wasn't expecting a call back so soon.

Cookie sounded upbeat. "You wanted me to call?" she gleefully asked. "I heard your message. I left my billfold at the bar last night and came back to get it. The phone was ringing when I walked in. I listened to the recorder. You've a nice voice, Tex."

This made Clint uncomfortable although he felt sorry for the girl. Adrift without an anchor, Cookie was a wayward soul. He could see it in her eyes when they talked.

"I was wondering if I could stop in to see you tomorrow for a short chat."

"Absolutely. Come before my shift starts at noon though. That's my best time." she excitedly recommended.

"That works for me. I'll see you tomorrow then," Clint said quickly, wanting to cut the conversation short.

"Sure thing, Tex."

Clint cringed, aware that her parting remark referenced his cowboy attire, his disguise. While it seemed unnecessary to wear the getup any longer, an inner voiced warned him it was.

When he hung up, he called Farley. "Sorry to be calling so early. I didn't know if you'd even answer the phone." Clint apologized. "I was wondering if it'd be okay if I stopped by later this morning? There's something I'd like to run by you. A development at the orphanage I'd like to discuss."

"Certainly," answered Farley. "No problem. I have an appointment at three but that shouldn't interfere."

"Great," replied Clint feeling relieved.

"See you later," Farley replied. Shooting the breeze with Clint and getting to know him better had been gratifying. The fact this man, practically a stranger, was looking out for his best interest, gave Farley a sense of well-being. He was acutely aware that since Clint had taken the reins, less chatter filled Farley's head. It was still there, but only on occasion, as opposed to before Clint got involved when it was in constant competition with Farley.

Clint continued to the library. Bonnie was expecting him. Within seconds of Clint walking in, Bonnie handed him a glossy printout of Ann Hill. The lady in the photo was wearing a chiffon blouse with red petite roses scattered throughout pine green leaves. Her shoulders bare, an embroidered scarf caressed her pale skin, her shiny ebony locks stylishly swirled into a bun.

It left no doubt that Farley's painting was a replica of this portrait. At the bottom, the image was signed by Charles Lewellyn Hill. Catching Clint's immediate attention was her eye color. Dazzling blue, just like K.C.'s.

"I did some checking over the weekend. I think you might find what I uncovered especially interesting," Bonnie began, leading Clint to a table at the back.

Laying four other photos side-by-side, she stated, "That picture I gave you, it's only one of a handful. Apparently, Charles Lewellyn Hill was gaining in popularity, once a starving artist, today his work is highly prized, sought after not only in Louisville. People have begun to collect his work. He sold many pieces prior to his death, at bargain basement prices. Not so today, he had one painting sell for three thousand dollars the day after his death. Later, this one," she tapped the woman's portrait, "sold for five."

"I knew it," proclaimed Clint. "That's why they hired an executor of their estate, believing Charlie's work would take off some day." Clint examined the photos on the table. "He's extremely talented. I'm surprised it took so long, but again the art world can be fickle. Authors and musicians as well as other artisans become more popular after their deaths than when alive. I can name several. Think of Edgar Allen Poe and Charles Dickens."

"Charles had few pieces on the internet, but what was there, got scarfed up in a heartbeat." Bonnie pulled a face, thinking he words inappropriate. "I didn't phrase that well."

Clint smiled. "Yeah, that's okay, under the circumstances. His heart seems to be doing quite well." He slid a second photo closer. The landscape appeared to be of the British Isles. The sea sparkled like diamonds, the coastline magnificent with steplike cliffs, steep plateaus, dotted by caves and coves on the seaward side of what Clint guessed to be the Irish Sea. He wondered where this place was and determined Charlie must have seen it firsthand to have depicted it so magnificently.

If June Bennett is correct, Ann was born in Wales. Black hair and blue eyes are common over there. "Is there a way we could look up a birth certificate on her?" Then Clint laughed. "I mean, you."

Bonnie nodded. "Certainly, Sherlock, I'll look into it."

Clint grinned. "This situation is becoming even more complicated if you can imagine. I need to have as much ammunition as possible under my belt going forward. My guess is Charlie painted this on location," Clint pointed to the image. "In Ireland, or maybe Wales. The geology is region specific." Confusion filled his mind. "It seems hard to believe Charlie only had a few paintings when he died. Not likely, would you agree?"

"Yes," agreed Bonnie. "The same thing occurred to me. There must be more artwork somewhere that haven't surfaced."

Clint considered the stacks of paintings at Farley McDougal's cabin, finding it difficult to grasp Charlie had inspired Farley to paint nonstop yet had only a few paintings finished of his own.

"Bonnie you've been a tremendous help. Thank you," said Clint. He had one more question not yet put forth. "Did you find out anything more about Thaddeus Andersen?"

"Nothing. Sorry. No more notices in the papers or on the internet. Maybe he showed up." She considered what she had said and added, "It's not like you can go to his parents and ask them. Right?"

Her words sparked an idea. "Bonnie, you're brilliant. Yes, I can and will. If you can find me an address, I'll pay them a visit." Clint wondered exactly what he would say or how that meeting would play out. "Maybe all I'll do is cruise the area, but at a minimum, I'll find out where they live. See what kind of neighborhood Thaddeus had been raised in."

"Had been raised?" repeated Bonnie. "That sounds like past tense."

It dawned on Clint that he hadn't told her about the man in the alley. The one being hauled away by his cousin. That man was, in fact, Thaddeus Andersen. And he was definitely dead. The problem that remained was where did Axel take him?

He remembered the L&N locomotive. *Could that be where Thaddeus was taken?* wondered Clint. *Buried somewhere around that locomotive?* He was onto something. *That's it! Thaddeus is buried in or around that abandoned engine. Where deserted train cars are found.*

"It's just a figure of speech, Bonnie," he replied. "I couldn't know. Could I?"

Clint left the library knowing much more than he did walking in. Headed down US 150, Clint was on his way to Farley's. At the doorstep, he listened to Winston and Cocoa barking. *Those dogs are better than any doorbell.* He laughed. When the door opened, the dogs scooted up the steps so fast it was comical. "They see me, and off they go," hooted Clint. "Rudy in tow!"

"Aren't they funny? I'd like to know what goes through those little heads of theirs," snickered Farley. "Glad you stopped by. I wasn't sure what I was going to do. A bit bored, I'm afraid. Winter has a way of putting a damper on any outside chores, so I work crossword puzzles and watch television. Not much exercise there." He chuckled heartily. "I do work out, upstairs in the exercise room, but wasn't inclined to do so this morning. I love the solitude of this place, don't get me wrong, but there are times I feel lonely."

Farley's face transformed from pleased to see Clint, to a sadness without description. He was thinking of Violet and Vincent, his deceased two-year-old twins and how he missed their giggles, hugs, energy, and sweet smiles. "That's another way of saying I'm glad you came?"

Without articulating, Clint recognized what was on Farley's mind, and felt a deep sadness for the man sitting across from him. Losing two little ones to a drowning accident would be hard to endure. He waited giving Farley's emotion time to pass.

"A revelation surfaced yesterday. At the orphanage. I'd like to share it with you."

"Sounds intriguing. Please..."

"Do you recall the boy I talked to you about, the *special* one?" Clint hesitated, "Casey?"

"That sounds unsettling," replied Farley, concerned something had happened to the boy. "I do. Is he alright?"

"Sorry, didn't mean to alarm you. Yeah, he's fine." Clint wondered if that was a factual statement. "It's just that his name isn't Casey. It's K.C. The initials stand for Keelan Charles." Clint gave his revelation a minute to sink in and then tagged on, "Hill."

Initially Farley appeared perplexed, not certain of Clint's meaning but then his confusion quickly gave way to unmistakable transparency. "Keelan Charles Hill," he repeated, "as in Charlie

Hill's kid?" Farley was astonished at his own words.

"Precisely," Clint replied, glad Farley understood. "He's Charlie and Ann's child. We've been calling him Casey because that's what we heard, when in fact, he was saying, K.C. His parents must have called him by his initials."

"How did you manage to figure this out?" Farley asked, astonished and leaning in he waited to hear how Clint figured out the discrepancy.

"The orphanage phoned me and asked that I stop. The boy came unglued when his therapist tried to force him into spelling his name... incorrectly. As in Casey. He hit a breaking point. I went there to calm him. When things settled down, K.C. got up, took a marker, and wrote Keelan."

Clint's eyes grew large, still amazed at what he had learned. "Farley, this kid is smart enough to know how to spell his full name. I've had the impression he wasn't too bright. I no longer think that." Clint's smugness showed when he declared, "I guessed at the Hill part but was correct. I asked him what the C. stood for–guessed at Charles, and he confirmed it. Then I followed that up with, "Is your name Keelan Charles Hill?" and he verified that, too."

Farley seemed shaken. "He's Charlie's son? That means he witnessed his parents' murders. Good God, Clint. All this time, Charlie's boy has been in your care." He stood, pacing around the room, fidgeting, and agitated at the news Clint had delivered. More than Clint would have expected from an interested third party.

He took in Farley's strange behavior. From the table to the door, window, and back again, Farley rounded the room, unable to find a place to light. Eventually he dropped into the chair, folded his hands, and said, with a weird tone, "It's about time."

"What?" Clint responded, stunned and puzzled by Farley's curt response.

Blinking, Farley, in turn, explored his friend's quizzical query. "What do you mean, *what?*"

In an instant Clint understood Farley was not the one who had posed the question. It was Farley's other self, at last, finding his voice. *Charles Hill!* Realizing who was listening to their conversation, Clint said, "Can you imagine how I felt when he wrote Keelan? Honestly, Farley, I was blown away. There is more to K.C. than what meets the eye."

Clint thought a moment, remembering what he had earlier witnessed. "K.C. had math equations jotted on his tablet. Before I could take a good look, he hid them away, behind one of his drawings. He didn't want me to see them, but I did. The boy is not ordinary, not by a long shot."

Clint got up, grabbed the coffee pot, and sat back down. "But here's the thing, he is an incredible artist, like you. I've not mentioned it before because it didn't seem relevant, but it does now. K.C. has been creating drawings. I have three in total, two in the office. The first he gave me was of dinosaurs, but it was a truly disturbing image. Blood was everywhere, which I now understand must have been his way of describing the murder scene he'd witnessed. Only with fictional characters could a child relate. Unable to come to grips with his parents' deaths, K.C. drew dinosaurs. As you'd expect a child might do."

"What was the other one?" inquired Farley, extremely fascinated.

"The second one was a garden scene with a lovely lady sitting on a bench under a trellis. He drew flowers all around her. It was outstanding, as far as talent, a serene scene no ordinary child his age would normally create. The woman looked like an angel, a beautiful woman with dark hair and stunning eyes. The third one, though, is lying in my desk drawer. I'm not quite sure what to make of it if I'm honest. I know what it is and why he drew it. However, what it represents is beyond me. It has a strange connection to you, oddly enough. The subject of the image is what I can't make sense of."

"Really?" Farley replied, surprised there could be a connection between him and the boy. "Poor kid." Farley abruptly stopped speaking, appearing dazed, literally bewildered. "You want me to see his third drawing, in person."

"Yes," shrugged Clint. "Would you be interested in taking a ride to the orphanage? Now?"

Farley got up, pushed his chair under the table and declared. "I'm ready if you are."

The two men grabbed their coats and headed out.

Feeling nervous when the drive ended, Farley got out of the truck, attempting to take in the entirety of the view but found it impossible. With anticipation he strolled the lane to the entrance of Radcliff's Children's Home. He had not stepped foot inside the building but was appreciative each time he drove by it. Clint had done a beautiful job of designing his orphanage. The west wing remained under construction. Winter months had slowed progress, but the home remained on target for completion mid-summer, 2006. The next project on the list was a carousel.

A team of workers were hammering away, fashioning extra extensions to the already impressive structure. Farley was impressed to no end. He walked inside, Clint at his side. When they passed the receptionist desk, Clint waved, moved to the elevators, and pushed the fifth floor. Getting out, he walked to the locked door on the left, punched in his secret code, and stepped back, waiting for Farley to start the climb to the tiptop floor of the orphanage.

"Clint, this place is truly impressive. I had no idea how eloquent it was indoors. Matches its outside beauty. This surpasses any orphanage I've ever seen."

"Yeah, well, nothing is too good for my kids. They deserve everything they get." He unlocked the door to his office, holding the door ajar for Farley. Going straight to the desk, he pulled K.C.'s drawing out and handed it to Farley, waiting for his expected reaction.

Farley's face turned ashen. With a shocked expression, he asked, "How can this be? This is a near duplicate to my drawing. It's bizarre!" He searched Clint's eyes for an explanation. "We drew the exact same image? Clint, that's impossible."

"But, it appears you did," he replied, appearing as shocked as Farley. "Your drawings must be enormously important is all I can say. It can't be a coincidence." Clint wrinkled his forehead. "A specific location I'm supposed to find? But where? And how do I find it?" A puzzled expression appeared. "When I do find it, what will it reveal?"

Farley thought long and hard. He walked across the room and looked out the tall window that overlooked the grounds. "It's clear now that this boy and I are strongly linked. K.C. is Charlie's son.

Charlie saw the murder in the alley. I have Charlie's heart. Maybe it's Charlie's way of directing your actions through us, his only way to make contact. It was certain to grab your attention."

Clint considered what Farley had suggested, revisiting his experience inside the mirror. He glanced over at it across from him thinking about the backside portal he had entered. A piece of the story Farley knew nothing about.

"I agree that it is a vital clue. One I will keep close, however, for the time being, it's of no help." He examined the drawing, "This is an abandoned rail yard area with derelict trains, cars, and a locomotive. The type you see all over the country these days, except L&N locomotives are relatively local, so it's close by, is my guess."

"I concur, otherwise, why would we both draw this specific engine? It would hold no relevance, otherwise." Farley contemplated the situation as an outsider. "Here's what I think," Farley speculated. "Whoever the man in the alley was, he's been buried around this railroad track and engine. More than likely a remote location people won't find."

Then, Farley tapped K.C.'s drawing several times, demanding Clint's undivided attention. A recognition, not seen before, appeared on Farley's face. Deep in his eyes, Clint saw someone else speaking in place of Farley, strongly recommending, "I'd start looking for abandoned railroad yards that surround Louisville, outside the metropolitan area."

Clint considered the proposal, agreeing with the logic. Axel would not have disposed of his victim's body anywhere near Louisville. It would have to be a place where people wouldn't happen upon it, a location known only by Axel Drako.

They rode down the elevator in silence, both men reflecting on Charlie Hill, and his son Keelan, who was somewhere in the building.

Clint and Farley parted ways, both having plenty to think about.

On his way back home, Clint tried the best he could to shake the feeling he was being called in a different direction.

Chapter 34
Critical Error

Restless through the night, Clint awoke to snow outside the window. Jules was sound asleep when he slipped out of bed and shuffled to the kitchen to begin his daily routine. The aromatic scent of Columbian bean drifted down the hallway as he moved toward the restroom.

Dark outside, the hour was earlier than usual. The pot had not begun to brew, set for 5:47 a.m. Clint preferred setting the clock at an odd time rather than on even minutes like 5:30, or 5:45. He pushed the brew button and went to the living room to wait for the coffee machine to run its cycle.

What more would he learn after driving to Louisville today, providing the weather held out. Lately, clues were streaming in from all directions. Keeping his ear to the ground, not letting anything get past him, was hard. Staring into the flames of the fire, he heard Jules stirring in the bedroom.

It wasn't long before Jules was sitting next to him in the kitchen scarfing down a quick bite before rushing off to Josie's Diner where she'd spend the better part of her day. Choosing her schedule had its advantages, but the downside was longer hours and on the days she did work.

Clint kissed her goodbye then headed to the shower. An hour later he was set to leave. He had to use the time available to him wisely. Cookie said her shift started at noon. If he could arrive before eleven o'clock, she'd buy him lunch.

Placing his travel mug into the cup holder of his truck, he revved up the engine, letting it idle before pulling out into the street. Concerned the weather wasn't going to cooperate with his objectives, he threw extra bags of sand and fire logs into the bed of the truck as a precautionary measure. Although the snow had let up, he couldn't count on it staying clear for the rest of the day. According to the weather map, it would be hit and miss the entire day.

Clint ran untold scenarios through his mind as he rumbled down the highway in the direction of inner-city Louisville. To keep his wits about him wasn't easy carrying the heavy weight of making the right decisions. Should Axel Drako catch wind he was asking questions, it could be unhealthy for anyone associated with Clint. He'd cover his tracks to make them less obvious.

Clint turned the truck onto Washington Street and slowly continued deeper into the heart of the city. When he saw Beans a' Brewin' he pulled up to the curb and parked. A distance from the coffee shop and alley he waited. A 1974 truck would be easy to spot if someone was looking for it.

Wearing his Gambler cowboy hat, duster, and boots, once again, Clint moved in the direction of Cell Block #49 to speak to his informant. The dark and seedy street had an unpleasant staleness no snow could camouflage. It was as though Clint had left his *other self* in the truck and his alter ego had stepped out onto the street. Sidestepping the crumbled sidewalk, he listened to his clacking boots hitting the pavement and wondered if boots were a good idea when his intention was to not be noticed.

The next time I'll wear my hiking boots, he sensibly decided.

Clint checked his watch: 10:55 a.m. Cookie had requested he be there at 11 a.m. He didn't want too much time to lapse between his arrival and their conversation. The less chance of being seen, he figured. As he passed by the window, he heard the door click. She'd been waiting for him. The door unlocked, allowing Clint access before hours.

"Good to see you, Tex," she said. "I love that Gambler hat you're wearing. We don't see many of those around here." Cookie smiled. "You're a handsome dude, you know that? A sight for sore eyes this early in the day. By nightfall, the roaches come out, loud and boisterous, and they don't look like you."

For the first time, Clint noticed Cookie's chipped front tooth. Surprised by it, not meaning to stare, he was caught red handed, causing her to wilt.

"Yeah, Axel did that," she confessed, embarrassed. Dropping her shoulders, the wind was let out of her sails. "He pushed me into the wall with his fist." She showed him to the table and sat down. "I was certain my jaw was broken but it turned out all I had was a chipped tooth. And a black eye. I guess I should be thankful." Shrugging, she said with a less bright smile, "I was going to have it fixed but didn't have the dough. That's why I don't smile much. You may have noticed. Makes me look ugly."

"That's not true, Cookie. Your smile can be fixed!" Clint stared long and hard at her, and then said, "Find out the cost and I'll cover it. A pretty face like yours shouldn't be hampered by a problem that can be easily corrected."

"Seriously?" Cookie responded, close to tears. "Why would you do that?"

"Because you're worth it," Clint asserted with concern for her well-being. "I don't know your full situation, but I can say this. If you'd like to stop working here, and come work at a place for needy children, I have a job. You won't work directly with the kids, I have therapist for that, but there are plenty of other jobs at the facility. It's in Salzburg, several miles from away, on the Indiana side of the river, but I believe you'd love the town and its people. Sleep on it, let me know… whenever. No pressure. Either way works for me. You need to know other opportunities are out there. This isn't the only game in town."

She put her face down, weeping silent tears. The kind offer Clint had presented was overwhelming. Finally, she said, "Needy children is right up my alley. What would I be doing? I have no skills." She gave him a sideways glance. "None to speak of." Again, she lowered her eyes. "I'd take any job that didn't require me serving liquor. You won't believe me, but I don't drink. I pretend to drink, sorta like you did the other day. Don't think I didn't notice."

She took a labored breath, extending a knowing smile. "You're a standup guy. Aren't you? I can tell you love your wife because of the way you get so uncomfortable around my off-color comments. I'm sorry for acting so forward." Her face filled with anguish. "It's all I know. I promise I'll not flirt no more."

Then, getting to her feet, she asked, "Want a cup of coffee, or a tea? That's what I drink. Only not in a teacup, a whiskey glass." She chortled. "I'll do the same for you if you ever show up again, only I wouldn't suggest you do that."

She sat on the edge of the chair. "Axel came in here after you were here, hot under the collar, asking who you were and what we talked about, warning if I ever spoke to you again, it would be the last time I talked to anyone. He was spittin' mad!" she scowled. "He twisted my arm so hard." She pulled up her sleeve to show him her bruise. "See."

Her face tightened. "I'll take that job you offered, you bet I will, whenever it's available. I can start Monday if you like. Jerry, my boss, won't like it but I don't care. He treats me like crap just like Axel. I owe him no more than a week. There're gobs of girls wantin' my job, at least that's what he says." Her expression showed her anger and grit when she declared, "Axel ain't running my life. I told him I'd do as I pleased." She walked to the bar.

Clint watched her behind the bar, performing a routine performed hundreds of times before of fixing drinks. He'd suggested a hot tea would be nice, and she was busy preparing it when his phone buzzed. He let it go to voicemail, then listened.

Scott had left a message saying the pocket watch would be dusted for fingerprints, that afternoon. If Clint would give him a call, or better yet, stop by that would be great. When Clint slipped the phone back into his pocket, he felt uneasy about talking with Scott, realizing he should have filled him in sooner. If time permitted, when he returned to Salzburg, he'd stop in. Otherwise, he'd call tomorrow.

Cookie came back to the table toting two cups of Earl Grey. She set them and herself down, directly asking, "So why are you here? There must be something more you want to know about me and Axel. This ain't no social call."

"True. I have a few more questions. One," he stated as though he'd been rehearsing his lines. "Where does he live? Two, did you live there? Three, if you did, how do I find the stolen property you mentioned? And, lastly, I assume there are weapons in the house. Do you know where he keeps them?"

She appeared shocked, wondering how to answer such pointed questions. She glanced over at Jerry who had come out of the back room and was staring at them with extreme interest. "We need to be cautious because Axel got me this job. He and Jerry's pals. Neither one of 'em like me spending time with my cowboy friend." She winked. "I figure that's how Axel knew about you. Jerry snitched on us."

With sparkling eyes, reacting to her last remark, she grinned big, but it quickly faded. She warned him, "Look, Axel don't want me, but he doesn't want anyone else to have me neither. Ya know? That's how men are, especially ones like Axel. Possessive and all. He can fool around all he wants, but not his women."

Clint nodded, grasping her meaning. "Okay, let's do this swiftly. Home address? I'd like to have it." Clint's attention drifted toward the bar, realizing her advice was timely, because Jerry, who was on the phone conducting a somber conversation, was shooting daggers through him.

"Weapons?" Clint questioned with urgency. "Do you know where they are?"

"Yes," she replied while writing down Axel's address on a receipt pad she'd taken from her apron. She cautiously slid it over to Clint making certain it was directly in front of her and not seen.

"Like I mentioned, Axel created a hidden area beneath the basement. A place no one would ever find or notice. In the kitchen pantry, which is a descent sized room, you'll see water spots on the floor. Those are loose boards. You'll have to squirm your way through that section down to the basement below. You'll find yourself in a walled off room."

She glanced at the ceiling as though picturing the area. "Once there, moving from the outside east wall with the window, you see a section of bricks about midway. Look for the chipped ones. The middle top brick is discolored. Press it and a series of bricks will release, one at a time. Located behind those bricks you'll find steps which lead to another chamber. I suspect whatever it is you're searching for," she whispered, laying her hand on his, "you'll find it in there."

"I won't ask how you know so much about an area he took such pains to hide," stated Clint not wanting to push her any harder than he already had, "but thanks. That's enormously helpful."

Cookie pretended to wipe down the table. "Don't." She grinned cunningly. "All I can say is liquor is a fine mouthpiece to make people say stupid things. Axel's an idiot, always bragging about how clever he is. Especially when he drinks Jack Daniels. That man will talk nonstop, if asked the right way."

She lifted her brows and her eyes twinkled. "While he was passed out, I did some exploring. Sure enough, he has some serious stuff hidden below the house. Holy smokes! You wouldn't believe what he's stashed away. I helped myself to one of the coins. Figured he'd know if I took more. One missing wouldn't be a big deal. He'd just figure he dropped or misplaced it somewhere."

Acting as though she was prepping for the customers soon to arrive, she spoke purposefully, as though something just occurred to her. "By chance, does this have anything to do with his cousin? I haven't heard his name mentioned lately. He's not been in for a while. I asked Axel about him, and if they made up. He told me to shut my trap. Not to mention Thaddeus to him or anyone else. Ever again."

Her face contorted with disgust. "He was with saucy Sally that day, not DeArra D'Amelio his current squeeze, running off at the mouth about expensive things he'd been buying." Her fiery eyes flashed. "Couldn't buy me nothing, but now he's throwing money around like it's grows on trees. He thought he could buy my silence. I told him to put his money where the sun doesn't shine. I didn't need him, or it."

Clint looked uncertain if he should answer her question, while taking in her other comments about Axel's sudden wealth. "I'm afraid it does. It would appear Thaddeus has gone missing."

"Oh," she squealed, unwisely, considering there were listening ears. "It's not what you think. He's not missing."

Clint watched the barkeeper pull a pint and set it on the bar, sipping while keeping a close eye on them. Jerry's gaze darkened.

Prepared to cooperate any way she could, Cookie told Clint what she knew about Thaddeus. "Thaddeus went to Montana. Someplace called Eureka, to buy an old Vette. A C-2."

Puckering her lips, she tried to recall the details of her and Axel's conversation. "It's a super special sports car." Her attention shifted in Jerry's direction. He was on the phone again, with his back turned to them.

"Thaddeus loves cars and tinkering with them." She laced her fingers, steepling her forefingers. "Some old guy has pieces of it in his barn. He was in a bad car wreck and his legs got messed up so he decided to sell it."

She scowled, thinking a moment longer before injecting, "I was told Thaddeus has a new girlfriend. That's why Axel said not to talk about his cousin anymore. She's married." She thought back, then said, "Axel wanted to tag along on the trip, but Thaddeus said it would cramp his style." Now, talking with her hands, she explained, "With them sleeping together in the motels, Axel would be a third wheel, I suppose. She would be the front seat—you know how it is with new lovers." She acted embarrassed talking about such matters.

"Cookie, his parents don't know any of this because they put a missing person's ad in the paper back in January. If they were told where he'd gone, why would they place a full-page ad asking for information as to Thaddeus's whereabouts? He didn't show up for Christmas or New Year's."

"Really?" Confused, she said, "You'd think he would have told them he was taking off. Thaddeus has a close-knit family, as I recall. Irene, Axel's mother, never remarried after she divorced her husband, Jay." Cookie smiled sweetly. "She's so beautiful. The nicest woman on the planet. Dorian and Jessica, Axel's uncle and aunt, they're nice people too. Everybody's nice 'cept Axel! Well, and Jay... he's in prison."

She made a gesture as though what she was about to mention held no significance. "You gotta remember, me and Axel, we've not been an item for a while. He dumped me around the same time Thaddeus and he got into their fight." She considered the coincidence of those two events. "Other than when he comes in here to act like a celebrity. Like the other day. He'll come in to show off his latest *arm candy,* trying to make me jealous."

Clint looked down at the paper where Axel's address was written—945 Hardin Street. "Thanks, Cookie," he said appreciatively. "I want you to be extra careful from now on. Do you hear?"

"Sure," she acknowledged, thinking Clint was overreacting. "Nuttin's gonna happen. I'm one tough cookie," she joked, laughing loud. "Get it? Cookie... is one tough cookie?"

"I'm not kidding, Cookie. Axel may be more dangerous than you think or has shown in the past. Will you do as I ask? Please." Clint stood, pushing his chair under the table. "I'll inform the human resources department at Radcliff's Children's Home to be expecting your call. Are we on the same page?" He tilted his head, "They'll want to set up an interview. It will be a service job. Are you okay with that?"

"Sure. I'll give my notice today," Cookie responded, beaming from ear to ear, glancing over at Jerry who was looking mighty unhappy. "I can't tell you how happy this makes me. I've been wanting to move on, to blow this popcorn stand." She put her hands on her hips, excited to turn in her notice. "You, Tex, are sent from heaven above. An answer to my prayers."

Clint's brow creased, not at ease with her assigned nickname for him. "You do realize you won't be able to call me that when you start work at the orphanage. My name is Clint Reeves, Mr. Clint Reeves to you, as with any other employee I hire."

She saluted stiffly, addressing him properly. "Oh sure," she replied, flashing a sweet smile, "got it. It's Mr. Reeves from now on." She thought a moment, and then winked. "I won't tell anyone how we met, ya know... in a tavern. You have my word. That'd be bad. I'll be careful. Act like a proper lady, I promise."

"Cookie, this isn't a game," Clint scolded, holding his ground. "If you want the job, you must behave with dignity. Do you understand and agree?" Clint stated firmly, worried he might have gotten in over his head. In that moment, it occurred to him he should explain who Cookie was to Tom Sanders, as well as how they had met, and to his wife, prior to Cookie being hired.

"Don't you worry, Mr. Reeves. I get it."

"There is *one* caveat to my offer. My wife needs to be told about you and how we met. Like you said. I don't want any misunderstandings. If she's uncomfortable with this, so am I. She'll have the final word."

"That's fine," Cookie replied showing her disappointment. She would have to wait to give her notice. "Leave a message. I'll wait till' I hear from you, before telling Jerry."

Clint finished his tea. He walked out into the street, waving as he passed the display window, aware that she had an eye on him.

Cookie yanked the door open before he got out of earshot to run after him. She stretched on her tiptoes and kissed his cheek before he knew what had happened. "Not trying to be forward with ya, Mr. Clint Reeves, only want to say thank you again for believing in me. I won't let you down." She looked as though she might cry, "please tell your wife I'm a good person. I know I'm rough around the edges, but I'll make you both proud."

She turned away, but then tagged on an important distinction. "My real name is Carla! Carla Lynn Crenna. My mom thought it was the prettiest name ever. She died when I was twelve. I vaguely remember her. But what I do is all good. She had smiling eyes and loved me a lot." Tears formed in her eyes from recalling her loss. She rushed away.

To Clint's shock, while speaking, Cookie had slipped something into his hand.

She turned, stealing a quick glance with a keen eye. "Axel's house key. I'd forgotten I had it until you started talking about his place. Thought it could come in handy. I won't be using it anymore. He's forgotten I have it." Then with an air of apprehension, she too warned, "You be careful, Mr. Reeves. Axel ain't a nice guy, especially when you piss him off."

Clint watched her disappear back inside Cell Block #49, happy and expectant of a new career opportunity. His heart ached for what he'd gathered from her words. A motherless child who had been struggling to survive in an unkind world.

Chapter 35
Unanswered Prayers

Sounds clacked against the pavement, gaining an edge over Clint's hastened pace. He progressed quickly through the dark alley, passing Beans a' Brewin' on the way back to his truck. Down the side street he hurried, breathing hard as he homed in on the noise and its distance.

Swinging open the door to his vehicle, he jumped inside and locked the doors, acutely aware that his boots weren't the only footsteps to echo in the silence of the shadowy street. The clatter had dissipated by the time he reached his truck, but Clint was certain he had been followed. He'd heard someone's, other than his steps keeping pace as he dashed close to the building through the empty street.

Clint suspected the phone call Jerry was on was with Axel and that Jerry could have notified him Clint was at the tavern pumping Cookie for information.

He leaned over and opened the glovebox, removing the road atlas. He flipped to Louisville, finding Hardin Street. Turning over the engine, he headed that way navigating the city's unfamiliar inner city. Slowly he pulled from the curb, checking his rearview mirror to see if he was being tailed. Motoring toward the busier streets of downtown, he made rights and lefts until, at last, twelve minutes later, the address he was searching for appeared.

Eyeing Axel's home, he was surprised by its size, smaller than expected. Having been told it had two lower levels underground made it more interesting.

Clint slid the key out from his pocket, the one that would unlock the door if he chose to be that brave. He had no plans of going inside or even talking to anyone coming or going, but later was a different matter. For now, all he wanted was to observe the property.

Ten to fifteen minutes had passed with Clint unsure what he was going to do for an encore. But then a car pulled into the drive. Clint drove further down the street, out of eyesight.

Driving a Lexus LS 430 Sedan, a shapely woman in a skintight, black dress stepped out of the car, stiletto high heels digging into the soft mud by the drive, jewelry dripping from her ears, neck, wrists, and ankles. A noteworthy, heavy, gem-laden, gold chain clasped her ankle, glinting as she fumbled at the vehicle, prying packages from the back seat.

Clint watched with fascination as she swayed this way and that finding it difficult to stand upright. He even laughed out loud at one point when she severely lost her balance dropping a couple bags and swearing, as best he could tell from the distance he was sitting, at her difficulties. DeArra D'Amelio, he deduced, given Cookie's description of Axel's *current squeeze.*

With hours of daylight remaining before he had to return to Salzburg, Clint drove on to his next location.

Bonnie had left a message while he was in Cell Block #49, providing him with a current address for the Andersen's. He was more than a little curious where they dwelled, presuming it was nicer than Axel's shabby abode with its peeling paint, crumbled steps, and large exposed patches without grass.

Clint chuckled. If Axel's a rich man, which Cookie seems to believe he is, the man certainly isn't putting his resources in his home.

Away from city limits, where smooth blacktop driveways, gated communities, and high-end homes were sprawled, Clint searched for his next destination. Closing in on his desired location, Clint checked his phone one last time to the corresponding address before him.

Straight ahead, a monstrous stucco-sided, cream-colored mansion, crowned by a sienna tile roof, loomed in the now fading afternoon light. Shadows stretched across the yard. He estimated the house to be a minimum of ten to twelve thousand square feet. Manicured yards and gardens, and a glimpse of a large lake behind were barriered by an exquisite wall. Clint was in awe.

Thinking about his modest home, and the money available to him through his newly acquired Reno Gang unearthing, he felt no envy. Rather, an appreciation of what money could do when used for others, like Cookie Crenna, in offering her a job opportunity and new life. In a small-town environment on the other side of the river, where less cars and more land awaited her.

Clint lifted the disposable cell phone he'd purchased, not wanting to use his own to make the call. He dialed the number he had written down on a pad sitting by his leg. He silenced the engine, hoping residents would assume he was a laborer or possibly a landscaper. His F-100 fit the bill even if he didn't. Nervously, he awaited the person on the other end to pick up. One ring led to eight, without success. Voicemail picked up on the ninth. Leave a message came on, disappointing Clint greatly. He laid the phone back on the seat after he'd left his name and number followed by a brief message.

Patiently waiting for a returned call while watching the activity at Andersens' mansion, Clint witnessed only two cars pull in and out, passing his parked truck. Then, just as he was about to throw in the towel and fire up the engine, the phone vibrated, jiggling on the seat.

Clint answered without hesitation, not giving the man a chance to leave a message, or get cold feet.

"Hello," Clint said, trying to act like he didn't know who it was.

"I believe you just called my number," the caller said. "Who may I ask is calling?"

Clint froze, not prepared to give his name, "Is this Dorian Andersen?"

"Yes, and who might you be? Why have you called this number? You should know, it's a designated line."

"I know, sir. I'm sorry Mr. Andersen, but I'm not at the liberty to divulge my identity. I do possess information I believe you will want to hear. It's concerning your son, Thaddeus Aaren Andersen."

"I must have your name before we talk. This is a sensitive nature. I've had countless calls, cranks, or worthless leads. Nothing to date has developed into anything worth my time. Why would yours?"

"You must be dreadfully tired from your quest for valuable leads. My heart goes out to you." Clint continued, not giving Andersen a chance to speak. "What I know is vital and worth listening to. However, I am not giving my name or my informants' names. Only what I believe to be facts. Are you willing to listen? Because I am not willing to meet in person or go on record."

A heavy silence hung on the line. Clint thought for a moment Andersen might very well disconnect the call, but, likewise, he suspected Andersen may be thinking the same thing. It was instinct that pushed Clint to say what came next.

"Your nephew, Axel Alrik Drako, killed him."

He heard a gasp on the other end, a whimper, and then sobs.

"Mr. Andersen, Dorian... I can't tell you how sorry I am to deliver such horrific news. I know what I say comes as a shock, but something inside me believes you already suspect your nephew."

Dorian tried to breathe, laboring for air, not certain if the person he was speaking with was telling the truth or, for reasons unknown, lying. "Where does this accusation originate? Are you someone wanting revenge? Someone Axel has offended?"

"None of those, I'm afraid. Just someone who thinks, after all this time, you are owed the truth about your son and that he is not coming home."

Again, the silence weighed, lasting for what felt like an eternity.

"I need proof," demanded Dorian, barely able to speak.

"Axel's father, Jay Erik Drako, is in prison for life. Selling drugs is Axel's nature as well. It's what he knows. Your yacht safe was broken into. The one docked at Skippers Haven off I-265 in case you have others. I understand you're wealthy, an influential man. The contents of your safe contained precious high denomination bills, several $500, and a few $1000. Should I go on?"

The sound Clint heard coming from Dorian's side of the phone was agonizing. Instead of putting the man through additional torment, he volunteered, "Dorian, this is more than a call to give you information about your son. It's to track down who murdered him. Your nephew has left a long calling card of victims. He stole from you, turned your high numbered bills into hard cash, and is living the high life." Clint stopped before asking, "Haven't you noticed? He believes he's sly, but he's made mistakes and they will trip him up."

"I want to know more. Tell me, please," Andersen cried, throwing Clint off his game, until it occurred to him the call would soon be traceable, and it was possible Andersen had been instructed to keep callers on the line. If he was trying to engage Clint in conversation, Anderson could later hand his phone over to the authorities. After thinking through the comment, Clint had no doubt what the man was attempting. To do it by the books.

"I will, but not now. I'll be honest, I only have one aim, and that is to see Axel Drako arrested." Clint let the stillness build, before he firmly stated, "Dorian, I cannot allow this call to be traced." He hung up, checking the minutes the phone displayed. Less than two minutes had passed, but it was too close for comfort. He'd destroy this phone with the hammer he kept in the truck. Inwardly he knew Dorian Andersen was beside himself, anxiously awaiting the phone to ring again. Having provided enough ammunition to get the ball rolling, Clint had set the bait.

He reached over and opened the second throw-away he'd purchased for the same purpose and dialed. This time Andersen answered on the first ring. "Hello, hello?" he exclaimed franticly.

"I have one question," Clint said, "an option really, and an opportunity. Are you interested?"

"Yes, yes, please..."

"You will do as I request?"

"I will," Andersen submitted, too scared not to conform.

"First, the police cannot be involved. I know that's hard because you've been relying on them heavily to help locate your son. This brings me no pleasure, sir. In fact, it distressed me greatly to deliver such heartbreaking news." Clint gave his words a minute to penetrate the grief he could hear on the other end. "You'll have to trust me if you want to learn the truth. Believe me, I'm not a crank call, nor someone wanting to get even with Axel."

Andersen's breathing was strained when he answered. "I do, and I will. How will we talk?"

"We could meet face to face, but I have no guarantee you'd keep the cops out of it. I'd probably have them in the wings, if I were in your shoes, but that can't happen. Their natural reaction could be to point the finger at me, rather than at the true person responsible for taking your son's life. That's the way things are often done. The first line of inquiry is directed at the discoverer." Clint shared what he knew. "I got your number from the ad you placed back in January. Is there another number we can use, besides this one? If we do move forward, you'll have to trust me. There is no other way."

"Do you want a reward?"

"Don't insult me, Dorian. Money is irrelevant. I'm as wealthy, or more so than you are, sir. On my end of the equation, this has to do with two people who were brutally murdered, by your nephew as collateral damage ensuing your son's death, I'm sorry to say. Are you willing to work together to bring Axel to justice? Or do I hang up?"

Clint could feel Dorian Andersen sweating it out, aware that a decision must be made at that exact moment. No second chances would come again. Impulsively, relying on nothing more than his instincts, he'd have to decide. Being a good businessman, with exceptional instincts, Andersen swiftly replied, "Yes, I am. What do you want me to do? I promise, the police will not be brought into it. You have my word."

"Good," replied Clint, aware that when most men of Andersen's reputation gave their word, they stood by it. "We are on the same page then. I'll be back in touch soon. You can depend on it. Likewise, I must warn you, and it doesn't come lightly, not one word, or action, can flag Axel's notice. You must treat him as you always have, or my suggestion is to avoid him altogether. Make up business trips, meetings, anything to keep the two of you separate. I'm afraid if he looks into your eyes, they'll reflect suspicion."

"Okay, I'll do anything you say. I'll watch for your next call."

"Goodbye, Dorian. Again, I'm terribly sorry to be the one to break such terrible news. Rest assured I'm strongminded and will even the score."

Clint wanted to say more but felt confident he'd done the right thing in ending the call. He'd given Andersen plenty to think about, which was enough for now. He drove three miles out. On a gravel road, he stepped out and smashed both phones.

Chapter 36
Lingering Spirit

Dorian Andersen's conversation was tossed into a bucket of fragmented loose ends, burdening Clint with one more person to fret over. Aware he'd poked a hornet's nest, he hoped soliciting Andersen's involvement didn't come back to bite him. He had done the honorable thing by telling the man the truth of his son's circumstance. There was no turning back now.

If I were in Dorian's shoes, I'd want to know, Clint thought, concerned that he might have made a mistake.

An urgency to locate Thaddeus's body was crucial. Where Andersen had been blindly asked to put his faith in Clint, for both men trust was a tall order. A gut-wrenching realism was dropped in a father's lap. Andersen's son was forever lost, the starkness of Clint's words cut to the core.

"I'll find that kid's body and deliver it to his father if it's the last thing I do," said Clint resolutely, ready to phone Andersen when he was on the Indiana side of the river. Nothing Clint had done was without consequence. Untrained in detective work, he second-guessed every move. Andersen had probably thought of little else since receiving word of his son's demise, and Clint was responsible for delivering the bad news, an unenviable position by anyone standards.

Two floors below the main level of Axel's house, if Cookie could be believed, lay damaging evidence. Did he have the nerve to trespass onto someone else's property? He'd soon know. Brushing concerns aside, Clint slipped the key from his pocket into the glove compartment, aware of the firepower it possessed. He hoped for incriminating evidence but had no guarantee.

Fading light framed the western sky on Indiana's side of the Sherman Mitton Bridge. Setting earlier each day, shorter days lay ahead. At the 7-Eleven Clint pulled in, parked, and dialed Andersen with his remaining burner phone. "Would you want to set a time to meet?" asked Clint when Andersen answered the phone… again, on the first ring.

"Certainly, if you don't have a place in mind, I do."

"It's better we talk in person, though I must insist you honor your word," said Clint.

"I swear to it," promised Andersen. "At the marina, we can talk below deck. During winter months not many people go there."

"Good location," Clint replied, relieved to have the privacy. "Nine, Thursday? After rush hour traffic clears?"

"I'll make myself available," Andersen immediately responded.

"Slip number?"

"B-14"

"See you then," agreed Clint, wasting no time to disconnect the line, a fissure of excitement bubbling below the surface.

Driving along US 150, he thought about how he was going to explain Cookie Crenna to his wife. Leaving Jules in the dark for the time being would have been his preference but his honesty with her was more important.

When he pulled into the driveway, his mobile sounded, surprising Clint. He saw Farley's number. "Hey there," said Clint. "Is everything okay? You don't normally call me this late."

"Everything's fine," Farley declared excitedly, clearly having something on his mind.

"What's up?"

"I had the strangest day ever," Farley jovially declared. "This morning, I got to thinking it would be nice to visit the orphanage again. Walk the grounds and take a closer look inside."

"That's nice to hear," said Clint. "I hope you enjoyed yourself. If you want to come again, we can always use readers," Clint joked. "I read once a week. If you have any interest, let me know, and I'll get you set up."

"I can't believe you said that. That's kind of what I've been thinking. I'd like to help support the kids, and you. The smallest job would suit me fine, don't care what. Volunteering in whatever capacity will add quality to my life and give me a purpose."

Farley sighed, ready to confess he was feeling down. "Painting is a grand hobby. I get great satisfaction from it, but I'd like to repay my good fortune in other ways too. I was going to bring it up the next time we talked but today something happened that took me by surprise. My plan was to stroll the grounds, but things changed."

"What exactly has you so wound up?" asked Clint, his curiosity piqued, having never heard Farley so animated.

"Well, when I went to speak to the receptionist to ask permission to look around, this young boy came running up and hugged the daylights out of me. Clung to my leg like glue."

Clint knew who *that boy* was. "Keelan?"

"You guessed it," Farley laughed warmly. "He said the darndest thing, Clint."

"Really? What?"

Farley chuckled. "You are not going to believe this… the boy said, 'I knew you'd come. I've been waiting.'"

Clint gulped, grasping the insinuation of K.C.'s words. "Wow! I'm not sure how to respond. What do you think he meant?" he questioned Farley, knowing full well what the inference pointed to.

"C'mon Clint," razzed Farley, "you know as well as I do, the boy knows! How he could, is the million-dollar question, but he obviously does. Isn't that amazing? His father is part of me, and Keelan sensed it. And if that isn't crazy enough," Farley added, "Keelan acted like he was expecting me."

Neither spoke as both deliberated the gravity of the situation, and its apparent connotations.

"Farley, for K.C. to know you house Charlie's heart, he must have some kind of outside knowledge."

"Exactly," Farley enthusiastically agreed. "Believe me, it's all I've been thinking about since the child hugged me. You can't appreciate how stunned and pleased I was. But here is the oddest part. After that… Keelan didn't say another word. Rather, he turned and walked away, like he had no idea what he had said."

Clint could hear Farley breathing, and suggested, "Would you like to start reading to the kids this Friday? K.C. will be there. He always stands in the same spot at the back of the room."

"Are you sure?" Farley excitedly answered. "That would be fantastic. That way the boy could see me interact with other children.

He'd know I was an okay guy. Feel more comfortable around me next time." Farley expressed his next words gently, emotionally trying to release them. "Clint, I've missed my babies so badly. Today, when Keelan hugged me, it felt like they were there too. A little tiny bit of that hug was from them is how it felt. I wanted to collapse on the floor with joy."

Another quiet moment slipped by. "Forgive me, Clint. I'm just overreacting. Wishful thinking, you know? Keelan is such a cute kid. I suppose he ambushed my vulnerable side. Those big blue eyes of his would melt any man's heart he turned them on." Suddenly, Farley became pensive. "I don't think I mentioned it, but my twins also had blue eyes. The boy's eyes are nearly identical to that lady's portrait I painted."

"That's because the painting, I believe, is of Ann Hill, K.C.'s mother." Clint said waiting for Farley's reaction. "His dark hair and eyes favor her. There is no mistaking those eyes." He chuckled, glad to have made the association prior to Farley.

Farley smiled. "This whole affair is unimaginable. The way things have been evolving. Do you know what I mean? It seems like one coincidence after another have turned up since I moved to Salzburg, Indiana."

Agreeing with him, Clint wondered what Farley would say if he knew the rest of what he was keeping in reserve. "It does, I must admit. One thing after another."

"I'd love to interact with the kids on a regular basis."

"Well, here's the thing, we typically rotate reading days, but if you were interested in it daily, or at least three times a week, it would allow the staff to do other things. Until now it's always been whoever is free reads that day. If you wish, we could assign that job to you permanently. Or until you say otherwise. Providing you want to be pinned down." Clint chuckled. "With a voice of yours, you'd be perfect for the job."

"You're on!" Farley eagerly accepted. "It'll give me something to get enthused about." He smiled big on his end. "Thanks, Clint. I suspect this is what has been missing and I didn't realize it until Keelan laced his arms around me. Man, it felt good. Been a long time since I had one of those kinds of hugs. I've missed human touch, especially from little people. Cocoa and Winston make me laugh and give me immense joy, but it's not like a little kid squeezing your leg like Keelan did."

Hanging up the phone, Clint pondered what K.C. had said to Farley, believing in his heart the child knew his father's spirit lingered in the man. This situation couldn't continue. Clint had to bring an end to Charlie's resistance to move on. It was disturbing to think Charlie had been the instigator behind so many strange occurrences, including this last one with K.C.–all with a specific purpose in mind. Just as Rod Radcliff, Sr. had done two years prior.

The deceased shouldn't remain here. Like Rod had for fifty years. Just as Charlie Hill is now. Clint considered his cog in the equation. *This must be resolved. As it was with Rod. His soul suffered until the truth came out. When Hill's story is exposed, he too, will move on and find peace. What is it going to take to make that happen?*

He watched Jules pull into the drive, knowing it was time to stop his mental processing.

She got out of the car and walked his way. "Why are you still out here and not inside where its warm?"

"I was talking to Farley. He called just as I turned off the engine."

Jules reached in and took Clint's hand. "How was your day?"

"Interesting," he replied truthfully, aware the time had come to level with her. Both dreading and glad to unburden himself.

"Hmm," she replied, "sounds like we need to talk."

"We do. I agree, right after dinner." His tone emphasized something was bothering him, and he needed to unload.

They inhaled the meal she'd brought home from the diner in no time flat. They were both tired and wanted to get to the real meat of things. No dilly-dallying around. They took their cups to the living room and sat down before the fire, ready to talk.

"First of all, there's this girl," Clint started out, "a tavern maid at Cell Block #49, in Louisville. We should talk about her first. I offered her a job, contingent on your approval. She seriously messed up, Jules. Probably hasn't known happiness in her entire life. Cookie Crenna is what they call her, but her birth name is Carla. I thought we could find something for her to do at the orphanage. It could give her a new lease on life."

"How did you meet this girl?" Jules curiously asked, having heard the word, *tavern*.

"I was walking the alley where the first murder occurred. Can't really explain it but I had a strong feeling to check the surrounding area. I've been wondering how Axel and Thaddeus ended up there. Well, it turns out they had been in Cell Block #49, arguing and took that argument outdoors around the corner."

"She told you this?" asked Jules, unclear how Cookie Crenna fit in.

"Yeah, and tons more. Jules, I've met her twice. The first time she explained how the fight began and what it was over. They were arguing about the pocket watch. The one found on Charlie Hill."

Clint stopped a moment, took a drink, and then said, "The second time I went there I was after information regarding Axel Drako, like where he lived. When I told Cookie a missing person report had been released on Thaddeus Andersen, she was surprised. She also said Axel had been her boyfriend but wasn't any longer. Axel apparently mentioned his cousin went to see about a Corvette in Eureka, Montana. Of course, we both know that's not true. I witnessed his death while I was in the mirror. They were in the alley when Charlie happened on the scene."

"Good grief!" exclaimed Jules. "This gal has helped you a great deal. So how did you come to offer her a job at the orphanage?"

"I could say a lot of things to explain, but the fact is I feel sorry for her. The first time I talked with her I realized how lost she was, even considered sending her money, but thought better of it." His brow lifted. "I was afraid the optics might be misinterpreted." He reached for Jules's hand. "Cookie was born on the wrong side of the tracks. Lost her mother at an earlier age. I tell you, she's a good kid with a bad station in life. She doesn't know anything other than bars and survival. In my heart, I believe a genuinely good person is in there, and she'd fit in well at the orphanage. With a little help she could turn into a productive asset."

Jules stared hard at Clint not sure he hadn't lost his perspective on things. "It's your nature to try to help people. I have no problem, whatsoever, if you want to offer this girl an opportunity to better herself. My only drawback is she's tied to Thaddeus's murder, and the killer happens to be her ex-boyfriend. You can't pretend there isn't substantial risk involved if Axel finds out you are snooping around, asking questions about the fight and him. Do you really think it's logical to hire her under those circumstances? It's terribly risky, Clint. Think about what you are considering. If her old boyfriend can kill his cousin, what will keep him from turning on you? And her? Especially if he feels you're moving in on his territory. He might think you're hitting on her."

"Jules, that's harsh. Axel dumped her. He could care less about Cookie... Carla. Don't we owe her a break? To help her get off the Ferris wheel?"

"I get it, Clint," Jules said, terribly concerned. "I'm worried you might have opened a can of worms, stepped over the line, into his domain. Men are known to be territorial when it comes to their wives and girlfriends. If you don't know that by now, you should."

Clint sighed heavily. His wife had a point. It was something he hadn't considered. "So, your advice is not to get involved?"

"That's not what I'm saying."

Clint frowned. "Then what are you saying? I'm confused."

"After this guy is placed behind bars, if it happens, that is when you can offer her a job. You bring her on board after he's put away for life. Don't let the two overlap one another. You don't want him coming in the orphanage and shooting up the place or children. Is that blunt enough?"

"Good Lord, I never thought of that. You're right, of course. I wasn't thinking clearly. I'll let her know we'd like to hire her but not until we have an opening that fits a skill she's best suited for. Hopefully, she won't misread our objective and think we are trying to retract the offer. I told her I wanted to talk it over with you first and she might assume you're not in agreement. Are you positive you don't have an issue with hiring her?"

"Positive. I have no issues with helping young people. To give her a chance to move out of the city to the country, how could that not be a step in the right direction? If you want, I'll talk with her, so she understands I don't object to her. Just so we don't have any misunderstandings. I'll take her under my wing. Say there's a job we are creating specifically for her if she doesn't mind waiting until after the first of the year. After the holidays."

Clint leaned over and tightly squeezed Jules's arm. "You are a dream come true, woman. How did I ever get by without you?"

"We think alike, Clint. I want to give back as much as you do. We owe it to ourselves to *realize* our dreams. This girl is only one of many we'll help over the years." She stood, facing him, ready to refill their drinks. "Is there anything more?"

Clint squirmed in his chair. "I'm afraid there is."

Chapter 37
Filling in the Blanks

Wednesday, December 7

Driving into Salzburg, Clint now regretted the job offer he'd extended the day before, a flat-out misjudgment on his part. Tunnel vision had caused him to disregard the bigger picture of concentrating on putting the Hills' killer behind bars. Thanks to Jules, it was evident what had to be done. Recant the offer at least until he had completed what he'd set out to do. She was right, letting things settle down was a prudent move. He was glad he had Jules to course-correct him.

Scott had given the green light to stop by the station early. With so much going on, Clint wasn't sure where he'd begin. A good starting point, he figured, could be to confess he had Axel Drako's address. He wouldn't mention having a key to his house.

"Hey, Jeannie," Clint called out as he walked past the receptionist. "How are you today?"

"Doing fine, Clint. And you?" Both exchanged niceties without glancing up or looking at each other.

"A good day to be alive!" he joked, thinking that wasn't too far from the truth. "Scott's expecting me."

Clint climbed the stairs to the second floor, while Jeannie returned to her spreadsheet.

Arriving outside Scott's office, Clint saw him concentrating on a folder he was reading. "Knock, knock," Clint spoke.

"Have a seat," Scott replied.

"I'm glad we could find a minute or two to talk. So much has happened."

"Is that so," Scott observed Clint's demeanor for signs that he'd been pushing beyond the boundaries of their agreement. Appreciating his friend's personality, he didn't doubt Clint kept things to himself.

"Look, I know I said I wouldn't get in over my head, and I'd let you know of any developments, as they happened, but the fact is that's not as easy as it sounds." Clint started out, tossing his hands in the air. "Cookie Crenna gave me vital information. about the night the fight broke out between Thaddeus and Axel Drako and what the disagreement was about."

Scott grinned, "Well that is a load of stuff to lay on me right off the bat."

"Yeah, I know. Thought I'd just jump in. Those two were cousins." Clint leaned in. "She claims they were arguing over Axel's pocket watch. Then, when tempers flared, they went outdoors. She said they were both hot under the collar and saw them from the window turn into the alley behind the bar."

"Is that right? Useful information to know, but again, how does she fit into the picture?"

"According to her, Axel came into some serious cash. After that he dropped her like a hot potato, and then hooked up with some other woman." A smirk appeared on Clint's face. "I think that's why she was so willing to unload dirty laundry." Clint conveniently omitted how he had approached her, not the other way around, dressed like someone he wasn't.

"Hell has no fury like a woman scorned," quoted Clint.

Scott humorously grinned. Snickering, he replied, "You got that right."

"Anyway," Clint went on, "Cookie suggested Thaddeus went to Montana to buy disassembled Stingray parts from a man who'd had them listed in Autotrader. They struck up a deal and Thaddeus went to collect them."

"This is who you believe to be the victim? Bonnie's missing person's report verified Thaddeus Anderson has not been seen since the beginning of this year. So, he's still not shown up?"

"No, he has not," responded Clint, holding his breath, waiting for Scott to fire back, a response that came quicker than expected.

"And how are you so certain?"

"I spoke with his father, Dorian Andersen. I dialed the number from the ad. Called from outside his home. The guy lives in a freakin' mansion. He confirmed he hasn't had any communication with his son. The kid hasn't called or made contact. No texts, voicemails, nothing–totally radio silent! He pulled the ad sometime late spring, too many crank calls and leads that went nowhere. As you can imagine, the man was distraught and worried sick."

Eyeing Clint, Scott thoughts strayed. He was picturing what Clint conveyed. "Are you certain the kid isn't somewhere? Maybe he stayed in Montana. Liked the place and elected not to return to Kentucky. Was he alone?"

"Well, that's the thing, Cookie said Thaddeus took a girl along with him. Axel wanted to come but was told no." Clint became solemn. "Scott, he's dead. Axel killed him."

Disturbed by Clint's unsubstantiated accusation, Scott sharply replied, "You aren't sure of that. You could be wrong. Kids turn up after being missing all the time, by their own accord. They start new lives, new identities, away from their families. Doting fathers, controlling mothers, that sort of thing. It's not as unusual as you might think. Let's take this discussion a different direction," encouraged Scott. "I have a bit of information I'd like to share with you. It's why *I* asked *you* to stop by."

Scott watched Clint slide closer to the edge of the desk. "I'm happy to report we were able to lift two fingerprints from the pocket watch. A lucky break." Scott pulled a folder from his desk, sliding over to Clint. "They follow your line of thinking. Axel Drako is one, the other, Dorian Andersen. Other smudges were lifted but could not be isolated. Nothing definitive came from them."

Clint lowered his head, collecting himself. "I know where Axel lives, if you are interested," he said with closed eyes. "945 Hardin Street, Louisville. I drove by his house. Pretty much a dump. Doesn't appear he cares about upsetting his neighbors." Clint let that sit a moment.

Scott sighed in frustration. "You will say to me, you weren't seen."

"Correct. I was not," he replied.

"Good Lord Clint, you are going to drive me to the madhouse."

"Sorry," Clint said not proud to tell Scott he'd taken so many risks. "Let's suppose Axel killed his cousin, and then he went to Beans a' Brewin' and killed the Hills. Charlie was the only one who could positively identify Axel, so he erased him from the equation."

Clint looked straight at Scott, "The guy who killed Ann and Charlie went back to Bean's a Brewin'. He demanded that Mark Carlson, the owner, give him his copy of the police report, insistent on finding out the content of Charlie's effects. Even threatened Mark, demanding he not speak to anyone about the visit."

Shifting his attention, Scott commented, "Okay, let's delve into this Axel Drako character. Is there anything else you know about him?"

"Yeah, his father, Jay Erik Drako, is in prison for dealing drugs. A lifer. Axel wasn't an easy kid to raise. Dorian took him in after the sentencing. Apparently Axel was a difficult teenager. Started drinking in his early teens. Had a girl-of-the-week club, running thru them like a sieve. Irene, his mother, couldn't manage him any longer and asked Dorian to apply a heavy hand, try to guide the kid, but Axel didn't show signs of wanting any guidance. Apparently, his good looks played in his favor. Has an actor's smile and is the life of any party. Can turn the charm on like a faucet. Dorian says he can see right through Axel but could never bring himself to turn his back on the boy."

"Sounds like a real gem. I've seen the type, but in fairness, having your dad hauled off for drug trafficking couldn't have been easy. Probably has anger issues."

"Having a soft spot in my heart for kids, I would have to agree. A gut-wrenching experience in his young life. I believe he was nine at the time. Plus, Dorian mentioned Irene even bought Axel a house to help him get on his feet. Job hopping doesn't pay bills." Clint looked away. "I saw the place and he's trashed it."

Scott rubbed his jaw. "He'll have a record. I'll have it pulled."

"Cookie says he's mean as a varmint," claimed Clint. "I suppose you'll see that when you investigate. He was arrested twice that she knew of."

"Alright. Anything else?"

Clint thought about the key he had in the glove compartment of the truck. "No, I don't think so, but if something pops up, I'll be sure to let you know." Then the thought crossed his mind, on Thursday morning, he and Dorian would further their talk at his marina. Clint had no idea where that would lead, so he omitted it too.

"Does Dunn have the pocket watch now?" asked Clint.

"Not yet, I'll take it back tomorrow. Or have one of my officers do it."

"Would it be acceptable if I delivered it if I promise to be extra careful. Dunn knows me. He wouldn't have an issue with me bringing it back. Would you agree?"

"No, I can't do that. It's official police business."

"It wasn't when he gave it to us. Not until you found incriminating fingerprints. What if there hadn't been any?"

Scott stared at his friend, thinking about what he had said. He and Clint had asked David Dunn to borrow the piece for a day or two, under Scott's supervision, and then they'd return it. Dunn trusted them, so why shouldn't Scott trust Clint? Although he wasn't completely convinced it was a good idea, he might consent to it with one stipulation. It should arrive no later than noon on Thursday. If it wasn't there by noon, Scott would come looking for Clint.

Looking beyond Clint, Scott, grumbled. "I've got to think about it."

"Call Dunn?" suggested Clint. "If he doesn't care, why should you?"

Considering the suggestion, Scott picked up the phone on an off-chance Dunn would take his call. "Hello, may I speak to David Dunn? Police business." In no time flat the connection went through.

"This is David Dunn, how may I help you, Scott."

"I'm sorry to interrupt, but we're finished with the pocket watch. It's ready to be returned. Clint Reeves is here in my office. He suggested he could bring it by tomorrow," Scott looked up at Clint, "before noon. Would that be agreeable, or would you prefer one of my officers bring it by later today. Or me personally?"

"It's fine for Clint to do it," answered Dunn. "No need to go out of your way. If he's coming this direction, that works for me. Tell him to buzz me when he gets here so I can come out to get it."

"Thanks, I'll let him know," said Scott, "I appreciate your time." He laid the phone on the desk. "Guess he has no problem with it. Stay put, I'll get it."

A sigh of relief came over Clint. Now he had tangible evidence to show to Andersen. His shoulders straightened. With the inscription, *you only live once, but if you do it right, once is enough.*, it would leave no doubt. Clint's ace in the hole would prove Axel's thievery and involvement. It would explain why his son and nephew were arguing. Because Thaddeus would presumably tell his father. Axel couldn't let that happen. Andersen and Clint were to meet at nine in the morning. That would give him ample time before noon to drop it off.

Scott walked in holding a package. The watch was well disguised in a large brown envelope. He handed it over. "Take exceptional care, Clint. We could need it back as evidence."

"Count on it," said Clint, appreciating the confidence Scott had extended. When he got to his vehicle, Clint dialed Cell Block #49. "May I speak with Cookie Crenna, please."

"Cookies and Cream no longer works here," a curt voice growled.

"What do you mean? Did you fire her?"

Before thudding the phone back into its cradle, Jerry, Cookie's boss, laughed. "Call the morgue! Cowboy!"

Chapter 38
Follow the Numbers

Clint gaped at the phone, disbelieving what he'd heard, a sickening feeling rushing over him. Bile climbed up his throat. He immediately dialed Scott. "Hey," he said when Scott answered on the second ring.

"Are you okay? You sound frazzled."

"No, I'm not okay. I called Cell Block #49 to speak to Cookie," Clint realized Scott knew nothing about the job offer he'd proposed to Cookie, "because I had offered her a job but wanted to discuss it further. Jules and I decided last night we would start Cookie after the holidays." Clint's voice cracked. "Cookie thought she was starting right away."

"So, why are you so uptight?" asked Scott, noting a tone in Clint's voice.

"You are not going to believe this, Scott. The guy who answered the phone–her boss–wasn't too happy about me coming in there and talking with her. The last time I was in, he was staring daggers through us. He picked up the phone and called somebody. Whoever that was, and I suspect it was Axel, he talked to him the majority of time I was there."

"Clint, you still haven't told me what this is about."

"Give me a minute," he replied, trying to stifle tears. "The man told me Cookie wasn't there. When I asked him if he had fired her, he laughed and told me to call the morgue."

This time it was Scott's turn to react. Dumbstruck, he responded. "Are you certain you heard him correctly?"

"C'mon, Scott, I don't have a hearing problem. Would you check your incident reports? Her legal name is Carla Crenna."

"Holy cow, I'll get right on it."

"Cookie said Axel and the owner are good friends. She suspected Axel sold drugs at the bar, at a minimum, and supplied the owner. I think he's been keeping an eye out. She indicated Axel might not want her, but he didn't want anyone else to have her either."

"Clint, I'll call you as soon as I know anything."

"Please do. Hopefully the owner was yanking my chain. Trying to get under my skin." Clint thought through the situation. "I bet he let her go." Clint kept processing possibilities. "If he did, that's fine, I'll hire her at the home right away, not wait like we were going to." His voice faltered, "Scott if that woman is dead, I'm to blame. I don't know how I'll live with that. If it's true."

"Don't do that, Clint! You are not at fault. Her association to Axel got her killed if that's how this turns out. The truth is she may have been a liability for a while. You don't know. Her anger toward him and mouthing off, would have been an issue."

Scott stood, pacing the room, too nervous to sit still. "In my experience, if a person complains to one person, others have heard it as well. In other words, you weren't the only one. Think about it. I could have been the one asking the questions. The result would have been the same. The man is starting to feel cornered. That's my guess. Having said that, do I need to remind you to tread lightly? Stay out of his line of fire?"

"This trail of dead bodies is getting deeper. You don't have to remind me. I'm very much aware how dangerous Axel is, and I suspect he's feeling threatened. Like a caged animal. To be cautious, I won't speak with Mark Carlson again, either."

In his mind's eye, Clint walked back through his Tuesday's trip to the tavern. "When I returned to my truck yesterday, after speaking with Cookie, I would have sworn someone was following me. Through the alley and back to my truck. I didn't see anyone, but I could feel them."

"Let me get off here and do what I do. Watch for my call."

"I will," he said before hanging up. Clint pondered his and Scott's call, praying for good news so when the phone rang after only a minute or two identifying Scott as the caller, he froze, unable to breath.

"That was quick," he responded, not expecting the gravity of the call.

"She died of an overdose at 2 a.m. Wednesday morning," Scott said, mincing no words. "It's current on the incident reports from that area. I'm so sorry, Clint." Scott let a moment slip by, allowing Clint to absorb his words. "If Axel was into drugs, she probably was too. Emerson said, *as we are, so we associate.*"

"I don't believe that Scott. Not for a minute. She didn't drink. She faked drinking because people expected her to because she worked at a bar. She said she never touched the stuff. We drank tea together, for God's sake. She's never had glassy eyes or slurred speech," Clint said in a raised voice, on the edge of coming unglued.

"She didn't drink?" quizzed Scott bothered by a discrepancy he'd read.

"No. Never. She pretended to."

"Well, then, there's a problem. Her BAC registered .38. Mixed with heroin, that would be fatal. She might have been trying to relax before bed. People do that. But in Cookie's case she must have been drinking nonstop. Downing one after another until she passed out. There were no signs of a struggle–a typical overdose."

"Impossible for a teetotaler to have a blood alcohol concentration of .38. *No way*, Scott. She was killed, like the others." Clint felt like he was going to erupt, angry at himself for having put Cookie's life in jeopardy. "Look, I'll call you later. I can't deal with this right now. I'm feeling nauseous. Why did she have to die?"

"Don't do anything foolish Clint. Let me take care of this. I'll contact the Louisville police. Drex Mason is a friend of mine. I'll fill him in on the situation."

A troubling silence hung in the air, interpreted as a distressing signal for Scott. "Did you hear me? Stay clear of this. You've helped plenty. Your insights have put the law on the right track."

"I won't do anything to get in the way of your investigation. I want this monster caught before somebody else dies."

"I'm glad we understand each other," stated Scott, not sure if he believed his friend's promise, knowing how determined Clint could be.

Clint immediately called Jules with the shocking news, informing her Scott had taken the reins. They talked for a long while. Her trying to convince him he wasn't at fault, him desperately wanting to believe her.

"Look, I need time to digest this. I'm going over to the orphanage, if you don't mind, rather than head home. I might even go up to the roof," he suggested. "I'll be back around dinnertime. Do you want me to pick anything up?" he asked as a courtesy.

"No, I have a pot roast in the crockpot. Honey, take as much time as you need." She felt sorry for Clint, understanding the depth of pain this latest death had caused. Trying to do the right thing had turned on him as a snake's poisonous bite.

The orphanage was Clint's refuge, his safe place to release emotions without being observed. As he passed the staff members milling about, he barely acknowledged them. On his way to the fifth floor to hide from the world in his office until the tsunami passed, he figured a walk outside to let the cold air penetrate his senses would be good.

He stepped into a dark room, glad for it, choosing not to turn lights on. Instead, he sat in the shadows letting the pain of the situation seep in and absorbing it–owning it. Tears pooled, brushed away as they escaped the well of defeat. Jules and Scott both had said Clint was not responsible for putting the bar maid in danger, that he hadn't caused her death. He wasn't on that same page.

"Cookie Crenna displayed poor judgment, talked too much, and undeniably underestimated Axel's instincts to survive," were Scott's final words to Clint.

Some of what his friend stated may have been factual, but Clint was not about to let himself off the hook. What he *would* buy into was he had put that poor girl directly in the line of fire. He was responsible for putting the gun to her head. Consequently, she paid the ultimate price for his lack of discretion.

Amid the darkness, he heard Axel's voice mocking him, jeering at what a fool he'd been. That Clint was no match for his nastiness–to stay clear or more victims would fall if he didn't back off. If he chose differently, more would be laid at his doorstep. Interrupting Clint's guilt flogging, he heard a soft rap. He whipped around, surprised, not certain whether it was the door, or the frame of mind he was in. Then he heard it again.

I'll pretend I'm not here, he told himself, not wishing to be disturbed. But then he thought, *The only people who know I'm here are those I saw on my way in. Must be important.* Getting up, he walked to the door and opened it. K.C. was standing outside the door, barefoot and holding a piece of paper in his hand, a cat perched at his feet. He handed over the paper he was holding.

"How did you know I was here?" asked Clint looking up and down the pocket-sized hallway wondering where the cat had come from.

"Him," he mumbled directing his attention to the butterscotch tabby with brilliant eyes at his feet.

Clint glanced at the cat and grinned. "The cat told you?" When K.C. didn't respond, Clint glanced down at the paper. Before he knew it, the boy was gone, running with his cat–disappearing into the elevator.

Expecting a new drawing to hang on his wall, Clint was blown away by what he saw. A jumble of random numbers.

3804030 380225

8484576 8450447

In a flash, he charged down the hall, pounding the elevator button repeatedly, waiting impatiently for the doors to open. When they did, K.C. surprised Clint a second time. Standing inside, as though he'd been waiting for Clint, the boy softly said, "Frankie."

Clint's confused look displayed he was trying to interpret the boy's cryptic words. "Oh, I see. Someone named Frankie sent you."

K.C's eyes narrowed, his attention glancing at the cat in his arms.

"Frankie is your cat?" Clint said pleased to have guessed correctly.

The boy's face beamed with delight, his lips curling at the edges.

Clint had answered properly. "K.C., what do these numbers mean?" asked Clint, aware there was a reason he had them.

The boy shrugged.

"Who told you to give them to me?" Exasperated at how much work it took to have an exchange with the boy, Clint inserted, "Please don't tell me the cat told you."

Their eyes locked, K.C. frowning all the while. Unable to form the words his head had collected, he took the paper and wrote, with the crayon he'd taken from his pocket, the answer: T.

"T? What does that mean?"

"Him."

"The man who instructed you to give it to me?"

K.C. confirmed Clint's guess, speaking so softly he was barely heard. "Fr-a-nk-ie's mi-ne."

"This T person, is it someone who lives here?"

Finished with the conversation, when the doors opened to the second floor, which Clint didn't realize had occurred, K.C. and Frankie made a run for it.

Clint tailed them. Out of exasperation, Clint blurted out, not knowing why, "Is it a friend of your fathers?" Why Clint said it was a mystery even to him.

Recognition flashed on K.C.'s face, voicing what he was unable to articulate.

Clint felt like he was playing a game of pantomime. Gestures and guesses that he and K.C. exchanged in only one or two syllables. Or, if Clint was lucky, through written words or letters. An idea popped into his head. "Please sit down with me. In your room, that's where you're going. Am I right?"

The boy did not confirm Clint's presumption, but he did point in that direction which was at the end of the hall. When he walked in, Clint followed. Taking station at the desk, K.C. fanatically started to scribble, while the mysteriously acquired feline sat erect on the desk pad, watching him as he wrote. It was as though K.C. was taking dictation. Oddly, the cat jumped up in sync when the boy sat down, like it was a coordinated move.

He handed over more numbers.

16 689043 4212476

551 1659 1988

"Son, I wish so badly I understood what you're trying to tell me. I just don't. What do these numbers mean? Please help me understand."

The cat's blue eyes intensified, connecting with K.C.'s until the boy suddenly shouted out, "Young," he stammered over and over, "Young, Young, Young!" When the cat backed away, the boy relaxed, but cried from the exertion. The cat snuggled, licking his arms and face.

Seeing the pleasure in K.C.'s manner, Clint admitted his mistake. "I'm so sorry, I didn't mean to push you so hard." He walked over to where the two of them sat, the same place as Clint's last visit, where they had both fallen asleep. He lowered himself to the floor, just like last time.

K.C. rocked his body from side to side a distance away but stopped when Clint leaned against the wall. "Won't you join me?" he asked, patting the spot beside him. "I won't say another word. I promise. Just you and me, no more questions."

Gradually K.C. scooted in Clint's direction, his eyes feral when he embraced Frankie around the neck and shoulders. The cat pushed into K.C. lovingly.

Clint couldn't help but notice the cat's intelligent eyes were now directed at him. The name K.C. had assigned the cat was uncanny considering the boy could not know about Frank Sinatra and his amazing blue eyes. If one didn't know better, they would assume maybe that is where the name originated but Clint knew that wasn't possible.

When K.C. slid next to Clint, his cat in tow, he instantly leaned in, collapsing on Clint's lap like a ragdoll, just as he had done the first time they were in this position. Clint felt sad, unable to relate to the degree of damage the young boy had endured.

A sickening feeling came over him when he recalled why he had come to the orphanage. It hit him hard. Two wounded souls comforted by the other's presence. "How did you know I was in the building?" he whispered.

K.C. looked up, unable to supply the answer. A glint sparkled in his eye before burying his face in the cat's yellow fur. Clint lifted the boy to bed. Fast asleep under the covers, Clint stroked his forehead, telling him how much he was loved.

Departing K.C.'s room with a page of cryptic numbers, plus one letter, he wondered what any of it meant. Then he remembered K.C. shouting, "*Young.*"

The name, Clint determined, held meaning.

Chapter 39
Home Is Where the Heart Is

Clint opened the door to his office and walked over to the desk to lay K.C.'s latest scribblings down. When he sat in the chair, sinking into the soft leather, he felt worried and uncertain, defeat consumed him. Fallible, he felt the walls closing in. He was over his head, lacking what it took to go toe to toe with a man who housed a heart of stone.

Clint believed himself a brave man, possessing a curious mind, and fit body. Proud, when Jules once said, not long after they first met, "You don't have an ounce of fat on your entire body, Clint!" He worked hard maintaining his stamina and lean body. His nature was rooted in tradition, coupled with a solid moral compass.

Although convinced that a can-do attitude transcended the worst of problems, Clint's confidence had waned since yesterday. Likening his skills to what he now perceived as a calculated, coldblooded killer's resolve, was foolish. Mind over matter was not enough firepower to jump into the arena with Axel. Furthermore, if he stepped over the line Scott Edwards had set, Clint's head was going to roll. Although he wanted to take this journey alone, he was more aware than ever Scott and he must walk it together.

A glint sparked on the far side of the office, holding his attention. Half expecting to see someone, or something, in the antique mirror when he swiveled it around to face him—as it had the last time the wall danced with a flickering light—Clint felt disappointed when he saw nothing out of the ordinary. Both sides of the mirror were normal. But then again, how could the word normal, and the antique mirror ever be used in the same sentence, considering he'd purchased the mirror in a shop that didn't exist. Still, the room felt unnatural, alive even, as he took a step back and stared at his reflection.

His eyes restlessly circled the room, landing on the quartz crystal on his desk—Rod Radcliff, Sr.'s parting gift to him. His turned his head and narrowed his eyes. Golden rays radiated from the crystal's core.

Fanciful thinking maybe, but for a moment, it was as though a voice breathed. *Numbers hold the key.*

"I need protection," he voiced to the empty room. "You brought me into to this. If I dive into the deep end, will you be there?"

A clear and succinct manifestation rang out. *Frame of mind affects outcome. Step out of the way. Let magic occur.*

Clint stood silently letting the words absorb into his consciousness, taking them to heart. Heeding the advice. *These injustices must be rectified so I can free myself from the pain of knowledge,* he told himself.

He shivered, thinking about Cookie Crenna and how she must have felt in her last moments. "Did you beg? Bargain? Make promises, before whoever did this to you robbed you of your future dreams?" Clint said, choking back the tears that refused to be held. "I'm so sorry," he cried. "How could I have..." he let the words drop knowing they were futile. But then a terrifying thought crossed his mind, *Cookie must not have given Axel my real name or he wouldn't still be calling me cowboy.*

From this point onward he'd rely on insight exclusively, without hesitancy. Get out of his head and tap into his sixth sense. Which meant, he had to move swiftly, with intent, and expel any doubt when it raised its ugly head. "The darkest hour is just before dawn," Clint quoted Fuller, the theologian of old. Lifting the crystal from its base, he gazed deeply into its core, beholden to the powers it held.

"A new day starts in a few hours," he proclaimed soberly into the darkness. "Let's see what it brings." Tightening his grip, he breathed. "Guess what? You are tagging along for the ride." Then he folded the page with numbers, putting both the crystal and paper in his jacket. He locked the door, headed for home.

Pulling up the drive, Clint stopped dead in his tracks, his heart a flutter. It had been an emotional day from start to finish and this latest development put a period to it. In every window of his house red cellophane wreaths glowed. Single red lights wrapped the house and conjured strong memories of his father. The powerful sight made everything he was thinking more intense. Grateful to see them, he was in awe of his lovely wife and her way of knowing what he needed before he did.

When he walked through the door, the house smelled like home. He was lighter of foot, ready to congratulate her on her ingenious idea. She was singing *Silent Night*, the sound generating from the restroom they had remodeled when she moved in. The adjoining facilities accommodated them both and provided privacy.

He tapped on the door and peeked around the corner. "May I come in?"

"Sure," she giggled delightfully from her 1800s clawfoot soaking tub. "I'm covered in bubbles! My hair too!"

Clint sat down on the commode, so grateful to see such a lovely sight after the day he'd had. "You are something else, woman," he said wearing a huge grin. "Where did you get them? We are talking 1950 vintage; they can't be purchased just anywhere."

Her face lit up, proud of her achievement. "eBay! Can you believe that? Came in multiple boxes during the week. Didn't want to hang them until I had enough to cover all the windows. I thought you'd be happy. You needed a pleasant surprise. Especially today, that's why I picked tonight to surprise you."

He sighed in gratitude. "Thank you. You have no idea how much it meant to me to drive up and see them. Touched my heart deeply. This house looks and smells so good. I love this place. And *you!*" With his shoulders higher than before he came home, Clint walked out of the restroom, bringing the door to a partial close in hopes she'd start singing again and he'd hear, her voice soothing to him.

Jules's eyes sparkled, exactly the reaction she had hoped for. "Guess what?" she called from the tub. "I bought enough for Rod's Apothecary, too. Forget the orphanage." She laughed. "Don't ask what I paid. They were worth every penny to see that look on your face. Let's drive around this weekend to look at Christmas lights. Have you noticed how decorative Salzburg is?"

Clint was sorry to say he had not, but answered, "We'll do that. Can't think of anything I'd enjoy more."

Later, after they sat down to dinner, wearing comfy clothes, conversing about a multitude of subjects including putting up the tree on Friday night, Jules said something that took Clint off guard.

"Hey, one of Charlie Hill's painting was sold—again. On the internet, it showed his brother with a lady, the painting between them. That's what Bonnie said, anyhow."

"Mac Hill is Charlie Hill's brother's name," volunteered Clint. "A half-brother."

"Do you think this Mac is selling personal paintings Charlie had given him? If so, that seems thick-skinned. Don't you think? I cannot imagine selling something my deceased brother gave me and profiting from it, but then again, we already know he left Charlie's boy on the orphanage steps, and that's beyond cold-hearted."

She tried to reconcile who this man was and how he could do such things. "The painting sold for a pretty penny! If I'm not mistaken, fifty-eight hundred." She turned, making direct eye contact. "They must not have been close to have done something like that?" She smirked, feeling disgusted. "Maybe he's got more than he wants or needs."

Clint frowned. Red flags flew. "To your point, Jules, unless he has an abundance of them." *Maybe I should poke my nose into it.*

Each day Clint became more interlocked with Charles Hill. Their bond stronger, their quest for justice unwavering. The unlikely partnership was inseparably linked, cutting into every waking hour, ferrying Clint miles from when he first heard of the man. Farley's revelation in the forest, later down in Little Goss Cave, was a remarkable story, an unbelievable one to be sure. A voice, overriding Farley's, demanding attention.

I'll check with Dunn, he told himself. *Get a full understanding of the Will and who got what.* He made a mental note to call Hill's lawyer. *I should ask Bonnie to make me a copy or direct me to it so I can show it to David Dunn. See if the painting was among the Hills' possessions at the time of their death.*

Clint grabbed his wife's hand. "Now that we know K.C. is Charlie and Ann's boy, wouldn't the paintings legally be his?" He thought for a moment, deciphering his thoughts. "Unless Charlie gave his brother a few and kept a few. Named them in the Will. It appears he saw his future and knew they'd be worth something." He shook his head, "Dunn will clear it up." He chuckled. "I'm tired of thinking."

Jules stood, pushing her chair back. "My dear, this whole affair needs to end so you can escape back into your life here with me." Then her face turned earnest. "You do what you need to do. I've put my faith in the influences that are driving you. I trust them, and you! I'd never want to be a ball and chain."

"Thank you, Jules. I couldn't, and wouldn't, do this without your support." His eyes grew dark, ominous in their meaning when he said, "This low-life must pay for what he's done." He got up and walked over to the jacket hanging on the tree in the foyer. Coming back, he placed the golden quartz crystal between them, atop a piece of paper.

"I have Rod's protection, Charlie's wisdom, and K.C.'s insights. How could I go wrong?" He made a slight gesture toward humor, "The boy is a little tougher to figure out than the other two, but I'm tuning my skills."

Jules moved the crystal to the side. Glancing down at the paper, she asked, "What are those?"

"I have no idea. I was hoping you could enlighten me." Clint shrugged in despair. "K.C. came to the office and said he was told to give them to me. I was at a loss for words. What am I to make of that?"

She moved the paper closer, trying to make sense of the poppycock a child's doodling and imagination would create, remembering the battling dinosaurs and the violence the drawing depicted, and of an angelic lady sitting on a bench under a trellis is a heavenly garden. It was hard to believe the same child created both.

"K.C. drew the same locomotive as Farley. Didn't you say?"

"He did. This boy is not a normal Asperger's case Jules." Clint turned proud, thinking how he enjoyed interacting with Keelan. "I forgot to tell you, Tom Sanders had him evaluated. The boy is highly intellectual, and his math skills are off the charts. So is his artistic talent, as you've already witnessed."

"What was his score?" she curiously asked. "If you look deep in his eyes, Clint, you can see there is more to him. It's like the wheels are turning and he's processing incoming data all the time."

"His test came back at 151. Tom sent the report over, I'll forward it to you." Clint looked shocked by what he'd learned. "Tom believes

Keelan sees frequencies outside normal range. He's been reading up on the condition and says it's possible for the child to identify with diverse types of shapes, and colors, that most people don't. Tom suggested K.C. might see things none of us do. Sanders wrote, 'K.C.'s imaginary friends very well might appear *real* to him.' I know that sounds bizarre, Jules, but to the boy they are as real as you and me, they talk and interact. At least, that is what Tom suggested. I haven't talked to Tom personally, but I plan to."

The hour was growing late. Both Jules and Clint were tired. She went around turning off the lights, until she came to the bedroom and living room. The back part of the house was dark. Clint asked to leave special lights burning, as he had as a child. Just as his father had agreed, so did Jules.

Thursday, December 8, Early Morning

With Jules working, Clint's meeting with Dorian Andersen at 9 a.m. at the Skipper's Vessel marina would put him under no pressure to return home early. Thursday was another late night for Jules, same as Tuesday. He hadn't mentioned his meeting the night before but after what Jules stated about trust, he didn't feel it was necessary which on one level was a huge relief. This way he wasn't lying or covering up.

As he was about to turn onto the highway, his cell phone buzzed. Taking the first right, he stopped in at a fast-food restaurant and parked to return the call.

Scott immediately answered. "Clint, you said Cookie didn't drink. Right? Could she have been lying? Trying to warm up to you? Thinking it would put her in your favor?" asked Scott with a sense of dread.

"Yes, she told me she didn't drink. Faked it so people at the bar wouldn't know. She drank tea instead or pretended to mix liquor with coke."

"I've alerted the medical examiner office, asking them to look for puncture marks based on what you've said. Since Cookie Crenna's alcohol blood concentration was .38, mixed with heroin in her

319

system, it was a lethal cocktail by anybody's standards. Presuming she was honest with you my feeling is she *was* murdered. Clint, that's the equivalent of seven to eight drinks an hour. For a woman her size and weight, which happens to be 5 ft. 1 and 110 pounds, it was excessive."

Clint pounded the dash with his hand, madder than he'd ever been in his life. "He did it. You know he did. Or had someone do it for him."

"I'm reluctant to admit it, but I think you're right. The girl was only twenty-four years old."

"That's shocking. I would have guessed mid-thirties," declared Clint angrily, thinking the pronounced wrinkles around Cookie's eyes were overly defined for someone her age. He closed his eyes, taking a breath to calm down. "We didn't talk about it, but I got the impression she'd lived a hard life."

"I just wanted to run this by you. Make sure you weren't going to reconsider. Throw in a *maybe she did take her own life.* The problem is, there isn't any proof she didn't do herself in. The people at the bar will say she drank and took drugs, no question about it. The coroner's report stated she had bourbon in her system and a bottle of Knob's Creek was on the nightstand. Considering there wasn't a struggle, according to the report, it will be regarded as suicide."

Pounding like a freight train, Clint's heart boomed against his ribcage. "Knob Creek," he shouted. "That's the bourbon I ordered the first time I was at the tavern. I had her fix me one, thinking it would be a common drink for a guy in Kentucky."

Numbness set in. Clint realized Axel had picked that brand on purpose to send a clear message. Nausea rushed over him. "Scott, Axel killed her with the brand I ordered the day I started asking questions. He's sending me a warning."

"As much as I'd like to disagree with your logic, your assumption is probably spot on. I'm terribly sorry you've gotten yourself up to your neck in this mess. Don't forget to keep me posted. I demand to be kept abreast of your whereabouts. Let's not add your name to the list. Do you hear me?"

"I hear," acknowledged Clint. "I will be in touch! You can count on it. Probably sooner than you wish." The idea of breaking and entering Axel's home made his heart race. The off chance to locate a murder weapon was everything he could hope for. He'd been told every bullet fired can be traced through microscopic markings back to a firearm. Bullets are as unique as a person's fingerprints.

"Okay, don't keep me guessing. And don't forget to take the watch back to Dunn. Before noon!"

"I heard you the first time, Scott. I'm not that old. My hearing is still intact!"

Scott's chuckle on the other end of the line made Clint smile. Never having experienced a sibling, he reveled at the idea that Scott was his sparring partner.

"That may be, but you'll always be older than me," were Scott's parting words.

Chapter 40
Skipper's Vessel

Clint withdrew the vintage pocket watch from his wool full-length coat and set it on the seat. He would keep Rod's crystal inside the glove compartment from this day forward until he was finished with all inquiries. Dressed for the part, the attire Clint wore presumably would match Andersen's appearance, best suiting the circumstance and the person he was about to meet.

Aware that Andersen was a man of means, and the patrons of the Skipper's Vessel would most likely wear high fashion–although he didn't expect to see many people in the dead of winter–Clint had layered a tailored sweater over a cream, button down oxford shirt. He carried leather gloves and wore a stylish fedora.

When he reached the waterfront, the parking lot was nearly empty. Only one car drew his attention, on the far end. A silver, SL500 Mercedes Benz. The driver was seated inside the running car, eyeing him. Getting out, Clint moved toward the door but stopped when the owner of the Benz, called out, "Would you happen to be Clint Reeves by chance?"

For a moment, trepidation seized him, inspecting the parking lot, and door, for undercover police waiting his arrival. When everything remained calm, Clint answered, "Yes. Are you Dorian Andersen?"

"Yes, I am. Thought it might be best to wait out here until you showed up. No need to go in if you developed cold feet." Andersen exhibited a hint of a smile hoping to lighten the mood.

"That wouldn't be so tough to do." Clint's expression matched Andersen's. "Meeting you is all I've thought about since we talked."

"Me as well, I'm afraid. It would appear we have much to discuss. Let's go indoors where its warm," he suggested, eyeing Clint's style and feeling more comfortable than before he arrived. "I told Harry to put breakfast together for us. Samplings of meat and pastries," he said growing closer. He wore a double-breasted, black wool peacoat, pressed dress jeans, and loafers.

"Thanks, I could use some coffee and something to eat. When my wife left home this morning I darted out and forgot to grab a bite." Clint slyly grinned. "Didn't want to be late to our meeting."

"I understand. I'm nervous too."

When Clint realized Andersen was a down-to-earth man and had honored their agreement, he sighed with relief. Walking into the building shoulder to shoulder, at about the same height and stature, he realized if the circumstances were different, they could be perceived as friends.

The head waiter and owner of the marina, brought a carafe of coffee and two cups, setting them down on a fine linen cloth spread over a circular table. "I'll have your breakfast choices out soon, Dorian."

"Thanks, Harry," he said, reaching out to shake the man's hand. Out of range to be heard, Andersen remarked, "Harry is a one of a kind. Would do anything for his clientele."

Taking in the easy manner of his companion, Clint tossed out, "I know a place to enjoy outstanding food and great service, as well… like here. Josie's Diner on the other side of the river, in Salzburg. James Patrick, the owner, is much the same. Everyone calls him Patrick. He's an outstanding chef, and person, in general. You'd like the place, I'm positive. My wife works there a couple of days a week." Clint grinned big, almost forgetting why the two men had come together.

"I'll do that, sir. A day trip, with my wife, Jessica." Andersen's eyes turned hollow remembering his son was missing, or if Clint was to be believed, dead. "Please start out, tell me what you know."

Clint took a deep breath, started at the beginning, leaving out large gaps of how he was able to arrive at the conclusion he held. When he was done, he said, "I have an unflappable witness who can testify to Axel's identity as the shooter. Axel returned to the scene and threatened the owner. He wanted to see what Hill had on his body the night he died."

Not easy to choke down the bitter truth, Andersen finally spoke, asking, "Why was that so important?"

Clint reached into his coat that was flung over the chair beside him and removed something from the pocket. Putting his hand over it, he closed his eyes trying to muster additional courage. "Because he was looking for this. Killed for it, in fact. Five people have died. Axel's greedy search to retrieve what I have here, caused their deaths. Your son was the first, the waitress at Cell Block #49, Cookie Crenna, died yesterday—a supposed overdose, which it was not." He slid the pocket watch to Andersen's side of the table, waiting for the man's expression to change from wonder, to wounded.

Andersen's breath caught, grabbing the watch off the table, opening it to read the inscription while a familiar tune played. *Moonlight Sonata* chimed delicately six notes before he latched it shut, lowering his head so Clint couldn't see his tears. "I love the Old West theme on the outside. Don't you? And Mae West's words crack me up."

"I do. It's all very distinct."

"Thaddeus is dead. Isn't he?" Dorian feebly asked.

"I'm afraid so."

"Do you have any idea where his body might be?"

"I'm sorry to say I do not," replied Clint. "Not yet, but I'll find him, Dorian. You can count on it. It's my single aim in life right now. To find your son and bring Axel to justice. The second person he killed is closely related to a friend of mine."

"Axel was the one who robbed me?" Andersen moaned. "My son must have found out." A measure of a man, heartbroken, leaned hard, back into his chair. "I knew the waitress. I went in there once. To tell you the truth, I liked the girl. I can't believe she's dead. My God, why?"

"Because she talked too much." Clint's faced looked pained. "Especially to me. Cookie was the conduit for how I was able to piece most everything altogether. I even offered the poor girl a job at my orphanage to get her out of the bar and the rat race."

Dorian's face looked startled. "You're that guy, the one who found the Reno treasure in Goss Cave. I remember reading about you! Your story. It was fascinating!"

"Fraid so." Clint shifted sheepishly in his seat, knowing he had a persistent reputation that followed him. "That's me."

"Good grief. I never thought you and I would ever be talking one on one, or ever meet."

"Well, that makes two of us." Clint agreed, looking toward the windows and watching the undulant river water beyond the docks where yachts were stored, rise and fall.

"No wonder I felt something was different about you, not just a typical caller. That you were on the level."

"I am, Dorian, and my current mission is to find your boy's body. Axel must pay for what he's done. I have my reasons why this is exceedingly important to me. Again, you'll have to trust my motives. They are noble, I assure you."

"What do you want with me? Other than to convince me to stop looking for Thaddeus?" Andersen's eyes filled with tears; not sure how to continue. "This is doubly hard on me. Irene, my sister, Axel's mother, was devastated when her husband was hauled off to jail. She lived on tranquilizers for what felt like forever. Probably still uses them. She won't hear of anyone speaking negative about her son. She thinks her kid walks on water, and he encourages it, so long as she dishes out spending money to support his fancies. She even bought him a house," Andersen grimaced, feeling older than his years. "But I may have already mentioned that."

"Your watch was the reason they fought," said Clint. "When Thaddeus saw it, according to Cookie, he got extremely angry, started pushing Axel around the room, like a madman. It didn't take long before the argument was taken outdoors to the alley behind the bar."

Shifting his gaze, Clint chose not to observe Dorian's pained countenance. "The second victim of Axel's crimes was Charles Hill, a pedestrian who happened on the scene. Axel darted off when he saw Charlie, not aware Thaddeus had lifted the watch from him. Before Thaddeus died, he gave it to Charlie."

Clint pointed to the masterfully crafted gold timepiece, adding, "When your nephew came back, intending to retrieve it, and to remove Thaddeus's body before the police arrived, he figured out what had occurred."

Recalling his conversation with Cookie, Clint inserted an additional comment. "Cookie questioned Axel as to why Thaddeus had not been coming around and he invented a cockamamie story about a corvette in Eureka, Montana, and Thaddeus going there to haul it back here. A morass of lies."

Dorian laid his trembling fingers atop the gold case. "Axel always was a difficult kid," he retorted. "Would never take *no* for an answer. I'm afraid he's like his father that way." He smiled pleasantly, caressing the watch tenderly. "Those boys, when they were young, were like brothers. When they got older, they'd bungie jump from bridges and skydive, things I'd never had the nerve for. Both were insanely fearless." His eyes sparkled from the memory.

It was hard to listen to Andersen. He was walking down memory lane to a better time when his influence held weight.

"I found a gold toothpick in the alleyway where the fight continued. It was the first item that made me suspect your nephew. The black velvet case it was in bore the initials A.A.D. Cookie enlightened me as to what the initials stood for and to whom the toothpick belonged. She recognized it right away, said A.A.D. stood for Axel Alrik Drako. Alrik was your father's name if I'm correct."

Clint lingered a moment before stating what he had on his mind, "I'll never know why I went into Cell Block #49 that day, or why I set the toothpick casing on the table."

"That's easy," Andersen replied with confidence, "because you were meant to." The man conversing with Clint, firmly charged, "From what I read about you, I gather you are a determined fellow who follows your instincts. That's how you found the treasure, I dare say. This is just another example. Gut feelings are never wrong, my friend, *never!* That is what I've learned, and why I didn't hang up on you when you called the first time."

"Point taken." Clint nodded, in full agreement of the assessment put forth. "That's what I'm doing. It's why I'm here. Dorian, I will need you to testify at some point. The watch belongs to you, that shouldn't be too hard considering its markings, inscription, and uniqueness."

Taking the watch back from Andersen, Clint noted, "I understand you filed a report. It'll be used as evidence. The good news is some of your items will hopefully be returned, including this watch, but not today. It was found on Charlie the night he died and is part of his estate. Until I can prove otherwise, that it wasn't his to begin with, it must stay a part of the Will."

Clint observed Andersen's puzzled expression, quickly making a promise. "It will end up with you. If I'm on the right track, and I believe I am, I'll be returning more items taken from your safe, not just your father's watch. Right now, with Cookie out of the picture, and Charlie Hill gone, I have my work cut out for me, to prove connections between events."

Clint intentionally withheld information from Andersen. He had omitted Thaddeus's dying word–*Axel*. While inside the mirror Clint witnessed Thaddeus's death and heard him desperately utter his killer's name. It was something Clint couldn't disclose.

He patted the table, declaring it was time for him to hit the road. "Will you keep what I've shared under wraps? At least for the time being? Hopefully, I proved my case against your nephew and provided tangible evidence to substantiate my theory."

"Absolutely," Dorian concurred. "I'd like to ask how you know so many details about that night Thaddeus, and the rest of the victims were murdered. You talk about it as if you were there. It's conjecture, I'm aware, but it doesn't sound that way."

Caught flat-footed, Clint replied, "Oh, I've replayed it dozens of times in my mind. I've read police reports and talked to witnesses. It's not so hard to piece together, really." He lifted his eyes. "As a sidenote, a young police officer was also shot that night, leaving a widow, and his children fatherless. Four people died in succession on December 21, 2004."

Reacting to the abridged answer he'd received, Andersen commented, "I suppose you've done your homework. I commend you." Softly speaking, he made an apology. "I'm sorry we had to meet under these circumstances, but I will say, I'm glad we've met. Please keep me informed of any developments. I'll be sitting on needles and pins until my boy comes home."

"No problem," Clint replied, thinking he planned to do so anyway. You are one of my top concerns."

Clint moved to the bar area to compliment Harry on the excellent food he had served and for his hospitality. "I appreciate your efforts, Harry. Thank you, it was a kind gesture and a treat I assure you."

"Take care, Dorian." Clint waved at his companion, registering his miserable expression. Harry and Andersen shared a word. Although they appeared to be talking business, Clint knew Andersen's mind was elsewhere.

Clint sat in his truck, wondering what would develop over the next few weeks. His journey was not a linear one. Many varied factors and people affected it. Heavy on his mind was the painting Mac Hill had recently sold, knowing that action felt seriously off. It didn't set well with Clint, and although he knew it was none of his business, he had to understand why Charlie's brother would give up such a priceless possession.

Leaving Skipper's Vessel marina, feeling less burdened than when he arrived, Clint felt Dorian Andersen had taken the shocking news as well as could be expected. He turned out of the parking lot and noticed Andersen leaning against his car, looking as though he might collapse.

In his heart, Clint believed he'd made the right decision in telling Andersen the truth. Now Clint would direct his attention on finding Thaddeus's remains. He had no greater mission than to bring Dorian's son home.

The timepiece was tucked back inside his overcoat. Glancing at the dash, the digital clock registered 10:32, ample time remaining before noon to drop the package off, call Scott to let him know *mission accomplished*. After that he'd spend a short while staking out Axel Drako's residence.

Using Cookie's key to sneak inside a known killer's house triggered enormous fear. How would he ever be able to garner enough nerve to execute the plan he entertained? It was an idea without advantage unless it was executed perfectly.

For now, he'd observe the household occupants' comings and goings, just as he had done the last time. Around this same hour, only that time Cookie was still alive, which brought grievous regret. If he ever expected to venture beyond the front gate, he'd need to consider Axel's routine and anyone else who lived there.

He turned onto Liberty Drive, moving east bound two blocks until he reached Third Street, where he made a sharp right turn into the parking lot of Dunn and Murphy Law Offices. Sandwiching his truck between two fancy cars, Clint jumped out and made a beeline to the side entrance of the building.

The receptionist greeted him with a bright smile. "How may I help you, sir?"

"I'm here to see David Dunn."

After a moment, she instructed Clint to take the elevators to the second floor. "The law offices are midway down the hall, Suite 204." He didn't mention he'd been there before, knowing precisely where it was, when she finished delivering her instructions.

When Clint entered the lobby, David Dunn was graciously awaiting his arrival. "Don't have but a minute, but thought I'd come out to greet you and receive the heirloom personally."

"Great," Clint replied, handing the package over. "I was going to ask you a question, but if you don't have time, I can come back another day."

"I'm sorry, didn't mean to be rude, Dunn said with a wave of his hand. "I have a solid fifteen minutes. Would you like to come to my office to talk? Don't like to conduct business in the lobby."

"Have a seat," Dunn said as they walked into his office. Sitting across from Clint, he asked, "How may I help you?"

"Well, it has to do with Charles Hill's paintings. Did he leave any in the Will? We didn't really go into that the last time Scott Edwards and I were here."

Dunn's face turned inquisitive. "Interesting question. And timely. I did not go into detail the first time but that is why Charles hired me. He believed someday his work would pay off. His art would hold substantial worth." Dunn's face brightened. "Every artist's dream."

"May I ask how many were there? And where are they now?"

Dunn's brow creased, "There were only three. I'm certain Charles meant to leave more, but his time ran out, unfortunately. It was his intention to leave a legacy for his son. I awarded them to his brother just this week. The anniversary date is nearing so I released them early, considering there were so few. Didn't turn out like Charles thought it would unfold, but they will be treasured, I'm certain. Mac, his brother, seemed incredibly pleased." Dunn glanced out the window into the bright morning sky, "Everyone always thinks they have another day, month, or year. Doesn't always happen that way."

Clint felt defeated after hearing Dunn's revelation. "Okay. Just so you know Mac sold one of Charles's paintings for $5,800. So, Charlie wasn't too far off in his belief that someday he'd gain in popularity. Poor guy, he dreamed of the day his name would be recognizable and his grandioso beliefs, may in fact, be coming true."

What Clint had said didn't set well with Dunn. He leaned back in his chair. "I hope that wasn't one I turned over to him at the first of the week. Could you tell me what the subject was?"

"Not really, I only know a lady purchased it for that amount. The article and picture are on the internet. You can look it up."

"I might do that. Because if he sold any of the ones I gave him, those were meant as a gift, not intended to be sold."

Suggesting there may be a reasonable explanation, Clint offered, "My wife thinks it could have been one he didn't particularly care for, or he just has more than he knows what to do with."

"I don't think so," Dunn responded promptly. "Mac said he only had two of his brother's painting and was thrilled to receive the three I gave him."

"Oh," Clint reacted, surprised. "I suppose that puts a nix on my wife's theory."

"Yes, I'd say so. I should check into this," Dunn announced, pondering the situation with rebuff. Glancing at his watch, he stated, "I need to wrap this up, but you might consider this. Mac Hill locked his brother's house the night he died and contacted me right away. He stated nothing was touched and everything was awaiting this law firm's representative to show up to evaluate the property and itemize what was inside."

"So, it's possible he removed articles prior to someone getting there? Is that what you are proposing?"

"I'm suggesting its possible is all. My point is, if a loved one only has maybe five of his brothers painting, would he sell one of them? Would you?"

"No, I don't suppose I would. To be transparent, this is the second one that has been sold since his death, not the first. One sold the day after."

Dunn raised a brow, disgusted by what he had learned.

They went their separate ways, both wondering what kind of man Mac Hill might be.

In the truck, Clint devised a plan, a way to determine if Charlie's brother did indeed remove paintings from his house prior to David Dunn's representative arriving on the scene. If so, that would explain why Charlie had so few pieces of artwork in inventory. Especially since Farley McDougal, who held Charlie's beating heart, was producing them right and left. Layers upon layers of them.

What didn't make sense to Clint was why would Charlie use Farley to paint so prolifically after his death but do so little prior to it? Hiring a lawyer to keep track of his life's work, and then have none? Seemed more than a little odd.

Chapter 41
A Light in the Darkness

Parked a fair distance from Axel's home, Clint slouched in his seat watching carefully for any movements, inside or outside the house. A pattern was surfacing. Little went on during the day. Assuming Axel and his lady friend were night owls, Clint's best chance of entering the property would be after dark. Which meant one of Jules's late-night shifts would provide the right timing.

Assuming Axel slept during the day, he decided to stop by a nearby coffee shop to formulate phrasing for a local advertisement to be placed in one of the many smaller local Louisville papers. Later he'd drive back by Axel's to see if anything stirred.

Carefully Clint wrote verbiage for an ad. *Dedicated collector seeking Charles Hill's artwork,* it read, *willing to deal fairly for the right piece.* Giving the name Jake Reeves, attached to a burner phone, designated to the purpose, Clint was ready whenever the call came in. He placed the ad in four small publications. Now, all Clint had to do was sit and wait.

He aimed his truck back through the streets of Louisville, to 945 Hardin Street. This time, his reward for waiting an extra hour proved to his advantage. A Lexus LS430 Sedan was parked crooked in the drive–DeArra D'Amelio, *blondie in a box*–as Cookie Crenna had described her–was home.

Clint kept a close eye on the LS, and in the two windows of the house he could clearly define movement. An animated interchange was turning violent, he deduced. And if he didn't know better, Clint would have sworn the couple was fist-fighting. Then, his suspicion was confirmed when he saw Axel at the window backhanding DeArra into the darker part of the room that couldn't be seen.

Within seconds, *blondie in a box* hightailed it out the door, her wig wonky, clinging to one ear, screaming obscenities over her shoulder that would cause a sailor to blush. She slammed the door behind her so hard Clint heard it a block away.

Blondie peeled her Lexus out of the drive so furiously Clint was positive she was going to hit the parked car opposite Axel's house or blow a tire from hitting the curb violently. It threw gravel several feet into the air.

From the truck, Clint saw serendipity come knocking when Axel bolted from the side door like his pants were on fire. He flung his hefty weight into a shiny black Cadillac Deville, the door not completely shut as he ripped out of the drive, just as his lover had done two seconds before. The chase was on!

So was Clint's window of opportunity to perform the devil's work. Sliding down into the seat an inch further, he peeked over the steering wheel, observing until he was certain the neighbors had lost interest, and the coast was clear. The time had come to swallow his fear and pin on the badge of courage or leave.

"'Tread lightly and carry a big stick,' was Teddy Roosevelt's recommendation," Clint quoted, as he reached for the tire thumper he kept behind the seat. Used as a tire pressure gauge, the tool could also serve nicely for a weapon.

Clint opened the door and stepped out of the truck. The bravest thing he'd ever done, notwithstanding, walking into Salzburg in knee-deep snow when he was five years old back in 1953. The memory was a strong reminder of what he was capable of when he put his mind to it. He looked up, "Hope you're hanging around, Charlie. I might need you."

Morphing before his eyes, dense clouds shielded what sunlight remained of the day. Approaching four o'clock, December's sun set in an hour, which could work to Clint's advantage. Securing the weapon under his coat, Clint rushed behind the house. Laying low, he listened for any other sounds generated from inside the house. Convinced no other occupants remained, he tugged on the gates of hell, slid the key into the lock, and turned it. The door clicked, unlatching on the first try.

He knew if Axel returned too soon and caught him trespassing, his name would undoubtedly be added to the list of casualties already notched into Drako's belt.

With determination he advanced through the kitchen and into the backroom where Cookie described floorboards that would lead him to a lower level. Clint kept his mind sharp while swiftly eyeing the darkened pantry, until at last, the space he was looking for appeared.

Taking a deep breath, he placed the boards that camouflaged the entry to the side. His heart thundered as he stared down into the abyss. He uncradled the flashlight attached to his beltloop and aimed the beam into the pit. Just as he had done two years prior when the shack presented an alternate entrance into Goss Cave.

Turning, he lowered his body down into the hole, determined to locate the place Cookie had mentioned. Now standing in the basement beneath the pantry, Clint's next hurdle was to locate the center brick that would release yet another opening. He moved away from the window. Using his hands, he felt every inch of the surface for the entrance to the next level down but found nothing that would indicate another room existed besides the one he was in.

None of the brick features gave way to any other compartment. The darkness, wrapped in a veil of oppression and wickedness, permeated the small cubicle. The air reeked with the stench of evil.

"Don't lose your objectivity," Clint voiced. "Stay focused on why you are here. Don't think about how it feels. Think about the mission."

He inspected the bricks closely and noticed something irregular. Using his fingers to apply more pressure than the first time he'd examined them, he was gratified when the first brick loosened, setting off a sequence of others. One by one, they released from the wall, exposing steps to a hidden chamber.

The secret space below the basement was made visible. He placed a foot into the cavity, realizing Cookie must have done the same. He would have to exhibit more bravery than he ever had to continue his forward progress. Did he have what it took to move downward, and onward, into what could be a death trap?

Everything in him screamed *get out of there*. His heart was beating so hard, it felt like it might explode in his chest. No one would ever know where he was or had gone. The worst possible outcome awaited if he made a mistake. He had to remove a significant piece of Axel's stolen property to show conclusive evidence, and then get back to his truck pronto.

The part that scared Clint the most, however, was the void of nothingness that surrounded him. It occurred to him no magical support had arrived as he'd anticipated. *Was I insane to have believed my own nonsense? That my back is covered?* Clint lamented with aggravation, doubting his choices and himself.

In this hole beneath the basement, hunched where the window above should be, Clint became his own cheerleader. *I can do this.* The cranny was cramped, but the contents it held were immense. Valuables to be sure, but no knife, gun, or any other weapon Clint had hoped to find. He felt deflated, his disappointment was obvious.

Did I really risk my life for this? he thought. *Doesn't matter, take what you can and leave.* He listened for sounds coming from the upper levels but noted nothing of consequence. Stacks of rubber banded paper bills, including $500s and $1000s, fifteen or so gold coins, silver dollars, and a handful of jewels were scattered about. He headed for the opening with a $500 bill in his back pocket. Evidence to show Scott. Enough to get a search warrant.

He slipped through the hole, emerging back in the basement where a heavy stench hung. It smelled as though something had died, but Clint chose not to think about it. In haste he scurried to the wood slats to make his escape through the pantry.

In the quiet, a sudden storm of loud voices erupted. People had entered the house, slamming a door against the wall so hard the reverberation was felt in the basement.

To make a run for it now would be stupidity. His only option was to put the boards back and hope they weren't noticed. He prayed no one went into the pantry rummaging for food or snacks.

Placing his face against the floorboard, he observed light on the wall generated from the front of the house. The kitchen was dark, showing no signs of activity. In the adjoining room is where Clint focused his attention.

Now what? he questioned fretfully. *I guess if push comes to shove, I'll stay here until they leave again. I don't have another option.*

He heard, presumably DeArra, spewing obscenities at Axel. In turn, Axel was attempting to coddle her, not wanting the argument to escalate any more than it already had. Clint shook his head, thinking what a volatile, explosive couple they were. He knew some people fed on the disfunction of a bad relationship and actually preferred it to a healthy one.

Too bad they didn't stay away another ten minutes, he grumbled, *I would have been long gone by then.*

Jules came to mind. *I'm one lucky guy.* Suddenly, he remembered his cell phone was on mute. *What if it had rung?* he grimaced, moving further into the darkness. *Good grief, man,* he scolded himself, *that could have turned ugly.* Repositioning the last wood panel back into position to hide the fact it had been tampered with, Clint's confidence waned.

Advancing through the labyrinth of junk scattered about on the basement floor, Clint peered at the window to his right and found it unduly safeguarded. Thick bars braced the window on the inside and out. The assumption might be to deter breaking and entering, but Clint knew better. Axel had a lot more to lose than pilfered goods from the upper level should his hidden stash of incriminating property be unearthed.

The sun had forfeited its dominion over to the moon, offering Clint no warmth from the window located on the east wall. With the flashlight switched off, exposure, or detection, was unlikely. A permanent delay in the investigation was at risk–at least on his side of the equation.

A chain is no better than its weakest link, Clint reminded himself. Cradling his knees, Clint breathed hard. Filled with dread, Clint realized he could not hide from the fool-hearted decision he'd made, which had placed him in serious jeopardy. This predicament could easily cost him his life if he didn't find a solution, which happened to be unfathomably absent at present.

Keep your wits about you, Clint's sensible side lectured, marshaling the grit he had going in back to the surface.

Taking a step toward the pantry, he took another one in reverse, lowering himself to the concrete floor. He'd already established to try to escape now was a dangerous move and could prove fatal.

With the flashlight off, the room turned blacker than the blackest night. A darkness he'd only experienced once, in Goss Cave. Fear seeped through the cracks of his armor. If he was forced to remain below ground for an indeterminate time, what would he do? He thought about the room's repulsive smell and wondered if he might not be the first person to be trapped down here.

What about food, bathroom needs, and water? He cringed at the idea. An unexpected event to an impossible situation, occurred. Clint chose to quiet his mind and focus on anything other than his predicament.

It was in that moment an unknown energy entered the space, something quite indescribable.

In the darkness, an illumination appeared.

Clint was not alone after all.

Chapter 42
Dangerous Interlude

Sitting perfectly still, his attention moved to the window where the unnatural light entered. In that instant, Clint experienced an event outside the realm of even his believability. The black iron rails barricading entry began to alter.

The window creaked open, slowly allowing a draft of nighttime air to flow in from outdoors. He inhaled a cold, refreshing breath as the staleness shifted away. Air never smelled so sweet, or clean.

Ecstatic, Clint dizzily exclaimed, *Thank you. Thank you. Thank you.* Flying across the room, with a burst of energy he didn't know he had in him, Clint repositioned a stool under the window he had located on the opposite side of the room.

From the floor he lifted his weight to the window. A difficult maneuver for anyone. Grateful to have a fit body, Clint pushed into and past a space barely large enough for a child to manage. Determined to escape the prison he'd locked himself in, Clint forcibly rammed his mass through. Once he'd landed on the other side, a gash bled from under his ribcage, deep enough to cause excruciating pain. A willing exchange for freedom.

Lying on the ground, his face pressed against the soil, Clint rolled over, touching but quickly withdrawing his hand from the severe injury he had incurred. It felt deep. Time would tell. Blood trickled from the wound, and he felt it ooze down his side.

All the while, snowflakes floated in the breeze, swishing this way and that, softly landing on his skin as he watched them zigzag through the dark sky. A glorious feeling after inhaling stale, smelly, rotten odors in the environment he had come.

Hushed words entered his consciousness, clearly spoken, leaving no doubt to whom they were directed. *You are never alone. Look to the stars for answers.*

Rod? Clint spoke inwardly, joyously elated at words he recognized from another time. *You opened the window? Parted the bars so I could escape?*

The messenger vaporized so quickly Clint had no time to process what he'd witnessed. He credited Rod Radcliff, Sr. for intervening, keeping in mind the phrase he'd heard was so similar to words expressed to Clint when Radcliff separated from Salzburg over two years ago.

But Rod had not been Clint's benefactor engulfed in light that night, nor was it Charlie Hill's essence come to call. Destiny with a different name had saved him.

Tiptoeing across the rough, uneven ruts trenched into the lawn, Clint slithered his way over the shadowy ground and held his hand against his bleeding side to spring over the back gate, adrenaline propelling him to heights that amazed even him.

With knees bent and his back hunched, Clint lowered his frame beneath the fence line. He snuck forward down the darkened alleyway that separated Hardin Street from Tetters Drive. From end to end, he snaked through the rough gravel while his feverish pulse kept pace with the life-saving adrenaline that helped him hyper-focus until he reached the mouth of the alley. Catching his breath, he stood at the side street that crosslinked the two roadways.

Two blocks away snow blanketed his truck. As he approached, an inner warning activated alarm bells. Alongside the door and back panel words were etched into the paint.

I KNOW YOU ARE HERE AND I WILL FIND YOU.

Interpreting the threat was easy, though synchronicity had played its hand. Axel must have seen his truck prior to pulling into his driveway and tailing his girlfriend indoors.

A huge weight slipped from Clint's shoulders. True, his truck was trashed, but currently Axel was indoors mending bridges with DeArra. He didn't have time to canvass the streets in pursuit of Clint. There was no time to lie in wait before Clint could hop back into his truck and make a run for it.

He felt comfort in knowing Axel had no idea who the *cowboy* was that pursued him. Nor was Axel aware his nemesis had evidence that could place him behind bars. It, most likely, was a temporary incarceration, but with Axel in jail he'd be powerless to cause harm. Clint could search for Thaddeus's body without fear of retaliation.

The hour had turned late. Clint had been detained less than two hours, but that would be enough to cause Jules to worry if he didn't phone. Uncertain how he should address the telltale signs of his injury, Clint considered rational explanations as he tackled the slippery roads back to the highway. He debated on how much to share. He could lie, of course, and say his truck slid off the road, or that he'd had a flat tire, but none of that would do. He owed Jules the unvarnished truth, no matter how distasteful.

Motoring along I-64, Clint called Scott before phoning his wife. He left a message on voicemail stating he had important news. Clint requested Scott return the call as soon as possible.

Before he could dial Jules, the phone rang. "Scott, thanks for calling back so quickly."

"I told you I'd be watching for your call. What's up?"

"I have evidence."

"Evidence… explain, please."

"One of Dorian Andersen's $500 bills taken from his safe is in my possession. It should be traceable."

A long silence lingered between them.

"I need you to tell me how you came upon this evidence."

"I lifted it from Axel Drako's place. Only one but enough to show he stole it from his uncle."

"For the love of God, Clint, tell you didn't break into the guy's house?"

Again, a heavy silence settled.

"I didn't exactly break in. I used the key Cookie gave me. So, technically I didn't trespass in the true sense of the word. I walked in after unlocking the door, but the house doors weren't all locked. I went in the back, and it was locked."

Scott had no words for what he had just heard.

"I am going to pretend I didn't hear what I just heard." Scott said frustratedly. "I will call you back. We will talk. We will meet. We will discuss this in person, face to face."

"Okay," Clint agreed, thinking that was best. "I'll watch for your call."

Clint stared at the clock. Did he call now, thinking Jules was probably close to pulling into the drive? *I should,* his logical side instructed, so he dialed.

"Hey, lady," he chirped, more jovial than normal. "Where are you?"

"I'm sorry," she apologized, "we got so busy I didn't have time to check my phone. It was one whale of a day. I haven't even clocked out. Should be home in forty-five minutes. What did you make us?" she teased.

"Pizza? Is that alright?" Clint sighed with relief. "I didn't figure you'd want a ton to eat at this hour."

"Pizza is God's perfect food. In my opinion." Her voice was upbeat and spirited. "Every night should be pizza night in my book. My body wouldn't agree, but my taste buds would."

Clint couldn't get a word in edgewise, listening to Jules's animated conversation made him laugh. He was delighted when she continued, carrying on about her day.

"I bet we broke our all-time-high sales record. Josie's is so popular these days, especially with people out Christmas shopping, it's hard to keep up. Customers don't seem to mind waiting a few minutes longer. Everyone sits around and chats. It's sort of fun to watch them interact. On occasion they reel me in."

"I'm glad it pleases you, Jules. I keep thinking it's time for you to give Patrick your notice. Are you certain you want to continue working since the place is getting busier? Heavens knows you don't have to."

"Absolutely, I thoroughly get into the place, and the people. When customers walk in, they leave their troubles at the door, I've noticed. Don't you feel that way?"

Thinking about that, he wished it could be that easy. "I do. But remember, whenever the time comes to pull the plug, just say the word."

"I will someday, but not now. The holidays make Josie's Diner a place to spread Christmas cheer. Everyone can use that. I even thought about suggesting a day trip for the children. Bring them over around 2 p.m. when things are quieter. Serve them their choice of ice cream and toppings, like we did with our grandkids. You know how they loved Josie's ice cream."

Clint laughed. "We even shared an ice cream sundae after we first met. When things started to get serious between us."

"We did. I fixed it for us. The start of something wonderful."

"You betcha!" agreed Clint. "I will say, your idea is an excellent one. The Christmas season is a great time for the orphans to bask in the spirit of the holiday."

"Done. I'll call Terence or Sue tomorrow and get it set up. Tonight though, this lady needs her feet rubbed. You up to the task?"

"Absolutely. Your wish is my command."

Jules chuckled. "That's music to my ears."

Once home, Clint moved at lightning speed to defrost the last frozen pizza in the freezer, placing it on an oven rack before his wife arrived. Without a minute to spare, he set the table, tossing a quick salad, and placing two wine glasses beside their plates before dashing down the hall to dress his wound.

A stroke of luck had allowed him extra time. To explain his tardiness would have been awkward. No way was he going to spoil her good mood by dropping a bomb into her lap. The details of his day could wait until another time.

He rushed to the restroom for the bottle of iodine kept in the medicine cabinet. He wanted to dress the wound before Jules arrived.

First, he drizzled the antiseptic over the cut, dabbing every inch of the gash, followed with gauze and an extra-large Band-Aid to cover the large section the wound encompassed. The cut was deep and much nastier than Clint had imagined. It had bled down past his waistband into his trousers, soiling his shirt and pants.

Throwing everything in the tub, he dashed to the kitchen for a trash bag, to deposit his ruined clothing. Besides the fact they were bloody, they stank, reeking with the odors of Axel's place. It had been a narrow escape for certain, one Clint was appreciative to have executed—thanks to an unknown hand. The very thought of that gave Clint reason to pause.

After collecting his soiled clothing, he used a washcloth to wash his body.

When Jules walked through the door, Clint was in the restroom with the door closed.

"Your honey is home!" she called out. "Smells good in here."

"I'll be right out," he called back, glad to have put soap and water to the stench he'd carried home. Quickly, in the sink he tried to wash his hair, lathering it the best he could. It was important to smell fresh and clean. The last thing Clint wanted was for Jules to detect any hint of Axel's basement.

Walking into the kitchen, Clint pulled the pizza from the oven and set it on the table, waiting for Jules to return from the bedroom. He had flung the garbage bag out the backdoor just in time.

Jules called down the hall, "I'll be there in two seconds. I need to wash my hands."

"Take your time," Clint replied, relieved to have a few seconds to regroup and position himself in such a way his wife wouldn't notice what he'd been up to.

Chapter 43
Day of Reckoning

In the *Importance of Being Earnest*, Oscar Wilde wrote, "The truth is *rarely* pure and *never* simple." And so it was for Clint as he sat across from Scott Edwards, trying to explain how he happened to be in possession of the $500 bill that he was now turning over to his friend.

"So, how exactly did you manage to come up with this?" Scott inquired, knowing full well he probably didn't want the answer.

"Like I said, I used the key Cookie handed me. I went inside Axel's home while he was gone. He'd had a fight with his girlfriend, and I used the opportunity to make my move. I located the area Cookie described but didn't find any weapons. Not the knife he used on Thaddeus, or the gun that killed Charlie."

"Clint, what am I to do with you? You cannot keep throwing yourself in front of buses and think you are not going to get run down. How can I use this as evidence? You broke into the guy's home. Not to mention Kentucky versus Indiana law."

"What about probable cause, a search warrant? Don't you have a friend on the Louisville police force to confide in?"

"A judge would have to sign the warrant. I'd assist only. Couldn't serve as leading officer. Clint, we can't just waltz into this guy's house, or the judge's office, for that matter, without strong evidence to back up allegations."

Clint looked away, ready to lay his cards on the table. "I met with Dorian Andersen before I returned the watch to David Dunn. Andersen positively identified it. A gift from his father, he said it was a family heirloom always kept in the yacht safe, the one that was broken into."

"Alright, but that doesn't positively prove Axel took it, or give me a reason to search his house."

"I understand. Look, Cookie Crenna said Thaddeus and Axel were fighting over a pocket watch the night of the altercation. Thaddeus and Axel took the fight behind the bar in the alley. Charles Hill surprised them, Axel ran, leaving Thaddeus, who was fatally injured, alone with Charlie. The watch ends up on Charlie's body that same night. Cookie's reward for telling me all of this is she too, is dead. Silenced like everyone else that comes close to exposing Axel. Don't you see, at Cell Block #49, Axel stupidly flashed the watch around, bragging about it. When Thaddeus saw it, he knew exactly how it landed in Axel's position. That's when the fight broke out."

"Grant you, it makes sense, but no matter what the circumstances, I can't just force my way into Axel's house without justification.

"The watch is the key. Axel wanted it back because it would incriminate him. Now five people have died because of it." Clint tapped the $500 bill. "This is only one of countless bills rubber banded underground. I saw them. I took only one to prove to you he has his uncle's stolen goods. I suspect he's turned some of it into spendable cash–maybe a gold coin or two, or more. That's how he was able to pay cash for that brand-new truck of his and hook his current girlfriend. Money talks. Axel is a rich man."

Clint assessed the situation with intense clarity. "What if we set a trap?"

"Like how?" responded Scott, shocked Clint would suggest getting involved in uncover work.

"Blackmail. I'll tell him I want money in exchange for my silence. Believe me, he knows I exist. He keyed my truck yesterday. Scratched a warning onto the side panel, driver's side, telling me he would find me. He knew I was there."

Scott's face turned pale. "He did?"

"He certainly did. Thank goodness I had the presence of mind to hang fake tags on my truck when I went into Louisville. He won't be able to trace the plates back to me. I've taken a lot of precautions."

"That was clever," Scott responded, complimenting his friend.

"In the beginning I wore a disguise. That's why the owner called me *cowboy* when he told me to look for Cookie at the morgue." Clint winced, remembering the conversation and how alarmed he felt.

"Anyway, I need to take the truck to the garage. The new owner, Brian Jeffries, used to paint cars at a big dealership in New Albany, as well as do body work. Hopefully he can help or find someone who can. Don't know if you've used him since the place got sold, but he's a good guy. Fortunately, I believe the repair work will be a simple fix."

Pondering the proposition Clint had just made, Scott stated, "You understand I'm not fond of you sticking your nose into places it doesn't belong, but the truth is, I have no idea how to catch him without tripping him up. I'll bring David Andrews up to speed. He'll be needed as backup if things go south, which they probably will. These things are never cut and dried."

"David with us will strengthen our resolve and success."

"Okay, here's the deal, I'll ring Drex Mason. I've used him on a few of my cases, this side of the river. If we present our case concisely, deputization is a possibility. Most of Drex's and my interactions have been drug related, but crime is crime, no matter how you slice it. It could be I'll assist only, so we don't get ourselves in legal trouble. And we want the charges to stick."

"That sounds promising. Let me know how your talk goes. We could lure Axel to the bar," Clint said after much consideration. "Public places are less dangerous, I imagine. The sleaze bag owner at Cell Block #49 knows my face. He's a piece of work, I think Axel runs drugs through there, so maybe we can kill two birds with one stone." Clint sneered. "If only it were that easy."

"We'll need to set a trap. Hopefully, you can convince Axel to continue the conversation, and the pay off, at his residence. Can't say why, but my feeling is he's not too bright. A bully yes, but smart, it doesn't appear so. If he was, he wouldn't have killed Cookie. That was a big mistake on his part."

"Why did you say that?" Clint asked curiously.

"Because the coroner found puncture wounds. One at the nap of her neck, the other behind her right knee. He said it was consistent with an administered overdose through unnatural means. They weren't all that hard to find once he started searching. Rather obvious, he said, not well-disguised. I was going to mention it, but our discussion took off in a different direction."

Clint didn't comment. The pain he felt associated with Cookie's death ran deep.

"Let's circle back around after Drex and I discuss the situation and how best to proceed. Until then stay out of Louisville. The next time you go there, I expect to be with you. Will you promise me that?"

"I will. I've had enough of Louisville for now. I need your help to put this guy away and don't want to jeopardize the outcome. Making Axel pay is my top priority. The thing that bothered me is the murder weapon wasn't found in the house. Cookie said he kept weapons around, but I didn't see any of significance, one in a drawer and another under the mattress. That's disheartening considering if we can't locate either of the murder weapons, we can't prove he's a murderer. Even Cookie's death can't be linked to him."

"I'll reach out when I know something more." Scott got up to walk Clint down the steps to the lobby. "Clint, you've done an amazing job in uncovering vital information. Because of you, Charles Hill's case was reopened. We'll get this guy. Count on it."

Outside in the open air, Clint felt his mindset lift. Friday was a day he and Jules relaxed, and on occasion invited friends over. The idea appealed to him, so he called his wife to clear the idea.

She was out running errands. Getting groceries, filling the tank, speaking with Sue Johnson at the orphanage about a date for the children to visit Josie's. When the phone buzzed, she quickly answered, "Hi, honey."

"Hey, would you be up for playing Mille Bornes tonight with maybe Bonnie and Farley? I haven't called either one but thought it could be fun. I could use a break. What do you think. Sound appealing?"

"I'd love that. I'll call Bonnie to see if she's available."

"Alright, sounds good. Let's shoot for seven. I'll pick up some wings and snacks on my way home." After hanging up, he dialed Farley. He was surprised Farley didn't answer. He left a message explaining why he had called, saying he hoped Farley could join them. After Clint ended the call, he headed for the orphanage.

Jules had sent a quick text stating Bonnie had accepted their invitation and would bring dessert.

Radcliff's Children's Home always warmed Clint's heart. It was his home away from home and felt like an old shoe when he walked through the doors. Earlier, before meeting with Scott, he called to say he'd be stopping by to check out the decorations the children had put up. The lobby was festive. The children had participated in coloring Christmas-related pictures for the walls. A tall tree was arranged in the corner of the room making it impossible to miss. It stood at least eight feet high and supported homemade decorations, weaved around bubble lights and red, green, and gold garland. Large wreaths hung on both sides of the receptionist desk.

Shocked when he poked his head around the corner of the reading room, Clint saw Farley sitting up front and waved in recognition. "Good to see you. Can't say I expected to see you here, though. I called your house and left a message."

"Did you forget what day it was?" inquired Farley with a large grin.

Suddenly Clint remembered their agreement. Starting today, Farley would begin reading to the kids, a standing engagement. "I did. I totally forgot." Clint scanned the room and saw an unusual number of kids mulling about. "You won't be reading until 2 p.m. if I recall. Why are so many here already?"

"Because I sent a bulletin out announcing, starting today Farley McDougal would be the permanent master of ceremony and would have three reading sessions. One at noon, three and seven." Farley's smile broadened. "I sort of felt the kids might enjoy having a story read to them at various hours during the day, more options to choose from I suppose was my thinking. Also offering an opportunity to hear a story before turning in for the night felt right."

The idea of story hour being spread out over the day was an excellent idea and Clint quickly let Farley know how he felt. "I can't believe I never considered it. That way if a child is doing something else, they can choose a different hour to hear a story. Brilliant! Will you read the same story?"

"I was thinking I'd choose any book that spoke to me. The last reading of the day will always be one that lends to a nighttime theme." His lips curled at the edges, "I don't have anything else penciled in on my calendar and can't think of anything I'd enjoy more. You're okay with me changing the routine around here? I hope."

Looking slightly uncomfortable for not having the change he made approved beforehand, Farley volunteered, "I probably should have asked before sending out the notice." Farley reached over and handed Clint the page he had designed. A delightful message on Christmas green construction paper. Pictures of books, cats, dogs, and kids. "I made it at home and delivered it at each door before eleven o'clock. That way everyone would have plenty of time to see it." He looked embarrassed, when he stated, "Sorry, Clint, I should have run it by you first. Don't know what I was thinking. I guess I took our friendship too far."

"Don't give it a second thought, Farley. I'm thrilled to pieces you took the initiative. You'd be surprised how much of everything falls on my shoulders when it comes to implementing new policy. You'll be a good one to have around."

"Super. I've been looking forward to this all week." Sheepishly he admitted, "I had a sit down with Keelan. You don't mind if I call him that, instead of K.C. Do you?"

"Not in the least, things got started on the wrong foot anyway. It'll be a refreshing change. But he'll be the one to let you know. One thing I've learned about K.C." Clint grinned realizing he used Keelan's nickname. "I mean Keelan. The boy has no problem letting you know if he doesn't like something. If he doesn't object, he approves."

"I agree, it was the oddest thing, when he saw me in here a little while ago, he came in, didn't say a word, but sat down beside me on this bench. Like my little shadow." Then Farley chuckled, saying, "he even got up and got both of us a glass of water. Isn't that something?" Farley boasted proudly. "For a boy who doesn't talk much, he sure knows how to communicate."

"I'd say, I'm amazed because he doesn't come into this room until the last minute, right before our designated reader starts the session and stands at the back of the room as close to the door as he can possibly get."

"Like I said, he surprised me too."

"Sounds like I'll need to call Patrick for our fourth in Mille Bornes tonight. That's what I called you about. Jules and I thought we needed a break, have a little fun. Sorry you'll not be able to join us, but I have this feeling you'd rather be here with the kids."

Farley's face lit up, matching the excitement of the season, and of the Christmas tree in the corner that donned decorations of handmade ornaments and construction paper garland.

"It feels like I belong here."

"I'm glad you feel that way," Clint said pridefully, "because I do too. I love everything about the orphanage. When you see positive results reflected from your efforts, it is the most rewarding feeling on earth."

Just as his words passed between them, Keelan Charles walked into the room, a success story in the making.

Chapter 44
Casting Bait

Before leaving Radcliff's Children's Home, Clint reluctantly visited the medical clinic for a professional assessment of his wound. The tightness and slight sting in that area was becoming bothersome.

Nurse Penelope didn't like what she saw. She questioned him on what he had used to clean the cut. She asked when the accident occurred, and *how* it had happened–which, of course, required a fib. She searched for telltale signs of infection and determined none had taken root. She cleaned the wound thoroughly and then applied a fresh bandage designed to close lacerations without sutures. The injury was properly attended to in quick order, to the best of her ability, with an attached warning that Clint should call her asap if redness or swelling occurred.

On his way out, Clint felt relieved to have had an onsite medical clinician at the children's home to evaluate the damage without having to make an appointment with his regular doctor.

Rather than calling or texting an invitation to the card game that evening, Clint preferred to speak with Patrick face to face. Besides, cherry and lemon meringue pie were the *pie of the day* at Josie's Diner every Friday. Comfort food sounded wonderful after the morning he'd had. Jules had sent a message saying Bonnie was informed that Farley would be their fourth in the Mille Bornes game. Clint figured he had a perfect replacement.

"Well, look what the cat dragged in," Patrick goaded humorously, greeting Clint fondly when he sat down at the counter. Rarely did he see his friend on Fridays, if ever, so he knew something was up. "What brings you in at this hour?"

"I have an invite for you... if you're interested. Jules and I were thinking it'd be a load of fun to play Mille Bornes tonight. Boys against the girls!" he joked knowing fate had no favorites. "Would you like to join us? Be our fourth?"

"This afternoon my uncle is stopping by, but that shouldn't interfere. I'd love to. Thanks for asking. A frolicking night with friends. Doesn't get better than that." He laughed, accentuating his rugged, youthful dark features. "Boys against the girls, huh? That ought to be entertaining. I assume Bonnie will be there," he deduced knowing she was Jules's best friend.

"You know it. Those two are fierce. They won't be taking prisoners. You'd better bring your 'A' game," teased Clint spryly. "Don't bother eating beforehand. Bonnie has dessert covered, Jules is making homemade fries, and I'll be picking up wings. Just bring a winning team attitude."

"No way am I coming to your home without pulling my weight," Patrick kidded, thinking of something fun he might make. "I'll surprise you." He teased, thoroughly enjoying the conversation. Patrick had never been married, instead he elected to work in his youth, devoting every waking hour to Josie's Diner. His parents had deposited their lifesavings into the endeavor, taking a second mortgage on their home. Sadly, they passed two years apart, and only four years into the venture, never seeing the diner's popularity.

Patrick had moved to Salzburg in 1969, working doubly hard after his parents' deaths hoping to prove their investment wasn't in vain. He believed they would have been proud of him—their only child—and his extraordinary accomplishment, had they lived.

The nostalgic railcar-style diner, with its Wurlitzer jukebox was a novelty in Southern Indiana. Featuring Elvis Presley, Marilyn Monroe, James Dean, Humphrey Bogart, and a recent addition of the Rat Pack, lent extra charm to its 1950's Formica countertops, lunch car booths, barstools, and red and white vinyl square tiling.

Patrick and Jules had been a winning combination that paid off, but now, seven years after he and Jules joined forces, they could both sit back and bask in their hard work and dedication to Josie's Diner. Patrick was aware *all work and no play* wasn't a recipe for happiness. A fulfilled life required equal parts of work, play and honoring spiritual values. He had been so focused on building a business he had neglected to carve personal time out. He wanted to pursue activities away from Josie's and this invitation from Clint was a great place to start.

"I like surprises," joked Clint, "bring it on!" He reached over the counter to shake Patrick's hand. "See you at seven."

"Looking forward to it," responded Patrick, snatching the receipt for pie and coffee before Clint could lift it from the counter. "Thanks, pal."

Outside, just as Clint opened the door to his truck, his cell phone vibrated, taking him by surprise. Not his normal phone, but the throw-away phone he'd purchased for the ad he'd placed on Thursday morning.

"Hello," he said, anxiously waiting the voice on the other end.

"Afternoon," a man responded in an upbeat tone. "I'm responding to the ad you placed in the Daily Journal. It says you are looking for artwork by the artist, Charles Lewellyn Hill?"

"Yeah, yeah, I am. Thank you for calling. I've been searching for second piece. I have one already. Love his work but haven't been able to locate any more pieces," lied Clint, aware his limited knowledge of art could expose his ignorance. "Are you calling from a gallery?"

"No, I'm a private investor. I too appreciate his style, but I have a few I've been thinking about selling. I'm sticking with a central theme so I'm willing to part with a few that don't fit."

"Gee whiz," Clint said enthusiastically, "when did you start collecting? To have so many, I mean?"

"Back when he first started exhibiting his work on street corners, small venues, exhibits around Louisville mostly, street fairs, that sort of thing. The day before the shooting, he participated in his first and sadly his last gallery show." Mac spoke with reservation, "I don't mean to be rude, but I thought it odd to find an ad soliciting Hill's work. In truth, in the big scheme of things, he's not that popular."

"Oh, I know, but his style is loads better than other artists I've come across. Been looking for another piece these many years. My wife and me, we bought a Christmas picture unlike any out there. A one of a kind—by him. For a present this year, I thought I'd surprise her with a matching piece for our bedroom. She's crazy about the one we have."

Clint thought he'd ham it up a notch, and added, "My woman ain't that easy to please when it comes to gifts, but she'll love anything I find by him. To answer yer question, it just so happened someone suggested I place an ad, so I did. Seems that was a good idea cuz you called. Would you have any Christmas pictures you're wanting to let loose of?"

Taken aback by the Southern accent and back woods, rural, dialogue of his potential buyer, Mac Hill struggled not to laugh. He had neglected to do his due diligence of checking credentials. The buyer sounded so eager to get his hands on one of his brother's paintings, he figured this transaction was a slam dunk.

"The only thing is, Mr. Reeves, would it be alright if I called you Jake?" Mac requested politely.

"Oh sure, Mr. Reeves is way too formal. I prefer first names. What's yours?" Clint fired back.

Fast on his feet, Mac replied, "Jordan Cane. You can call me Jordy." He thought the nickname matched his caller's mentality.

"Well, Jordy, where can we meet? If you want, we could meet at a McDonald's somewheres. Are you in Louisville? I'm in Jeffersonville, this side of the Ohio."

Mac kept himself in check, trying not to howl outright at the idiocy of Jake Reeves. His ad, claiming to be a *dedicated collector* was such a ruse, nonsense, Mac concluded considering the guy couldn't even speak proper English. Comically, he determined someone must have written the ad for him. Owning one painting did not make Jake a collector.

"Just to make myself clear, Jake. Charles Hill is no longer with us, he passed away two years ago. Had you heard?"

"Gosh, no," grumbled Clint. "I had no idea. Sorry, I must have missed that part. Bet that changes things. Don't it?"

"Yes, I'm afraid it does. Hill's work has gone up substantially in price and value. I'm not sure you'll be comfortable with today's going rate. I'd cut you a deal but even that might not make it affordable for you, I'm afraid his work could be outside your budget. May I ask what you paid for the piece you have?"

"My wife bought it," Clint shot back, sounding as though Jordy could be right. Couldn't say for sure. Maybe four or five hundred?" Clint made a warbling sound, "She never tells the truth about what she buys. Thinks I don't pay attention. Could have been more."

"I'm sorry to say, the artist's work runs in the thousands. He's grown in popularity. People are scarfing up pieces right and left. Soon there won't be any available anywhere. It might sound like *humbug*, but I'm not too fond of Christmas art. They don't trip my trigger if you know what I mean." Mac used a term he thought Jake could associate.

"Oh, I get it. Me neither but she's loopy over that sort of thing. Better never come home with what I want... a barn scene with a twelve-point buck standing in the field. I'd love to have that rack hanging in the den." Clint nearly laughed out loud at his silliness but kept his cool.

Not sure he could meet this man face to face without revealing his disdain for his hillbilly manner, Mac exhaled, "Jake, the only thing I have in my collection that matches your description of a rustic scene, isn't for sale. Sorry. But I do have a Christmas picture I'd be willing to negotiate. Just so we are clear, and I'm required to be upfront–don't want to waste your time, or mine–is I believe the canvas is approximately eighteen by twenty-four, which means it could run up to three or four thousand dollars, maybe more. I'd have to check the size. Can't say for certain. May not be what you have in mind, or in the price range you were expecting."

Under this breath Mac guffawed, having a hard time getting his next words out. "Santa Claus is in it."

"I can't believe it," hailed Clint. "That's perfect, Mr. Cane, I mean Jordy. My wife's nutty about Santa Claus scenes, although it's got to be a serious Santa Claus picture, nothing silly, ya know what I mean? Seeun's Charles Hill painted it, it'll be a good one, I'm sure."

"You guessed it. It's a serious Santa painting." Not able to suppress the laughter that had welled up, Mac's hilarity could not be harnessed. Without regard to how Jake might react, he pulled the phone away from his mouth not to make matters worse.

Just as quickly he rebounded, extending an apology. "I'm sorry. Don't take offense, Jake. I'm a little slap-happy from burning the midnight oil last evening. One too many beers I'm afraid." Although Mac didn't drink beer–he preferred fine wines–he assumed his potential client did. Backpedaling, he wisely appealed to Jake's desire to acquire a sample of Charles Lewellyn Hill art.

"This could be your lucky day, though. I believe you may have found the perfect gift for your wife. Can't top this oil, it is about as unusual as they come. But you'll be the judge. I'll not do it justice if I try to describe it. It's way too unique."

"Alrighty, I'll come your way, where's the closest McDonalds? Those places are a dime a dozen."

"No, no, that won't do," Mac protested. "I never transport paintings away from the house. I have so few for sale, I wouldn't dream of taking a chance of damaging one. Could you drive to Louisville?" Taking a minute to reassure himself he wanted to do a deal with this person, Mac stalled for time. "Jake, can you hang on a minute, I need to check my calendar." He held the phone at an arm's length while shuffling papers around his desk. "Would you be free this Thursday?"

The wager of letting too many days pass without direct contact didn't set well with Clint. "Darn it, I can't. The missus has a hair appointment that day. She's got me watching the grandkids. How about Tuesday? Only day I got free this week. If that doesn't work, we could shoot for next week. If that picture is as good as you say, I'll have it under the tree on Christmas morning. You and me can hopefully set a meeting prior to the big event."

By that time Mac was ready to hang up and ditch the call, but a handsome payoff hung in the balance. *Don't look a gift horse in the mouth*, he jested inwardly. "I suppose I could move things around, how about ten o'clock, I have an appointment at eleven thirty. Should be able to squeeze you in beforehand."

"Works for me. Sorry my schedule is so tight."

"It's okay," Mac replied, irritation reflected in his tone, "just make sure you're not late. Be on time, if for some reason you can't make it, call. Do you have a pen and paper? I'll give you my address."

"Sure do, Jordy. Fire when ready." Clint listened while the man gave his address and then repeated it back. "Oh, you can count on me. I'm a *Johnny on the spot* kind of fella. See ya at ten on Tuesday."

"Looking forward to meeting you," Mac cringed, not meaning a word of it, other than to take the fool's money come Tuesday.

Carrying on a ridiculous conversation with a man he already disliked, Clint felt like putting his fist through the door.

Tuesday was going to be an interesting day. With lady luck at his side, Clint expected to have a better understanding of just how many paintings Mac Hill really possessed, betting Mac lied when he told David Dunn, only three were in the house the day Charles Hill died.

Clint suddenly remembered he'd intended to put the tree up prior to company arriving. He called his wife to suggest they work together getting it decorated, but she didn't answer her phone. He left a message.

"Farley can't make it this evening, but Patrick jumped at the opportunity to join us. Hope that meets with your approval. Farley is heading up story hour. I had forgotten about our arrangement for him to take over on Fridays. He's doing three readings instead of one today. The guy jumped in with both feet, Jules, and the most remarkable part is, K. C came down and sat with Farley in between readings."

Jules's car was in the drive when Clint returned to the house. She was standing at the door holding her phone, "I was just getting ready to call you. I was getting the decorations down."

When seven fifteen rolled around, they saw car lights coming up the drive. Patrick got out, carrying a box tied with red and green ribbons. Directly after Clint departed Josie's, Patrick had gotten busy creating a holiday treat with a French flare, complementing the French game they were about to play with a French pastry–chocolate éclairs.

Soon thereafter Bonnie joined the group carrying a can of whipped cream. She had made chocolate pudding cake. Collectively they agreed, they loved chocolate.

The game was afoot, women battling the men. They told jokes and embellished stories. The women, although they jabbered throughout the entire game, beat the men two out of three, racing their cars to the finish line of some unknown destination. In one of their two games, they used all four coup-fourrés, meaning *counter thrust* in English, astounding the men. Bonus points continued to pile up, ending the decisive conclusion in a speedy finish.

During dessert break, Clint took the numbers K.C. had given him, spliced together on one sheet, and put them in front of his guests.

3804030 380225

8484576 8450447

16 689043 4212476

551 1659 1988

"What do either one of you make of these?"

Patrick frowned deeply, looking up at Clint wearing a bewildered expression. "I have no idea. You say K.C. wrote them?"

"He did. I think they are supposed to mean something."

It was Jules and Bonnie's turn to examine the figures with a discerning eye. Jules had already scrutinized them to the nth degree, unable to decipher any meaning, but Bonnie's observation stunned them all.

"Could they be coordinates, all jumbled together?"

The other three people at the table stared at the digits, thrown off guard, thinking... just like in the game, wheels were turning.

"How do you figure?" quizzed Patrick, looking at them with a fresh pair of eyes. "You mean like UTM, zone, easting and northing coordinates, and longitude and latitudes written in succession without proper spacing?

Bonnie quickly answered, "You guys know I read a lot of research papers, and to me, these look like coordinates, only the decimals are missing. Could be degrees in minutes and seconds. Zones? North, south, east, or west? I'd start with breaking them out, placing a plus or minus at the front to represent decimals, followed by a period after the first two numbers, if they are, they could give you a location somewhere.

She spun the paper around, "Like this, +38.04030," she wrote. "You might also want to entertain length, because 551 1659 1988, placing spaces between the numbers, looks suspiciously like lengths. That 1988 tagged on at the end, could be a date. If it were me, I'd start there."

Eyes shifted around the room, Bonnie thinking nothing of what she'd said. The rest however were blown away with her insights.

"If you give me a day or two, I'd be glad to play around with them at the library. On my downtime."

"Would you?" replied Clint at lightning speed. "Truth is they are driving me nuts. K.C. said I was supposed to have them, but you know how the boy is. Always to the right or left of center. They might mean nothing, but my feeling is they do."

Bonnie rewrote the numbers on a separate piece of paper and put them in her purse. "I'll get back with you in a few days."

"Thanks, Bonnie," Clint said, appreciative of the help "Give me a call if anything comes of them."

The night ended on a positive note. They made promises for a rematch and divided up dessert. Though the first time this combination of foursome had been together, it would not be the last. The laughter was intoxicating and so were the desserts.

For a few short hours Clint was able to push the aspects of his endeavors to the back of his mind. It was much-needed break from the investigative world he had entered, which was growing more unpredictable with each passing day.

After poking two hornets' nests, he was certain he'd caused a stir. He was grateful to have K.C.'s numbers in the hands of someone who perhaps had a better chance of interpreting them.

Chapter 45
A Bold Move

While Jules readied herself for bed, Clint went to the kitchen to boil water for tea. Carrying the mug into the living room, he set it on the end table and lowered himself into his favorite leather recliner, with the one he bought for Jules to match beside him. He smiled, remembering the day they were delivered before he proposed, praying she would accept his hand in marriage.

The room had become comfortably cool. Clint remained by the fire until the flames in the hearth had died down.

Jules put her arms around his neck and kissed the top of his head. Sweetly, she advised, "Don't stay up too late, honey. We have tickets for *War of the Worlds* tomorrow. Tom Cruise stars. It's your type of movie, sci-fi, and action packed. Afterward, if you feel up to it, I'd like to check out the Christmas lights around town."

"Sounds fun," he agreed amiably, delighting in the joy he saw on her face. "We haven't been to a movie in I can't remember when." Gently stroking her arm as she moved past, the feathery aroma of lavender dangled in the air. "I'll be in shortly. I promise."

When he checked in on his wife a few minutes later she was comfortably asleep on her side, the arm under her chin extended from the bed. He returned to the kitchen to refill his drink with a mind full of *what ifs*. He chuckled at her reference to him liking action movies, and thought, *I'm living one of my own.*

Before noon on Monday, he'd phone Axel… toss him a bone, a bribe in hopes of setting a trap where Scott Edwards, David Andrews, and Drex Mason could move in to make an arrest.

A robbery felony would keep Axel in jail, or under house arrest if he paid whatever bail the judge set, buying Clint time to continue his task. The goal was first-degree murder, not to simply slap Axel with a felony. Nothing less than murder in the first degree would do.

Nevertheless, Clint was under no illusion. They'd require substantial evidence to make a charge like that stick. Until then, theft would suffice. Stashed somewhere, other than in the place

Cookie was certain weapons would be found, Clint's search for one or more murder weapons would persist.

The large bill Clint had turned over to Scott, should be traceable to Andersen's police report of stolen property from his yacht. At the very minimum, tying that crime to Axel, would buy Clint precious time.

Carla Crenna would be laid to rest at week's end. Clint had paid in advance for a proper funeral, covering the gilded inlay mahogany casket, burial plot, and suitable headstone. He spared no expenses. In a state of interment, the person who had helped Clint the most had paid the highest price. Like a rusty hinge, the stark reality of her death gnawed at him. The dread of seeing the young woman in a casket made his stomach turn. Robbed of the life she imagined, a happier future away from the city, would always be one of Clint's greatest regrets.

With fingers steepled close to this face, Clint plotted his next moves, envisioning probable outcomes. He'd need to painstakingly execute each step. Monday was certain to usher in uncertainty. With his head rested against the back of the chair, Clint closed his eyes.

Monday, December 12

The weekend passed by pleasantly enough, offering Clint a much-needed hiatus from the tension he'd been concealing. They drove through town, enjoying house decorations and streetlights, that made Saturday night extra special.

They listened to oldies, worked around the house on Sunday, and phoned Wade and Rusty about upcoming holiday arrangements, plus finalized arrival dates with their Beech Grove family. The proverbial three-legged stool that kept everything in balance: family, work, and spiritual strength was stable once again. The ego serves well to support, but when it becomes the master, trouble looms.

Jules swept a kiss past Clint's cheek as she charged for the door, late for her 9 a.m. appointment with Sue Johnson, Radcliff's

Children's Home's Planning Coordinator. Keys jangling, her bag drooped off her shoulder, she was dialing Sue on her way out.

Jumping at the opportunity he'd been given, Clint finished his toast, pushed the newspaper aside, and took the last sip of his coffee and started to draft the note he would pin to Axel's door around noon if the gods were willing.

On the way to Louisville, he'd purchase another burner phone for conversations between him and Axel. Keeping it brief and leaving space at the bottom for the new phone number, the words simply said:

> Talk to me now, or the authorities
> later. Those are your choices.
>
> Cowboy

He tucked the creased note inside his jacket pocket, ready for delivery. If things went as planned, Clint would find himself inside Axel's home again, but this time the police would be waiting outside when the ruckus Clint intended to start, began. They'd determine the date and time of the confrontation. When it was set, Scott Edwards would be notified.

On the way to Louisville, he stopped in at a big box chain store in New Albany to purchase, and activate the phone he intended to use, tossing it on the seat when he got back to Farley's Land Cruiser at the far end of the lot. Borrowed for the day, he had told Farley his truck needed new tires put on. Farley was more than happy to oblige. Truth was, it was having fresh paint applied. No way was he about to explain why, in the middle of December, he'd have someone paint his truck.

Lying wasn't something Clint felt good about, but then again, telling Farley what he intended was not an option either, especially since it had a direct link to the person responsible for Farley receiving his life-saving heart. Clint was safer behind the wheel of a Land Cruiser since Axel wouldn't associate the vehicle with him, giving him added protection.

As he motored across the Indiana-Kentucky bridge, pillowy clouds lazily moved across the winter sky, drifting in from the northwest. Six to eight inches of fresh snow, starting in the late afternoon, over what was already on the ground, was in the forecast.

Gazing out at the black river water, Clint garnered every ounce of courage he could muster. Although he fought hard not to permit foreboding images to enter his mind, fragments of his own demise edged his vision. An arm outstretched, lying on a bare floor, his face disproportionate and his body crumbled.

Frozen from the fear of possibilities, his thoughts brought waves of terror. Confident in his abilities and believing he wasn't in this alone, Clint passionately clung to his convictions, not letting panic stand in the way of uncovering the unvarnished truth.

Slowing in advance of where he would have normally turned, Clint rotated the wheel the opposite direction of where he expected to head. Turning left, he traveled west, a block over. On Walker Avenue he pulled into an open space that straddled two homes, a yard or so from the corner side street.

A direct line of sight to his target was out of the question, too many houses and obstructions stood in the way on Hardin, which forced Clint from the vehicle on foot. Strolling as though he belonged to the neighborhood, he casually rounded the side street and continued until he was a few yards from Hardin Street.

At last, Axel's residence came into view. He scanned the area. The LS430 was parked in the drive, so DeArra D'Amelio was home, but Axel's black Cadillac was nowhere in sight.

The front windows of the house faced east. That area wasn't what he was interested in. Fortunately for Clint the section of the house visible to him was the one he'd hoped to see. The angle of his position was nothing short of ideal. Having been inside Axel's home had given him a definite advantage. Light from the kitchen door illuminated down onto the side porch and driveway.

Clint stopped at his vantage point, eyeing the side door with hopes Axel would appear. Obviously, he couldn't hang around, loitering without reason. Someone might notice him and become suspicious. The last thing he wanted was to have the cops called.

Although he hated to walk in circles on a blistering cold day, he had no choice. He would return to this spot every five to ten minutes waiting for the opportunity to tape his note on the door. If he had to warm his hands and face, he'd jump in the Land Cruiser for a few.

After wandering the neighborhood, looping back, and standing longer than he should watching the house, his wait finally paid off. DeArra stepped through the side door, carrying an oversized brown leather handbag, and a cell phone pressed to her ear.

Patiently Clint waited for the Lexus to rumble to life, back out of the drive and proceed down the street. Headlights disappeared beyond the four-way stop, affording Clint the chance to make his move.

Swiftly, his muffled footsteps moved over fresh and packed snow. Clint made his way to the side of the house, hiding at the edge of the back yard until he knew for certain he could continue. At fervent speed he taped the message to the glass. The problem was he fled so quickly from the porch, he lost his balance on a patch of ice at the top of the steps and fell forward. The edge of the concrete dug deep into his hip. He wanted to yell an assortment of colorful words but swallowed them.

Hobbling away, adrenaline helped him scale the fence. He then dashed down the same alley he had used to escape Axel's the first time he was there. On the brink of panic, he felt relieved to unlock the Land Cruiser. He turned the engine over and hightailed it away. Mission accomplished.

It was only a matter of time. With his hand placed on the phone he'd conduct business with, the game clock was now ticking. The rotation of the tires against the pavement when he passed over the Sherman Minton Bridge, back to the Indiana side of the border, hummed in time with the rapid beat of his heart.

Anticipating the phone would soon ring, likely by day's end, Clint counted on Axel not having the intellect, nor the connections to trace a call. Therefore, whatever interactions took place, they'd be conducted worry-free.

Donuts! Once inside Greenville's city limits, he aimed the Land Cruiser toward Sticky Buns Pastry where he set a much-needed cup of coffee, coupled beside a pecan roll, on the table. The adrenaline high Clint was on didn't need a stimulant, yet his brain screamed for *comfort food*.

Traveling on to Josie's Diner fleetingly entered his mind, but he dismissed the idea without a second thought. Running into friends from Salzburg was not something he desired. If by chance the phone rang, it was imperative he was alone and without distraction.

Sitting in the booth at Sticky Buns Pastry with his nerves on edge, he observed the two phones lying on the table. Both felt intimidating, but when his personal phone rang, it startled him. Not sure he should answer it, he studied the name displayed on the screen and hit the answer button.

"Well, good morning," he said as nonchalantly as possible.

"Hey, Clint, do you have a minute?" asked Bonnie.

"Sure, what's up?"

"I mean in person. Could you stop by the library sometime today? Didn't know what you were up to this morning but hoped you might carve out a half hour or so to come by here."

"No problem," replied Clint, curious as to the nature of her request.

"I think I've figure out what those numbers mean. Not all, but a big block of them."

"Are you kidding me, that fast?" exclaimed Clint, excited to hear more.

"You are going to be shocked," Bonnie predicted, still surprised K.C. had written them. "When it dawned on me what they represented, I was dumbfounded. I'm still in the process of interpreting the last few but the first ones, I know what those are."

"Bonnie, I can't believe this. I'll head that way soon, shouldn't take me more than an hour. How about twelve thirty?"

"Perfect. I'll have my lunch before you get here. See you in a while," she said pleased with herself for solving the problem so quickly and being able to enlighten Clint.

The phone he wanted to ring lay silently on the tablet. Realizing he couldn't just stay in hiding all day and finding it impossible to avoid people, he lifted both phones from the table and headed out the door.

When he reached the library, he called Jules to check in. However, it went straight to voicemail. Trying to operate around her schedule, he left a message saying he was in town if she needed him and to text if she was coming home early.

Feeling uneasy as to the timing of Axel's call, he put the phone on vibrate and stepped inside the building.

Bonnie was sitting at the desk with her head bowed but when Clint approached, her eyes glanced up. "Good, you're here," she said folding the document she'd been reading, and putting it back on the pile where she'd taken it.

"Sara, can you come relieve me for fifteen?" She asked the young lady with her back to Bonnie, standing at the shelves and reorganizing misplaced books.

Indicating Clint should follow her to a table under the windows, Bonnie said, "I thought it would be best to talk over here rather than take the chance of being interrupted. This won't take long."

Anticipation escalated as Clint discerned Bonnie's manner to mean something not only unusual but extraordinary was about to be spoken. He pulled out a chair, and touching the phone inside his pocket, he sat down.

Bonnie did the same, only she opened a folder she'd been carrying. An odd expression appeared on her face. "Take a look."

Inside the folder was a map of Louisville and surrounding counties. Clint gazed at her, uncertain what he was looking at. "I don't understand. Why are you showing me this?"

"Because…" she answered, pushing the numbers K.C. had written and given to Clint to his side of the table, "this is their meaning."

Heavy frown lines accented his curious, thoughtful, blue eyes as he studied the scribbles Bonnie had made next to the numerals and on the main map in the folder. "Are you telling me these are coordinates?"

"I am."

"No way," Clint replied, surprised at Bonnie's deduction, "how did you arrive at that? I don't see it." Still shocked, Clint asked once again," You're saying those numbers the boy gave me–3804030 380225–indicate a location?"

"They do if you break them out to decimals, and then by degrees." She saw the perplexed expression Clint held and said, "I have no idea how K.C. saw these numbers in his head but the first seven are decimal degrees followed by six numbers of degree, minutes, seconds." She continued believing Clint would eventually catch up. "In other words, 3804030 and 380225 represent the same in decimal and degrees. The second set of numbers, 8484576 8450447 continue the coordinates to a specific location in the same way."

With eyes narrowed, Clint stated, "Are you telling me these are latitude and longitude numbers?"

"Yes," she replied with raised brows. "Clint when I got home Friday night, I just couldn't get those numbers out of my head. They were driving me crazy, as though they were speaking to me."

Stunned to have been shown a correlation between K.C.'s scrawling and a location on the map, he smiled and said, "Bonnie, I have no doubt they were."

"I'd seen something similar years ago where a remote viewer jotted down numbers and eventually those numbers were put into more precise coordinates. When I rearranged, breaking out K.C.'s jottings, into UTM parameters: +38.04030, -84.84576, vs. 38°02'25" N, 84°50'447" W, they pointed here."

Bonnie put her finger on a spot on the map to indicate where the numbers aligned. "I have no idea right now, but I will figure it out, I can assure you. I'll put money on it the other numbers follow the same pattern."

Raised an inch from his face, Clint stared intently at any areas he might recognize. Then he shifted his attention to Bonnie. "The coordinates point to Tyrone, Kentucky."

"Yeah, I looked it up on the internet. There's an article that claims thrill seekers use the abandoned bridge for all sorts of activities. Young's High Bridge happens to be close to an old distillery. I suppose the kids find it tantalizing, and daring." Bonnie shrugged, finding it unimaginable to jump from a high bridge no matter how tantalizing the location.

"Anyhow," she continued, "Louisville Southern connected Lexington, Kentucky to Lawrenceburg, Indiana, prior to 1937. Then a derailment at Tyrone Power Station occurred and, of course, the automobile became more attractive, which meant fewer passengers, which spurred its eventually closure."

Clint shielded his eyes, stumbling on his words, he cleared his throat, "The name of the bridge they jump from is Young's High Bridge?

"Yes, why?" asked Bonnie with strange curiosity after seeing Clint's face turn ashen.

Recalling K.C.'s breakdown in his bedroom the night he handed the numbers to Clint, saying he was told to deliver them, Clint realized he had forgotten K.C. screamed in frustration, words the boy tried to communicate verbally but was unable. Clint had discounted the episode, giving it no credence.

Young, Young, Young... K.C. had shouted in a temper tantrum rage at Clint from his inability to put his thoughts into words. Clint shook his head now, bowled over by how vital that miniscule piece of information had been.

"K.C. is an amazing boy, a one of a kind," he said to Bonnie, patting her hand. "Gotta go," he said, fearful the phone in his pocket could ring any second. He didn't want to take a chance on losing his opportunity to set a trap for Axel.

"Let me know if the other numbers tell as an enlightening revelation as these have. I have total confidence you'll decode them, no matter what." He smiled, shocked by how Bonnie's brain worked regarding problem solving.

"Bonnie, I cannot express enough gratitude for how much you've helped me. I've always known you as a friend. Never did I consider how resourceful you can be. You are an incredible lady. You've helped more than you can imagine.'

United in their efforts to look under every rock and keep Clint's pursuit on target, Bonnie promised to get back in touch, as did Clint.

Chapter 46
Unforeseen Exchange

The hours passed in silence with no call from Axel were a nerve-racking affair. With a head primed for cagey dialogue of cat and mouse with his adversary, Clint felt worried Axel might not take the bait. Was it possible Axel realized he could be making a colossal mistake should he call the number Clint had left on his note? Possibly. Either way, a solution would come even if he had to change directions.

Clint drove to the orphanage. He needed, not wanted, to see K.C. The boy had a treasure trove of information in his head and Clint badly wanted to extract it, without, of course throwing him into fight or flight mode.

Radcliff's Children's Home had proven dreams do come true. He'd first visualized what he wanted brought into existence, and then stepped back and let the universe do its work. The secret was trusting something greater than himself. He came to realize God was in the driver's seat, not him. The last two years had proven, forces unseen had a vested interest in his welfare. He felt a protective shield he hadn't sensed before Rod Radcliff, Sr. entered his life, or Rod, Radcliff, Jr., for that matter. What a pair they had been in orchestrating the discovery of Reno treasure from Goss Cave. The man showed Clint that realms outside what his eyes could detect, really do exist.

Something Clint had learned along the way was not to discount paranormal experiences. No matter how much he didn't believe in them at the start–unlike Elise, who subscribed to that way of thinking in their youth. The odd thing was, the more he opened himself to messages the more they materialized. Lucid dreams, clairvoyance, sounds, smells, déjà-vu where he was certain he had experienced a splice of time prior to having it manifest, even seeing himself *walk into a mirror*. Call him crazy, but he was plugged into the unexplained.

"Clint are you there?" his wife asked when he didn't directly acknowledge her on the phone.

"Sorry, honey, my mind wandered." He chuckled. "I forgot I answered."

"That's weird." She laughed, thinking it wasn't like Clint to be so absent-minded.

"Your brain needs a rest," she joked at his silliness. "Goofball."

Reasoning it was not best to tell her about his and Bonnie's conversation quite yet, he answered, "Not playing with a full deck, I'm afraid. Can I blame it on my age?

"Sure, on someone else. I'm not drinking the Kool-Aid, though," Jules teased.

"Didn't think so," he replied in jest. "What are your plans for the rest of the day? I've been thinking about taking you to dinner. You up for barbeque?"

"I'm always up for Paoli's BBQ!"

"Alright then, what time?" he asked.

"I'll be finished up here by three-thirty. Should be home no later than four. An early dinner suits me. I haven't eaten all day."

When the conversation ended, Clint was relieved. It was high time he took Jules out to eat and spent some personal time with her. He'd been so preoccupied with solving Charlie Hill's wrongful death he'd let his husband duties fall short. Never did he want to put anything in front of Jules. Ever! Her bright smile and positive, supportive attitude had brought him back from the brink of despair. Never could he repay her for seeing in him what he didn't see.

The phone in his pocket felt like a brick. The weight of it chipped away at his confidence he'd outsmarted Axel, not wanting to admit his plan had failed. Minutes turned into hours with Clint considering maybe the note he had placed on the side door had blown away, was removed by DeArra, or simply tossed in the trash by Axel. Finally, Clint conceded defeat.

With limited time before joining Jules, he hurried up the path to the orphanage, watching his step not to slip for a second time. Battered and bruised from the side wound he'd incurred and now his hip banged up from falling off the porch at Axel's, Clint's body ached. It would have to take a back seat. He didn't have time for nonsense.

Inside the warm building, he searched for signs of K.C., knowing he preferred the corner table when he wasn't in his room. The safe place didn't require he interact with other children. It made Clint sad that in all this time K.C. had not become more comfortable with the kids in the establishment, but he accepted K.C. was a special case.

On the administrative level, Clint asked to see Tom Sanders, an unannounced visit. Tom stepped out of his office, "What an unexpected surprise, come on in," he indicated with his arm pressed against the door for Clint to join him.

"We haven't had an opportunity to talk in any length about K.C.," Clint commented, leaning back in his chair. "Your notes were intriguing. Do you have time now to discuss the tests? I'd like to hear your assessment. Putting the boy through anything outside his norm couldn't have been easy."

Clint broadly smiled, recognizing what he had said to be an understatement. "Although, I believe necessary." He already knew firsthand K.C. was gifted but wanted to know to what degree. "Your opinion, please, of his abilities." Clint raised a creased brow in anticipation of Tom's response.

"That's easy. Me personally? I think the boy is a genius, without an ability to express his intelligence." Tom shook his head. "Clint, we suspect K.C. is what was historically referred to as an 'idiot savant' only with a twist. His nonverbal tests suggest ASD, but I suspect something more."

"What's ASD?"

"Oh, sorry. It means Asperger's Syndrome Disorder, which is associated with autism." Tom leaned in, "I definitely recommend we take testing a step further." He tapped the file on his desk. "This report reveals extraordinary findings. The psychologist who wrote it recommends K.C. be retested. She literally didn't know what to make of him."

Tom saw a perplexed expression on Clint's face, and quickly explained himself. "At certain stages of the evaluation, K.C.'s right hemisphere became highly active. It was firing on all cylinders a few times. The left one was close, which denotes whole brain activity."

Tom's eyes narrowed. "We all know that's not possible. It's why Dr. Tillman wants to retest. She believes the equipment malfunctioned. She stated if the results were accurate, it would be like K.C. can tap into a gateway to higher consciousness. The test revealed unimaginable intelligence. His IQ test could not be completed."

"Don't savants excel in memory, and rapid math calculation? Often, they possess amazing artistic ability, even map making, and musical talents?"

"They do," answered Tom. "One of those, I suspect in K.C.'s case, is art. Have you seen any of his drawings? That kid is seriously talented."

Clint became distracted, thinking about extrasensory perception, knowing the child possessed it too. After a moment he asked, "Were they able to isolate color discernment associated with numbers or objects, different from what an average person perceives? Irregular numeral shapes for instance?"

"Clint, you're on the right track. The psychologist noted that when asked to describe numbers one through ten, K.C. didn't articulate, which she expected, but on the Comprehensive Test of Nonverbal Intelligence or CTONI, he portrayed numbers as shapes swathed in very specific colors."

Tom's face turned animated. "Dr. Tillman told me in private, it's as though K.C. was communicating with objects she didn't see in the room. He was intuitive beyond anything she'd experienced in her professional career." Tom looked over his glasses. "Before you ask… yes, I had her sign a nondisclosure agreement prior to working with K.C. Besides, she's in the medical field and knows not to share private information. She'd be looking at a lawsuit if she did."

"That's good," Clint responded. "Even so, we won't be conducting anymore experiments on the kid. My curiosity has been satisfied." Clint punctuated his meaning by making direct eye contact, aware that Tom rarely saw this side of him. "Now that we are mindful of his condition, no matter how Dr. Tillman, or anyone else frames their requests, the answer is no. Got that?"

Clint's bidding was not a negotiable directive, it was a command. "You made yourself clear," Tom acknowledged, thinking K.C.'s protection wasn't the only thing at stake. The orphanage's privacy could be compromised as well.

"Great, thanks for the fine work," Clint complimented Tom. "I made an excellent choice when I brought you on board to run this place. Your attention to detail is commendable. Conversely, I don't want K.C. treated with kid gloves. Take a cautious approach and tell the staff to do the same. He's a fragile child."

"Will do," responded Tom, standing to walk Clint to the door.

When Clint reached the lobby, he was taken aback when he saw Farley McDougal sitting at K.C.'s special table. He hadn't been there when Clint boarded the elevator.

"What are you doing here?" inquired Clint aware this was not story hour day.

"I'm pleased to see you too," answered Farley with a grin. "I'm hoping Keelan comes down. I have something for him and don't want to drop it off at the desk. I've learned not to surprise him."

The thought entered Clint's mind, *That's an understatement.*

"Is that it?" he asked, pointing to a book about dinosaurs.

"It is," answered Farley, turning the book around so Clint could examine it. "I think he'll like it. There are tons of images. Just his sort of thing. You know how he is with visuals."

Both parties turned when the elevator doors parted, and K.C. walked out taking in the area that surrounded him. When he saw the two men he admired most, he moved in their direction, stopping short of the table. Behind his eyes was a world of mystery.

"It's nice to see you Keelan Charles," Farley gently spoke, not giving Clint a chance to interact with the child. "I brought you a surprise. I hope you like it." He pushed the book toward K.C.

When Keelan touched it a reaction of glee flashed on his face. He offered no "thank you," but from what Clint observed in Farley's demeanor, the boy's appreciation was obvious No words were needed to convey his pleasure.

"What a delight to see you K.C." Clint glanced over at Farley, uncertain if he should say what was on his mind. Then he realized anything he wanted to voice was safe with Farley. He knew K.C. as well, if not better than, Clint. "I want you to know the numbers you gave me last week have been immensely valuable. So far, they have identified a location. I truly appreciate the gift of insight you've shared with me."

A sharp alertness appeared on K.C.'s face, causing alarm in both men. The boy's eyes darted from one direction to another. Glancing over Clint's shoulder, he said with extreme clarity, "Yo-ung..." Then he tilted his head to the side as though he was listening to something, or someone.

Clint had learned the child's ways. With his new knowledge about K.C.'s IQ, he asked, "Is there anything else you can tell me?"

Again, the strangeness in K.C.'s manner could not be understated. "Tra-ck-s," he replied definitively.

Then the daddy of all questions was hurled at the only person who had answers that mattered. "K.C. are you able to tell me who is giving you this information?" Clint waited his heart in his throat.

K.C.'s face twisted as though someone had put a lemon in his mouth, his entire face squinched, like he was in pain when he stuttered, "Th..a..," he started out but stopped, his face perplexed and strained.

"It's okay K.C., just do the best you can. No hurry, take your time," Clint encouraged calmly, surprised by the word K.C. was trying to pronounce. A racing heart accompanied the prospect of what he imagined K.C. was struggling with.

A long, miserable moment passed. K.C. frowned, uncomfortable in his own head. Then, at last, he uttered the remainder of the word, "d..e..u..s"

Clint knew not to touch him but wanted so badly to hug the child. Leaning in, very close to K.C.'s body, he closed his eyes and said, "Are you trying to say Thaddeus?"

K.C.'s entire body went limp, falling into Clint's arms, a full weight collapse. The relief he felt was immeasurable. "Uh-h-uh," he moaned, nodding, grateful not to have to speak again.

"Thaddeus gave you those numbers?" questioned Clint, "Just use your head for yes or no," he instructed without excitement reflected in his voice.

Looking like he might cry, or buckle even more, again K.C. nodded.

"Thank you, K.C. you've been a tremendous help," Clint said. He lowered his head, shocked and almost speechless. "I know I've pushed you a great deal. Son, you can't imagine how much this means to me," declared Clint, his eyes drifting in Farley's directions with a message not to ask.

"Keelan, why don't you come over here. Sit with me," suggested Farley with a pat of his hand. "We'll look through your new book."

The child almost knocked Clint over to get to Farley.

"That's a good lad," Farley cooed, touching the top of Keelan's hand, stroking it only for a moment before releasing his touch. He smiled back at Keelan, who was smiling at him, his eyes wide, a boy who circumnavigated two worlds of incoming information, currently pushed aside to live in the moment.

"Farley, I'll explain later," promised Clint, giving his word.

The two men's gazes locked. Without speaking, Clint walked away.

Chapter 47
Bait and Switch

With signs coming faster and closer together, Clint mentally catalogued Thaddeus Andersen's sentient message, interpreted by K.C., along with a backlog of other data still to piece together, having no doubt the latest information was aimed at discovering a buried body. Bonnie had provided crucial details, a starting point, and a means to an end.

Snowflakes drifted through the air, landing on the hood of the truck, the sound of the wipers crossing the windshield as distinct as the voice in his head telling him Andersen's body would be found where longitude and latitude lines intersect. By all accounts the man's remains would be uncovered somewhere near abandoned railroad tracks around or in Tyrone, Kentucky.

While in school, learning came easy with Clint retaining information effortlessly. Possessing an exceptional memory, he was observant of the world around him, all of which had served him well. And, although Jules had once told him, poetically, his intelligence reflected the undercurrents of his stare, the following day, he would pretend to be a simpleton with little ambition other than to buy his wife a Christmas present. A challenge he must rise to.

Clint confirmed with Jules, he'd pick her up at five o'clock at the house. They drove to Paoli to dine at their favorite BBQ restaurant. Over dinner he informed her of the developments in the case, including what he had learned at the orphanage, sharing the absolute, but not entire truth.

Jules, likewise, brought Clint up to date regarding the outing preparations she and Sue had put together at their 9 a.m. meeting last Monday. Jules had been so excited about organizing holiday day trips for the kids, including one centered around Christmas at the Zoo in Indianapolis, she did not fully register the depth of Clint's news, nor the potential danger involved.

At home that night, once Jules retired for the evening, beaming from the inside out in anticipation of Wednesday's outing, Clint sat before the fire as he often did. She routinely turned in earlier than him and arose later. But for Clint, sleep never came easy.

Visualizing how different scenarios would play out the next morning when he was scheduled to meet Mac Hill, Clint depended on him delivering the best performance of his life, or he'd be exposed for a fraud that he was. Neither situation sounded gratifying, other than to catch Mac Hill at swindling his own brother. It was one thing to pretend to be someone he wasn't over a phone conversation but an entirely different matter to keep the charade to scale in person.

As he had done so many times before, he'd keep his feet grounded and his eyes peeled while navigating through the maze of deceit. The answers were written in the stars of his life, and with each step he took, he followed their otherworldly guidance.

After the third cup of chamomile and ginger tea, still disappointed the phone he designated for catching Axel never sounded, Clint shuffled off to bed to join his wife soundly in slumber.

Tuesday, December 13, 8:45 a.m.

The time had come to expose Mac Hill. Clint walked through every situation he could imagine and what he might do to combat any awkwardness should the scene turn sour. Sweaty palms held tightly to the steering wheel as he practiced his accent to perfection, believing it might well rise to the occasion, same as his determination to uncover the facts about Charlie Hill's artwork.

Feeling forced to follow through on his commitment, Clint made every attempt to slow his breathing and heart rate down to normal. With Jules at the diner, he had ample time to play act in Louisville with Mac Hill, alias Joran Cane… or as Mac preferred in the sham–Jordy.

He followed the directions he'd been given. The truck zigzagged its way through the slippery Louisville streets to 269 Tuxedo Street. Oddly, Clint believed Mac Hill's house strangely inconsistent with others that, from the outside, appeared unoccupied. Although the house was presentable and the yard groomed, oriel windows that opened to a second-floor porch seemed completely out of place in a neighborhood where chipped paint and crooked window coverings were the norm.

He's using this house as a front to do business, concluded Clint, wondering if the inside was as nice as out. There was only one way to find out.

He pounded the door knocker, stepping back on the porch waiting for an answer, nervous but ready to put this show on stage. When Jordan Cane opened the storm door to let Jake Reeves in, heavy cologne wafted through the air, matching the interior room they found themselves.

Managing to keep his voice level, Jake greeted Jordy enthusiastically. "Good day, sir," he said, moving to Mac's side and stopping abruptly. Right off the bat, not giving Mac a chance to return the greeting, Clint blurted out, "I'm sorry, but those guys looks just like you. Are they your relatives?"

Pointing to the strong family resemblance of the pictures hanging on the wall at the base of the staircase, he was uncomfortably aware the three men appeared to be looking down as though waiting for the interlude between Jake and Jordy to start, Clint was stunned into silence when he realized one of the pictures still had the remnants of a price tag attached the bottom left corner. These pictures were purchased rather than personal photographs.

The striking man with a bony face and gray hair showing at the base of his temples, hair brush back to cover a bald spot, was formidable and not to be taken lightly.

"You have a keen eye," Jordy complimented Jake on how observant he had been. "The man on the right is my father, the other two are uncles."

Turning away to hide the disgust written on his face, Clint examined the portrait more closely to buy time. Hung strategically to catch the eye, he noted, in an innocent voice, "Well, I sure can see the family's resemblance in *you*, Jordy, with that strong chin of yours."

"Thank you, Jake," replied Mac with an edge to his voice, anxious to get the man before him out of his house in record time. The house was used only to sell paintings, brought in five at a time, and designed for quick turn-around so as not to draw unnecessary attention to his operation. "If you don't mind, I have another appointment in less than an hour. We only have a small window before I need to leave."

"My apology. Didn't mean to waste time. I've got some things on my plate to attend to as well." Clint did his best not to clip his words too finely, fearful of exposing the underbelly nastiness of the transaction the two men were engaged.

Mac Hill led Clint into a room eloquently furnished with antiques and rich oriental rugs. The windows were heavily covered in dark material, letting no light in, although they brought a richness to the room that was hard to describe. He'd chosen a baroque European motif to hide what went on here.

In the next room, a handful of paintings in assorted sizes hung on the walls, light fittings centered above each one. The dim room accentuated every detail of the canvases, bringing out the magnificence of Charlie Hill's work. Clint staggered at the awesome display on the four walls that surrounded him, finding it impossible to believe anyone could be that talented. Then, just as quickly, he remembered he was Jake Reeves, and slipped back into his act.

"Man, those pictures sure are pretty," he said in appreciation of the paintings in a truer sense than he could have anticipated.

"Is that the one you told me about?" he asked, pointing to the canvas of a train depot at the base of a snow-capped mountain, the landscape backdrop, painted in silvers and dark blues, graduated downward to emphasize a steam engine positioned on railroad tracks.

Steady snowfall, evenly placed over the canvas, landed atop a locomotive, steam bellowing into the frigid air. With train cars connected–parallel to a warmly lit scene of windows–two older gentlemen faced one another, the conductor of the train, and Santa Claus, whose reindeers and sleigh were parked behind the depot, barely visible. They were chatting while enjoying a cup of coffee and piece of pie.

Behind the counter stood a solitary man in the diner clenching a dishcloth, ready to wipe the bar clean after his customers departed. Leaning on the counter, as though participating in the conversation with the other men... on bar stools opposite him, the younger man, in his fifties Clint guessed, brows creased in concentration appeared engaged in the discussion.

Clint stared at the title, mesmerized by the talent of the brush strokes that had created such a masterpiece, his breath catching. **MIDNIGHT BREAK**, it read. Captured by the message, Clint found himself without words. Totally enamored, from the moment his vision absorbed what he was viewing, he said, "I'll take it!"

A deep frown appeared on Mac's face. "You don't know the price."

"I know, but I know you're an honest man and will shoot me a fair price." Clint grinned. "My wife is going to love it. I'll never outdo this. Geez, Louise, did I ever hit the jackpot."

"Mr. Reeves, I'm afraid it might be out of your price range a wee bit. Seeing it in person was essential because, on the phone I could never begin to describe how unusual this painting really is." Mac put his fingers to the wooden frame created to enhance the image. "As I mentioned earlier, I'm not into Christmas pictures or anything to do with Santa Claus, but I do have other people who have shown interest in this piece. As a matter of fact, I have some due here at 3 p.m. A young couple looking for something special for their parent's fortieth anniversary on December 23."

Shuffling his feet, swaying slightly, Clint tried to look as uncomfortable as possible. "So what price are you asking?"

"Jake, look, I'll make you a deal because I can tell you want it badly, and I like you. It is the perfect gift for the missus. Am I right? You'd love to see it under the tree for her. Wouldn't you?"

The contempt Clint felt for the man before him, trying to make a quick buck from his brother's work, could not be overstated, yet in his pretense Clint was forced to resort to the farce of being a layman uneducated in art world affairs.

"Yeah, I do but depends on how much you're asking."

"For the reasons I stated, I'll cut twenty-five percent off, and set the price at $4,400. Because of its size, I would be remiss to ask a dime less. Because this specific piece, and Charlie Hill's paintings in general, are in such demand." He paused for emphasis, and then continued. "All of them rare, and hard to come by, especially now that he's gone. Most paintings in this canvas size, 24x28, go for much more than the smaller ones. Do you understand my dilemma? Can't drop the price too far below market prices."

"Boy, that's a big number, Jordy. Would you be willing to meet me at $4,000? I brought that much along, in cash, thinking it wouldn't cost me no more." Clint did his best to appear uncomfortable, without stooping to groveling. In the event he needed additional cash, Clint had brought extra funds just in case. "Don't have four hundred more in the account without Gertrude finding out." Clint stepped back, putting distance between them, as he knew he should. Clint wanted to give the impression he was ready to walk away.

"I've never seen anything like that picture, in my entire life. Nothing out there compares. I'd be sick to miss out on something so grand. Maybe we could come to some arrangement over the balance. Let me squirrel some money away without her knowing? Ya know how it is with women. They have eyes behind their heads. That's how my ma was too, just like my wife. Could we work out an arrangement, Mr. Cane, please? I'd be willing to make installments if you like. I'm good for it."

Mac was ready to pull his hair out, believing this man was able to fork over much more than $4,000. *A bird in the hand is worth two in the bush,* he reminded himself, ready to accept any deal that would escort Jake Reeves out of the house... $4,000 lighter.

"Alright, Jake, *Midnight Break* is yours, you lucky dog you, at an even more reduced price. I'll take your $4,000 and call it a sweet deal for you." Mac nodded toward the chair across from at his desk. "Sit tight while I wrap it. Please have a seat over there. Plus, we have a little bit of paperwork to do. I'll be back in five minutes."

Clint was now directly facing *Midnight Break* reverently, his eyes bright with anticipation for reasons Mac would soon learn. "You have no idea how much this means to me. Jordan Cane, ya made my day."

While Clint waited, the desk drawers and the papers sitting on it became too much of a temptation to not peek. Hurriedly Clint rifled through as many stacks of loose papers as he could, until one stood out among the rest.

A rent charge from a warehouse storage facility in Wellington, which Clint happened to know was less than three miles from their location, showed not only Mac Hill's name, but Charles Hill's on the receipt as well.

Interesting, thought Clint. *Why would the brothers need to share a warehouse?* he pondered, wheels turning in overdrive. *Possibly Mac is keeping additional pieces of his brother's work at a separate location, not upstairs as I imagined?* Slowly he sidled over to the remaining canvas hanging on the walls so when Mac returned, he'd be as far from Hill's desk as possible, giving no inkling he'd rifled through his papers.

Viewing Charlie's additional pieces caused his stomach muscles to tighten, a painful thought that this poor man had sacrificed his life because he was at the wrong place at the wrong time.

Clint reeled with anger, not understanding how anyone could be so cold hearted as Mac Hill. Not only did this man cast off his responsibility as an uncle by dropping his brother's only child at the orphanage with no identification, but he was currently profiting from Charlie's death. *Who does things like that?* Clint incredulously thought.

Mac Hill rounded the corner from the living room carrying Clint's new artwork cradled in his arms, making certain not to hit any corners. He smiled and said, "Ready to go. Where will you hide it until Christmas?"

"Over at my ma's. She's good at keeping secrets," Clint squinched with delight. "When she sees what I bought from you, she'll be trying to talk me into giving it to her." He snickered as if what he had said was funnier than it was. "Better get going," heralded Clint in a relaxed tone, dawdling to the door. "We need to let you get back to your day."

Earlier when the teller at the bank counted the money, Clint was shocked just how much $5,000 really was, which also presented a problem. He tried to stuff the money into his billfold and money clip, however, it was painfully clear he wasn't thinking straight. What would a back woodsy, down to earth man like Jake Reeves be doing carrying an expensive Lucchese crocodile leather billfold like the one Jules had given him on their first anniversary.

Red flags popped up all over the place. He had been on the verge of making a gargantuan error, fortunately caught in time. Contact with Mac required Clint to think like the man he was portraying, Jake Reeves—a local rural guy—not Clint, the pretend private investigator who created this elaborate deception.

An hour ago, when he pulled up to the curb at Hill's house, Clint had money bulging from every pocket on his person, all but one thousand left in the truck. On the cusp of sheer entertainment when handing cash over to Mac in payment of his purchase, providing all went as planned, was only minutes away.

When they reached the foot of the stairs, Clint's hand drew Mac's attention to a photograph resting against a clock. "She's pretty. Your wife?"

"No," answered Mac impatiently. "She's a friend."

No, she's not, more like a picture picked up at local hodge-podge store, mocked Clint in defiance of the liar who was trying his best to shove Clint out the door now that he had made a sale.

"You need to pay me, Jake. The painting isn't free." Mac's beady, unfriendly eyes had almost narrowed to nothing.

"Gosh darn," Clint fired back, ashamed of himself. "I almost forgot. Tsk-tsk, nuttin is for free. Is it? Shame on me," he joked, laughing loudly from his embarrassment. "Just too excited I reckon." Clint stepped back. "I got your money right here." He turned his pockets inside out, dropping the bills on the table, many falling to the floor.

"Too bad about those folks coming to see you at three, they'll be disappointed, I bet." Jokingly, he punctuated his remark with a phrase he thought fit. "Early bird gets the worm!" he said with a kind smile, digging into his pockets for the last bit of money. "Sorry," he apologized, "I suppose I should have got you a cashier's check but didn't know how much to make it out for."

Stunned at the wads of cash piled on his table, Mac laughed. "Nope this will do just fine." Pushing Clint toward the door and then through it, Mac cheerfully said, "Good doing business with you, Jake. You and your wife have a Merry Christmas!"

"You too, Jordy," mirrored Clint in his greeting.

Back in the truck, Clint swerved to miss a car that pulled out unexpectedly. He held tight to the wheel and had to stop a moment to calm down. Three houses down, he let his emotions settle after catching a glimpse of the wrapped package behind him, feeling on top of the world to be in possession of a Charles Lewellyn Hill painting, one he was certain was not on any inventory list.

Looking down at the address scribbled on the wadded piece of paper pulled from his shirt, Clint aimed his truck in the direction of Wellington. He'd show the painting to David Dunn in due time, but at this moment Clint was drawn to the jointly rented warehouse space that Mac Hill now rented alone.

Chapter 48
Removing All the Stops

Pulling his truck into the D&J Warehouse complex, Clint observed the moderate sized structure, comprised of multiple individual units, numbers, and letters affixed to the doors. Circling the facility to the northeast corner, soon the address he was searching for came into view, H-J24. For reasons unclear, Clint opened the glove box and withdrew the golden crystal he had carried from his office, putting it on the dash, at eyelevel.

With no intention of lingering, he drove his truck slowly past the bend, and then parked into a space alongside the facility's dumpster, observing tenant activity as they came and went. To have his truck spotted outside the H-J24 entrance would not be smart. The further back he set the vehicle the better. Not a busy place, few vehicles motored by, in and out of the well-maintained repository.

Deciding to exit before finding himself in a compromising position, Clint focused on the tubular steel security gates at the west end, ready to flee. Having a mental picture of D&J Warehouse, and its exact location, was an unexpected development one more piece of the ongoing puzzle Clint was trying to fit together.

Confident his presence was undetected, Clint turned right at the gate, continuing to the four-way stop, following the signs back to the highway. Glancing ahead, he noticed an advancing blue Suburban. Quickly he made another right-hand turn, running his F-100 east as fast as it would allow without drawing unwanted attention to his hasty departure.

Steering to the side of the road, over a gravel pull off, north of the business complex, Clint watched the full-size SUV maneuver the building's parking lot, before stopping at glass door H-J24 where Clint had just been. He was shocked, although ecstatic, to see Mac Hill step out of the vehicle, Clint knew this was not happenstance. He was led here by design.

He reached for the golden crystal on the dash which surprisingly seemed to change. Grasping the quartz to his body, Clint felt its vibration travel outward to his fingertips. He had read–after the stone came into his possession–if a crystal is squeezed, electricity flows through it.

When electromagnetic force is applied to crystals, they vibrate. Called the piezoelectric effect, the same mineral crystal composition found on the surface of the Earth is also known to be present at its core. Crystals transmit and receive electromagnetic energy pulses, which highly attuned individuals claim to experience. Clint understandably accepted this claim since humans, likewise, house an electromagnetic field. Although some might argue the subject as invalid, Clint knew, firsthand, the quartz crystal Rod Radcliff, Sr. had left him had undeniable powers.

He watched as Mac stepped out of the vehicle swinging his keys, and then unlocked the door and went inside. Clint waited, watching the door Mac disappeared behind, thinking, *Why is he here?* His answer came minutes after asking. With two paintings clenched in his hands, Mac looked from side to side before placing them into his SUV, behind the seat. Carefully, he backed up, stopping before moving onward, his head down, presumably looking at his phone.

So, this is where Mac took Charlie's artwork? decided Clint, glad to have inadvertently discovered the location of Charlie's paintings, taken from his home before David Dunn's representative could be dispatched after Charlie's death.

Adding two and two together, Clint figured each time Mac sold a painting he would replace it with another stored at the warehouse, telling his clients only a few paintings existed. Then he would pull from his backup supply, thereby running up the price with a story about how scarce Charlie's paintings were.

With the truck idling, Clint waited for Mac to disappear down the street before putting his own vehicle in gear. His next destination was the estate lawyer's office, wiser than when he had arrived at the warehouse. Looking at the two phones resting on the seat, he wondered if Axel would ever call. Picking up his personal phone, he dialed David Dunn.

"David Dunn," the lawyer answered unaware of who was waiting on the other end of the line.

"David, it's Clint Reeves, would you happen to have a couple minutes to spare? Something important has arisen."

Surprised to hear Clint so animated, he replied, "Sure, I'm not too busy this afternoon. Anytime will work."

"Great, I'll be there in about thirty minutes," he said, thanking David for taking his call.

Glad to have timed every green light perfectly, Clint pulled behind Dunn and Murphy Law Offices and parked his truck between two cars. Sliding out, he reached behind the seat to lift his newly acquired canvas out, leaning it against the truck while he locked the doors.

As Clint approached Dunn's office, David stared at Clint in dismay, wondering what he was up to and why he was carrying a large package down the hall. "Come on in," he advised, holding the door for Clint to enter.

"Thanks. I need you to see this," he said when they were both on the other side of Dunn's office. "Regretfully, I feel you're going to be alarmed, more than anything."

"What is it?" inquired Dunn.

"Hang on," Clint replied while unwrapping the painting. When done, he turned to face Dunn, observing the odd expression the attorney wore, which grew more exaggerated as he examined in detail what Clint had brought.

"Please explain, because I clearly have no idea why you brought this here and how you happened upon it."

"That's the thing, and I hope you won't be upset, but I met with Mac Hill this morning under pretense, posing as a man named Jake Reeves." He let his words float, and then continued, "Last week I placed an ad in the local paper, stating I was searching for Charles Lewellyn Hill artwork. Mac replied, as Jordan Cane. We met at a location I suspect is only used to turn his brother's artwork."

Dunn's face turned livid, flushing a deep pink when he asked, "Are you telling me he sold you this painting?"

"I am."

"For how much?"

"Four thousand," replied Clint. "And that's not all. Four others were displayed in the same room, designated to exhibit Charles's work. The lighting was exquisite and perfectly placed. It reminded me of an art gallery."

The bill of sale, signed by Jordan Cane, was attached to the back. Dunn went to his desk and pulled a folder from the file, checking signatures of Mac Hill to Jordan Cane. The handwriting matched. Then he pulled an inventory of items removed from Charles and Ann Hill's house the night of the murders. The canvas Clint had brought in did not line up with any item on the list.

Seeing the frustration on Dunn's face, Clint volunteered, "Mac, alias Jordan, or Jordy, as he requested me to refer to him, said this painting was part of his personal collection no longer wanted and that he was willing to depart with it since Christmas images weren't his thing. Neither were the other themes he had hanging on the walls. He gave me a line about appreciating the artist's style but had collected too many."

Sitting down at his desk, Dunn turned away, facing the windows, apparently thinking through the problem.

"Good grief, Clint, what would possess you to do something so outrageous?"

Clint responded, "Don't you recall I mentioned the librarian in Salzburg noticed an article where Mac sold one of Charles's paintings for five thousand eight hundred? Then another sold by someone else, sometime later. Not to mention the day after Charles died, one sold for three thousand, and then another for five thousand, according to Bonnie. Don't you find that suspicious, I sure did, and I was right to think that way. Mac is selling his brother's work under assumed names, at astronomical prices. From an undisclosed location."

Then, from out of the blue, Clint remembered a dream Farley McDougal had described early on, where he vividly saw himself in an art studio that resembled a warehouse. Unused canvases were sitting everywhere. But the thing that was especially odd was he was attaching an envelope behind the lining of one specific painting, as though concealing a package for safety reasons.

"My question is since I paid four grand, can I keep it?" asked Clint, expectation showing in his eyes. "Is it rightfully mine?"

Searching Clint's eyes, Dunn asked, "Neither man exists, but you have a bill of sale, I'll keep it as evidence until I decide what to do about this. Keep the painting, for now." David shook his head, "In all my years of practice, I've never run into anything so devious."

In turn, Clint wrote down the warehouse address and pushed it toward Dunn's side of the desk. "David," cautioned Clint, "we must walk through this slowly. We have no idea what is stored in that warehouse."

"No doubt. Just give me time to think through this situation," Dunn quietly advised, "I'll give you a call, soon." He looked at the Christmas painting. "That is one unusual painting. If I had seen it in a gallery, I would have bought it myself. I had no idea Charles had that kind of talent."

"If you had been in my shoes today and had seen the others Mac had on the walls, you'd be even more impressed. Charles Hill was a gifted artist."

Walking out under laden skies, a bounce to Clint's step, his relief was measurable. Disclosing information to David Dunn about Charles Hill's brother and the deception Mac Hill was committing, made Clint's burden lighter, ticking one complication off Clint's list and adding it to Dunn's.

From here on out he'd let the estate attorney and law deal with Mac Hill. He'd been told by Dunn that in Charles's Will, Mac was to receive five paintings in total, Clint wagered countless more were unreported. All worth ten times their original value.

In the truck, words came out harsh and calloused, without pity for the man, "He deserves whatever he is handed," Clint mumbled. "Was it jealousy, envy, or pure greed that had caused him to stoop so low? The hubris and confidence to profit from his brother's death is sickening."

Mac's story would eventually see the light of day, as most cons do. Believing the man would receive his comeuppance was one thing, but what hurt Clint the most was how anyone could have discarded a helpless child, Mac's own brother's child. It was beyond cruel. It was evil.

Leaving Louisville, the grin Clint held while toting the whimsical painting at his side, was comical. The picture had transported him back into his childhood. Good thoughts were generated from the few good memories he carried. He'd hang the scene on his office wall, year-round, or at home, should he decide to surprise Jules with it as a Christmas gift, which is what he imagined he'd do.

Maybe I'll bring her to the orphanage before our Beech Grove trip, he considered, *and give it to her then. Either way, this is one painting that won't be stored away or be displayed only during the Christmas season.* Rolling into town to Radcliff's Children's Home, Clint hummed "Santa Claus is Coming to Town" as he carried his painting into the building, past the Christmas tree and onto the elevator.

When he stepped off the elevator onto the fifth floor, a peace cascaded around him. He had done a good thing, and every fiber in his body felt proud of his undercover work. Then, just as quickly, his mood switched when Axel Drako came to mind. He was disturbed that the plan he had derived had failed miserably, and the huge risk he had taken had been in vain. He proceeded to push the thought aside. Up the winding staircase he carted his new prize, excited to find a new home for it. Although it had been a truckload of money to purchase, Clint felt it was worth every cent.

Snow had started to fall outside the tall thin windows overlooking the grounds. Jules had done a fine job decorating his office, and Clint was exceedingly proud. It felt comfortable and warm, especially with the Santa painting directly across from him to the right of the antique mirror where nothing had been hung on the bare wall. He couldn't believe he had been so fortunate to have come across the scene, no matter the cost.

Tonight's plan was to drive to the diner for an early supper while Jules waited tables. He carried a Travis McGee novel in his truck that he'd read so he and Jules could be under the same roof until her shift ended. A monumental day behind him, Clint was ready for downhome cooking, and a slice of one of Patrick's superb pies.

Climbing back on the elevator, Clint disembarked at the lobby, surprised to see Farley in the story room with Josephine, Joseph, and K.C. gathered round. When he poked his head in, all four looked up, simultaneously.

"Good afternoon, my friend," said Farley wearing a broad grin, delighted to be surrounded by children hanging onto his every word.

"Good day to you," replied Clint. "Are you getting ready to read?" He glanced down at his watch, thinking it wasn't normal for story hour to begin at 4:30 in the afternoon.

"Not until seven," answered Farley, "We're just goofing around." He chuckled, hugging Keelan's shoulders, and leaning in toward the other two children. Clint couldn't help but notice K.C. had returned Farley's hug with one of his own.

"Looks like everyone is enjoying themselves." An excellent idea popped into Clint's head. "Hey, would you guys like to see something very, very special?"

Before Clint could say another word, Farley was on his feet. "Ready to take an adventure to a magical land only the skipper knows about?" he asked, a gleam glimmering in his eye. Noticing Clint smiling at him, Farley said, "We're ready."

Farley is so perfect for this job, reflected Clint, turning to wait on the gang who would accompany him upstairs.

Talking so loud people in the other room turned their heads, Joseph was first to reply. "Ready to board, Captain," he directed Farley, pulling his sister from her chair. Keelan adorably fell in line, the smallest of Farley's ducklings.

Returning to the elevator and taking it up to the fifth floor, he negotiated the spiral staircase to his office at the head of the group. When they arrived, he opened the door, and everyone stepped inside. The elegantly carved fireplace, accented by two of K.C.'s drawings, under an arched open beam ceiling, all reflecting Clint's personality. The pride on K.C.'s face was thrilling to witness, until he saw the painting on the adjacent wall.

Farley instantly realized the boy was upset.

Suddenly, K.C. was clinging to the painting, stroking the bottom of the frame repeatedly. He rocked and bawled, whimpering as he banged his head against the wall, crying, "Mine... mine!"

Clint was stunned, as were the other three. No one knew what to think. What had happened? The only thing he knew to do was remove the Christmas scene from the wall. He rested it on the floor in front of K.C. thinking he might find comfort in its closeness.

That's when the craziest thing that day occurred.

Chapter 49
Camouflaged

K.C. dragged the Santa scene to the middle of the room. Had he not been stopped he would have lain on the canvas. The child refused to be comforted no matter how much Farley and the others tried.

"Papa," he cried laying his body near the frame while trying his best to stroke the painting.

Farley asked, "Keelan Charles, how do you know this painting?"

"Mi-n-e," the boy thundered, turning belligerent when the other children tried to touch or comfort him.

Farley felt an indescribable tug on his heartstrings, grasping the painting on the floor had once belonged to Keelan, created by his father, Charles Lewellyn Hill. How Farley knew this was an unknown, but he did.

"Keelan, did your papa paint this for you?" Hitting so close to home with his guess, Farley thought the child had gone into a seizure until K.C. stopped thrashing around and curled into a ball. Sounds Farley had never heard came from the boy, anguish, pain, torment, and grief bellowed from his core.

No one had any idea what to do. Clint stood, saying, "I think we need to leave and let K.C. settle down before story hour."

"I agree," said Farley, his face pained in empathy for the boy. "We do need to get to the bottom of this, Clint. It could damage him emotionally if we don't address the problem, right away."

"I'll set an appointment with Tom Sanders and ask him if he can help."

Nodding, Farley lifted the boy from the floor.

Bewildered, the group uncomfortably headed for the door, Clint's surprise ruined by an incident no one understood. Before locking up, Clint walked over to the painting now leaning against the wall, ready to place it back on the wall, at least for now, but then something caught his eye. The top right corner wasn't completed sealed. He detected a nearly imperceptible bulge. Remembering Farley's dream, he stepped out into the hall and called to him. "Hey, Farley, could you come here for a minute?"

Returning, Farley said, "Sure, what do you need?" K.C. stood at his hip, holding his hand. Josephine and Joseph moved to the side.

"Didn't you tell me you had a dream, saw yourself sealing something between a canvas and backing board?"

"I did," Farley answered, his face changing, a shocked expression replacing the disturbed one he walked in with. I didn't remember the painting at first, but I think this is the one I saw. The subject was vague, although what I was doing was vividly clear. I was hiding something."

"I think you were hiding something behind this canvas. Take the children downstairs. I'll join you as soon as I can," suggested Clint, glancing down at K.C. "It's going to be alright. We will take care of you, and your daddy's painting. I'll have it hung in your room as soon as I'm done here. Is that okay?"

K.C. nodded, a smile covering his face and an inner glow shining through. Clint watched happy tears roll down his cheeks. "Pa-pa... min-e," he muttered. A sparkle of light, like that of a glistening ocean appeared behind his eyes, as the child leaned into Farley. "Papa."

"I know," comforted Clint, wondering if K.C. was referring to Farley as *Papa*. A curious thought. "Your Papa painted it for you, and it will remain with you. No one will ever take it from you again. I promise."

Clint saw something enter K.C.'s eyes he'd never seen before–a sense of well-being. "You're a good lad." Although Clint was hesitant to touch the boy, he lightly tapped the top of his head and was pleased to sense no resistance. "Go with Farley for now, your Santa Claus painting will be on your wall when you go to bed tonight." Clint bent down. "I love you, son, and will do everything in my power to protect you from any more harm."

The two men moved apart. Farley turned toward the door, aware of Clint's intentions. What Clint was about to do would be earth-shattering, he suspected.

Locking the door, Clint walked over to the painting, carefully starting to detach the mounting board from the stretcher. What he found astounded him, a handwritten note scripted on the backside of the canvas:

> To: Keelan Charles Hill,
> My beloved son and light of my life. May the sun forever shine down on you. I'm proud to call you son. Merry Christmas, Your forever, loving, Papa

Below that was a handwritten signature, Charles Lewellyn Hill, dated, December 25, 2002. To Clint's surprise he found another smaller version of the same painting neatly attached to the back of the canvas, beneath a six-by-nine manilla envelope. Also signed.

Carefully, Clint removed the contents of the envelope out onto the desktop. A key fell out onto the desk pad. Written on a smaller envelope were the words, Safety Deposit Box 428, Wellington Credit Union. A multipage note followed naming a list of paintings Charles had completed, titled, dated, and numbered. All were to be given to his son Keelan Charles Hill in the event of his death. A copy of a mortgage deed and car title were also enclosed. A typed message stated a duplicate copy of everything could be found inside the safety deposit box. The note listed, Macalister Eugene Hill, Charles's brother, as having a matching key, safeguarding the property.

Ann, his wife, signed a similar document listing her wedding ring, mother's locket, and Aunt Betty's diamond ring and ruby necklace, to be distributed to her three nieces, Abagail Malcomb, Jillian Malcomb, and Daisy Malcomb, respectively. The remainder of her jewelry, hairpins, scarves, and any other items in the home, to be given to her lifelong friend, June Bennett.

A sadness swept over Clint. *They probably never thought these documents would be opened before they were old.* An ounce of protection had turned valuable in the puzzle Clint was working. Enough to convict Mac Hill of committing fraud, theft, and misrepresenting his brother, plus a mountain of other crimes.

Dialing the law office number, Clint was pleased when Dunn answered on the second ring, bypassing the receptionist. "Has something come up, so soon?" asked Dunn without saying *hello.*

"Yeah, I'm afraid it has. Do you have any time on your calendar tomorrow?" asked Clint knowing Jules would be on an outing for the entire day with the children from the orphanage.

"I'll make time. Can you tell me what this is about?"

"You know that painting I showed you? Well, I found an envelope behind the backing material. Totally by mistake. It's revealing though, plus a safety deposit key was inside. Thought we could visit Wellington Credit Union, find out what's inside box 428."

Dunn was stunned. "Is that right?" His voice reflected his excitement, "Of course, I have legal representation so there won't be a problem."

"David, Charlie had a list of his paintings stapled together, pages of them. *Midnight Break* was one of them. This will shock you. Charles painted *Midnight Break* for his son, Keelan, even had a handwritten note directly on the canvas. Mac jumped the gun. He'd been better off waiting for what was legally his. Forces were playing against him." Clint didn't elaborate on his meaning, but quickly said. "The document says all paintings were willed to his son. At the bottom, in a separate note, is your name and law firm listed as Keelan's executor of his affairs. It was notarized and dated, January 1, 2003."

"I need to see this, confirm its authenticity. If what you say is accurate, it updates the Last Will and Testament I have on file."

"Thought it might. Look, if you have an opening around ten, I can be there then. Need to wait for my wife to leave before I head out. Does that work?"

"I'll move my schedule around or have one of my colleagues fill in for me if need be. I don't mind saying, this whole affair has been like one big roller-coaster ride. Starting with the Hills' unexpected deaths. See you at ten."

When they hung up, Clint gathered his things and headed downstairs. Tom Sanders was given the painting and he promised to have it hung immediately, no questions asked. A good man.

He walked out and aimed his truck toward town.

Josie's diner was relatively quiet. From outside Clint watched his wife scurry about, filling drinks and chatting with the customers, a smile on her face the whole while. *What a jewel*, thought Clint, glad to be able to call her his own.

Jules grinned big when Clint walked through the entrance, making his way to the back and his assigned booth. Tipping his hat before removing it, he spoke, "Love you!"

"Likewise," she mouthed back. "Be right there," she said lifting the coffee carafe for him to see.

Clint held up his hand, "No more. thanks."

Taking a book from his coat, he started to read, starting from an earmarked page. Tales about a drifter who solved mysteries wherever he went, living on a vessel docked by the ocean, the character was elusive and proficient at his job. Grinning when his favorite character found himself in an impossible jam, it occurred to Clint the reason he liked this series so much was it reminded him of himself. Far from a perfect investigator but filled with courage, the man was unconventional, and possessed an iron will, resolute to do the right thing.

Thirty minutes later, Jules clocked out and sat down across from her husband, "What a day, it's been like a three-ring-circus until you arrived. People swarmed in the moment the doors opened, carrying packages, loaded with Christmas spirit, and tipped well," she sheepishly smirked. "It's been fun."

Following Jules home, Clint felt let down. Happy to have made K.C.'s day, he was sorry to have tapped into so much pain. Drained from the affair, his consolation was to find a second image, pretty much identical to the original, tucked behind it. At the very least Clint could frame that one for Jules. No longer did he want the scene at his office. Home felt like a better choice. He'd give it to her at Christmas just as he had imagined.

Darkness had set in, and Christmas lights were brightly lit at every corner in Salzburg, even out of town on the rural roads, in remote locations miles from US 150. His sadness had lifted, replaced by gratitude to have Jules in his life, to have thoughtful children and

Jules's family, now his, and to have helped Farley and K.C. come together. Plus, so many little guys at the orphanage, like Joseph and Josephine who had settled in quite nicely.

Clint chuckled out loud recalling when he left the orphanage that Farley was readying himself for the upcoming story hour session, putting decorations out, and setting books on the tables.

K.C., on the other hand, was sitting at his normal table, alone. That surprised Clint greatly considering the mood he'd last seen the child exhibiting, expecting to see K.C. glued to Farley's side. An odd couple those two made.

The strange thing that caught him off guard, was K.C. appeared to be having an animated discussion with some imaginary friends. Clint hadn't seen him do that for a while, not since Farley appeared on the scene, so it struck him odd for K.C. to be conversing with dinosaurs or some other mythical creatures only seen in the boy's world.

Clint had waved goodbye, but before moving outside into the blistering wind, he heard K.C. chortle sillily and say, "Okay." Then he started to sing out loud. "This old man he played one, he played knick-knack on my thumb, with a knick-knack paddywhack give your dog a bone, this old man came rolling home. This old man he played two…"

What was it about that song that children seemed to like so much, he wondered?

Just as Clint pulled into his driveway the cell phone he'd been waiting and hoping would ring, did. Axel was calling.

Paralyzed for a moment, he had to regroup, bring himself back to ground zero, no emotion. The *Cowboy* was about to answer. He lifted the phone, his heart pounding like a drum.

"What took you so long?"

Chapter 50
Walls Start Tumbling Down

Right off, the background noise of Axel's boisterous location revealed his whereabouts, coupled with slurred words, and a cocky attitude he'd found in the bourbon he was holding–Cell Block #49, his favorite tavern to push drugs and fondle women.

The jukebox blasted, intermingled with loud voices nearly as earsplitting as the person on the line, making it tough for Clint to hear Axel's threat on his life.

"Oughta put a bullet through your brain, just like I did…" Axel ceased speaking, thinking it best to give himself a moment. He shifted his position, lowering his compact body onto the bar stool at the far end of the bar, out of earshot where his diatribe of unprintable words was not so easily heard.

"It's best to be thought of as a fool then to speak and leave no doubt. That's my version," responded Clint. "Good thing you shut your trap, smart boy, instead of speaking and proving me right."

Seething at the insult, Axel saw red, warning, "Others who talked to me like that were just as stupid as you are, Cowboy. Don't threaten me. You have no idea who you're dealing with. In case you're interested, I tried hard to get Cookie to tell me your name, figuring she knew it. Even told her she was a *dead woman walking* if she didn't, but that little back-stabber just wouldn't cooperate. To tell you the truth, she surprised even me. But we both know she had it coming. Turncoats rarely fair well."

Clint's stomach knotted, twisting in horror at the image Axel had painted. Identifying a ring of truth associated with traitors, he shuddered at the thought but did not back down. Icily furious, he firmly delivered his next blow, eyes hard, fully aware of the line he had crossed, yet confident in his own strength. "Oh, but I do know who I'm dealing with," Clint struck back. "You're the guy who was reckless enough to leave puncture wounds in two places on her body, proving it wasn't an overdose. Uh-oh! Dumb move, smart guy. Sloppy snuff job, Axel."

Absorbed in the unasked question, while wrestling with the uncertainty of where to take the conversation, Clint flung another insult to buy time. "So that's how you treat your insubordinate lady friends."

"Could get your ugly mug caught in the crosshairs of your virtuous nature if you keep pushing your luck. See where that leads ya, Cowboy." A weighted pause passed, "You got a death wish or something," Axel sarcastically asked?

"Pointing an accusing finger is easy when I'm dealing with a cold-blooded killer." Clint fired back. "A natural, I'd say."

"How flattering for you to notice," spewed Axel's venom at his antagonist. "What do you expect to achieve from all this, not a feather in your cap by bringing the *bad guy* down, surely? If you had in mind to rat to the cops, you'd already done it, so what's your game?"

"It's straight-forward, simple, really. Moola—and plenty of it." Clint's southern drawl was executed to perfection.

"What makes you think I've got that kind of money? You're barking up the wrong tree, moron."

"Come on, Axel, you're not talking to a halfwit here. I've seen your stockpile of rainy-day currency. Stolen goods out the wazoo. I spotted lots of extortion funds, including articles slipped from your uncle's yacht. A prized little stash of goods you've got tucked in your basement… oh, excuse me, the level below your *stinking* basement."

"You were in my house?" Axel argumentatively shouted into the phone. "A dead man, that's what you are."

"Nope, not so long as I have your uncle's fascinating pocket watch. Anytime I feel like it I could enlighten Dorian Andersen to what his nephew has been up to. Couldn't I? Tell him how I happened on his grandfather's watch in a dead man's personal belongings. Maybe go on to share what I know about his kid's disappearance. Your cousin. Tell him why I don't think Thaddeus will come to call, ever again. Should I go on, bright boy?"

"You have my pocket watch?" spat Axel, outraged at Clint's revelation. "Where'd you find it? I want it back."

"Did my homework," grunted Clint satisfactorily, aware Axel was obsessed with it. "It didn't just fly in on the noon balloon, and drop in my lap," he scoffed. "I have friends in high places. Bodies have been dropping like flies over that timepiece. Wasn't tough to figure out what was going on. Call it my bargaining chip. We both have something the other one desires."

"Meet me here, tomorrow night at 9 p.m. We'll discuss it in person," demanded Axel through garbled words, bordering three sheets to the wind.

"Don't think so. I'll not be a sitting duck like the others. Make sure DeArra is home when I stop by your house tomorrow. I'll let you know when. Good to have a witness present to level the playing field."

Laughing so loud Clint had to move the phone away from his ear, Axel's rebuttal was swift and uncompromising. "No can do, Cowboy. Ain't riding that horse. You come here, come alone. I'll meet you at the same time you flirted with my girl, Cookie. Eleven in the morning."

"Don't screw with me Axel," warned Clint with equal hostility. "Okay not tomorrow. I'll give you two days to decide. Don't underestimate me. I'm not walking into a trap. I've seen your friend Jerry and suspect his associates could be called on anytime, if required."

Not hearing resistance, Clint unequivocally stated, "It's your house or nowhere."

"Sounds like in another life we could have been friends," howled Axel understanding he was backed into a corner.

"Oh, and by the way, that friend I told you about, the one in higher places, he's no nicer than either of us. Cops seldom find what they are already convinced can't be found. Especially if they're told not to. Get my drift? Might turn his head the other way at the right price. I'd rather not bring him into this, but I will if necessary."

Clint could hear Axel seething on the other end. "Keeping it simple suits me," Clint advised, "but it's your choice. Cookie's death has been investigated and so far, there aren't any leads. That doesn't mean an anonymous one might not fall into the right hands."

He waited for the weight of his words to register inside Axel's thick skull and then said, "You only live once, but if you do it right, once is enough." With his thumb, he pressed the end call button.

Behind the storm door, Jules stood wearing a puzzled expression, *Why isn't he coming in?* she wondered. Just then, Clint stepped out of the truck, slamming the door with punishing emphasis. *Whoa, he's not a happy camper.*

Clint walked into the foyer, hugging Jules as he entered the house. She instinctively knew not to ask what was on his mind, but did say, "Hey, Bonnie called, said she figured out the last of the numbers." Jules's face brightened, "She's like a female Sherlock Holmes, loves to solve a good mystery." Jules laughed, seeing an immediate shift in her husband's attitude. "She asked you to give her a ring."

"That's music to my ears," admitted Clint, displaying his first smile since entering the house. "Bonnie has impeccable timing. I can't believe how fast she deciphered those numbers I gave her at the party. They represent a specific location. The order was off but the sequence, although spaced incorrectly, once rearranged, were accurate."

Seeing he had Jules's full attention, Clint went on. "The general location is Young's High Bridge, Tyrone, Kentucky, named after a county in Northern Ireland. The bridge was built in 1889 but is unused today. Tyrone is virtually a ghost town on the Kentucky River. At one time a functional distillery operated there. Louisville Southern Railroad transported passengers from Lexington, Kentucky to Lawrenceburg, Indiana, last used in December 1937."

"Good grief, why would K.C. have written those coordinates down and give them to you?"

"I believe with all my heart that's where Thaddeus Andersen is buried. Dorian, his father, told me the boys visited the bridge when they were young men. It's a place Axel and his cousin are extremely familiar with." He stopped a moment, "I should rephrase that. *Were.*"

Large green eyes observed Clint's blue, telling ones. Jules, in an instant, understood the implications of his disclosure. "So, who will accompany you there. You'd better tell me you're not going alone. Scott, and who else?"

A gentle embrace caressed her shoulders. "Don't worry. If you want, I'll let you tag along," he suggested, lovingly. "I'm open to that. You are part of everything I do, or ever will do. Scott might not be too happy about you coming with me, but if you want, I'll talk to him. Please understand, though, this is a murder investigation, no longer just me speculating about Thaddeus's disappearance."

Jules nodded, "I know. Truthfully, I don't want to be anywhere near that place. If you find that man's body, I'd rather find out about it from you, right here at home at the kitchen table. No, thank you."

"Granted, I prefer that too. Although, it's important to me that you feel included, to have your blessing in all this is paramount to my own happiness. I didn't ask to be involved, but here I am."

"You are immersed in the case, sucked in from day one. Ever since Farley entered the picture and told you about his heart dilemma. Charlie Hill was and maybe still is reaching out." Jules's appearance grew dark, not liking the sound of her own words.

Seems to be more than one of those hanging about these days, thought Clint, aware that Thaddeus had passed on the longitude and latitude geographical coordinates of where his body would be found to K.C.

Had K.C. not been an autistic savant with the ability to see and hear things outside a normal person's range, Clint would be no further along or knowledgeable about Thaddeus's body. The mirror only revealed so much, and the rest came from the boy. How could Clint ever explain something as bizarre as what he'd experienced other than to his wife who had participated in the Rod Radcliff, Sr. incident, at his side?

No matter, this was the world in which Clint found himself. Tasked as an extension of an unseen domain, Clint had a higher purpose. One that involved placing a spotlight on injustices. He was at peace with his inner calling.

First Thing the next morning, Clint phoned Bonnie to ask if it would be all right with her if he stopped by when the library first opened. She agreed.

When he entered, she was there at the desk waiting. Obviously, something of importance was on her mind.

"Alright, woman, I'm waiting to hear what you've come up with now," he teased, seeing the gleam in her eye.

"Bridge length, 1,659 feet. Largest span, 551 feet. Built in 1889. 16 689043 42124767 took me a little longer, but I finally figured it out. It's the zone, easting, and northing lines. Where the bridge is erected, its exact location. I've got to tell you Clint, that was not easy. About drove me crazy." Bonnie placed her hands on the desk, and leaned in, emphasizing, "My brain is toast."

"I must confess," admitted Clint, "I read online about the bridge and when it was constructed and what railroad service primarily used it before I stopped in to see you. So, the 1988 number I figured out. But the others, no way."

"Geez, Louise, Clint. Why did K.C. give you all that. What were you expected to do with it?"

"That's another subject for another day, I'm afraid." He smiled wily, not about to explain the complexity of his situation. The time was coming when Bonnie would be brought into his confidence but today was not that day.

"Okay, master sleuth." She laughed with a sly grin. "But you owe me!"

"I do. That's a fact. For now, a big thank you will have to do." He reached in and hugged her, saying, "Seriously, you've been a tremendous help."

Getting back into his truck, Clint then dialed Scott. "Got a minute," he asked after being transferred to Scott's office.

"No," he answered with a smile waiting for Clint's response.

"You might want to find five minutes in that busy schedule of yours," chortled Clint.

"Sure, but let's not meet here. How about Josie's in fifteen?" suggested Scott, pushing the report he was reading aside.

"I have so much to tell you I don't know where to begin. I have thirty minutes, tops. I'm headed back to Louisville for a meeting with David Dunn at 10 a.m."

"You don't say. You have my interest piqued. I'll see you at Josie's in five."

Five minutes later Scott and Clint were conversing over a hot cup of brew.

"First, I caught Mac Hill red handed defrauding his brother's estate, swindling proceeds that belong to K.C. Currently, I have no idea the extent of the theft, but soon will. I plan to explain in detail whenever you are available, just not now."

Frowning, bewilderment written on his face, Scott replied, "Do pray tell your plan to do that?"

"I bought a painting from Mac, under pretense, and later stumbled on a separate letter of intent, in essence, a second Will, behind the painting's backboard. Long story short, the canvas painting was meant for his boy, prior to his parents' murder. When K.C. saw it in my office, the kid went berserk. After he left, I saw the backing was oddly misshapen and removed it. That's when I found a list of Charlie's paintings and other items to be distributed to people he and Ann cared about."

"Okay," grunted Scott, glancing down at his watch. "Let's move on. Next item?"

Scott was about to be bowled over with Clint's next revelation, Clint felt certain. "I know the general location of Thaddeus Andersen's body. It's somewhere in the vicinity of Young's High Bridge, in Tyrone."

Watching Scott's face closely, he then dropped a bombshell. "Lastly, your expertise to catch Axel Drako is paramount." Their glances locked. "Didn't you say your colleague's name in Louisville is Drex Mason? You might want to give him a head's up soon, since things are about to get ugly."

Chapter 51
The Tangled Web We Weave

After he left his meeting with Scott, and following a courtesy call to David Dunn, Clint dialed Jules. "Good luck today, sweetheart, hope you and the kids have a blast. The ideas you shared last night for the field trip sounded fantastic."

"Thank you," replied Jules, excited for the day to begin. "I'm about to walk into the children's home. Don't expect to see me much before eight. The movie doesn't start until 3:10. By the time we get back to the orphanage, unload the children, and give them a snack before bed, it will be after seven."

"I forgot to ask. Will K.C. be among the ones going?"

"As a matter of fact, he will be on the bus, along with twenty-eight other children. Quite a crew, four adult chaperons, including Farley, and of course, me." Jules's face lit up when she said, "Josephine cried when she heard we had tickets to see The Muffet Christmas Carol, a special airing in New Albany and were stopping for breakfast at the diner beforehand."

Making a sound of appreciation, Jules followed up her thought. "Patrick is such a sweetheart. He closed the place until 1 p.m. to give us plenty of time to get in and out without being rushed or disturbed. He knows I'm planning a small awards presentation. My boss has the biggest heart of anyone I know."

Clint coughed, chuckling, "What about me?"

"Sorry, Clint, you come in a distant second." Listening to his laughter, she had the good sense not to ask him where he was or what he was up to, other than to speak to Charlie and Ann Hill's attorney at 10 a.m. about the deception Clint had told her about the night before.

"You're off tomorrow for a change. Let's do something super special. Maybe go Christmas shopping together. Pick up a few additional presents. We should take Faith a separate gift for hosting us," suggested Clint with the mindset he'd be making his wife happy to focus on a house gift for her sister.

"How does that sound?" he asked, remembering Christmas Eve was a week from Friday. "December has flown by. I initially wanted to get our Salzburg family together. Time has run out. Maybe this gang here should do a New Year's celebration instead. They all have families too. I suspect they will be just as busy over the holidays as we are."

"That's a great idea. I switched Thursday for Friday. Thought a day between to rest up sounded good. We'll be able to spend it together, excellent. I hope you don't mind I moved Thursday to Friday," commented Jules, sounding rather chipper for so early in the morning. "FYI, Faith is expecting us around noon on the twenty-third. It'll be great to spend the night in Beech Grove, and to see Dad, Diana, and everyone. Faith said the family is taking us to dinner at a new Italian restaurant downtown."

"Is that right?" Excited at the prospect of seeing downtown Indianapolis again, especially at Christmastime, Clint remarked, "I'm looking forward to that. Indy decorates the Circle spectacularly. It'll be a festive celebration."

Jules's enthusiasm was contagious. She had been in the Christmas spirit for weeks, which had prompted thoughts for an extra nice day on Thursday. He switched gears. "How does an early afternoon dinner in French Lick sound? I could take you to West Baden's jewelry store to look around. Maybe an early Christmas present."

"Are you kidding me? That will be perfect. Something to look forward to," Jules's voice reached the next level of bubbly. She glanced down at her watch, remembering the time. "Oh… Clint, I've got to go. See you later sweetie. Sending you a hug!"

Jules had a way of lifting her husband's mood. Normally her contagious personality lingered, but not this time. When the truck crossed the state line, Clint's tension returned in spades, escalating to new heights. His wife had no idea the pressure he was under. Left unsaid, he struggled not to let it overwhelm him. For the first time since getting involved with Farley, Clint weighed how many crooked, dishonest people must be in the world and how drained he was from encountering only two, unable to conceive the type of stress police dealt with daily.

Passing the law office's receptionist on his way to the elevators, the thirty something handsomely dressed woman nodded in recognition as Clint got off the elevators. As with the previous visit, Dunn was in the waiting area ready to take Clint back to his office.

Reaching into his pocket, Clint placed an envelope, Box 428, Wellington Credit Union written on the front, with key, to the far side of the desk. When Dunn glanced at it, Clint said, "That's the key I found behind the painting."

He stated with raised brow, "It is, dated December 25, 2002." He also showed a phone image of Charles's message meant for Keelan scripted on the back of the canvas.

"As I mentioned, a second smaller version of Midnight Break was behind the original. I'd like to keep it for my wife if you have no objections. We should be able to retrieve the four thousand I paid for the larger painting when Mac Hill is arrested. I've already had the original painting hung on K.C.'s bedroom wall. It belongs to him."

"That's not a problem," agreed Dunn. "You said there is a multipage numbered list of Charles's work, with titles and dates, in here," he asked tapping the envelope.

"Yes, you should have found some of those paintings at his premises the day after his death. You'll also find a mortgage deed and the title to his car. Duplicate copies should be in the safety deposit box. Plus, Ann's wishes for her jewelry and other things. His brother, according to this account, has a duplicate key."

Dunn sighed, leery of what might be found inside the box. "Let's have a look."

Walking out together, Clint's hopes were high. Either way, he felt confident the Hills' wishes would be upheld in court with a notarized copy of their intentions in David Dunn's hands.

Turning into Wellington Credit Union, the two men anxiously went indoors and stood in the lobby. A few minutes later they were escorted to the manager's office where they explained their purpose for being there. Dunn showed his credentials in advance of being taken to the vault where the manager applied her matching key alongside the one Clint had given Dunn to open the safety deposit box. A security guard stood outside the door waiting while the two of them scanned the materials inside the box.

Set on a metal table next in a room of other secured boxes, David and Clint combed through the contents of the Hills' safety box, finding more than they anticipated but none of what was expected. The mortgage deed and car title were missing. No list of paintings. However, there was a sealed letter to Keelan Charles Hill, a small bag of old pennies and dimes, silk pouch with jeweled hair pins, and several loose Indian head nickels. A half dozen or so small silver spoons with certificates of authenticity were arranged in a black box lined in red velvet.

"Looks like Mac's been here," guessed Dunn, his irritation undeniable. "Since I was unaware of this location, and Mac was the only one with a key, other than Charles, Mac undoubtedly assumed the other key was hidden somewhere in the house. He might have unsuccessfully searched for it when he removed whatever paintings Charles did have there, other than the three we removed a day later."

"Ann's mother's locket isn't here, nor is the ruby necklace, or her Aunt Betty's diamond ring." Clint said, "I got the definite impression June Bennett was to have more than just a few nice hairpins. Unless you have Ann's jewelry, scarves, and pins in inventory somewhere."

"No, I don't have any of those items listed. We'll have to do another thorough search of the house," replied Dunn in a clipped tone, his face visibly disturbed by the sequence of events. "I'll send one of my associates over. Ann told me she would list her jewelry as an addendum to the Will but never did."

Attorneys often color their moods and personalities to match that of their clients but in this case the conversation and temperament of Dunn and Reeves were in complete harmony, repulsed by the lack of moral character Charlie's brother exhibited. Angry and exasperated, the muscles around Dunn's mouth tightened, reflecting a harshness in his eyes.

"This will be set right. I want you to take me to the warehouse. I'll find us an escort to unlock the facility door. Before that, I need to call a judge who will be willing to aid us." Dunn signaled for the person standing by to assist them with putting the safety box back in its cradle.

"I have a phone call to make," stated Clint. "Do you want to call me when you're ready to move forward? I would also like you to see where Mac Hill is doing business from."

"We'll visit that location after we see the warehouse merchandise. Make your call, said Dunn. "I'll text you when I'm ready to head over."

"That works," agreed Clint knowing what he was about to do wouldn't take long.

Walking across the street to a small café, Clint pulled out his other phone and dialed Axel's number. To his surprise, a female voice answered on the first ring.

"Hello."

"Is Axel there? Tell him its Cowboy."

"Sure, I'll get him," the heavy Brooklyn accent said, putting the phone down.

In the background Clint heard two raised voices.

"Go outside and shut the door," Axel demanded.

"It's too cold," complained the woman. "I don't want to. Can't I go in the bedroom?"

"I told you to go outdoors. *Do it! Now!*"

"Axel, I've had it with you!" Clint heard the woman say as the door slammed excessively hard, their quarrel not ending well on her side of the equation. A closer, more colorful version of their relationship told Clint the bare facts he needed, paying heed to DeArra's fussiness could prove in Clint's favor, turning out to be Axel's weak link.

"What?" yelled Axel, impatience in every word being delivered, "I'm done playing games."

Annoyed, Clint was on the verge of saying more but thought better of it. Instead, he charged, "I'll be at your place on Friday, you pick the time. Make it fast. I'm a busy man." Clint was hoping against hope Axel wouldn't agree, thinking that was too soon.

He was watching in the mirror that was hung behind the counter and saw David Dunn approaching his BMW. Soon Clint heard a text message come through. He quickly paused to review it. Dunn was ready to drive to the warehouse.

Clint raised his voice, as Axel had his. "Make up your mind, man," Clint angrily stated, "And… I swear if you step outside our agreement, my friend has been instructed to release damaging information that *will* put you behind bars for life."

"I'm not doing this anymore," protested Axel. "You either get over here right now or I'm coming after you. And I will find you Cowboy, count on it. I have friends too, you know!"

Running out of time, Clint said, "You have five seconds. Five…"

"No, come here now, or the deal is off," demanded Axel who intended to stand his ground, no matter what.

"Four, three, two… I will hang up."

"Alright, alright. Two o'clock, but can't we do this on Monday?" Axel peppered his words with hard emphasis, aware that Friday was DeArra's tanning, hair, and nails day."

The door he'd heard slam in the background was being pounded fiercely. Evidently DeArra wanted back inside the house. Threads of information filtered into Clint's awareness. Honing his greatest asset of decoding the smallest of details, he had reached the next level of insight. In a daredevilish move, he sent a torpedo aimed at Axel's soft spot.

"Best take care of your woman, DeArra D'Amelio. Not treat her like Carla Crenna was handled, because I will know, Axel. DeArra Drako has a nice ring to it. Wouldn't you say? Sounds like something you'd find in an Old Maid deck or Clue." Taking a second to let Axel think about what he had said, he tagged on, "Monday, works better for me."

Scoffing at Clint's boldness, Axel fired back angrily, "Alright Monday, but you leave her out of this."

"Make sure she's there, Axel, or as you said, the deal is off. If she's not, I'm not."

After he disconnected the call, Clint let out the breath he'd been holding. He was hoping Axel would settle on Monday all along.

Crossing the street back to Dunn's BMW coupe, he now had to contact Scott Edwards. Not able to call, he sent a quick text as he slid into Dunn's passenger's seat. Making an entry into a pocket-sized leather note pad, Clint was unmistakably preoccupied with another matter.

Noting Clint's clenched jaw, Dunn asked, "Is everything alright?"

Not realizing he had let his guard down, allowing his emotions to surface, Clint quieted the spinning turmoil of his own thoughts, "Yeah, sure. Nothing of importance."

Fingering the frame of his glasses, Dunn was a steady, insightful man who understood his turf well. He could tell when people weren't speaking the truth. Still, he found Clint hard to read. Taking Clint at his word, although not convinced of his truthfulness, Dunn replied, "Okay. Show me how to get to this warehouse. Someone on the police force will be meeting us with a search warrant at the address you provided."

Driving toward the outskirts of Wellington, Clint directed Dunn to the D&J Warehouse facility, which resembled a business complex more than a warehouse.

Stepping out of the car, they walked shoulder to shoulder to the secured, bolted door at H-J24. The good news was the bars behind the glass could be cut through, if the entry tools the police carried didn't pry the door open easily enough.

Two police vehicles pulled beside the building, their squad lights on, and Clint watched the operation of breaking in, saying to Dunn, "It's about to get real. We'll soon find out what Mac has been up to. I sure hope this wasn't for naught."

"I doubt it," stated Dunn confidentially, "after a while you start to get a nose for these things. I began my career as an insurance fraud investigator, oddly enough. There's no question you've rooted out a sham. If I were honest, I'd have to admit something seemed off with Mr. Hill when he stated he'd been to his brother's house to lock up straight away. That never did set well, and the fact Charles only had three paintings at his house seemed unlikely."

Just then the door burst against the frame, exposing a dark interior space behind it. Only a dim light illuminated what little there was to see. Escorted by a police officer, clutching the search warrant he had solicited, Dunn disappeared into the cavity of darkness, Clint close on his heels.

What they found exceeded any expectations they had walked in with. Arranged on tables and in organized compartments were unframed Charles Lewellyn Hill artwork. Countless more rested against the walls, in tubes, by theme classification. In the center of the wide space were small tables of art supplies next to shelves of blank canvases. Woodwork not yet carved into finished products were piled at the opposite end of the room.

"I think we hit the jackpot," declared Dunn, a fissure of excitement in his voice. "Charles had more than three paintings, it appears." He smiled, "This leaves no doubt that Mac was devaluing the Hills' estate."

"Did you notice his brother's art has been categorized into like images," mentioned Clint, pulling painting after painting away from the one it leaned on.

Still amazed at the sheer number of items scattered around the room, of every shape and size, Dunn was doleful when he speculated, "Charles must have painted nonstop to create these many images. All since the day he visited my office to have his Will prepared."

David shook his head. "And to think, Mac shared this place with his brother. From what Charles told me, Mac is a master artisan in his own right, makes beautiful furniture. I presume they worked alongside each other at this location. And now Mac comes here to replace what he is selling over on Tuxedo Street or elsewhere, to profit from his brother's passing. I don't know how anyone could do such a thing."

"Honestly, the man gives me the creeps. The pompous look in his eyes is repulsive," said Clint somberly, thinking back on his and Mac's interaction.

"I'll have someone stake out 269 Tuxedo Street if he is not there when we show up." Dunn walked to the front where the police were waiting to seal the entrance. "Let's do this thing."

Chapter 52
Justice Prevails

In Dunn's car, when Clint's phone rang, it startled him.

Farley was on the line, sounding winded. "Hey, Clint I hope I didn't catch you at a bad time," Farley apologized, his voice anxious, but excited.

Not knowing how to answer, Clint responded, "I am in the middle of something right now. Could I call you back in five?"

"Oh sure, it's nothing that can't wait."

Clint noticed David was pulling into a gas station parking lot. "I need something to drink," Dunn indicated. With a wave of his hand, he said, "Take your call, please."

Clint nodded thanks." When Dunn stepped out of the car, he said, "That's alright, Farley, go ahead. What's on your mind."

"Well, you know we are on the field trip today, and I've spent a lot of time with Keelan lately. I was wondering if you would approve him coming home with me when we get back. For dinner. I promise to have him back by bedtime. Thought I could read to him before bed at my place rather than at the orphanage."

Clint was elated, happy to answer in the affirmative. "Absolutely, that sounds wonderful for both of you. When K.C. sees your place, he'll flip out." Clint chuckled, with a smile so big that when he saw David returning to the car, he had to adjust back to the serious situation they were in, wiping the happy look off his face. "Can't talk right now but I'll text Tom Sanders with an approval. "Have a good evening with K.C. We'll talk later."

Having already noticed how close Farley and K.C. had become, it did Clint's heart good to see their relationship mature. They were both happier than before they met. Their joy was in direct contrast to the wickedness of Mac Hill, and his relationship to his half-brother, Charles Hill.

So he wouldn't forget, Clint immediately sent a text to Tom Sanders, followed by one to Sue Johnson, who was with Jules, stating K.C. could accompany Farley this evening when everyone returned from the field trip. Farley's call made Clint think about his wife and how her day was going with twenty-eight children, which prompted a grin.

No one was home at 269 Tuxedo Street when they parked a block from Mac's rental. It was imperative that Dunn catch Hill in his con. The problem was it could take days for him to return with another victim. Either way, David Dunn now knew, as well as the police, where the crime was being committed. After an hour they drove away with a police commitment to watch the house for activity. At which point, Dunn would be notified, and Mac would be arrested.

Two hours after Clint climbed back into his F-100, he was back in Salzburg. The call came through. Mac Hill had been apprehended and taken to jail. Dunn stated the police would contact him for a statement to which Clint gladly agreed.

Dunn went on to say that Hill had angrily shouted at him saying Charlie's kid was an imbecile, an idiot that didn't deserve his father's fortune. The man was strong-armed into the squad car, forced, even bullied, out of the house when he refused to cooperate, all while neighbors stood gawking from their yards at the commotion surrounding them.

Clint was on cloud nine, having accomplished one good deed on Charlie Hill's, and his wife, Ann's, behalf. Their Will would now be honored as it was intended. Having not felt Charlie's presence in some time, Clint wondered if the man knew his half-brother was a cheat and charlatan. That he had thrown K.C. to the wind in the name of profit, and unadulterated greed? Possessions found among the items in the warehouse had included Ann's jewelry and over sixty of Charlie's original works of art.

The saddest part of his and Dunn's conversation, however, was when he heard Charlie had a partially completed companion piece to *Midnight Break* with a note attached to the back, indicating it was to be given to Keelan, Christmas, 2004. Tragically, he and Ann were killed on December 21 that same year. Clint considered commissioning another artist to finish the piece so he might present it to K.C. on Christmas Day, if it felt like the right thing to do. Not a gift from his father, but heartfelt, nonetheless.

Clint badly needed downtime to pull himself together before he saw Jules later that evening. His heart had been racing since early morning and, at times, felt like it was having palpitations.

Things had gone as smoothly as could be expected. They had found exactly what Clint trusted they would, and more than enough to nail Mac. Dunn told Clint that Hill had been charged and was spending the night in jail.

In truth, David Dunn had turned out to be a compatible companion. He was incredibly knowledgeable and adept at his job. No doubt they'd be seeing one another again at Mac's arraignment, and sentencing. When they did, Clint would invite him to dinner as a thank you for playing a key roll in uncovering the extent of Mac's wrongdoings.

With his meeting set for Monday, rather than Friday, Clint had ample time to check out Young's High Bridge, especially with Jules switching her workdays. Unintended consequences could surface if his guard dropped. Therefore, he needed to move cautiously while keeping a clear head. To pretend, the angst amassing within himself wasn't a factor, would be an outright falsehood. Axel was not a mere thief like Mac Hill. He was a hardened criminal, several times over.

To date, they didn't have enough evidence to lay at Axel's feet, nothing to solidly convict him of any wrongdoing. Clint knew his work was cut out for him, but in the silence of his being, he saw a glimmer of hope. On the precipice of discovery, he grinned without amusement.

He'd start at the bridge and ride the wave of discovery until the day Thaddeus's body was at last unearthed. Remembering Henry Ford's words, Clint recited words of encouragement to help him in his endeavor. "Whether you think you can, or think you can't, you're right." But, first things first, Scott had to be updated. He picked up the phone.

"What are you up to?" asked Scott cordially when he answered Clint's call.

"Is it possible to see you today?"

"Not until 4 pm. I'm afraid? Does this have to do with Axel?" inquired Scott, his antenna on high alert, also aware Clint had been looking into circumstances surrounding Charlie Hill's paintings.

"I have several things to speak with you about, all of them important. Some more so than others," admitted Clint with a sound of urgency to his voice, thinking he'd like Scott to accompany him on Friday to scout the area around Young's High Bridge. Glancing at his watch, the dial showed 2:45, enough time to drop by Aces & Eights for an early dinner. "When you're ready, give me a call. I'll be at Aces & Eights."

"That sounds like a winner." Scott chortled, ready to drop everything to go enjoy a beer with his friend. "Plan on me no later than 4 p.m."

"You're on," agreed Clint, glad to have Scott's listening ear, and as a cohort. And hopefully, Scott's company on Friday. "You know where to find me."

After first putting the phone down, Clint picked it back up again, calling Tom Sanders, to make certain everything was set for Farley and K.C. when they returned from the movie later. He was glad to hear the papers were complete. Protocol was met for Farley to invite K.C. to his house for dinner. Clint thought about the bond that was building between them. They were both lost souls, carrying the torment of losing everyone they loved.

Clint knew he stood at a fork in the road concerning Axel. From here on out he would be silent, listen to his inner voice, pay attention to where his instincts led. Without it, he was certain to fail. Let empowerment activate all potential scenarios that may have played out when Axel was last in Tyrone, Kentucky.

Walking into Aces & Eights, Clint immediately found the table he typically occupied. He ordered chips and salsa as a starter, and a beer. Leaning against the high back bench, he closed his eyes to clear his mind. Minutes rolled by without Clint noticing the normal sounds of the bar and grill.

It occurred to him that to solve the case he would have to enter the mind of a killer. Think as Axel thought, the day he hauled his cousin's body away. To murder him in the alley behind Cell Block #49 when they argued. To take on the temperament of someone angry enough to lash out and do bodily harm would take courage on his part. To somehow stoop to the level of the person who committed crimes, would be next to impossible.

417

At last, Clint relaxed mentally and put another order in asking for two burritos and a pizza quesadilla while he waited on Scott. Not long after his food arrived, his friend slid into the booth across from him.

Scott's hand was in the air, ready to order his own food and drink. "Fill me in." Scott didn't waste any time. He then admitted, "It's been on my mind since we talked last. That was a teaser without a follow-up."

"Here goes nothing." Clint's eyes met Scotts revealing he had much to divulge. Clearing his throat, he stated, "I wasn't so confident we could catch Mac Hill in the act, but the guy had the gall to sell another painting today, right after selling me one on Tuesday. Can you believe that?"

Impatience read in his eyes when Clint sarcastically showed his disdain for Mac Hill. "For all his sneaky underhanded deeds, his reward was getting handcuffed and put into a patrol car. With his neighbors watching, he was hauled off to jail and arrested. Dunn's search warrant allowed us to inspect the warehouse he and his brother shared, when Charlie was alive."

"What an update." Scott scowled, a hint of a smile spanning his face thinking his friend sounded more like a colleague on the force than an amateur. "Was there any other incriminating evidence?" Scott asked, thinking as a cop would naturally do.

"David Dunn apparently has contacts on the Kentucky police force and a judge he was able to reach," Clint said matter-of-factly. "Did you know David worked as an insurance fraud investigator at one time?"

"I did not. He didn't mention it. How interesting." Scott took a swig of his pint, trying not to gulp it too quickly. Recalling their first meeting with the estate attorney and how knowledgeable Dunn seemed concerning police matters, Scott noted, "Attributes like that could come in handy in his profession."

"Yeah, and it explains his insightful decision to keep the antique watch with him at his office. He must have known the watch held significance. He sensed if Charlie had it on his person the night he died, it might be important."

For a long while, they studied one another and what had been exchanged. A man who kept law and order, the other, a man of principle, pushing for justice.

Finally, Clint broke the ice. "I had a feeling Mac was hoarding Charlie's work. After he sold me the Christmas painting, I followed him to the warehouse and watched him go inside the business complex. He came out with two paintings. I figured one was to replace mine, and the other, a standby."

"I assume your gut feeling was spot on since you are telling me all of this."

"Yes." Clint nodded. "Charlie made a mistake when he gave his brother a duplicate copy to their safety deposit box because Mac emptied it out. He relocated their valuables to the warehouse. Other items taken from the Hills' home were also found there."

Scott looked revolted as he listened to Clint's account of what had gone down. "The house where you bought your Christmas painting is where Mac sells Charlie's work? Then, he replenishes the house inventory from what he had stockpiled at the warehouse?"

Folding his napkin, Clint carefully laid it beside his plate. He replied, "Honestly, Scott, I can't believe this guy thought he'd get away with it? Eventually someone was going to catch on to his scheme."

Scott snorted in laughter. "There are a lot of stupid people out there, Clint, Mac is just one of many." His eyes narrowed, peering across at Clint, his head lowering with a question. "So, what developments have arisen concerning Axel? You said you think his cousin is buried near Young's High Bridge? What brought you to that conclusion?"

Creasing his forehead, Clint reluctantly answered. "What I'm about to say is totally illogical. Therefore, I won't even try to explain it. Because I don't understand it myself. You'll have to trust me." Clint followed Scott's eyes knowing he was closely observing him.

"Go on," urged Scott. "I'm listening."

"K.C. gave me a set of numbers that someone else had given him. He said a man asked him to write them down and deliver them to me." Clint conveniently left out the man's name was Thaddeus.

Noticing he had Scott's full attention, Clint continued, "That same person asked K.C. to bring the numbers to my office. How this *someone* knew I was there, is anyone's guess." Clint's eyes searched Scott's but only an intense stare reflected out. He could see Scott was waiting for a plausible explanation for the numbers and their relationship to Clint's story.

"It turns out, thanks to Bonnie, the numbers apparently correspond to latitudinal and longitudinal lines of Tyrone, Kentucky." Clint shifted his weight, leaning inward, "I hope you don't try to make me explain how I know, *I just do*, that this is where Thaddeus Andersen's body was taken. Somewhere near Young's High Bridge. A place Axel and Thaddeus explored in their youth."

Clint looked hard into Scott's eyes, "I'm telling you that's where the man is buried. And I plan to go there early Friday morning to start a comprehensive search. I wondered if you'd like to join me?" With pursed lips, he firmly stated, "I'm headed that way at 7 a.m."

Scott wholeheartedly agreed, not hesitating to answer. "Yes, I would very much like that. I'll put in for a personal day. Don't know how my superiors would view this since we will be in Kentucky. That's why I'm going to involve Drex."

"I forgot to mention something else. Axel and I set a time to meet. He thinks I want money for my silence. Monday, 2 p.m., his place. He wants the antique watch. I told him there is proof Cookie Crenna was murdered." Clint folded his hands, asking, "Could you and Drex Mason be there? And possibly David Andrews? I'm pretty sure I'm going to need backup."

Hanging on to every word, Scott peered at Clint, wondering if the man had completely gone mad. With a stern eye of righteousness, he said, "Yes."

Chapter 53
Tensions Escalate

After leaving the restaurant and his conversation with Scott, Clint headed west on Grandview. Rounding the bend, Radcliff's Children's Home came into view. Drawing near, he rolled past the heavy iron gates, up the paved drive, amidst mature trees that banked the lane that as he approached *the orphanage of his dreams.*

Stepping outside the truck into late afternoon grey skies, an expanse of pillowy, freshly fallen snow blanketed the grounds presenting a magical quality to the frosty air. He looked up at the country mullion windows he and his wife had selected for the structure's frontage. A sense of pride enveloped him at the utter beauty and elegance the windows presented.

Pulling the collar of his double-breasted peacoat around his neck, Clint left the top button of his shirt unbuttoned, wanting to feel the brisk air against his warm skin. His favorite season was soon to bridge the winter solstice come December 21.

The Christmassy atmosphere in the home the orphans had created with handmade decorations was an endearing sight. Signs of their handiwork were everywhere, which lifted Clint's spirit to new heights. Apart from an occasional employee walking about, the place showed no signs of activity.

Rather than drive home and wait for his wife there, Clint had decided to go to the orphanage until the bus arrived. Besides, he wanted to personally give Farley his blessing, in respect to his first homemade meal at the cabin with K.C.

In truth Clint was curious if the boy had accepted Farley's invitation but knowing Cocoa and Winston were part of the equation, he figured Keelan jumped on board. The child Farley interacted with, and the Keelan everyone else knew, were two different people.

Meanwhile, a bus full of children was headed homeward bound from today's field trip, sang Christmas carols, and chatted about their remarkable day. Clint sat on a bench anxiously awaiting Farley, and Jules's return to Radcliff's Children's Home.

Sipping on a cola while watching the front entrance, he at last saw the bus turn into the roundabout, unloading the children at the door. Clint stood, waiting for the laughter and clatter to start.

"Hey, you," Jules called out with a huge smile on her face when she saw her husband waiting close to the door. "I'm so happy to see you. Can't wait to tell you about our day. The children had such a fabulous time. My mind is made up. I'll do another field trip right away, not wait so long in between outings. Valentine's Day might be a good time to plan one. The movie was delightful, and the children completely behaved themselves." Jules stopped talking when she saw the big smile on Clint's face, realizing she was talking nonstop without hardly taking a breath.

"Sorry," she laughed. "I'm on top of the world right now from seeing how happy this trip made the children. It did my heart good to witness the healing power of togetherness, support, hugs, and kisses."

"I can see that," grinned Clint. "I'm pleased too. That's why we have an orphanage. Helping a parentless child is an amazing feeling." Just then, over Jules's shoulder, Clint saw Farley heading their direction. Stepping to the side, Clint spoke, "Welcome back. How was your first time to help chaperone a busload of kids?"

"Cakewalk. Easy-peasy!" laughed Farley. "I've already signed up for the next gig." He moved in to give Jules a hug. "This woman is amazing. A natural leader with young people."

Clint was proud of Jules, but hearing someone else brag on her so robustly brought home what an excellent choice he had made when asking her hand in marriage. Early on he saw her effortless manner in relating to his grandchildren, knowing she would be a perfect fit with the kids from the orphanage.

Jules excused herself from the conversation to help finish signing the children back into the home. They had to do a headcount. That left the two men alone to discuss Farley's intention to have K.C. accompany him for dinner and a story. The lobby, jammed-packed with commotion and loud talking, showed no signs of the child Clint was most concerned with, causing him to wonder if something had gone amiss.

"Where's K.C.?" asked Clint.

"Oh, he needed to use the restroom. He'll be here in a minute so we can go gather a couple of things from his room before we leave." Farley saw concern in Clint's face and added, "You alright with this, still?"

"Sure," replied Clint quickly so he did not give the wrong impression. "I was afraid something had come up that might have changed your plans."

"No, not at all. Keelan doesn't speak words much, but he has no problem communicating," joked Farley. "He's looking forward to seeing my cabin. I told him about my dogs, Cocoa and Winston, and his eyes lit up like a Christmas tree." Farley chuckled. His face was as bright as the scene he described.

"I'm relieved to hear it," confessed Clint. "You two will have a super time. K.C. hasn't been anywhere like your place. He'll think he's at an amusement park. Notwithstanding Cocoa and his ferocious bark and evil eye. Let's hope K.C. doesn't draw Cocoa's wrath like I do."

At that moment K.C. came around the corner, walking silly, and talking to an imaginary companion. He approached slowly, looking up at Farley but eyeing Clint oddly.

"How's it going K.C.," inquired Clint. "Did you enjoy the movie? And the field trip?" Although Clint wasn't expecting an answer, he didn't expect the boy to run off.

Farley stared at Clint in surprise, wondering what K.C. was up to. "I wonder what that is about. He looked like something was on his mind." Before Farley could continue his thought, K.C. returned with a sheet of paper. He had gone to his special table and written a word down, and then came back to hand it to Clint.

"H-er-e," said K.C., deeply aware of who he was giving the paper to.

Clint and Farley examined the word written on the paper, "Angered."

"K.C., I don't understand," responded Clint, bothered by the idea he might have hurt K.C.'s feelings. "Are you angry with me? If so, let me try to fix whatever I did to upset you."

Squinting, K.C. vigorously shook his head, frustrated by the suggestion. For the second time, he ran away, back to his drawing table. Seconds later he was back, handing Clint another piece of paper.

"He-re," he said.

Clint saw the word, 'enraged', printed in red crayon. Clint's deeply creased brow and eyes showed how disturbed he felt. "Son, I don't understand. Why did you give these to me? What do they mean? Are you upset?"

K.C. didn't look up, nor did he try to reply. Instead, he grabbed Farley's hand, with his head lowered, he looked at his feet on the verge of tears. Wanting to help, Farley bent down to Keelan's level. He put his fingers on his chin to pull the child's head up. "It's okay, Keelan. You have special gifts." Farley took Keelan's hands in his. "Can you tell me where these words came from?"

Inspecting the words, realization of their meaning intensified into translation. Gazing into the deepest faraway corners of Keelan's dark intense eyes, Farley suddenly understood. Anagrams. *Enraged* and *angered,* both held the same number of letters, rearranged to form separate words. An intellectual connection joined Farley and Keelan to one mind. Farley tenderly probed for an answer. "Him, meaning... Thaddeus?" he asked. "Are these Thaddeus's words you've written?"

K.C. nodded briskly, looking up at Clint, with sad, pleading eyes, crying out for help from a mind that couldn't speak words.

Clint stroked the boy's head. K.C. didn't flinch as he would have normally done. "I understand, even if you don't, son. I promise to do everything in my power to figure this out."

With that said, K.C.'s shoulders relaxed, once again returning to his quiet, introverted self as though nothing out of the ordinary had happened.

Farley's inquisitive eyes stared across at Clint. "I won't pry, but this guy Thaddeus. Does he have special meaning to you?"

Unaware of the name of the person killed in the alley the afternoon Charlie Hill died, Farley was in the dark. However, Clint felt no need to explain the backstory. Casually he answered, "Yes, I know of him."

"Alright, we'll leave it at that," responded Farley on a lighthearted note. "If you have no objection Mr. Reeves. Mr. Keelan Charles Hill and Mr. Farley Liam McDougal have an engagement."

Farley and Clint gazed down at the boy and were surprised to see K.C. was oblivious to their exchange or Farley's funny remark. Taking his hand, Farley appealed to the youngster's sense of adventure. "You ready to go see where Uncle Farley lives? Have a hamburger at my place. Meet my doggies?"

Keelan wiggled in place, squirming wildly, waiting for the car ride he was promised to begin. Holding Farley's hand, he pulled and yanked until Farley stated, "Think it's time to hit the road."

"You two have an excellent evening," Clint said, reaching out to shake Farley's free hand. "I predict a successful outing is in store. Do let me know how it goes. Send a quick text if you don't mind. You know I'll be curious."

Although he didn't say as much, Clint felt an undercurrent of emotion roiling steadily below the surface. Fueled by fear, he worried he might not be able to deliver on the promise he'd made to K.C. moments before. Determined not to let uncertainty affect the end goal, he'd stay the course, trusting in the powers that had driven him to this juncture.

Friday's undertaking would be a day like nothing he'd ever experienced. Even so, with a little luck, a breakthrough in the case would surface. Even though he anticipated the search on Friday, the day before on Thursday with his wife, he'd shift gears back to family man and companion. He'd do his best to stay in the moment and enjoy every second of their time together. They'd Christmas shop and fine dine in French Lick, without thinking about the scum of the earth for a day. A complete departure from the man he had once been, inwardly Clint felt more like Dr. Jekyll and Mr. Hyde at times than his old self. He'd adjusted to the change with little difficulty.

Standing in the lobby waiting for things to settle down, Jules and Clint combed through the day she'd had with the orphans and other chaperones. She elaborated on every detail of the field trip, describing the excitement the group had generated was like any normal family, only on a grander scale.

She relayed to Clint that K.C. had been a perfect angel, not once causing a disturbance, describing how he had laughed loudly during the movie, shoveling popcorn in his mouth, and drinking his soft drink like no tomorrow. As did the other children, including Joseph and Josephine. She was pleased the boy remained at Farley's side the entire trip. At the end, Jules ruled the outing a complete success.

Driving home they made plans for Thursday, followed by Jules suggesting they roast hot dogs when they got home. Within an hour they were stepping outdoors and wrapping themselves in blankets beside an open fire pit enjoying the bright stars of winter. The stars were more pronounced than in the summer months when Jules and Clint typically enjoyed nighttime views. They ate two hot dogs apiece, potato chips, and smores for dessert. Afterwards, they retired to the living room to enjoy tumblers of Baileys Irish Cream over ice before the inside fireplace. Thirty minutes later they stood and dragged their weary bodies to bed.

Jules slept well. Clint not so much.

The next morning Jules was up and out of bed before the sun topped the trees in the east. Pouring a mug of steamy hot coffee while the maker was still in brew mode, she watched the sun rise through the decorative window in the kitchen. She sat down at the table, eager to go shopping, and waited eagerly for her man.

Smelling the delicious aroma of bacon and eggs that wafted through the house, Clint followed his wife's lead and moved toward the kitchen. With unkempt hair, and a loosely wrapped bathrobe, he fumbled around in slow motion, trying his best to wake up.

Their day together promised to be pleasant, something they had both looked forward to. By night's end, again they would fall into bed, exhausted from a pleasurable day of shopping, and enjoyable time together.

Chapter 54
Young's High Bridge

After a superb day on Thursday and a successful field trip the day before that, Jules was ready for whatever challenges came her way at Josie's Diner. Fridays at Josie's were always busy, but during the Christmas holiday, it was twofold. She didn't mind, though, because a lot of new and old faces would pass through the doors.

Finishing the yogurt and toast she'd made for a quick bite before leaving the house, Jules strolled to the foyer to move the beautifully carved hall tree Clint and she had purchased from a specialty shop in West Baden for Faith's thank-you gift when they spent the night. Carrying the coat tree to the back of the house, this item would not be wrapped. Only a bow would be placed on top.

Wrapping her arms tightly around her husband's neck, and then placing a kiss on his cheek, Jules was out the door by 5:47 a.m., leaving Clint ample time to prepare for the day that lay ahead. Grateful Jules's work schedule was a full one, keeping her late into the day because of the season, Clint readied himself both emotionally and mentally for the out-of-town trip to Tyrone, Kentucky, thankful for his sidekick.

Clint was at the door when the headlights from Scott's squad car pulled into the drive. He was out the door in no time, carrying a thermos of hot coffee they would share on the trail, aware the trip had earmarks of a long day.

Stepping next to Scott's vehicle, Clint said, "I hope you don't mind but I'm going to follow you to Tyrone. I have other things to do later today and would like the liberty of my own truck. You okay with that?"

"That's up to you. It's your gas you'll be burning," joked Scott, thinking his quip funny. "I wouldn't drive separately, but I've always been the adult in the room between the two of us."

The bare tree branches of Hoosier National Forest distinctly took shape as the vehicles progressed over U.S. 150, motoring southeast to the Ohio River, destination Tyrone, Kentucky, seventy-six miles from Salzburg, Indiana, an easy two-hour drive with traffic factored in. The countryside, frosty and clean smelling, shown like stained glass in the morning sun. Vibrant and vivid shades of winter spread out over the land.

Dressed for the occasion, they traveled beneath the wide sweep of a chilly dawn, mentally preparing themselves for a long, brutally cold day outdoors walking the desolate terrain of uneven ground and quiet reserve as they searched for the impossible.

Crossing to the Kentucky side of the bridge, Clint followed Scott, making a quick stop at a gas station for wrapped sandwiches to have in reserve, plus a restroom break before proceeding southeast to Tyrone, where Young's High Bridge was located. The drive had taken longer than expected due to an accident just north of the bridge, slowing rush hour traffic to a frustrating crawl.

At last, the squad car turned into an empty parking lot, after reading a road sign stating the ghost town, previously named New Tyrone, and the abandoned Young's High Bridge, was a mile and a half from the start of a trailhead northeast of the parking lot on their right. Getting out and walking toward Clint's truck, Scott asked, "You ready? Appears to be a way back there."

"I am," Clint decisively answered, convinced his efforts had cumulated to be at this very spot at this exact moment. "He's somewhere out in these woods, I'm positive. Our job is to find him. Near the bridge where Thaddeus and Axel hung out in their youth is where we should start our search. But I'm relying on your professional insight to guide us. You'd have a better feel for this sort of thing than I would."

"Not really, Clint," stated Scott, speaking his truth in the matter. "You give me too much credit. It's true, I have a policeman's sense for things not quite right, but something of this caliber, we'll have to follow our instincts. It's all we can do."

Walking cautiously up the wet trail scattered with leaves, fallen branches, undergrowth, and remains of snowfall, twenty minutes in they stopped, unsure how much longer the hike was going to take before they reached their destination. Other than assaulted, exposed facial skin, both stayed warm under layers of clothing.

Moving onward, Scott took the lead, followed by Clint who kept a reasonable distance behind. The sound of footfalls on the hard, packed ground was invigorating, and seducing. Birds chirped noisily in trees that rustled in the breeze producing an eerie, beguiling tone of tranquility, as they pushed deeper into the darkness of unfamiliar territory.

The hour appeared late, even though they knew the time fell well short of noon. December, in this region of the country, always carried a look of twilight no matter the time of day, shadowed by overcast skies, especially in a place like the one they were crossing.

Scott kept his hand close to his .45 pistol ready for anything unplanned. Until, at last, the enormously high, decaying, broken bridge appeared from the behind the trees to take center stage. Both men stood stationary, shocked at what they had found. A cantilever bridge, steel beams anchored into the ground, was clearly abandoned decades earlier, from its rusted and aged appearance. Towering over the Kentucky River, Clint thought about the dimensions K.C. had provided.

"The length of this bridge is 1,659 feet, of which the main span is 551 feet," declared Clint as they stood observing one of the oldest truss bridges in the United States, constructed in 1889, considered an engineering marvel in its day.

"Sounds like someone has done his homework," teased Scott, surprised Clint cited the information so readily.

"The bridge cost two hundred thousand to build, named after William Bennett Henderson Young, the president of Louisville Southern Railroad. Used for passenger excursions, until the automobile appeared on the scene, eventually halting passenger travel. That was in 1937." Clint turned to Scott, "If you want to know more, you'll have to look it up."

"No thank you. That will do." Scott laughed feeling like he was in a history class.

"This is our starting point," announced Clint, certain of his convictions. "Axel and Thaddeus used to come to his location, like I said. I believe this where we will find Thaddeus's body. Do you want to split up?"

"No, absolutely not," replied Scott without hesitation. "We can venture apart a short distance but that's it."

"Alright, let's get to it." Clint looked at his watch. "It's 10:17."

Looking northbound, Scott asked, "What do you think that run down building is?"

"Dorian Andersen said there is a distillery around here. My guess is that's it."

"Okay, I suggest we head that direction, but we need to mark our progress as we go. U.S. Route 62, or Tyrone Pike passes over, continuing east and west of here. My compass will keep us on track." Scott swung around to face Clint. "Do you realize Lexington is due east of here, twenty plus miles? Fifty-four back to Louisville? This is a very remote location."

"Yeah, we need to keep watch on our time. It could slip by quicker than we think if we don't stay mindful," noted Clint realizing lost hours could present a tricky problem.

The two friends aimed for the distillery but soon came upon corroded railroad tracks not noticed from their earlier vantage point. Covered by overgrown foliage, a lengthy line of deserted railroad cars fell in succession, colorful graffiti drawn over each one. As far as the eye could see, train cars chained to one another were rusting away. Neglected passenger cars lettered with L&S spoke of a different time when train travel was in demand.

"Good grief, Scott, can you believe this? I've never seen this many train cars in one place before, ever. It's like they were brought here to hide the ugliness of erosion."

"An ideal place to hide a body, wouldn't you agree?" Scott replied, raising his brows, indicating this was where they should start searching for the body they had come to find. "There is not enough time in the day to go through all of these. I can't imagine how many train cars are out here. Andersen's body could be anywhere, taking us days, if not months to find it, if we ever do," he calculated, his voice discouraged, even overwhelmed with the task of searching this extensively.

"I have to agree," concurred Clint, also feeling disheartened with such a massive job ahead. It was like the adage, *looking for a needle in a haystack*. He sat down on a stone the color of melted caramel. Hands interlocked on top of his head, he asked, "Still want to do this?"

Scott chortled with surprise. "Are you kidding, of course I do. I want to find this man's body almost as badly as you do. Especially since Axel thinks he found a place devoid of repercussions. We will prove him wrong and bring him to justice. That pocket watch you have is going to be his Achilles' heel. Mark my words."

"I sure hope so," declared Clint, knowing he had used it as a pawn in the game he and Axel were engaged in. Come Monday at 2 p.m. he'd know if his plan worked.

With anxious eyes, Clint confessed, "Dunn loaned me the watch, wishing us success. It's reassuring to know you'll be there Monday as back-up. Drako is a calloused maniac with a dark soul. Lacks any kind of conscience. I owe Cookie Crenna everything. If it weren't for her, we wouldn't be here on this trail. She pointed me to Axel."

"I'm truly sorry, Clint," responded Scott with genuine sorrow. "She, along with the other people who have died at his hand are why we continue to search for concrete evidence."

With conviction, the two friends began combing the terrain, train tracks and cars, one by one. They searched for anything out of place. Anything that might indicate Axel had been here.

Scott, trained at observing anomalies, tirelessly moved down the chain, checking car after car. Although failing in his efforts to find the smallest of clue, he did not give up.

Clint, even with his improved investigative skills, also fell short. Climbing over and under seats, checking around rocks, looking for disturbed ground, hoping to find any sign of Axel's presence yielded nothing. Discouraged but pushing onward, a sinking feeling passed through Clint, but he refused to admit defeat. Hours passed with not the slightest bit of encouragement or clue to set them in the right direction. Finally, to Clint's chagrin, Scott said the words he hoped not to hear.

"Clint, we've got to leave," Scott said. "Do you realize the time?"

"It's 2:32, I know," Clint replied, disappointedly. "Friday, plus rush hour traffic back over the bridge will be a nightmare. I get it. I agree with you, but hate to leave so soon."

"We'll come back," Scott assured Clint. I'll check my schedule and plan a return trip. For now, let's concentrate on Monday and Axel Drako. First things first. Putting him behind bars should be our priority. You understand the importance of crossing every T and dotting every I with that situation, I hope. No slip-ups, my friend."

"Yeah, I do," remarked Clint feeling discouraged not to have found the slightest disturbance or clue in respect to Thaddeus Andersen's remains. Walking away, after such high expectations felt like failure.

They adhered closely to Scott's compass, retracing their steps until the parking lot came into view. They conversed the whole while on how they would change directions on the return trip and search elsewhere. When they reached their vehicles, both prepared to leave. Clint held back as Scott drove away, texting him to say he was going to contact Jules and didn't want to text and drive.

With an immediate response back from Scott, Clint stepped out of his truck to stand alone in the parking lot. Letting his emotions settle before driving home, the last thing he planned to do was call Jules, especially in the downtrodden mood he was in.

Aware Axel Drako had more than likely been in this exact parking lot, carrying or hauling his cousin's lifeless body somewhere out there in the woods, Clint bellowed at the top of his lungs, full of anger. No one would hear in a place where no one journeyed in the dead of winter.

Except... something did hear... and move.

Chapter 55
Mysterious Insight

A measured distance from the truck, a large, stealthy animal stood in the woods peering out. Observing from snow damp ground, the animal slipped through the undergrowth, materializing from the opposite direction of where Scott and Clint had been searching. Differing from the deserted, unused passenger train cars, and long forgotten tracks where the two well-intentioned men had been, this animal guarded the southern section of the forest.

With a shiny coat, black as night, and a gait so eloquently quiet and stealthy, Clint easily identified the cat's approach. Affectionately named Picasso–the feline was embedded in his childhood memory– and now here he was awaiting Clint at the edge of the woods.

Clint studied the incredibly beautiful cat whose focus was locked on him, his brilliant green eyes messaging, *I'm waiting.*

In his younger days, Clint had thought the cat both terrifying and captivating. For a little boy of five, the feline seemed larger than life, the object of comic books. He'd fall asleep to tonal sounds imbued in the night, conjuring adventures he and the puma shared in dreamland, devoted allies on a mission. Back then, he embraced the howls Picasso made, thinking he was being summoned by the animal to come out and play.

No longer did Clint understand this elusive creature as he once had. As a child the cat's appearance was simple and direct, but Picasso had evolved since then. Shuddering at the realization he was about to trail a feral animal who had died over fifty years earlier into the forest without regard to consequences, was the indisputable definition of insanity but he would do it anyway.

A few steps in, staying several feet behind the puma, Clint reconsidered his purpose in trailing the cat.

What am I doing? I need to get back. Hightail it out of here, he advised his logical side. *While I still have some sense and daylight. I'll come back with Scott later. As he suggested.*

Clint desperately wanted to find Thaddeus's body, thinking it'd give him additional ammunition, leaving no doubt as to Axel's guilt. Certainly, it would bring more to the table to pressure Axel with than a mere pocket watch.

Aware if Axel was arrested for Dorian Andersen's stolen goods, it would only detain him in jail for a short while, probably until bail was set which was better than nothing. In the meanwhile, Scott and he could continue to search for Thaddeus's remains.

Clint's misguided steps had caused him to use poor judgment. It was dangerous to be out here alone without a partner. His intuitive side insisted he go back to his truck and leave the forest. Come back another day.

Ironically, with birds chirping, warbling late afternoon tweets and trills, indicating evening was closing in. Clint had calmed down and no longer did he doubt his decision to move forward to wherever it was Picasso was taking him. He heard animals moving in the forest. A deer and her fawn, stationary behind a band of pines made note of him and stopped their progress.

The puma had turned southbound while Clint deliberated. The cat had set out for an area Clint would not have found in a thousand lifetimes.

Not certain what he was going to do, keep walking or turn back, the decision was made for him. Shuddering from the guttural growl that reverberated from deep within the woods, Clint recognized the signature screech pumas were well-known for. The second timbre intensified up an octave, causing the hairs on the back of Clint's neck to stand on end. A blood-curling noise, likened to a woman's scream, created a terrifying, ungodly cry, heard in all directions.

As fast as his legs would allow, Clint sprinted to the parking lot. He hastened to his truck and dialed Scott. "Hey, man, can you turn around, come back," pleaded Clint knowing his request would not be received well. "It's vitally important. I understand the traffic conditions, and all that, but something has come up. You need to be here."

"What's wrong? Can't you just tell me over the phone?" Scott asked testily, thinking Clint must be overreacting to something he'd seen or heard.

"No, I can't." Going out on a limb, Clint made an unsubstantiated claim he hoped he didn't have to grapple with later. "I know where his body is located."

"What? How could you know that?" Scott questioned feeling confused with the information Clint claimed.

Hearing reservation in Scott's voice, Clint declared, "I will do this alone if I must. I already told Jules I was in Kentucky and would be a bit later than usual this evening. She's working late anyhow," Clint lied but would soon rectify his statement. "It's not that late. Plenty of daylight remains. I guarantee this will be worth the trip back here."

"Awe Clint," Scott complained, "come on. I'm a good six miles away from there. Are you one hundred percent certain about this?"

"Well, no! I'm not, but no one is one hundred percent certain of anything. Are they?"

Heaviness hung between them like a weighted blanket, neither speaking. Finally, Scott put out a warning. "You'd better know what you're talking about. Not take me on a wild-goose chase!"

"I do know, and I won't," countered Clint with confidence, thinking no way would Picasso have appeared or make himself heard if it wasn't a sure sign.

"I propose we stay here in Tyrone until after Louisville's rush-hour traffic clears. We leave around five, and still get home by seven or a bit after. We'll have two hours of daylight to our favor. What'da you say," queried Clint, his eager voice revealing a hint of betrayal that his outlandish claim had no legs to it but was a hunch.

Before Scott could reply, Clint brazenly injected one last comment. "Just trust me. Won't you? I wouldn't have called if I wasn't certain I knew what I was talking about."

"I wish you would just tell me what has you so wound up. That way I could judge for myself."

Answering Scott without hesitation, Clint replied, "You are going to have to take my word on this because I cannot explain it over the phone."

"For the love of God, Clint. Alright, I'm turning around. Should be there no later than 3:20. We leave... on the dot, no matter what, at 5:30. Got that? I'll call Wende to let her know I'll be late."

"I'll be here by the truck waiting," replied Clint, relieved Scott had changed his mind. "Thanks, Scott, for putting your faith in me. I don't give my word lightly. You know that."

"I do and that's why I'm coming back. See you in a few minutes." The phone disconnected leaving Clint on the other end wondering if he would have to eat crow before the night was through.

Before Clint's next breath was taken, the cat reappeared, moving toward his truck. In the dim late afternoon light, the cat approached silently on the pads of his paws. The solidness of his body almost appeared touchable.

Watching each graceful step, Clint felt compelled to reach out to pet him but of course, did not. When Picasso strolled back to the place he'd come, turning only once to make eye contact, it was as though he'd delivered a message–*Follow*.

Turning toward the truck, Clint withdrew a shovel, leaning it against the back panel, in anticipation of what was to develop. He then climbed inside to wait on his friend's arrival. Dropping temperatures had caused his hands to grow stiff, and warming them before going back out into the woods made sense.

Before turning the engine over, to warm the cabin, he noticed a weird vibration. He was alarmed at first until he realized where the strange tremor was generated. The glove compartment where Rod's crystal had been placed.

He reached inside, removing the quartz crystal he usually kept in his office. Immediately he realized the stone's color was not the same as when it sat on his desk. The color had turned a dark amber shade. He slipped it inside his coat pocket and within seconds the vibration quieted. He glanced at it and was surprised to see it was now a soft golden shade, its typical appearance.

Clint scribbled on his note pad, organizing his thoughts and suspicions while he waited on Scott. It had given him a few minutes to contemplate, reflect, and ponder what was yet to come along with other elements of the case. He considered the many unexpected developments that had emerged since Farley first told him about his transplant and the anomalies his new heart presented.

Around the bend Scott's squad car came into view, pulling into the parking lot beside the F-100. Looking over, Scott wore a suspicious expression as he stepped out of the car. Not saying a word, he strolled over to Clint who was now outside his own vehicle, leaning against the door, his hands in his trouser pockets.

Although it had never been expressed in words, including to his friend, Clint, or any co-workers, Scott had an uncanny knack of seeing the perspective of the prey. This latest victim he and Clint searched for in Tyrone, Kentucky, in the vicinity of Young's High Bridge was no different. Brought up to speed on each incident file that involved Axel Drako, prior to hooking up with Clint, Scott had extensively delved into all five executions he had committed, starting with Thaddeus, but not ending there. God only knew how many people Drako had killed in his short existence. All of them, malicious acts of evil.

Scott appraised Clint as he neared, seeing a determination in his eyes not there when he drove away earlier. His deep blue intelligent eyes did not reveal the stern severity of his mind. It had all but vanished when he said, "Alright, let's start searching."

Behind a wall of trees and into the shadowy vegetation, canopied by tall oaks, pines, sycamore, walnuts, ash, red maple, and hickory, Clint lead Scott Edwards, Salzburg's Captain, into a different and deeper part of the woods than they had been in previously.

Moving down the path he had seen Picasso disappear into, the cat's impressive stride had advanced through the forest. This southern part of the woods would cause anyone to hesitate. But with a policeman trailing his footsteps, Clint forged on into a place he'd dare not venture alone at this hour.

"Is there a specific reason you are taking me this way," Scott asked, not sure why Clint brought them this direction verses the area to the north.

"Yeah, but you won't like my answer if I tell you."

"Okay, I don't even like that answer." Laughed Scott from behind Clint. "I do need to know. You're not going to get out of this."

Just as Clint was ready to give an abbreviated version of the truth, warm sunlight beamed lazily through the trees, illuminating the area they were walking and giving it features that appeared enchanted. A ravine was off to the right, steep and full of sound as the trees rustled in the breeze.

"What a place. Can you believe how serene and perfect this is? Looks like something you'd see in a nature magazine," observed Clint, admiring the view. "Widens into a substantial gorge further up. See?" He stepped to the side for Scott to see.

But a magnificent gorge is not what Scott saw. His trained eye had picked up on graffiti poking through the distant trees. He found the colors in direct contrast to the forest's serene beauty.

Conversely, Clint saw a pair of emerald, green eyes about fifty feet ahead on the left, peering through the weeds, and undergrowth, crouched, waiting, and watching for these two men to arrive. The eyes that seemed to be staring into oblivion as Picasso stretched to full size and made one long stride, making certain he was seen by Scott and Clint.

Scott gulped.

"Yeah, that's the answer to your question. Picasso. He's the reason I came this way." Clint turned to Scott, expressing admiration when he glanced over his shoulder where the puma had been. Picasso had moved back into the shadows, though his brilliant green eyes were impossible to veil by undergrowth or the wildness of forest foliage.

"Now do you believe me?" asked Clint with a proud expression when the beauty of this animal came to mind. "I've told you about him before, back when we were exploring answers to the Reno Brother's lost treasure, my father's and Rod Radcliff, Sr.'s deaths, but now you've seen him for yourself. With your own two eyes, and I must admit I'm relieved, for whatever reason he chose to materialize to you too. For that I'm grateful."

Dumbstruck, stunned, astonished, dazed, and any other word that might describe his intense disbelief, Scott knew the reality of what he had seen, therefore believed what Clint had claimed. His eyes grew wide when he asked, "So, that animal over there was your dad's feral cat? The one he fed when you were a kid?"

"Yes," replied Clint feeling as awe inspired as his friend. "It would appear Picasso is still hanging about," he dryly joked understanding what a shock this must be to Scott.

Scott didn't speak, only stared at the place he knew the cat was crouched, hidden in the lush dense folds straight ahead of them.

"I saw the puma before I called you. Knew if Picasso was here, it was a sign to keep searching. Not to give up. We've been looking in the wrong place, Scott," exclaimed Clint. "The last time the cat appeared it was a big deal too. I don't want to go into that right now."

"Yeah, I remember you telling me how a black puma led you to the shack the night you hosted the treasure hunt for your grandchildren. The cat, and Radcliff, were involved that night in you finding the entrance to Goss Cave."

Clint's face showed that was not what he meant. He saw the shock in Scott's eyes when he replied, "No, my friend, I'm not talking about back then. I'm speaking of this year, in November."

"This year? I don't understand. You never said anything about it," stated Scott, expressing his concern.

"I know," replied Clint, turning from a disturbance he'd heard, and then seeing Picasso stand to full height, gracefully moving away from them. He twisted around toward Scott. "All I can say, is when I heard Picasso's wail, I knew it was him. The cry came from out here, in the general area of where we're standing. I figured a solid mile from the parking lot."

Recalling his childhood once again, lying in bed as a small boy waiting to hear Picasso's unique sound, resonating from the forest before drifting off in slumber, Clint's face brightened, and his heart warmed. He said, "I haven't heard that sound since I was a kid. It's something a boy never forgets. Ever."

Chapter 56
A Call from Beyond

Searching one another's faces for acknowledgement they were indeed ready to step even deeper into unknown territory, Scott indicated he was moving further up the trail. With Clint, close on his heels, they searched in all directions for anything out of the ordinary, notching trees to mark their progress.

Disregarding how late the hour had turned, Scott called over his shoulder, "Man, it's a lot darker back here." He watched his step not to trip over dead branches and declared with certainty. "In a million years, I'd probably not come this way." Then, with a hint of trepidation to his voice, Scott followed up his remark with a joke, "Glad I'm not scared of the dark."

Glancing over at the ravine and hearing a sound that reminded him of a tuning fork, Scott questioned, "Do you hear that?"

"I do," answered Clint, surprised at how the lighting had changed. His vision sensed a deep blue, purplish radiance coming into focus at the same time the quartz crystal activated, vibrating softly in his top pocket.

Breathing in a scent unknown to his sense of smell, Clint speculated, "I suppose the trees could cause that rustling drone," he said, addressing Scott's question. "The air has a scent like the ocean."

Drawn to the sound, they trekked further south toward an opening that echoed like rippling water. Moving toward the disturbance, they became distracted with their surroundings, with Scott pointing out, "The trees don't have enough leaves to make *that* sort of sound."

The forest wasn't nearly as dense as in summer months, other than the trees that naturally kept their leaves and needles throughout the winter, which did not explain the unusual area they had entered. This section had an extraordinary number of Weymouth pines, standing easily one hundred fifty feet tall along with smaller pitch pines, jerseys, and an extraordinary number of junipers, hemlocks, and northern white cedars, but most surprisingly, several Leyland cypresses.

Likeminded, Clint stated an observation he, too, had made. "I was wondering if you'd noticed how many sassafras trees there are, seems strange for this far into the forest. Wouldn't you say?"

"I have no idea. Never cared much for forestry," Scott replied honestly.

A few steps up the path they happened into a section of split railroad ties and tracks that had separated from their original configuration. Those led to a train's engine, rusting in every conceivable corner, but no graffiti. They saw a line of abandoned rail cars twenty feet ahead.

Out in the woods, Clint spotted Picasso's remarkable eyes staring out through the undergrowth, a stone's throw away, guarding an area that held unique features. Circling around to Scott, Clint suspected the direction to take and whispered, "Hey, follow me."

Disturbed ground of an unmarked grave was evident. The dirt appeared tampered with, different from elsewhere. A gravelly surface revealed spots darker than the rest of the area, barely visible, but clear enough to identify old blood. A decorative pile of stones, and other manmade items, were arranged in a chain, creating an imperfect circle. Of all the items lying atop this precise section of rails, the key fob poking out from beneath the wet soil drew Clint's interest.

Evidence of a violent death, a cadaverously thin victim awaited discovery. Under ordinary conditions Clint would have felt elated to have uncovered what they were out searching for, but not in this circumstance. Replacing jubilation, nausea extinguished any pride in their find.

In anticipation of what they would soon dig up under the rails, so ritually disguised, doubt nagged at Clint. Was he up to the job of seeing Thaddeus Andersen arranged with his arms flung out, hastily buried to get his body out of sight as quickly as humanly possible? He was not.

Shoots of tree roots ran up and below the damaged rails, literally pulling them asunder. In the dim light of a late afternoon, a flicker of light shown through the branches, underscoring that on the outskirts of civilization, a good man had been tossed aside like a piece of rubbish. Other than what few things were scattered as a final farewell from the man who had dropped him into a makeshift grave.

Kneeling in reverence, startled by the sight before them, Clint lowered his head, saying a prayer he had formulated, should the situation arise.

Scott followed suit, except, while his friend said a simple prayer in lieu of painstakingly unearthing the body, Scott attempted to tap into the mind of the person who lay beneath the cold, hard clay of winter, isolating why in cold blood this man had to die. He envisioned random glass fragments, although he could not confirm his insight in that moment, he soon would.

Scott's voice cracked, making a solemn promise. "If it's the last thing I do, I will avenge Thaddeus Andersen for this appalling act."

The effort of excavating dirt, parallel steel rails, ballast gravel, pebbles, and slag, from under the railway ties, along with all the braces and fasteners needed to hold the rails together, was a drudgery that had already been performed by the person who came before them.

Clint lifted his eyes, signifying, "I'm ready if you are."

"I am. Let's bring the man up," Scott replied, his eyes damp with emotion.

Clint pushed the shovel in the ground, removing soil and tossing it aside. "I'm glad I had the presence of mind to bring the spade," he said, pleased with the forethought he drew on at the start of the mission.

The two men placed tactical and military grade, super-bright flashlights against the trees behind them and began the chore of removing dirt that wasn't as compressed as should be. Still loose from earlier removal, the job of extracting soil went faster than either one anticipated.

With the top layer gone and the remains of a human figure near, Clint became uncertain on how protocol should be handled. He had confidence, though, that Scott would take charge since he was experienced in such matters. Clint relaxed as best he could. He'd never seen a corpse, or a grave, like this one.

Without flashlights, it would have been hard to see their hands in front of their faces. Both men had lost any concept of time. They were too engaged in uncovering Anderson's body to be concerned with the late hour.

For the second time in less than fifteen minutes, Clint stopped clearing dirt long enough to scan the immediate area, thinking Picasso could still be near. But he wasn't– Clint's instincts imparted the cat had gone. His beloved animal had removed himself from the scene. Having shown them where to look, his job was finished. Picasso had returned to wherever it was he had traveled from.

A melancholy sadness rushed over Clint. I wonder if I'll ever see him again. My black, majestic, wandering, troubadour of yesteryear. My childhood talisman, he thought lovingly of Picasso. Clint noticed Rod's crystal had gone dormant as well, weighted in his pocket but otherwise a mere stone.

Scott glanced over at him, peering into Clint's wistful moment. His friend's startled expression caused Clint to wince. "What?" he asked, afraid of the answer.

A look that could only be described as pure terror, flushed scarlet on Scott's face, exhibiting abhorrence. Scott used the back of his palms to wipe tears away that were rolling down his cheeks. Thaddeus's burial site was a shared pit.

The corners of the dog's mouth were twisted and burned. The German shepherd appeared to have been poisoned. Beautifully marked, this animal resembled Scott's dog, easily passing as her twin. Fighting the urge to retch, Scott pulled his head away fiercely, sparing himself the embarrassment of seeming less manly.

"I need to phone this in," he stiffly stated, wrestling with the physical reaction evoked by the decaying dog and person. "The body has identification on it, plus something else you'll be glad to see."

Kneeling at the split rails, alongside Scott, what Clint saw shook him to the core. The German Shepherd, by all indications, had been poisoned. Although he was ecstatic at what lay at his fingertips– wedged into the pit's soil at Thaddeus's side, was a switchblade knife, dried blood on the handle and blade. A handgun had been flung on Thaddeus's chest, dusted prints waiting to be disclosed.

More than either man could have ever anticipated, or hoped for, they now had enough evidence to connect, and presumably convict Axel Drako for his cousin's death, both Charlie and Ann Hill's murders, plus the off-duty policeman's death who had chased Axel from Beans-a-Brewin the night he shot the couple. Proof Clint's reasoning had been on target. Charlie Hill had been vindicated.

"Give me a minute," Scott said, his hands trembling, resting on the knees as he contemplated how he was going to explain why he was here, at this hour, at this exact location on a Friday night. He wasn't about to reveal a phantom puma was responsible for the discovery, and not him.

Shards of glass from a smashed picture frame, shattered to smithereens over Thaddeus's body, lay everywhere. Scott felt certain this was the broken glass he had perceived as a premonition prior to finding the man's grave. In his entire life he had never experienced anything of this scale. Being in Clint's presence had influenced his ability to see things outside his normal scope of perception.

On the verge of suggesting Clint wait in his truck or go home until a reasonable story could be constructed, Scott stated, "I need to call Drex Mason. We're in Kentucky, not Indiana. He'll be the one to notify forensics and the coroner. We've trampled the ground more than we should have." His voice well-modulated, Scott reminded Clint, "You've never been involved in a serious murder case. Please understand this is an extremely complicated case with many facets that must be addressed through proper channels."

"I expected as much," Clint replied fully comprehending the spot Scott was in.

A warning tone cautioned, "Do not allude to any of your experiences. They would not be well-received or be believed by Drex Mason, or the police force in general. On occasion I've known an associate or two who commissioned a psychic, on especially hard-to-crack cases, but this goes way beyond any I am aware of." He splayed his fingers. "Truthfully, I have no idea what I'm going to say to explain how we found Thaddeus Andersen." A slight sign of humor crossed his face but faded in a flash.

"Believe me, I understand," concurred Clint. "Don't you recall when I told you and David Andrews how I found the Reno Gang treasure in Goss Cave? David was put off, ridiculing even, when I tried to speak the truth. You were confounded with my confession, not sure how to relate to me at the time."

"I do remember. Seems like a million years ago." Scott's eyes showed he had walked back in time to Clint's kitchen table and the day Clint reported a body had been found in Goss Cave. Clint believed it to be his father's, Eli Reeves, remains. Scott was all business.

Clint returned the smile he saw on Scott's face. "We've come a long way, you and me, since then. We're up to our eyeballs in things that can't be explained, like it or not."

"A fact," Scott laughed, "It's like diverting landmines, carefully–very carefully. My report will be heavily massaged," Scott admitted, ready to ask what he had avoided earlier. "Before Drex gets here, I'd like you to be gone. I have enough on my plate without explaining your presence at the scene."

Surprised at the directive he'd been given, Clint viewed the crumpled body in the crude grave beside them, and with remorse for the poor soul who lay there, answered, "No problem. I think that's best."

Clint waited at Scott's side while he phoned in the incident, reporting to the Louisville Police Station a body had been discovered in Tyrone, Kentucky, south of Young's High Bridge. At 6:07 p.m. the call was put through. Drex phoned Scott's private line a few minutes later. The two colleagues would soon meet in the parking lot in Tyrone.

Scott walked Clint back to the parking lot, both wearing grim faces. When Clint left, glancing in his rearview mirror, he saw Scott sitting in his patrol car with his head against the stirring wheel.

While Clint was negotiating Louisville traffic, crossing the bridge for home, Drex Mason was examining the body, removing both weapons, and tagging them as evidence. He bagged anything found around or near the body. Locating a wallet in the back left pocket of the dead man's jeans made Mason's job of identifying the victim less complicated.

Since Scott had no jurisdiction this side of the Indiana-Kentucky border, Detective Drex Mason was now in charge. Made aware of the connection between the body and the stakeout on Monday, Drex grew suspicious that an anonymous caller was behind directing Scott to Kentucky and Young's High Bridge as Scott had indicated. Although he questioned the relationship of the cases Scott described, he elected not to press the issue.

By the time Scott left Tyrone, he'd developed a thunderous headache. The crowded parking lot was full of police vehicles and medical personnel, including a transport van for the body. Soon it would be taken to the county coroner's office where later an autopsy could be performed.

The rumble of Scott's 4.6L V8 engine was powerful. As he concentrated on the sound, he contemplated his deception. Although, by the time he drove to the Indiana side of the Sherman Minton Bridge, he'd made peace with his decision to tell an altered version of the truth. With weapons to fill in the blanks of the investigation, the two police officers' jobs had gotten a whole lot easier.

Before arriving in Salzburg, Scott dialed Clint to fill him in on Drex and his conversation. When asked how he explained his presence at the scene, Scott replied, "I used the same lie you used on me." Scott chuckled, "I told him an anonymous lead is what had prompted me to drive there. I happened on the disturbed ground and body during an exhaustive search of the area."

"And he bought that?" Clint was surprised Mason had accepted Scott's excuse for getting involved with an anonymous lead that took him out of state to Young's High Bridge in Kentucky.

"Appeared so. I told him a sealed envelope was on my desk when I was leaving for lunch, not thinking there was much to it. I left the station early to check it out. Said I would have called him but didn't want to waste his time on some wild goose chase, especially on a Friday afternoon. People can get pretty elaborate with some of their leads and tips."

Scott took a moment. "Drex knows me well, Clint, and probably figured I wasn't giving him an accurate account. It's the same way I feel about you. I apologized and said I showed poor judgment by not giving him a heads up."

Scott hesitated briefly, and then added, "In my mind before he got there, I ran a scenario that I thought was plausible. If Cookie

Crenna were still alive and had vital information, she might have done such a thing, since she was close to both men, Thaddeus, and Axel, and had an axe to grind. Could have given you that kind of information and you might have dropped it on my desk."

Clint heard Scott sigh, and asked, "Are you, okay?"

"Not really. I can't get that dog out of my mind. The poor thing. It probably suffered." Taking an extra minute, Scott changed the subject. "I hope you don't mind me using that analogy about Cookie. It was all I could come up with on short notice. I saw in my mind's eye Axel slipping up, arrogantly alluding to what he'd done. To be honest I'm not completely certain Drex bought my story hook, line, and sinker, but he's a good enough friend to take me at my word." Not as worried as he had been an hour ago, Scott admitted, "He didn't seem too concerned with how I acquired the information."

Clint felt sickened by what they had discovered and the condition of the remains. "Who kills a dog and puts it on their victim? Axel's deranged, I tell you!"

"I have no idea, but I *will* nail his ass to the wall. That dog is a spitting image of my Amy. My heart is broken on so many levels. Thaddeus, and that poor animal, didn't deserve what happened to them. He's pure evil."

"Well, the good news," noted Clint, in better spirits now that Scott dodged a sticky situation, "is Mason has the switchblade and 9mm to put him on the right track, and you and I know where they will lead. Tying Axel Drako to his multiple crimes. And, to answer your question, no, I don't mind. Cookie wouldn't either, Scott. She would have been happy, like us, that the grave was discovered."

"Thanks. I figured the *anonymous* lie worked for you." He chuckled. "Thought I'd give it a whirl. Thinking about Monday, with concrete evidence of murder, in addition to theft of his uncle's property, we should have Axel right where we want him. Drex says he'll phone tomorrow with an update. I'll let you know, what I know, when I know it."

"Hey, thanks," Clint said in genuine appreciation of Scott's support and trust. "We've been able to accomplish quite a bit in a short amount of time. Today put us closer to the finish line. We make a pretty good team, you and me," he teased.

"We do," countered Scott, putting a thought out there that was worthy to be noted. "Remember that in the future. Won't you? This might not be our last rodeo." A moment slid by. "I'm not sure I'll ever fully comprehend what happened out there," he said, thinking about Picasso. "Seeing your puma with my own two eyes is hard to put into context. What a gorgeous creature, he was." Scott grinned. "That's all I'll say about that... other than I'll never doubt another word you say." He chortled. "Though I don't think anything will ever top that one."

With Scott's last comment, they made a promise to join forces on Monday at noon. At Aces & Eights, they'd map out their strategy.

Chapter 57
Breaking Point

During a late dinner in Paoli at Jules's favorite BBQ joint, Clint went over every minuscule detail surrounding Young's High Bridge and the adventures near Tyrone, Kentucky, where he, and Scott, spent the better part of their day.

To make it sound more glamourous than it was, he explained the bridge's type of construction, and its original purpose in 1889. The first cantilever bridge built in America the three-span continuous under-deck truss was utilized by Louisville & Southern Railway Lexington to Lawrenceburg Division. The first train crossed over the gorge on August 21. Most notably, the bridge had never been reinforced, improved on, or ever restored to strengthen it.

With wide eyes, Jules listened as Clint described Scott's approach to apprehending Drako on Monday afternoon–with Clint's assistance, of course as well as David Andrews, and a detective on the Kentucky police force, in collaboration. He divulged Scott's operation of pinning four murders on Axel Drako, using the evidence they had unearthed in Tyrone, to arrest him at his residence. What Clint omitted was the real instigator in this endeavor, and ringleader in the pursuit, was him.

He didn't mention the dog they had disentombed for fear of making Jules more uncomfortable than she already appeared. Clint noticed a flare of edginess on her pretty face with each word of his recap and thought better of bringing the slain dog into it.

Clear skies, and no precipitation other than the promise of a light dusting by daybreak which was predicted to melt by mid-morning. For that, they were relieved.

When they arrived at home, they sipped a cup of hot cocoa as dessert at the kitchen table while they relaxed. Sipping the savory drink, covered with floating marshmallows and a sprinkle of cinnamon sugar, Jules filled in what had transpired during her day at the diner. The flurry of hubbub at Josie's Diner and around town all circled around Christmas activities. It had been a pleasurable day on Jules's end, when compared to Clint's.

The schedule for the weekend just included basic household activities. The couple decided to remain at home both Saturday and Sunday to finish wrapping what few presents remained in the closets, plus starting confectionaries to tote along to Beech Grove. They also planned to catch up on laundry and start packing for following weekend.

Clint broke the lovely harmony that had settled between them when he said, "David Dunn has set a date to finalize Charlie and Ann Hill's estate. It's on December 22. He'll disperse the last of their possessions, leaving everything to Keelan Charles Hill." Clint grinned cheerfully. "Despite Mac Hill's derogatory opinion of the child."

"Oh good, it'll be nice to have that over with. K.C. should have everything that belonged to his parents. Its rightfully his by law," Jules replied, thinking how terrible Mac Hill had talked about his nephew, calling him an idiot and a worthless human being.

"Other than the three paintings and a few personal items originally earmarked for Charlie's half-brother, Mac, everything goes to K.C. I'm pleased to say Mac is sitting in jail awaiting sentencing on multiple felonies associated with his brother's artwork and finances."

"Does the list include what he pilfered from the lockbox?" asked Jules, irritated that this man had been so self-serving and spoken so cruelly of his family.

"A ring June Bennett had given to Ann, considered a sentimental piece," Clint mentioned, his forehead wrinkled, remembering what Dunn had told him. "And a London blue topaz ring, I believe, were among the items Mac had taken. Ann had the ring listed in her Will, to give back to June. Mac took it from the Hills' home and hid it in his safe at the warehouse, along with other pieces she had earmarked for her nieces, and June. They are all now on a list of stolen merchandise in the case against Mac Hill."

"Clint, how does anyone do something like this? It's as if the man doesn't have a pulse. He's so greedy."

"I know. It is hard to believe he could have been so calloused. Dunn said the ring matched a bracelet Ann had given to June. Inside the ring box they found a letter stating how much June's friendship had meant to Ann. Even though they weren't biological sisters, they were sisters in spirit. Of course, she had no idea the letter would be read by June so early in life."

Jules's face was cloaked in gloom, apparent she was being impacted by their conversation at dinner, and now felt worse because the Hill's deaths hit closer to home than she was willing to admit. It was tapping into Jules's worse nightmare of losing Clint.

"Hey," Clint said in an upbeat tone after noticing Jules's gloomy face, "let's look on the bright side." He reached for her hands, holding them tight. "June Bennett, and the nieces, will now get what they were meant to have. Keelan inherits his parent's estate and Mac Hill faces jail time. Embezzlement is a serious crime, Jules, twenty to thirty years." Clint leaned back in satisfaction, "The Hill's wishes will be honored. Their son will be provided for. I can't tell you how happy that makes me feel. It could have turned out quite differently."

With a hint of a smile, Jules said something that entertained Clint when he contemplated the boy's abilities, the child's stunning eyes, and his overall cuteness. "It's easy to see where K.C. gets his artistic talent," she noted, "not to mention that face of his is a dead ringer for Ann Hill."

As anticipated, they relished a weekend of quiet solitude, with Christmas carols played on the stereo, cookie baking, and wrapping presents for family and friends. On Sunday, Jules served a pot roast smothered in au jus, using the gravy on mashed potatoes, plus the fixings that accompany a good old fashion meal like Jules's mom used to make. The house smelled of Christmas cheer that lingered well into the night.

While sugarplums danced in his wife's head, Clint was restless, tossing and turning through the night.

Monday, December 19

When Monday rolled around, Jules had made plans to spend the bulk of her day at the orphanage. She had called ahead to ask the staff to purchase ingredients to prepare the kitchen for cookie making-and-baking. All the residents were invited to participate. The feedback she received was one of jubilation.

Everyone was elated, including Jules, except her reasons were different from theirs. She needed an absorbing distraction from worrying about her husband's goings-on in Louisville. At home she would have been a wreck, nervously piddling around the house while Clint and Scott confronted a man who she knew was capable of violence. In her heart-of-hearts, Jules felt Clint had fallen well short of revealing the entirety of his involvement in this matter. Although she understood him to be a complex man, Clint ignited worrisome emotions in her.

By the time she reached Radcliff's Children's Home, a calm had cascaded around her. Jules decided to trust Clint's intuitions. They had proven reliable in past affairs, and today would be no different.

At home was a different case. When the phone rang, Clint was ill-prepared for what he heard. He stood speechless by the sink, and his jaw dropped, looking out over the yard while painfully digesting the information.

"The German shepherd buried alongside Thaddeus," Scott stated, his voice edgy and tired, "it was Thaddeus's own dog."

The good feelings Clint had fostered over the weekend flew right out the window when Scott added, "The dog was poisoned approximately the same time as Thaddeus's demise. The report concluded both victims were most likely killed within hours of one another. The coroner faxed the report over this morning."

"I'm nauseated," grumbled Clint, expressing his honesty in the rawest of terms. "How could he? What purpose did it serve?"

"Who knows what goes on in the mind of psychopath," offered Scott, not having a logical explanation for a madman. "If I had to guess I'd say the dog was Axel's parting gift. Like an ornament. He gave him his own dog to be buried with." A low scoffing sound was evident when Scott said, "for eternity, that sort of thing. Like Thaddeus would feel better."

Scott abruptly cleared his throat. "Axel Drako must be apprehended today, Clint, before anyone else gets hurt, or killed. Enough people have died at this guy's hand, we don't want any more added to the list. I'll see you at noon, Aces and Eights. No beers, I'm afraid. We'll need all our faculties on high alert.

The suddenness of the conversation brought home the seriousness of their endeavor. The sound of silence seized his ability to think straight. The loathing he felt for the man he pursued had grown sharply, putting it at an all-time high.

Standing in a dark kitchen, peering out into a forest where dim light filtered through the evergreen trees and bare branches, softly accentuating early morning's arrival, Clint emotionally buckled, not believing himself competent to take down someone of this caliber. A man who had a taste for killing other human beings and pet dogs. Uncertain he had what it took, he muttered, "What am I thinking? Axel won't blink twice to shoot to kill. I will unquestionably hesitate."

He sat down at the table to steady his weak knees. At his breaking point, Clint assured himself, *Scott can handle this without me. The rest of those guys are trained police officers, I'll be the weak link.* He put his hands to his forehead and closed his eyes.

What if one of them get hurt because of me, or even shot, or worst yet, killed? How could I live with that? I can't take the chance. I'm a fool to think I can walk into this arena with them. They are in a different league than me. Clint buried his face afraid his inexperience would yield monstrous consequences. *Axel warned me...*

The deep rumble of conviction, from an unknown source–clear as a bell in his mind–spoke words he would not have thought himself capable of orating. "Keep doubt out of this," it said, "the winds of righteousness flow. Avenge those unable to do so. You're the only one who can."

With his eyes shielded, the color of contempt he saw was scarlet. This anger was not Clint's, nor was the voice that demanded that justice prevail. "Murderous acts cannot go unpunished," he had heard.

"Charlie?" he frantically called out in an empty room, convinced he was not alone... at the eleventh hour. A wordless exchange that lasted less than a flash of light, had left its mark on his resolve. The message, loud and clear, proved Clint wasn't going solo. Strength from a different source stood abreast with him in the battle he faced.

Clint walked outside for a breath of fresh air, badly needing to clear his muddled head of what had transpired. No longer was his and Axel's meeting a question of choice. This was about endurance and honoring a promise to Charles Lewellyn Hill, who had sought Clint's support to *right a wrong*.

Minutes slipped away so quickly Clint barely had time to catch his breath. He decided to drop in on Jules and the kids to see how they were progressing. To take in the sweet smells of Christmas in the children's home. The children who resided in his protected place were family, to he, Jules, and the staff who worked there. Their contribution to the less fortunate was the greatest gift of all.

Another reason he was going to visit was a yearning to reconnect. Never knowing how things might turn out, Clint ached to be with those he loved prior to tackling what promised to be a day of upheaval. He made his rounds, spreading what cheer he could muster.

A reserved look befell husband and wife. She, standing at the doorway to the kitchen on the far side of the room, a Christmas apron wrapped around her waist and flour on her hands, a smidgen on her cheek. Clint with his hand placed on the entrance door bar ready to leave.

Neither one spoke, nor moved. Hers was a penetrating stare. No question was asked or reply given to the unvoiced exchange of words that passed between them.

Chapter 58
Man Down

At Aces and Eight, the smell of fried foods, onions, and liquor saturated the air. Over strong coffee and toast, nothing more, Scott and Clint ended their discussion, ready to join forces with Sargent David Andrews, and then head to Louisville to assemble the rest of the team of Detective Drex Mason and a fellow officer, Theo Dickson.

When Clint exited the bar side door, behind Scott, his taut muscles forecasted the hour had arrived for them to move the operation forward. Clint was to play a major roll—sitting duck, a pawn. The power of emotion that whirled beneath the skin, ablaze with hypotheticals, pointed at a sting operation designed to trap Axel Drako into admitting one of his numerous crimes, subsequently leading to his arrest.

Fitted with a listening device, the rest of the crew would hear every word of Clint and Axel's conversation and would act instantly if required. Advised not to mention the initial bribe that had gotten him through the door in the first place, Clint was to stay calm, and under no circumstance, provoke Axel.

As he walked to the truck, Clint felt a confidence he'd never experienced, the incident in the kitchen had restored a belief in his ability to do the impossible. It stirred a cast-iron certainty to flow through his veins.

During their meeting, Scott and he had decided to drive to Louisville separately. Axel was familiar with Clint's truck and would spot the Ford the moment he arrived. The other unmarked police vehicles were to park on streets further away, so they were not detected.

The drone of the engine mirrored Clint's heightened anxiety. Restless but alert, he turned on a sixties station to settle his nerves. The diversion to suppress any wayward thoughts from entering his mind did nothing to bring his ragged breathing inline or erase the dubious expression that had settled into the tense contours of his face. Fighting for the upper hand over negative impulses that popped into his head, Clint counted the miles as they rolled by, singing along with sixties' tunes. He had entered yesteryear, his safe zone.

Turning onto the busy streets of downtown–the bridge in his rearview mirror–Clint navigated the same roads he'd used the last time he was in Louisville. The address he sought was east of downtown. Amid the crowded Monday afternoon traffic, Clint repeated the same rights and lefts until Tetters Drive showed on his radar.

Slowly Clint's vehicle rolled up to 945 Hardin Street, pulling beside the curb directly behind Axel's black Cadillac Deville, noticing Axel's F-250 truck was parked around back. Relieved to see DeArra's Lexus LS430 ruby red sedan by the side door, Clint smiled. *My witness is here.* His eyes quickly surveyed the front of the house, assuming Axel was awaiting indoors.

Peering out from behind the curtain, Axel had stepped back when Clint's truck showed. His girlfriend, seated on the couch by the wall, was verbally objecting to being forced to sit in the living room while her boyfriend conducted business.

"Shut up, woman," he yelled loudly enough for the next county to hear, very close to slapping her. "DeArra, I'm warning you." With fire in his eyes he threatened bodily harm, meaning every word he'd uttered. "Complain once more and see what happens to that pretty, made-up face of yours." He swung around, his eyes hard. "During my meeting, if I hear one peep out of you, that pretty head *will* fly. Got that?" He patted her poofy blonde hairdo. "Girl, don't think for a minute that I'm foolin'."

Pointedly glaring through her thick, black fake eyelashes, DeArra began to whimper, not used to Axel behaving this badly. He had notched it up a level. "You're a bully, Axel."

Axel gloated beneath the surface, taking her complaint as a compliment. "Just do as I say. I'll make it up to you later." With DeArra's lips pouting, silence bathed the room.

When Clint tapped three times on the door, almost too soft for anyone to hear, he speculated what Axel might be considering. The door opened, allowing him step into the living room. Clint glanced over at DeArra pushed into the couch, Axel's mood became apparent.

Something in her expression, though, felt off, a dreadful look in her eyes. They directed him to the kitchen.

Unnerved when he saw two shadowy figures standing in the darkness beyond the kitchen door, Clint realized both shapes dwarfed him. One grunted, the other cracked his knuckles. Once the front door was securely fastened, they moved ever so slightly into the light.

Axel, a typical rabble-rouser, coughed up a remark that riled his comrades, "This is the weasel I told you about," he mocked, staring out the window and searching for anything out of the ordinary while finding it hard to believe Clint trusted him not to bring others into the affair.

Double-crossed, Clint glared at Axel when the men repositioned themselves to the outer wall, arms folded. The square jaw of the taller one twitched while the shorter one shifted his weight to lean on his shoulder.

Bide your time, Clint inwardly coached, *backup is nearby. Just keep calm, I'm wearing a wiretap. They'll hear every word.*

Drex and his colleagues were indeed listening to the exchange inside the home. Fully engaged, they would know the exact minute to intercede.

Clint clenched his jaw, his sculpted cheekbones tightening when he noticed the uncanny resemblance of one of the men, too close not to be a relative. "Nice to see you invited a member of your unsavory clan to join us."

Worried about Clint's safety, DeArra cast a cursory glance his way, afraid he'd push Axel too far. She had never seen him this foul. She looked away when Axel turned her direction.

"Breathing down my neck," he pointed at himself, his eyes penetrating, "that wasn't your brightest idea." Axel turned away, agitated. "Did you really think the pocket watch was enough to get in here without repercussions, especially after knowing you'd been in my house rummaging through my things?"

Axel lifted DeArra to her feet. "Get in the bedroom." His voice was cold and demanding as he shoved her down the hall.

She didn't ask questions, but nervous tension simmered in her unemotional voice, frightful when she responded, "Okay." This was a side of Axel she didn't know existed, and it frightened her.

"If you planned to bring family members to our little pow wow–I presume from your father, Jay's side–why have DeArra here? I only asked for one witness."

Clint watched as she scurried to the bedroom, closing the door behind her, feeling concerned for her safety. Although he wasn't to broach the subject, he said. "Why don't you just hand over my side of our bargain, and I'll vanish into the night. You'll never see me again."

Axel spat his answer in Clint's face, derisively replying, "Cause you asked so politely. You demanded a witness, so she's here." A strange distortion crept into Axel's eyes, manifesting into pure evil.

Under ordinary circumstances Clint would have chided his displeasure, retaliated with a strike of his own, but instinctively he knew it wasn't wise. *Provoking him could have grave consequences,* he thought, sensing he was the target of the firing line. Although he didn't see a gun, the presence of it, and others, weighed heavily in the room.

"Hand over my watch," ordered Axel, edging nearer, closing what personal space they shared. With an unfurled right hand, he pointed with his left, indicating Clint should drop the pocket watch in his open palm.

The man on his right grinned, approving of Axel's antics.

"Sorry, it's in the truck." Clint's gaze shifted across the room to where the Paul Bunyan characters were holding up the burdensome wall. Attempting to match Axel's gruffness, he scoffed, "You don't really think I'd be stupid enough to carry it in here with me. Do you? It's all I have for an *even exchange,* cash for the watch. Remember? We made a deal. You have more than enough stolen goods in your secret vault to spare me a fraction. This doesn't have to get complicated, Axel, just a simple business transaction. That's all this is."

Axel's eyes flashed. "You try my patience, man," he said wagging his head low like a bull ready to charge. Far from pleased, he venomously questioned Clint. "And what exactly would keep me from putting a bullet between those bedroom eyes of yours, walk out to that piece of shit of yours and take my watch? I'm curious because that watch is mine, not yours. So why are we negotiating with something that belonged to me in the first place?"

This time Clint saw red, countering lightning fast. "It isn't yours, never was," he said, raising his voice. "It belongs to your uncle, your *mother's*, brother. Remember Uncle Dorian? Is this how you repay the man who raised you? You steal his property and kill his son?"

Axel became incensed, pacing back and forth, before swinging back around to face Clint. "You know too much! Nothing more than a pest problem that needs a permanent solution."

"You mean like Thaddeus's dog?"

Axel's eyelids twitched, his face purple when he blew smoke at Clint's face. "How do you know about that?"

"You poisoned his dog and tossed the poor animal over Thaddeus's body in an unmarked grave in the middle of nowhere? How could you, Axel?" Clint was as mad as Axel now, standing toe to toe with him.

"That dog was his right arm," Axel defended, justifying his actions. "The shepherd wouldn't have survived without Thaddeus. We camped in that area, the dog came along, always. It was the perfect place for them. At our special place." Axel turned, moved toward the two men, making a gesture they seemed to understand.

Clint stood unflappable, remaining steadfast. "Go on then, do it." A simple statement with no hostility tacked on, certainly nothing to incite a higher level of violence. Clint put his hand inside his pant pocket and held tightly to Rod's golden quartz crystal he'd brought. The rock was vibrating. Tightening his grip around it, he waited for the other shoe to fall.

An ugly Cheshire grin flashed on Axel's lips. His teeth were the shade of spicy mustard. Obviously entertained, he humorously grunted while walking over to the lacy curtains DeArra had hung at the picture window the day before. He held one of them aside for a clearer view of Clint's old truck parked behind his fancy Cadillac. He sarcastically said, "I assume you got my earlier message."

459

Their eyes locked. Axel's were like bottomless black pearls while Clint's remained firm. Beneath the surface Clint seethed, figuring Axel was goading him into a word battle–or something even worse. He sensed their tete-a-tete had escalated to an unhealthy level. "I read it, and then had it painted over, ready for your next memo."

Axel strolled back, looking down the hall. The door to the bedroom had somehow managed to open itself a smidgeon. Axel slammed it hard when he shut it for a second time. "I'm warning you, woman," he shouted from the hall. He cracked his neck with his hands holding his chin and twisting it from one side to the other, before walking back down the hall into the living room. His squinty, unblinking eyes critiqued Clint. "I don't see anything stopping me from claiming what's mine, other than *you*, and that's not much."

Clint fearlessly retaliated, "Could be by the time you get to the truck the authorities will have this house surrounded." It was a calculated risk Clint had to take if he intended to continue breathing. All the while he tightened his hand around the crystal in his pocket praying for extra courage to keep up the charade.

Having been taken by surprise, Axel's head pivoted, a stubby neck wrinkling under its weight, he charged, "What are you playing at?"

Adding a contradictory note, Clint hurled a less daring comment. "Or maybe not! I'm probably bluffing." His face displayed a lavish grin, his eyes bright.

Axel burst out with laughter. "I swear, you are my favorite person to hate." His brow creased. With his eyes fixed on Clint, said, "I have no idea what I'm going to do with you, but I promise you this, it'll be equal to your brashness."

"Anything as nice as what you gave Thaddeus will do. The others you've killed weren't as well cared for as your cousin, especially Cookie." Clint pushed his luck way past the boiling point when he added, "And to think she was your favorite gal for such a long time. So loyal."

Clint's eyes grew intense, speaking his words loud and clear to make certain DeArra could hear. He was aware Axel understood exactly what he was doing. "Don't worry. Cookie had a fine funeral.

She's been buried in a proper grave and has a beautiful headstone with her real name, Carla Lynn Crenna, inscribed on it. Hey, you should stop by to pay your respects." Clint's face grew provoking when he chided, "Not that you'd care."

He turned to the two men watching him and said, "That girl *was* a true angel." He swiveled back to Axel, "I just hope your current girlfriend doesn't rat on you like Cookie did. Could be bad for DeArra's health."

Stepping back, at an arm's length, and with his full weight behind his fury, Axel lunged forward, backhanding Clint so hard he slammed into the wall headfirst, bouncing against it before collapsing to the floor.

In his vision, stars appeared. Waves of sound reverberated through Clint's eardrums. Although he heard nothing, he managed to get up on one knee, blood oozing from the corner of his mouth, his jaw aching massively from the unexpected levelling.

Conceding to his poor judgment while trying to regain composure, Clint thought, *Now that was exceedingly foolish.*

Glaring down at Clint, Axel's point came through crystal clear. If Clint smarted off again, it would be the last time. Axel hissed, spewing his venom, "Awe, did I hit you a little too hard? Cowboy!" Sporting a measure of superiority, Axel looked over to his companions, "Get him out of my sight."

Unable to respond, even if he had wanted to, Clint lowered his body back down and tucked his head between his knees, staring at the hardwood floor hoping to regain focus sooner than later. Looking up at last, with dilated eyes, heavy echoes of laughter bellowing around him, he visualized the crystal giving him strength.

It took Clint a long while to register what Axel had referred to when he said, "Cowboy," but then remembered the persona he had invented at the start of his investigation when in Louisville and at the tavern. Clint made it to his feet, standing tall before Axel.

"I'm done with your smart mouth, man," Axel declared harshly, pushing Clint toward the kitchen and the two men who waited there.

Registering the threat and next action, Detective Mason gave orders to move in. One street over, on Bradbury, the team advanced to Hardin, cautiously circling the house, back, sides, and front.

Lieutenant David Andrews was situated at the rear of the property in the alley, lying low, below the fence line hidden behind trash cans. Captain Scott Edwards took the side door position, making it his vantage point from the next-door neighbor's shed. Theo Dickson was stationed on Hardin, squatting at the rear wheel of a parked vehicle. Mason took the prime location closest to the front door.

Hunkering down at their strategic locations, waiting on Detective Mason's command, Mason expected the pocket watch to take priority above all else to lure Drako out of the house. He knew Axel was obsessed by the timepiece, and had killed for it, so when Axel came strutting out the front door, Mason and the team shifted into high alert.

Axel boldly walked to the F-100, twirling Clint's keys on his forefinger. Feeling full of himself, he called back over his shoulder to his comrades, "You know where to go. I'll drive this rusted jalopy and meet you there."

"Axel Drako," Drex called out from the corner of the house, "you are under arrest for the murder of Thaddeus Andersen. Put your hands in the air," demanded Drex, who had his gun pointed at Axel's torso. "Slowly, put your hands on the truck."

To Mason's displeasure, the other two men walked out of the house at the same time Axel strolled out the front. They were forcefully ramming Clint out the side door.

Dressed in Italian leather jackets, the two men had Clint tightly clutched by his upper arms, shoving him toward the cargo van parked in the alley by the back gate where David Andrews was positioned.

When David jumped out and took a stand, pointing his gun and demanding the two men put down their weapons and release their hostage, declaring they were under arrest, gun fire broke out in an instant. David took a bullet to the shoulder and fell back while Scott leapt out from the neighbor's yard to distract the shooters.

Scott fired at the man closest to him. Another shot was driven into the van's rear tire. He meant to cripple the assailant, giving David Andrews time to move in and assist with apprehending the men, but things went south.

Scott signaled for David to call for backup, gesturing for Theo to do likewise.

Swiftly Clint made his move and hustled to the van for safety, literally rolling beneath its chassis.

From the side and rear of the property, gunfire continued to blast. Not one of the two accomplices had any intention of being taken in peacefully, which became painfully obvious when Mason saw Edwards scurry to the side of DeArra's luxury sedan.

Alongside the driveway, Mason heard the rapid fire. He had anticipated as much, knowing Scott Edwards would try to apprehend the men the second they walked from the house. He wondered how Clint was going to escape without harm, aware hostages rarely fared well in situations like these.

When chaos erupted from Scott's direction, it had caused Axel to stop and turn. He didn't comply to Drex's demand to lay down his gun any more than the other men had to David's.

Instead, Axel had slipped his 9mm from its shoulder holster and aimed it at Theo Dickson, trying to create a clear path to the Cadillac from the truck's driver door, grazing the officer's shoulder and forcing him behind the front wheel of the vehicle.

Just then, a shot whizzed past Axel's body, hitting the curb. It shattered into the cement—it was Drex's first and only warning shot. Axel spun around and pointed his weapon to where he believed the bullet had originated, discharging five rounds.

Mason darted back to the corner of the house, clinching his Beretta tightly with both hands and pointing it at Axel. But he did not pull the trigger. "There's nowhere to run, Axel," Mason shouted. "Drop your weapon. Kick it to the curb. No one needs to get hurt." Looking across the lawn to see if he had a clear path to a better position, if inclined to run in that direction, Mason waited.

Hightailing it to the Deville, Axel fled Clint's truck, agitated he would not retrieve his antique watch. Feeling incensed, he turned on Mason, firing at him, a sniper's aim, determined to eliminate the only deterrent standing in his way. His associates could handle themselves, he figured. Aware a level head and sure foot was imperative, he fired off two more rounds.

In response, an ear-shattering roar blasted from Mason's 9mm.

While shots were blaring up front, both men at the side of the property were being handcuffed. One was on the ground with Scott's weight heavy on his back, as he was read his rights. The other, David had faced toward the van while doing the same.

From the undercarriage, Clint had watched in awe at the precision of Scott and David's coordinated efforts. Clint had waited to emerge until the two criminals were apprehended. When he crawled out, Scott looked at him with reassurance, but Scott's eyes revealed something more, gratitude that his friend wasn't harmed.

Upfront, Axel glanced at the door and saw DeArra standing with her hand pressed against the glass wearing an expression that spoke of danger. Axel frantically waved her off, instructing her to stay inside, not to step out on the porch.

What is wrong with her? he screamed in his head. *Can't she hear gunfire.*

Moments before DeArra had entered the living room not fully understanding the explosive sounds from outdoors were coming from Axel's own yard, not from elsewhere as she had imagined. It wouldn't have been the first time to hear gun shots in the neighborhood.

Her arrival at the front door was enough to distract Axel, causing him to falter and take a bullet to his side, delivered by Drex Mason. Burning ribs did not stand in the way of him opening the Cadillac door and diving in, reaching for the extra keys he kept under the seat. Adrenaline pumped at impossible speed, triggering a battery of new rounds fired out the passenger window in the vicinity of where Mason held his ground. Two made contact.

Mason's tactical training had switched into high gear. Dropping low, he had crept toward the porch behind the shrubs with the intent of placing another calculated shot, this time into Axel's leg, but he hadn't acted quick enough. Axel had jumped into his car. The mistake Drex made was one of hesitation so he could gain solid footing, which allowed Axel's bullet to penetrate, slamming Drex against the house.

In hindsight, Detective Mason's hesitation to fire his own fatal bullet a split-second earlier when a clear shot was present, turned costly. Drex would pay the price for wanting only to obstruct Axel from escaping–choosing not to deliver his own deadly shot.

In a torrent of white-light heat, Mason's brain exploded in brilliance. The curtain of fire power of moments earlier vanished into a *curtain of darkness.* He groaned from the excruciating pain that traveled the length of his body.

A millisecond before passing out, he heard a trickle of sound from afar. It was like the scream of a banshee, an omen warning him of impending death. Drex relaxed into the trauma, feeling his collapsed body heaped on the ground, knowing he had lived an honorable, good life. As death's grip tightened, his mind begged for a miracle.

Scott reached Drex in a few swift strides, shouting to everyone in earshot, "Officer down. Call for an ambulance." On a dime Scott instinctively pivoted, planting his feet squarely, he brought his Beretta sight level and pulled the trigger, hitting Axel just as he pushed the accelerator to the floorboard trying to make a run for it. The Cadillac veered to the left into two parked vehicles. The police swarmed the car, yanking Axel from the front seat, bleeding from two wounds, but alive.

Less than two minutes later, sirens blared, barreling up the street at both ends moving at incredible speed. In a blur, paramedics jumped out, carried, and unfolded a wheeled stretcher. Hurriedly they lifted Detective Drex Mason from the spot he had fallen, leaving a black stain of blood on the ground. Bracing his head and neck, they cautiously strapped his body securely to the gurney, rushing him to the open ambulance doors. Ironically, the ambulance was headed for Grayson Hospital, the same hospital where Charles Hill had died the year before, almost to the day Axel had killed him.

When Clint saw the ambulance, the thought crossed his mind, *will June Bennett be part of the medical team to receive Detective Mason? If so, he's in good hands.* He turned, watching David, Scott, and Theo approach the blockade of police vehicles. Out of breath, Scott leaned in and said something to Axel who was handcuffed and sitting in the back of the squad car.

When the car moved, Axel saw Clint and sneered, wearing a cocky grin as though to say, *This ain't over yet, buddy, not by a long shot.* His other two co-conspirators were driven in separate police cars to Louisville's Police Station, constrained, and charged as accessories to murder.

DeArra sat on the step bawling her eyes out, a torrent of tears flowing down her cheeks. Long trails of black mascara lined her face from nonstop sobbing.

Clint observed Scott as he walked up and sat down beside her on the step. He spoke gently, giving her what comfort he could. Clint felt in awe of this man. Never had he seen Scott under pressure in the line of duty. Impressed with his composure and cool head, Clint walked toward DeArra and Scott, wanting to support them.

The horrific expression on Scott's face caused Clint enormous grief. He sadly expressed his regret, "Scott, I am so sorry."

With a mind that felt broken, Scott replied, his eyes dark and reflective, "Me too."

Chapter 59
Justice Served

With an onslaught of questions completed, and the last witness statement recorded, Captain Scott Edwards wrapped up his account of what transpired on the afternoon of December 19, 2005. Leaning back in the chair, fingers laced behind his head, the summation he had described pertaining to the arrest of Axel Drako and his multiple-count murder case was ready to forward to the Louisville Police Station.

The man's inevitable incarceration into the Kentucky State Penitentiary at Eddyville was simply a matter of time. The State of Kentucky's case against Axel Alrik Drako was rock solid. The list of crimes charged removed any chance of bail. The six deaths notched into his belt were only the tip of an iceberg they would eventually discover regarding his psychopathic nature.

The final nail in his coffin was at the hand of his own cousin, Leonard Drako, when Leonard willingly turned over the hypodermic needle used to end Carla Crenna's life, and a second needle used on Thaddeus Andersen's German shepherd. Having spilled the beans in exchange for a reduced sentence, he informed the authorities Axel had administered poison as an alternate method to kill in other instances.

When interrogated, Axel didn't blink an eye to the reference to his ex-girlfriend's death. Conversely, he lashed out, furiously insinuating, "Cookie got *exactly* what was coming to her. She was a blabbermouth and deserved to die!"

Adding to the felonies, the attempted murder of Kentucky's Detective Drex Mason raised the ire of every police officer on the Kentucky and Indiana sides of the border. Having already killed one police officer, Axel's name brought up strong emotions of outrage. The detailed account of how the team worked together seamlessly to bring Axel down and the events that led to his arrest was the stuff movies were made.

Detective Mason's survival rumbled throughout the Louisville and Salzburg police force. His team had been instructed to wear bulletproof vests, which appeared he had not used because he was found lying in his own blood, unconscious.

Scott had examined Mason seconds before the paramedics arrived nearly instantaneously supporting his head, as best he could. He determined the damage responsible for the pooled blood beneath Drex came from Mason's side, and although the situation appeared fatal, he had no way of telling for certain.

Mason had been wearing a vest but there was underlying moisture beneath the surface due to its age, which is what had compromised its integrity, allowing one of the two bullets fired by Axel to penetrate the material, thereby causing considerable damage, but only to Mason's side. Fortunately for him, the bullet to his right chest–the one that had propelled him against the house–did not break the vest's exterior. A deep muscle contusion was expected to be felt for months.

Upon arrival at Grayson Hospital, where Drex had been rushed into surgery, the staff gathered, placing their undivided attention to his care. His pierced spleen was removed, bleeding vessels were tied off, and where the bullet exited at his midback, the wound was sutured. By day's end, Detective Mason was listed in serious but stable condition.

The Hardin Street scene was cleared, DeArra was taken to a nearby motel, and the house and yard were barricaded with crime scene tape. After Scott spoke with Clint, he drove to see Mason who was coherent, pumped full of painkillers, and feeling mighty grateful to see him–his colleague, and friend.

"Hey, there," Drex slurred when he saw Scott enter the room. Slowly he enunciated, "Tissue damage and a little lost blood... survivable stuff–a small price to pay to catch the bad guys." He did his best to grin. "I'll live to see another day, Scott. Don't you worry. You'll not get rid of me that easily. I'm minus a spleen, but that's it. They are keeping a close eye for sepsis or any other developing infection."

"You are a walking miracle," proclaimed Scott. "Do you realize how close you came?" Astonished his colleague was still alive, he added, "Honestly, I don't know how you survived one bullet, let alone two." Sitting at the bedside, Scott said appreciatively, "Thank you for everything. We couldn't have done any of this without you. You were the glue that held the operation together. You're one brave SOB." Scott said, expressing his admiration with a huge grin.

With glistened eyes, Drex beamed but said nothing.

Soon Drex dozed off, leaving Scott to his thoughts. As he sat beside Drex in the darkness, breathing more calmly, he gave thanks to the Lord for the additional protection they had all received.

Earlier, before Scott drove to Grayson Hospital to check on Drex, he and Clint spent a few minutes at a nearby café to calm down. Both men's emotions were in high gear. From relief Axel had been arrested to how to deal with another death associated with the case, and then circling back again. Although at the time neither man knew Mason would survive.

Still processing the events of Axel's arrest, Clint oscillated back and forth between a myriad of feelings. A black and blue jaw, coupled with substantial swelling around his right eye and mouth made for an ugly sight. Painful, yes, but Clint knew they'd heal in time. He felt grateful to be alive.

If Clint was honest with himself, his battered appearance reflected a level of bravery he had no idea he possessed. He was proud not to have backed down under immense pressure. Scott expressed the same sentiments before heading back into Louisville, telling Clint he had done amazingly well under the circumstances.

"I don't think Jules is going to be too excited when she sees me," Clint confessed during their chat. "She was pretty worried when I left town this morning."

"I don't suppose she will, but seeing you walk through the door will supersede any fears she's been wrestling with," stated Scott convincingly.

Wagging his head, stunned by everything that had taken place over the last several hours, a broad smile crept onto Scott's face. "We do make a good team. I have to say, you surprised the heck out of me when things got dicey in there. Not backing down… that was a Cool Hand Luke moment." Scott's expression brightened even more when he said, "I never thought I'd say this, but you might be cut out for this kind of work." Then he broke into serious laughter. "Playing the role of a pigeon."

"No way," Clint objected passionately, laughing along with his friend. "I've had my fill of doing the honorable thing. I'm stepping back into my quiet, laid-back, charmed life. Besides, my barn needs a new coat of paint," he chuckled. "That's more my style."

Scott promised to keep Clint informed of any new developments surrounding Axel's case. Likewise, he'd report in with updates on Drex Mason.

On his way back to Salzburg, Clint was too riled up to make phone calls, figuring he'd phone Dorian Andersen the next day with the latest news about his son and nephew, and the stolen property they recovered beneath Axel's home. He also intended to reach out to June Bennett. He wanted to give her a head's up that David Dunn would be calling regarding the jewelry Ann had left to her.

Clint also planned to stop by Beans-a'-Brewin' sooner than later to speak with Mark Carlson personally. He wanted him to know he could breathe easily again. All three people had been extremely instrumental in bringing Axel Drako to justice.

Just as Scott had predicted, when Clint did arrive at home, Jules's expression was one for the record books. Stunned, she stood staring at him without saying a word. For Clint's sake she recovered quickly. She'd been preening at the bathroom mirror, combing her hair, and putting a fresh layer of make up on after her bath, getting ready for his arrival.

She walked into the kitchen and saw Clint seated at the table. She lightly touched his face, too shaken to speak right away. Kissing the top of the head, she finally whispered, "Hard day at work, eh?"

"You could say that." Clint smiled without a trace of humor, trying hard to control the tears that had welled in his eyes and were now running down his cheeks. He lowered his head and said, "But the good guys won!"

Jules leaned in, hugging him around the back of the neck so she wouldn't touch anything that might cause pain. "I love you! I hope you know how blessed I feel to have you in my life. Clint Reeves, you amaze me. You are a brave man and one of many talents. God outdid himself when he put you together."

Clint buried his face at her side, softly he said, "Jules, I couldn't have done any of this without your support and love. I honestly don't know where this hidden strength in me came from. But it exists, and I'm grateful to have followed through on my promise to Farley McDougal and," he grinned, "Charlie Hill's quest to expose the truth. His spirit should be put to rest since Axel was arrested and charged with not only Charlie's murder but, sadly, so many others."

Something out of the blue occurred to Jules–felt rather than seen. Quietly, with her emotions roiling, just as Clint's were, she claimed. "That son of Charlie's is far from average. Behind those eyes is so much expression and depth of feeling."

Clint looked up curiously, wondering what his wife was referring to, and if she was speaking of something specific. "What makes you say that?"

"Because he drew something today that literally blew me away. A picture. The power of expression was off the charts."

"Is that right? I can't wait to see it." Shaking his head, thinking everything K.C. did had meaning, he said, "That kid is something else." Clint stood and pushed his chair back. Gazing in Jules's watery eyes, he hugged her tight. "Don't worry, this thing is over. I'm back to my old self."

"Let me get you a root beer," she suggested thinking she liked the way Clint's words sounded. Grinning, she tagged on, "You look like you could use a cold drink."

Leaning against the counter, with his nerves still frayed, he asked, "How are Farley and K.C. doing?"

"Fabulously," she answered right away. "I didn't think you'd care, so I gave permission for K.C. to visit Farley's for the day. After we finished baking the second batch of Christmas cookies. Farley stopped by and helped for about an hour or so. When he got ready to leave, he asked if K.C. could join him. Said he'd bring him home after dinner."

"That's wonderful," Clint said, happy to hear they were spending so much time together. "I think I know where this is leading, but I don't want to get ahead of myself."

She smiled broadly. "When I asked K.C. if he would like to go home with Farley, he told me he loved it there. Clint, that boy has come out of his shell. He's starting to put coherent sentences together. He was so cute today, telling me he has friends at Farley's place. I said Cocoa and Winston are a lot of fun, aren't they? He answered, saying, "Them too." The minds of children are so endearing."

"That *is* cute." Clint smiled, pleased to hear they were doing so well.

"We have a big day coming up!" Jules turned with a flare of excitement. "Going to see Dad, Faith, and Rusty's family in just three days. Can you believe it? Christmas is this Sunday. I hope Santa got my letter." An enormous grin covered her face. Then it changed dramatically. "How are we going to explain your face?"

Clint burst out laughing, "That's going to require a *big fat lie*. And maybe some of your make-up. Maybe I'll say you hauled off and hit me with a frying pan."

"That can be arranged you know." She giggled, causing Clint to chuckle which hurt. "That's if you don't want to lie," she teased causing him to explode with laughter.

"You are something else, girl. Don't do that. It's painful to laugh."

Tuesday, December 20

The next day, Jules happily headed off to work, relieved Clint was going to stay at home, spending the day on the couch. This evening would be a late night, as they both were aware. The town was buzzing with excitement, packing Josie's Diner to the gills.

Clint, on the other hand, decided *not* to stay indoors and piddle around the house, packing for the trip, cleaning, and changing sheets–a habit of theirs before leaving town. There was plenty of time to finish those chores.

Getting dressed to fit the temperature where he was headed–a clammy fifty-five degrees ten feet below ground–Clint layered his clothing. He opened the back door and headed for one of his favorite places on Earth.

An overcast, snowy morning fell around him as he walked across the snow-blanketed yard. The forecast called for heavy snow. The day fit his mood of doing something he loved, as opposed to the sort of things he'd been faced with lately. Sucking in the cold air, everything he'd been working toward had come to fruition, in a very satisfactory way creating an enormous sense of pride.

With too much on his mind to perform menial tasks indoors, he ventured into the woods to his family's secret place at the back of the property in Hoosier National Forest.

Clint felt a sense of peace around his great-grandfather's things. He and Jules had discovered Earl Reeves's man-made spacious area two years prior, during the Reno Gang treasure episode. She was the one who had spotted the entrance near an outhouse, oddly enough, which led them below ground to a two-room area and a tunnel that connected to the shack and Goss Cave.

Clint lifted the hidden door, setting it to the side. He put his foot on the first step that would take him underground. He moved down a few more steps before closing the entrance.

When he entered the dark area, he turned on the sconce lighting he'd had installed. With the essence of his great-grandfather's things around him, Clint sat at Earl Reeves's desk. He wanted to make his final entry into the journal he'd been keeping.

He composed the crucial parts of Charles Hill's amazing story and thanked God for its rewarding conclusion. The ending, unknown the last time he jotted in the journal, was now recorded and part of history. The case had ended triumphantly.

Clint put the leather-bound notebook in his family's antiquated trunk, a legacy for his family and great-grandchildren. Jules had found this trunk unexpectedly two years earlier. They were surprised to find the trunk full of family history and stories.

Three books already stacked inside, chronicled the backstory of Goss Cave, the Reno Gang treasure and how the stash of riches was really discovered. He had freely written about Rod Radcliff, Sr, and Jr., Rod's New and Used Books, and everything that happened during that period. The story he'd just finished was no less spectacular.

By ten thirty Clint was climbing out of his underground retreat wearing a smile. Feeling unburdened, he called Farley, asking if they could meet. "I'll be in town today. Do you have a minute? Lunch somewhere? You pick the place."

Farley was delighted to hear from Clint. "How about here? I'll fry up hamburgers, and potatoes in the deep fryer."

"That sounds terrific, Farley. Thank you for the invitation. I'd much rather sit in the quiet surroundings of your place by a relaxing fire than go into town."

Clint was exceedingly pleased to have the invite extended to him. He didn't really want to be seen in public, but he also wanted to speak with Farley regarding what had transpired in Louisville the day before. At Farley's cabin, talking about Axel and his arrest would be much easier.

"There's only one caveat," Farley said, "Keelan is coming over too. Is that alright? I told him yesterday we would spend the afternoon together. We are setting up a train set today, tracks, steam engine, a town, trees, the works. We've been picking out pieces from a toy store. One I particularly enjoy."

Clint grinned, understanding Farley and K.C.'s relationship was moving in a healthy direction. "You know the answer to that," he jested. "I'm as fond of the boy as you are. It'd be extra nice to have him there. I think we might be his two favorite people," kidded Clint. "I hear he is doing much better with communication skills. Jules said he was stringing words together more coherently."

"It's true," Farley said, proud of Keelan's progress. "I've been amazed. I'll pick Keelan up around eleven. Do you want to meet us here at noon?"

"That's ideal. I have a stop to make at ACE Hardware. After that I'll be over."

With that, the two friends mutually agreed to see each other soon.

Yapping dogs greeted Clint in their usual manner when he knocked on Farley's door, with Cocoa carrying on like he was a hundred forty-pound Rottweiler as opposed to a ten-pound pint-size chihuahua, and Winston caring less, going his merry way.

Down the entrance hall, he noticed K.C. advancing with his arms extended, cannoning into Clint and brimming with excitement. "Hi," he squeaked in a small voice, his expression changing when he noticed Clint's battered face.

In an instant he vanished around the corner, running up the steps of the handsome staircase Farley had hand carved. Winston, and Cocoa were fast on his heels, bulleting up the steps behind him, racing to the top. Tossing toys to the second floor where he was headed, the boy fell short of the speedy animals. Cocoa arrived first, clutching Rudy, his stuffed toy reindeer in his mouth, waiting for Keelan to catch up.

Moving into the kitchen where Farley had already started the french fries, his fair complexion shone rosy from the light streaming through the window, framing his gray eyes that seemed to light from within, against his chestnut hair.

"Please have a seat," he suggested, facing Clint, surprised by his appearance. "Would you like something to drink? I have pop in the refrigerator and the pot has a least one more cup to relinquish."

It feels good to be here, noted Clint, feeling better today than yesterday. He glanced around the kitchen, sensing a radiance generated from every corner of the room. "Thank you for not asking about my appearance," Clint said. "What's behind this face of mine is a story I plan to relate."

"I'm very happy to see you," proclaimed Farley with an elation to his voice. "I have something I'd like to discuss with you as well. Was going to ask if we could get together. How ironic you called first. I was set to dial your number when the phone rang. Serendipity, don't you think?"

Thinking he knew what Farley wanted to discuss, Clint readily responded, "Sure, fire away. I'm all ears."

Farley went into the other room, opening a drawer to the credenza and pulling out an article before returning to the kitchen. Placing a picture on the table, his brows lifted high, looking at Clint in the oddest manner. "The worst nightmares can produce the greatest gifts," he said with a look of contentment.

"I don't understand," confessed Clint, not sure what he was supposed to recognize. "What is this?"

"In a minute my friend," Farley's face was difficult to decipher. "I'll call Keelan, let him tell you what those watercolors are of." Farley's eyes twinkled. "Your wife saw them."

"Oh, I know," Clint said quickly, "that's the picture Jules was talking about. The one where K.C. captured such depth of expression. He painted it yesterday. Correct? I see what she meant. That is a stunning portrait."

"I was with him when he asked for watercolors in lieu of his regular paints. 'Never used them before,' he told me. With almost an urgency, Keelan started brushing strokes on the page like it might vanish before his eyes if he didn't paint fast enough."

"Keelan, lunch is ready," Farley beckoned from the bottom of the stairs.

This old man, he played one, he played knick-knack on my thumb, with a knick-knack, paddywhack, give your dog a bone, this old man came rolling home. This old man… he played two…

He easily identified the song, coming from the room on the right at the upper level.

"Okay," Keelan answered, giggling when he came out of the room after seeing Farley standing at the foot of the stairs waiting for him. He barreled down the steps into Farley's arms, tightly holding on.

They walked into the kitchen, Farley's hand gently on Keelan's back leading him to the chair on Clint's right where the light illuminated the child's black, silky hair.

"Keelan, would you like to tell Clint about your striking picture." Eyes brilliant with inner knowledge beyond what the picture showed, Farley stated, "He likes it very much."

Keelan stuttered only slightly, his words clearly voiced, "Those are m-y friends, Vincent and Violet."

There in front of their eyes, Farley's children came to life in a watercolor drawing. Two small, wide-eyed innocent children, an exact likeness of Farley McDougal's twin two-year-old children.

"Please wash your hands before lunch, Keelan."

The boy scurried to the restroom in the hallway to do as he'd been asked.

Farley turned to Clint, wearing an indescribable look. "Clint, Keelan drew a portrait of my kids."

Chapter 60
Full Circle

When Keelan returned, Farley patted him on the hand. "Thank you for the beautiful picture. You did an excellent job."

Clint was astounded. He thought about Charles Hill and the heart transplant that had set things in motion. He pondered the connection between Farley McDougal, Charles Hill, and Charles's son Keelan Hill. Their amazing story was hard to believe or imagine.

The three of them enjoyed a lunch of hamburger and fries. They chatted while they ate, but then Keelan became fidgety.

"May I ask a question?" Clint requested, waiting until the boy had excused himself from the table, going into the living room to play fetch with the dogs. Running around, Cocoa and Winston chased Keelan through the house.

The pride Farley felt for his home reflected in his creation. It was obvious Keelan loved his surroundings just as much.

"Certainly, anything," answered Farley, pushing a tear away. "But before you do, I want to point out Keelan is not an ordinary boy. We both know that. He hears and sees things ordinary people can't. Things outside our perception and considered normal, but not in his world."

Clint felt the same. He had witnessed Keelan's abilities firsthand. In fact, Keelan's insights were directly tied to solving the case. Clint encouraged Farley to finish his train of thought.

"Look, I don't believe for a minute Vincent and Violet are here in this house. What I do think, is somehow Keelan can see and interact with them." Farley's face expressed his comprehension of what it must be like to be Keelan. "Even talks to them."

Farley looked out the window into the forest. When he turned his eyes to Clint, he said, "The only place he seems to be able to connect with the children, however, is in the room where I have their belongings. Keelan told me, on his second visit, he had friends upstairs–in that room. I dismissed it as seven-year-old's musings, not to be taken seriously. I'm aware he says he sees dinosaurs and such things." Farley grinned, thinking about his conversation with Clint and finding it comical. "So I passed it off as a young boy's fantasy world."

"A few boxes of playthings, pictures of the kids, children's books, that sort of thing are stacked in the closet in sealed boxes up there. Somehow, I believe, Keelan can tap into their energy because of those items, a realm outside our normal understanding. A place where my kids still exist. Call it another dimension if you like. How else do you explain this watercolor?" Farley pushed the painting closer to Clint, his eyes moist from seeing Vincent and Violet's faces before him, almost touchable.

"Farley, I think you are one hundred percent on the money," agreed Clint knowing he'd had too many things happen through the course of the recent case not to believe what Farley suggested to be true. "What about Charlie? Do you think he's still around?" he boldly asked.

"Funny you ask because yesterday I heard his voice after not hearing it for the longest time. I was thinking I might not ever hear it again. Things had quieted down so much. The thought crossed my mind that since Keelan was spending time here, Charlie had found peace."

Clint's face looked shocked because he hadn't mentioned a word about Monday yet, Axel's arrest, and the investigation's closure. "What did you hear?"

Farley leaned back in his chair, fingers interlaced on his head and an expression of joy covering his face. I swear I heard him say, "It's done." That was it, nothing more. But... I did have this remarkable feeling come over me. Clint, I think he's gone for good. For real this time."

As if he found murder easier to talk about than his unexplained experiences with ghosts, messages, and voices, Clint stated, "Well, that's interesting because I came here to tell you Axel Drako has been arrested for the murder of Charles Lewellyn Hill. He is in jail awaiting trial. It happened on Monday."

Farley's eyes lit up, full of excitement, "Really? They caught the guy who killed Charlie? And Ann?" His eyes narrowed, wondering, "Do you believe the case against him will hold up in court?"

Clint felt indescribable joy when he saw the sheer pleasure manifested on Farley's face. "Oh, I'm positive my friend, no doubt about it. The state of Kentucky has more than enough evidence to convict Axel. He'll be spending time in the penitentiary for the rest of his miserable life." He tilted his head, not saying what he was thinking, "That's if he's lucky!"

"Then that explains it! Charlie has moved on. Peace has found him." For a moment, Farley's eyes turned intense, deepening to a deep gray. "The man knows his son is here with me, safe and sound." He said gratefully. "And, of course, at the orphanage. That we are taking good care of Keelan."

"He does," responded Clint knowing how much the news he had delivered delighted Farley. Not only was Charles Hill's spirit released, but his departure set Farley free as well. "I, for one, am very pleased you and K.C have hit it off." Clint said something that startled Farley, "Like father and son. He seems at home here with you." Clint leaned off to the side, watching the boy pet the dogs, talking to them as though Winston and Cocoa understood every word he said. A bark from Cocoa, mirrored by Winston, echoed from the living room indicating it was possible. Dogs, like young children, appeared to have a sixth sense.

"Well, that brings up another subject I've been wanting to broach," declared Farley with happiness written on his face. "I'd like to adopt Keelan Charles Hill but don't know if there is an age restriction concerning adoption."

Clint guffawed, surprised by the question. "Farley, you're only thirty-eight years old, a young man with years of life left to enjoy a future with a boy seven years old. I'll start the paperwork today if that's what you want. In my heart I know you'll make the best of pals, a duo, knowing how to experience life to its fullest."

Enjoying the bantering conversation, Farley answered, "I'd love it if you did," Farley showed the emotion he was holding inside, "I can come to the orphanage today if you like. Whatever it takes, Clint. Keelan does feel like my child."

For a second, Farley became still, again thinking about something that had been bothering him. "Clint, I don't want to hurt your feelings, but would you mind calling the boy, Keelan, not

K.C.?" He waved his hand toward the living room, pointing in that direction. "Using K.C. reminds me of when the boy was identified by the wrong name. Now I know he wrote K.C. on the paper he gave you that day in his bedroom, but he also wrote Keelan and that feels more appropriate. Wouldn't you agree? New beginnings to his life and mine."

Then Farley's mood lightened, excitedly he continued, talking so fast he didn't give Clint a chance to respond to the question. "There's one other thing. Keelan and I will continue taking charge of story hour. Nothing will change in that regard, other than he will now be my assistant, and of course, he'll come home with me when we finish reading and enjoying our snacks afterward."

With glistening eyes, Farley choked out the words, "Keelan Charles Hill McDougal. Doesn't that have a nice ring to it?" He lifted his head when the tears began to roll down his cheeks. It was easy to ascertain who he was thanking.

"Absolutely, it does," replied Clint almost as delighted as Farley. "And, yes, we'll call him Keelan from this day forward. I'll alert the staff and mention it to Jules tonight when she gets home from work."

Clint shook Farley's hand to congratulate him. "I couldn't be happier for you and Keelan if I tried. This is the best news I've had all year. You know," Clint hesitated, and then said, "Keelan has always been special to me. But you know that. His beautiful little mind is a playground and a complete mystery. Farley, he's helped me in more ways than I can count." Clint thought for a moment, and then quietly said, "Pure souls seem to be easy conduits for messages."

Farley took in Clint's words. "Yes, I'd have to agree. He's a very unusual boy. Sometimes, when I look at him, I can see his wheels turning in that tiny brain of his." Farley joked. He anticipated what they were proposing. "We can approach Keelan's care as a team effort. He will continue his therapy at the orphanage, as always."

The two men stood, embracing in the kitchen before Clint turned to leave. "Will you bring this up to Keelan tonight?" Clint was very curious how the child would react to a huge change of this caliber.

An enormous smile appeared on Farley's face, his eyes glimmering with bliss as he answered Clint's question gladly. "He's aware, Clint.

He asked *me* to adopt him. Out of nowhere, yesterday afternoon, he sprang it on me. I laughed like no tomorrow because I was so afraid to tackle the subject. You know how he can be when things don't set well with him."

"I do." Clint chortled, remembering many occasions where he had to deal with one of Keelan's meltdowns. "Been there done that!" He grinned, agreeing Keelan could be difficult in some instances.

Walking to the door, Clint suggested, "Why don't you stop by tomorrow morning. I'll meet you at the orphanage around ten if that fits into your schedule. We'll discuss this with Tom Sanders to get the ball rolling. In the meantime, I'll place a call to David Dunn, see how we go about handling Keelan's inheritance."

"I don't care anything about his inheritance." Furrowing his brow, Farley then asked, "Can it be transferred, or kept at Radcliff's Children's Home?" Farley looked over his shoulder and saw Keelan standing at the end of the hallway, listening to their conversation. "To help young things grow, like Mr. Keelan here?" He smiled at his soon-to-be son. Keelan returned the gesture with a wave of his hand.

Tomorrow they'd meet again. In the meanwhile, Clint would stop by the orphanage to apprise Tom Sanders of the new developments. When he entered the orphanage, the place smelled of cinnamon, spice, and balsam wood, a lovely aroma Clint never tired of. The place had the appearance of a Norman Rockwell painting.

Thinking of David Dunn and how he would structure Farley into the equation as an adopted parent, Clint was going to suggest joint guardianship with the law firm, or the orphanage and Farley, on behalf of Keelan Charles. Legally he didn't see any problem since the orphanage was already named as co-executor.

Clint climbed the stairs rather than taking the elevator to his general manager's office. They had set an appointment for two o'clock. Quickly he raced up the steps, light of foot, pleased to have the discussion he was about to engage in. Tom would be told the truth of Clint's injuries.

Reading up on adoption procedures like this one was more complicated than a usual proceeding. Since Keelan Charles Hill had considerable wealth, there were more hoops to jump. Tom and Clint put their expertise to good use, looking for anything that would stand in the way. To their gratification, nothing did. By four thirty they wrapped up their preliminary meeting, ahead of the one they'd have with Farley McDougal the following day.

Afterward, Clint descended the steps back to the lobby where he grabbed a handful of cookies that sat strategically in ideal locations throughout the main area. He'd lifted his fair share before sneaking out the door, hoping not to be seen.

In the best mood he'd been in for months, Clint headed for Josie's Diner for a piece of pie and a glimpse of his lovely wife in action. He wanted to see the decorations there and around town she'd been going on about. After that he was going to drive to West Baden to pick up her Christmas gift, expecting to get home just in time for her arrival.

"Hey, darlin'," Clint chipperly called out from the doorway at Josie's Diner, flirting with his own wife. He tipped his cap to acknowledge Patrick, who was standing in the kitchen behind the food counter placing prepared hot plates in the window, ready to be handed out. He noticed Patrick's strange look after seeing his appearance, so he turned the other way. It was best not to remove his ball cap. "My table? Is it available?" he asked Jules wanting to hide away with his back to the door.

"Sorry, stranger, no can do. That's reserved for a regular. How about the counter?" Her smile revealed the joke. Most everyone there knew who Clint was, and chuckled at her response, watching her lead him to his preferred table.

After eating a generous slice of pumpkin pie and reading the several hours old, crumpled newspaper he'd picked up at the door, Clint readied himself to leave. "I'll see you in a little while," he said to Jules, his hand on the door.

"I'll bring chicken and noodles home for dinner. It's our special," she volunteered, pleased to see Clint looking so upbeat.

Just as he was about to leave, Clint tucked his hand inside his coat pocket to pull out a cookie for Jules, a gesture of fun, but quickly realized he'd forgotten the quartz crystal he'd been carrying in the pocket he'd placed the cookies. The crystal had crushed the peanut butter cookies he wanted to surprise her with, knowing they were her favorite.

The stone was meant to be placed back on his desk where it belonged before leaving the children's home. With limited time before Jules would clock out, Clint jogged to the truck, jumped inside, and drove back to the orphanage. He'd have to hurry to still make it to West Baden before they closed. If not, tomorrow would suffice.

Rushing through the glass doors of Radcliff's Children's Home, Clint rushed to the elevators, pushing the up button several times as though that would make an elevator arrive sooner. He impatiently waited but then saw Keelan sitting at his usual table, lights from the Christmas tree creating a glow to his appearance.

Clint decided to slow down. He walked over to the child. The lobby was empty and unusually quiet. Only Keelan was there, sitting alone at the corner table. When Clint sat down across from him, he realized Keelan had been creating a piece of artwork. Or so he thought.

Chapter 61
A Final Mystery

"What are you doing down here? asked Clint, concerned by Keelan's strange behavior, a distant look on his face not seen earlier when he was at Farley's.

Keelan cocked his head to the side as though he didn't know who Clint was. Then, he folded the paper he'd been working on, stood, handed it to Clint and walked away, without a word.

"Keelan, wait. Are you alright," Clint called to the boy, watching him disappear up the stairs without turning around to acknowledge Clint's presence.

Clint unfolded the paper Keelan had given him, his breath catching the second he saw what was placed there. The strangest thing he could have imagined was written on the paper he'd been handed. A border, in black outline, framed the words.

> Enjoy the present,
> Remember the past,
> The future is waiting,
> It's written in the stars.

Clint stared at the lines, disbelieving what he'd read. *What does that mean?* he questioned, confused, but familiar with the phrase, *written in the stars*, knowing it well.

He slowly rose from the bench, standing but not moving. He wasn't sure what to make of the paper he was holding. One thing he was certain of, Keelan had no idea what he had constructed, which was the reason he appeared detached. What he did know was Keelan was the link between Clint and a space beyond normal observation.

The elevator doors opened. He pushed the fifth-floor button. When the doors reopened, he walked the hall to the door that led to his office. There, he keyed in his code. He heard the familiar muffled click and pushed his weight against the door. His steps echoed on the winding staircase.

Clint unlocked the door to a place few had been invited–his private quarters. Although, Keelan once came there to hand deliver a set of numbers.

Stepping into his dark attic office, Clint chose not to flip on the light. He often sat in the dark in this room, loving the appearance of the light streaming through the tall windows, streaking the floor, and accentuating the blue swirls of the antique silk rug. Still shaken by the note but in the security of his secret place, Clint sat down in his rocker, trying to collect his thoughts.

In that instance Clint realized the room was different. Something was off. Although it looked comparatively the same, it was not.

A candle that wasn't there before had been placed on the mantel. It flickered as if a current passed through the room. That's when he noticed the furniture was not as it had been. The desk was in a slightly different position, though not by much.

Clint reached into his pocket, taking out the golden crystal. He walked over to the desk to put the stone back where it normally was placed on the left side. To his surprise a different, unfamiliar crystal was on the desk. An Amethyst crystal, nearly the same size as the yellow-gold one left at the doorway where Rod's General Store once stood back in 1953.

An uneasy feeling filled his senses, thinking, *When Rod's soul departed Salzburg, he left me a parting gift. Does this new crystal represent the same?* Then he recalled something about the note Keelan had given him downstairs that particularly stood out.

He unfolded the note and saw a reddish-purple amethyst crystal gorgeously painted at the bottom corner, featuring the exquisite geometric shape. What was depicted on paper was identical to what was before him. They were one in the same down to the tiniest detail.

Was this stone also an object of good luck, just as he believed Rod's crystal to be? Throughout the room he clearly noticed an undercurrent. In a crowd of witnesses and before God himself, Clint would have sworn he was not in the room alone. Someone was standing by the mirror. A shadowy outline, erect–but not moving.

Clint moved behind the desk and sat down. Over the last few years, he'd had so many paranormal experiences he couldn't count them all. This was shaping up to be one of the most memorable.

He stared at the gaunt figure, not certain if his eyes were playing tricks on him. Then a shift in the figure's position drew Clint's attention to the mantel. Keelan's pictures, the ones Clint had hung there himself, were missing, replaced by a breathtaking landscape showcasing Radcliff's Children's Home, stately, eloquent, heartwarming. The most beautiful painting Clint had *ever* laid his eyes on.

With trembling hands, Clint pushed the chair back from the desk and walked across the room. Although he hadn't started a fire, embers glowed as though someone had been there.

Above the fireplace, up close, the painting he saw from his desk was even more magnificent. Overcome with emotion, his eyes searched for a signature. With a flourish, the painter's name was indecipherably scrolled at the righthand corner. Illegible to most, but not to Clint. *C. L. Hill*. With a full heart, Clint stepped back from the mantel, shaken by what had occurred.

To his right, a whisper of movement was detected as a manifestation of snow shimmered against the wall. The figure vanished into the mirror, beckoned back to 7:32 p.m., December 21, 2004.

Moving to the rocker, Clint collapsed onto the seat. Sitting there, it occurred to him his strong connection to the astral plane was a double-edged sword that opened doors and demanded much. In a higher realm, where time doesn't exist, Clint's sentiments were noted. Much had been required of him, but he had risen to the challenge, demonstrating his sentient powers were finely tuned.

When the shock of the encounter settled, Clint got up, took one last look at the painting above the mantel, and whispered, "Peace awaits you, my friend."

He slowly advanced toward the door, ready to go home to his wife.

On Friday, The chorus of "Jingle Bells" and other Christmas tunes were enjoyed as they traveled on I-65, northbound toward their destination in Beech Grove, Indiana.

Time to resume an ordinary life.

Behind life's thin veil of the knowable, into a fissure undefined by time and its constructs, lies a place where souls move about freely without detection. A place where ghostly encounters meet angelic challenges and a desire to alter the foreseeable future is of paramount concern.

Stark changes that threaten all of mankind and what it means to be human are set into motion by a time when profit and greed outweighed concern for the future.

But none of this is known to Jay, a 14-year boy living in a rural town in 1947. Self-absorbed and mischievous, his life is upended when an angel and her constant companion interrupt his life. Soon he will be shown the future and the horrors it brings.

Provided a glimpse into a domain outside perception and beyond observation, Jay is transported from an uncomplicated life he has taken for granted so that he can see things as they really are. On his journey through layers of realities he will learn the errors of his ways and witness how his actions can influence humanities' future.

AUTHOR M. A. SENFT

Celebrates life's mysteries and joys in this tale of a middle-aged man who is forced to rectify an unjust legacy and free a trapped soul.

A family man, and widower, Clint Reeves is compelled to reexamine his buried past after a series of bizarre events occur in his hometown of Salzburg, Indiana.

At age five, on a snowy Christmas Eve, Clint's father failed to return home. Consequently, Clint was relocated to a nearby orphanage. Decades later, circumstances regarding his father's disappearance are revealed when an unlikely source leads Clint to the truth of that night.

Dating back to the days of the outlaw Reno Gang of 1868, the story gets its setting from a little known historical true tale of bandits, greed, and lost treasure.

M.A. SENFT'S The Unseen Player is a murder mystery that promises to elicit strong emotions. With engaging characters and unusual plot twists, it will engage you to the very end.

CPSIA information can be obtained
at www.ICGtesting.com
Printed in the USA
BVHW050210180323
660666BV00015B/690